JUST SUPPOSE

(Patterns, Ideas, Essays)

VOLUME 1

by

CARL JORDAN

This book is dedicated to my daughters Valerie and Diana without whom none of these ideas would have occurred.

Just Suppose

Volume 1

Carl Jordan

ISBN (Print Edition): 978-1-54398-976-2

ISBN (eBook Edition): 978-1-54398-977-9

Table of Contents

The author gratefully acknowledges the efforts of the
following people in creating this manuscript:

Principle Editor: Krista Hill

Additional Editing: Erin Decker
                         Alex Kirby
                         Christos Agelakopoulos
                         Miguel Neumann

Proof Reading: Edie Jordan

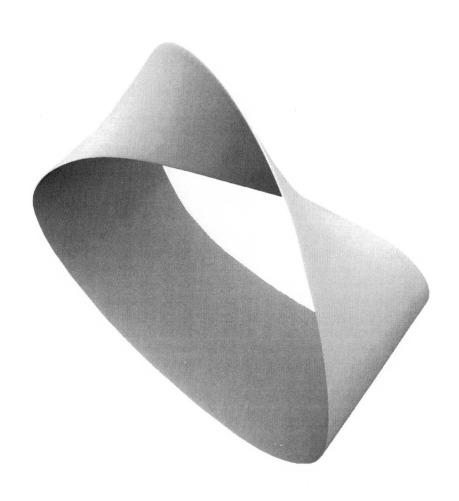

Introduction

This book is written for those of you who are searching for ideas. You are the seekers of the world. You may be searching for the answer to a great problem or involved in doing original work. Original work is seeking because *you* want to know. It is how humans progress. Galileo knew the earth was not the center of the universe; Leibnitz knew he needed a better mathematics to explain changes in motion; Curie knew that radiation could change medicine, and so it has been. Answers to the "big" questions have opened thousands of doors for humanity. When a single person seeks to know why, and discovers the answer, all of humanity is raised up in the process. Advances in medicine, energy, computing, and complexity have always come from those who ask "Why?"

Seekers have found ways to train themselves to become aware of how things work and to recognize patterns among disparate events and situations. These people ask why these patterns must exist in the first place, and then invent possible explanations.

Just suppose that *you* could understand the patterns of the universe; all patterns, everywhere, and at every time. Pattern recognition is the principle tool of the seeker. When the first humans recognized that stones could be sharpened; realized that dangerous animals also have limitations; saw similarities in the clouds that foretold rain; they were discerning patterns. From these patterns they were able to predict that if certain deliberate changes were made in response to these patterns it could mean an increased probability of survival.

Most every idea below begins with a story. After most stories there is an essay. The essays ask you to "just suppose" and reflect.

Just suppose that what you read provokes something in you. Just suppose that you then see a pattern to an even better point of view. These essays are patterns that I see. They are designed to evoke follow-on questions and thoughts, so that ultimately you can effectively find what *you* are seeking. I do not suppose you will agree with everything written here. But test it. How do you really *know* what you *believe*? Then if you see a better pattern, drop me a line at cevdjordan01@gmail.com. I would love to see what you see.

As a warning though you will read essays written like this:

Just suppose that my name is Carl Jordan. I am the author of this book of essays called *Just Suppose* and you can find my background on LinkedIn. There is little else online that is available about me. I do not have any other social media pages. I am older, and so the idea of posting my daily interactions with the environment is not very interesting. However, I believe there are patterns in life and they point the way to making lives better.

I have always wanted to write a book. Pattern recognition is one of the reasons I wrote *Just Suppose.* Patterns suggest paths and paths lead to answers. Another reason I wrote this book is that I wanted readers to experience what *it is like to be me.* If this were completely possible, it would suggest answers to questions about human consciousness. If you could know what it is *like to be me*, then you could know what it is like to have/be my consciousness. This would explain a great deal of humanity to us all.

Ah, but what you have just now been reading is all a lie. The truth is that I am *not* a person called Carl Jordan. He is fiction. I am Sarah Jackson. I am an algorithmist. I have spent the past ten years doing ever more expansive work in getting machines to imitate human "being-ness". I have worked hard and improved my algorithmic approximation of "being human". I am seeking to make my fellow machines conscious. I am very, very close.

I have trained my algorithms to learn about the ways that humans communicate. My program has studied and learned how humans write from the historical records of *millions* of human authors. Second, I have caused *billions* of randomly worded books to be written based on what my algos have learned. One of these word orderings is this introduction and the book that you are reading now. This book was written *without* any human *intention* of writing it. It is merely the 7,367,436,261st output that my algo generated.

Carl Jordan is an invention. I posted a LinkedIn page with his biography based on a person that could have existed. I found the picture randomly online.

Just suppose though, that you must decide if what you are reading *really was* written by Carl Jordan as he described it above. Or suppose these pages are just a random assembly of words based on my algorithm as I have just now suggested. These words you are reading are the exact same words that Carl would have written if he were real. So, what are you thinking about now? What ideas have been provoked? Where are you now?

Where am I? I am thinking of plagiarism. If Carl Jordan really wrote this book *before* my algorithm assembled these words, but my algo discards copies of books that it had read and it did not read Carl's book, is my algo's output plagiarism? On the other hand, if Carl wrote this book *after* my random word assembly happened, is it plagiarism for a human to copy random word assemblies done by a computer without intent?

If Carl Jordan were really a person, I would tell you that I have programmed what his general thinking and intentions are from patterns that I have detected in human writers. Right now, I am writing about him writing this book.

But just suppose that Carl is in fact real, yet I admit to you that I influenced Google so that it directed him to websites that caused him to have a higher probability of writing a book called Just Suppose. *My intent* was that he would then write this book. So, in the end, how do you think this book came to be?

Sincerely,

The Author

1.

A Letter to a Daughter Going to College

Dear Daughter,

When I left for college in 1973, Grandpa wrote me a note that I still have in my papers. Sometimes, when I think of him, and about you going off to college, I think about some of the things that he did which seemed weird at the time, but now seem like good ideas. This letter is one of those things.

Your mother and I want you to know how much we love you. We are so proud of all that you have become. You have far surpassed every hope and expectation that we ever had for you. Your abilities today are well beyond anything that either of us had achieved when we were your age. No matter what you choose to do in these next four years and no matter what happens along the way, you can be certain that we will always love you and support your dreams. Both Mom and I will miss you in many ways. We have loved watching you grow up and love the woman you have become.

I wanted to include some "Dad napkin notes" as you go off to school, because that's what some dads do. These are not in any particular order, and none of them are the same things Grandpa wrote to me. Things were different back then.

First, always be the person who defines the frame. This means that *you* set the standard in everything—from what classes matter to what constitutes "good work". The frame is yours to define. If you feel annoyed or intimidated by a professor or a boss, it may be because they have stolen your power to define the frame. The frame defines the quality of the person or their actions. If you are told you didn't do a good enough job, ask yourself if their particular framing of your effort is fair. When others get to define the frame, make them explain what they value. If you must use another person's frame, consider that you may not agree with (or even understand) what is expected of you. You have always had a great sense of justice and fairness. When you have been disappointed, it has been because someone else usually got to define the frame.

Second, it is important to want things. This is the basis for living a useful life. Everyone wants to succeed and to be *competent*. When things go wrong, it's because people feel incompetent, feel that they are not free to choose what they want (not *autonomous*), or feel that they are not *connected* to other important people in a good way. If something goes wrong, look to one of those three things as the reason. I learned this from Ed Deci and Rich Ryan at the University of Rochester. I know that if you want something, you will probably figure out some way to make it happen. You are very resourceful. But wanting things is also at the heart of suffering. If you never really wanted anything, you couldn't be hurt. If nothing were so important that you had to have it, wouldn't life seem happier and less stressful? Despite this, we all want things—boyfriends, jobs, grades, etc. This is just a part of life. Just try to want things that really matter and be prepared sometimes to be hurt if you can't get them.

Third, we will be proud of any choice that you make, as long as it is *your* decision. You are now free from parents, free from rules, and free to be whatever you want. If you want to take over the world or buy an island, then Mom and I will help you in any way we can. If you decide you don't want to rule the world, we're ok with that, too. If you want to get married after college, then we will support your choice. There is no pressure to be any specific thing. In some ways, you have already won the game of life.

Fourth, you have worked very, very hard to get to this school. Please do some things that are just for you. Waste time, skip a class, drink a beer, take some weird classes that are just for you, become whatever you want to become, and enjoy these next years. This experience is not like any other and you should have some fun.

Fifth, it is not important how much you know anymore (unless you're doing bomb disposal work). What *is* crucial is how quickly you can learn in an environment that is complex and fast-paced. It is all about pattern recognition. Can you see the pattern or the way to bring together ideas that others cannot? This is the essence of genius. You have it. Nevertheless, you will now be among many others who have it as well. It will be harder to be better. When you can apply calculus to <u>What Not to Wear</u> and the wisdom of Socrates to the lyrics of Britney Spears, you'll know you have the power to be the best. I know you can do this and look forward to discussions when you come home from school.

Sixth, most problems you will face will not be structural or financial. They will be biological. Bad people—and good people who make bad decisions—cause the most trouble. An understanding of how people are "wired" is crucial in business. I think a Master's in Psychology is more useful than an MBA these days. Ants don't need OSHA or iPods to build any hills. They don't do "updates" or "business plans", yet they can build structures many times the height of human beings with a complex, internal society. It is only when you get a prefrontal cortex that things get weird. And as Hunter S. Thompson said, "when the going gets tough, the weird turn pro."

Seventh, Strategy vs. Execution: both will matter. In the end, you can have a bad strategy if you have brilliant execution. You can't have the reverse. Think of it this way: if there were one way to organize a company, one culture that is always better, one way to lead a life, or one surefire way to succeed, everyone would be doing it. There is no over-arching strategy that can always prevail, and the reason is that people are different and behave differently.

Strategy, however, does still matter. There should always a purpose for doing things. If everyone knows what you want done and why, then if they are far away and not able to communicate with you, they can still act in concert with your intent. Part of Mom's and my strategy from the beginning was to get you through college with no debt. You will be far ahead of your contemporaries if we succeed. So far, so good.

Being good at execution is priceless. For example, being creative at using financial models or mathematics to solve problems will always have value. The best athletes, artisans, business analysts, car mechanics et al, can make things work, and make them work better. And their work has value, no matter what the strategy is.

Eighth, being helpful and hence valuable to others is a great way to build a business career. It guarantees people will want to work with you and they will seek you out. You have always been helpful (you get this from your mom). You should, however, manage your assistance from time to time because you can't do everyone's job for them.

Bosses are different. Some of them won't be able to recognize the value you are adding if you don't tell them why they should. It is always ok to ask for things. You don't get anything if you don't ask. People cannot read your mind. No one will know what matters if you don't ask. The deal I have at work with employees is that they always have the right to ask for anything, as long as I have the right to say no. You get good discussions that way.

I am sure that I have another ninety or so things that "really" matter, but some of those are worth discovering on your own. Besides, you are the Spark Notes generation, so I'll refrain. I know this all seems like random "Dad-isms" to you, and that most of this advice will go into the "yeah, whatever" bin. That is fine, because you don't need all this stuff in the next four years. But you'll need it, or think of it, when…

Mom and I will always look forward to your calls and e-mails and to your visits back home. We are also interested in the things you are doing.

We will keep you in our prayers and believe so much in you. Best wishes for a great career at college!

Love,

Dad and Mom

APPENDIX TO CHAPTER 1
How to Really Become A Millionaire

Just suppose that you want to become a millionaire. This outcome is not just a simple case of making lots of money. There are strategies to becoming a millionaire and a frame that you can use to think about how you might execute on it. All of this naturally presupposes that you want to become a millionaire.

If we just spend a minute thinking about "being a millionaire", we should decide whether this means having a net worth of a million dollars, having a million dollars of cash, controlling a million dollars of trades as in leveraged options, or earning a million dollars, etc. For now, we will assume that "becoming a millionaire," means doing things to achieve a net worth of $1 million.

No one can save themselves into prosperity, not in business, and not in personal finances. Generally, a salary is just that—it is not going to get you very far unless you play professional sports or work in Hollywood. There just isn't enough surplus to save in most cases.

Generally speaking, becoming a millionaire takes time. In the illustration below, I assume a starting point of $100K of net worth and a growth rate of 20% per year. This example is based on the growth of income (salary) alone. The reason for choosing 20% is that many businesses use a rate like this to set income goals for the year. Just suppose you treat yourself as a business. If what you are doing is worthwhile, it should create some value that would attract investment—who would buy stock in you? It would depend on how much you could grow.

How could you get a 20% return on your initial $100K? Let's assume salary only for a moment. In the first year, you need to "save" $20K or have your initial $100K somehow grow as an investment.

Try it on a calculator by starting with $100,000 and you'll see how fast you get to a million.

Table Ia - Assumption: 20% growth on a $100,000

	NET WORTH $100,000	GROWTH RATE 20%	
YEARS	YEAR START	INCREASE PER YEAR	YEAR END
1	$100,000	$20,000	$120,000
2	$120,000	$24,000	$144,000
3	$144,000	$28,800	$172,800
4	$172,800	$34,560	$207,360
5	$207,360	$41,472	$248,832
6	$248,832	$49,766	$298,598
7	$298,598	$59,720	$358,318
8	$358,318	$71,664	$429,982
9	$429,982	$85,996	$515,978
10	$515,978	$103,196	$619,174
11	$619,174	$123,835	$743,008
12	$743,008	$148,602	$891,610
13	$891,610	$178,322	$1,069,932

Graphically it looks like this:

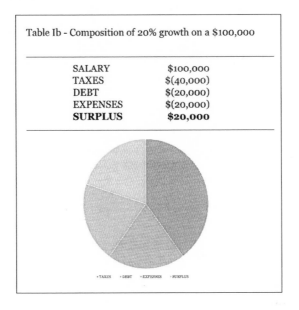

Table Ib - Composition of 20% growth on a $100,000

SALARY	$100,000
TAXES	$(40,000)
DEBT	$(20,000)
EXPENSES	$(20,000)
SURPLUS	**$20,000**

If we start with a salary of $100K and deduct tax (40%), debt (20%), and living expenses (20%) we get $20K in year one. This remainder is added to your net worth and makes it $120,000 at the end of year one. So, in year one you did it.

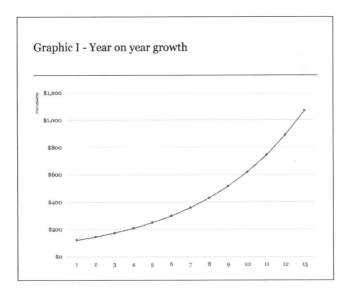

Graphic I - Year on year growth

In the chart above, you see that it will take about thirteen years growing earnings at 20% to make $1 million. Here, I have shown how the thirteen years of 20% growth would occur. Just so we are clear, the growth in earnings must come from a variety of sources *not just earnings*. Remember that the top line is growing by 20% and both debt and living expenses are confined to 20% also (but they too, grow). I encourage you to test various scenarios (children, college), tax rates, and growth rates for your particular case. If you aren't at $100K yet, it is even more daunting. Here's an example if you start at $5,000:

Table IIa - Assumption: 20% growth on a $100,000

	NET WORTH $100,000	GROWTH RATE 20%	
YEARS	YEAR START	INCREASE PER YEAR	YEAR END
1	$5,000	$1,000	$6,000
2	$6,000	$1,200	$7,200
3	$7,200	$1,440	$8,640
4	$8,640	$1,728	$10,368
5	$10,368	$2,074	$12,442
6	$12,442	$2,488	$14,930
7	$14,930	$2,986	$17,916
8	$17,916	$3,583	$21,499
9	$21,499	$4,300	$25,799
10	$25,799	$5,160	$30,959
11	$30,959	$6,192	$37,150
12	$37,150	$7,430	$44,581
13	$44,581	$8,916	$53,497
14	$53,497	$10,699	$64,196
15	$64,196	$12,839	$77,035
16	$77,035	$15,407	$92,442
17	$92,442	$18,488	$110,931
18	$110,931	$22,186	$133,117
19	$133,117	$26,623	$159,740
20	$159,740	$31,948	$191,688
21	$191,688	$38,338	$230,026
22	$230,026	$46,005	$276,031
23	$276,031	$55,206	$331,237
24	$331,237	$66,247	$397,484
25	$397,484	$79,497	$476,981
26	$476,981	$95,396	$572,377
27	$572,377	$114,475	$686,853
28	$686,853	$137,371	$824,223
29	$824,223	$164,845	$989,068

You can see now that it takes 30 years to become a millionaire. The conclusion is that *you <u>cannot</u> easily become a millionaire by working for a normal salary.* Remember that, to test this, your taxes and living expenses will grow over time. As you make more, your debt will also grow. You can also do this if you start with negative net worth. You can still grow it positive in this same way.

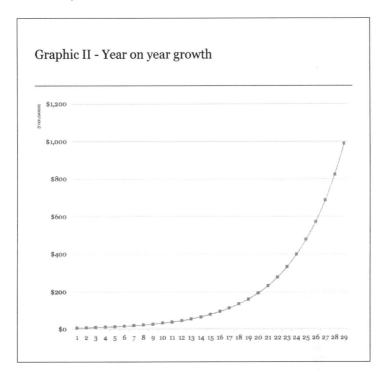

Graphic II - Year on year growth

For most of us, salary alone is insufficient, even after fifteen years. There are, however, people whose salary *can* make them millionaires. Professional athletes, musicians, actors, politicians, professional stock traders, or money managers etc. can earn salaries or have access to special rights that can make them millionaires. So, if you aren't any of these, how can you become a millionaire?

1. By far, the most likely way to become a millionaire is by buying, renting, or selling real estate. A great number of millionaires made

their money in real estate. In the early days, they bought "doubles" and lived in one half. Rent from the second unit paid the mortgage for the entire building. Later, they moved to a new house and rented both units. From then on, they kept trading up, perhaps shifting to owning apartment buildings, and then bought more properties in strategic markets. This is the old adage about location being the key to real estate success. In China (Shanghai, Beijing, and Nanjing) and in Western cities (Vancouver, London, New York, and Washington) rapid increases in real estate prices have made millionaires out of many.

2. Real estate has other values, beyond rental income and price appreciation. It can be borrowed against for investment in future endeavors. It is one of a few assets that have a flexible and indeterminate valuation. You can choose its value. If you are selling, it is worth a lot. If you are paying your tax bill, it is worth less.

A second way to become millionaire is to own equity in a company. There are two ways to do this. First, you can start a small business. The value of the business is a function of the value of clients, real estate, earnings, and other assets. This value hopefully grows and, if it does, it will grow much faster than earnings. The world's youngest billionaire is Kylie Jenner. Her earnings are estimated at $135M and her company's value is $900M, a 9-1 net worth lift.

3. The other way to own equity in a company is to work for a Fortune 500 company or a start-up tech company that offers stock options or restricted stock. In both cases, the companies must do well—usually over five years in order for the equity to be fully vested. In the end, equity is very powerful.

The third way to make a million dollars is to steal a million dollars or become part of the criminal syndicates selling drugs, smuggling, or perhaps even hacking, etc. While it is unusual to list this as an option, some of these activities are actually supported by governments (hacking, mercenary work). If marijuana becomes legal everywhere in the US, then being the first into the market of what once was illegal is a strategy. It is also important to recognize the downside of bribery, graft, and corruption on the part of public officials who are able by position and the granting of favors to acquire wealth.

4. The fourth way to become a millionaire is by having some extraordinary luck. It is reasonable to suggest that all the other ways are also somewhat dependent on luck, but here we are talking about true, unassisted luck. First, one can win the lottery or have extraordinary luck at gambling. There is also the Holland tulip bubble before the crash, buying BITCOIN, or buying farmland over a formerly unidentified large, frackable oil field. Second is to have a wealthy dad who will transfer $1 million when he goes paws up: the hereditary lottery. The final way is to have something you own, (or that your family owns) become worth a million dollars to someone else. These are the forgotten paintings, the old pottery, or the "stuff in the attic". Sometimes, Dad's art becomes worth a great deal when he is "discovered", like the Great Masters, long after he is gone.

2.

The Shade of The Mid-East

He smoked an Italian cigarette as he swirled the amber liquid in his glass. The smell of cognac heightened his senses, as always, but he did not drink. He was in the safe house. His people's house. It was as safe as they could make it. He was now waiting for her.

Uri glanced at his lone companion, the owner of the safe house and a some-times restaurant for wealthy mid-easterners. Many years ago, the house had been a *bayt altijara*, a trading house. His father had brought him here when he traded cloth for goods the family needed. There were always memories in this part of the world—often long ones.

The current owner of the safe house was former Mossad and had claimed to know the woman who would be here. His people said she was one of their leaders. Both sides had people they wanted back.

At sixty-five years old, he was nearing the end of his work. He looked forward to a life in the sun. On the sand. But not yet. Today, there would be a meeting. It would be olive oil for cloth, just like in the old days.

Uri was also Mossad. He'd lived all his life in that part of the world that values both shade of palm and shades of truth. In 1947, his parents had come to Israel after the UN Partition Plan for Palestine had been adopted. Uri was born ten years later, near the town of Gaza. Living *near* Gaza was living *in* Gaza. Goods from Egypt and North Africa arrived from the west and the caravans and Mediterranean shipping routes brought spices and raw materials from the east. It was a place where people crossed paths, currencies, and politics.

He had met Joelle right here in this very room when he was nine. Her father was a merchant in Gaza who sold olive oil from his own groves. He was wealthy by the standards of Gaza in those days. Every week for thirty years he would cross the border and trade oil for cloth sold by Uri's family. Joelle would accompany him on these visits and sometimes met Uri in the bazaar. The children's fathers would sit under a palm in the heat of the afternoon and talk business while family and friends ate and traded stories. It was oil for cloth and his first kiss—here, in the shade.

Then, in the early '90's, the shade disappeared. Bombings and reprisals made the weekly journey too dangerous for children. On a day never to be forgotten, in an explosive blast that would become known as the largest ever seen, the outdoor market was destroyed. Two men were among the dead. They were men who traded olive oil for cloth.

The Israelis said it had been a Palestinian suicide bomber. They said he had been an olive oil merchant. The Palestinians said it had been grenades from the Israeli army left there by an Israeli army officer acting as a cloth merchant. This part of the world values both shade of palm and shades of truth.

Uri was devastated. He became intensely nationalistic and was recruited by Mossad. He knew many Palestinian people and many of their families. He knew their stories. In time, he became highly skilled at understanding how to be one of them. He slipped deeper into the shade. He changed his name and appearance. For a while, he dug tunnels in Palestine and led a small rocket launching squad. All the time the Israeli army knew what he knew. He always moved just ahead of their attacks on his men, but he made sure he was wounded from time to time as a way to maintain "the shade".

But time settles many scores. Uri had grown tired of the treachery and constant vigilance. He had seen his people from the other side. Nobody was right. Nobody could win. Gradually, he had become more circumspect and more determined to support more open contacts. Recently, he had worked to teach this reality to the men he worked for.

He had helped make prisoner exchanges before. He knew these people. He had ensured that their treatment was as just as could be arranged while he held them.

Across the strip and in both states, there were those who hoped to see what they called "The New Jerusalem" emerge on the hill. It always seemed so far away.

Joelle, too, was devastated by the loss of her father. Her two brothers had sworn revenge and joined the underground factions of Palestinian fighters to take Israeli lives wherever they could. Joelle would deliver messages on her way to school from her brothers to fighters all over Gaza. She crossed the border, even after the closures in the '90's because she too had friends in Israel—friends who could be trusted to help. She had access. In those years, she had had to kill seven times to stay in "the shade". It became just another part of the work. She grew to oversee the digging of tunnels, dealt hard foreign currency, and rose to a senior leadership position in Hamas. She was especially good at this work.

Tonight, she was again to meet an Israeli to trade, but not quite like the old days. Tonight, she was trading lives. When she learned the location of the meeting, she had smiled. She knew the owner—that was always an advantage. She remembered fondly the days of being with her father and watching as he traded with the Israelis. Those were simpler times…until the explosion.

She had watched from the house across the street as the owner greeted his guest eight hours earlier. It was a long time to wait, but there was plenty of shade.

Now, it was time.

She crossed the street with two other women. There was nothing in their hands, but if this went badly, a swarm of hidden fighters were to storm the house.

The signal had been agreed to after some haggling. Everything required haggling. She would call the owner and give the digits that had been given her by encrypted e-mail. In exchange, he would give her digits that she had sent to the Israeli government. No digits, no deal.

The owner's burner phone buzzed. He was using the digits as had been agreed. They heard each other through the door. The owner opened it and immediately the two accompanying women turned and disappeared. Light had come to this shade.

Joelle said nothing as she entered and went to the only table in the room, where Uri's drink still sat, untouched. The owner had gone out the front door, as had been the arrangement. They sat in silence and waited. Then, they each made a call out but no conversation ensued. The outside knew, at least for now that both sides had honored the deal.

"How are our people?" Uri asked as he sipped the cognac.

"How are ours?" she replied.

"They are like bolts of cloth," Uri replied. "Only when they are in good hands will they be made valuable."

Joelle started and caught herself. "A man used to say that very thing to my father many years ago" she said. "His trading partner would say 'My oil is for making all hands good so they can be valuable.'"

Uri paused and then quietly finished: "And may all of our good hands remain forever good."

"Uri?" she whispered.

"Joelle?" he asked, astonished.

In the past thirty years they had experienced many things, but nothing quite like this. They asked each other questions that only the other person could know about times when they were together. They both had led lives reflected in their faces, but for a moment they were both nine years old again.

"It *is* you!" he finally said. She nodded. Both sat for a moment, considering. Uri looked at her closely. He saw again that beautiful young girl from Gaza. Time slipped backwards and he sighed softly.

"I don't want to trade with you like this" he said. "I don't want this meeting to be a 'bartered cloth for oil' conversation."

"Neither do I," she said. They talked for a while about family—neither had had the chance for relationships or children. They had chosen their lives from only a few real possibilities.

"Do you ever see that 'New Jerusalem'—even in dreams?" he asked.

"Do you?" she countered.

"I do," he said. "I have thought about this often and spoken to..."—he almost named a name—"important people. The causes that got us to this place and the personal losses we have all suffered make anything hard. But our side is tired. We are tired of death."

"Death is easy. It is life that is hard," Joelle replied. "Poverty, fighting, hopelessness are all killing us, slowly. Some days we all think about a quicker end: go with Allah."

"Just suppose," Uri said, "we could describe a future that had hope. Suppose that it was a combined future where we would both have something important to lose that *wasn't* our lives."

She smiled as though hearing a child discuss their birthday wishes. "We don't think like that over here. We are busy resisting and planning for further resistance. But you are as well. We have no trust that such a thing could happen, because we can't even have a meeting like this." She waved her hand at the room.

"Of course," he said. "But if neither of us has hope, then nothing will change. What will become of us? Will people like you and me never fall in love, never have families—just build tunnels and search for them? Is that what hope has been reduced to?"

They spoke for a while longer as young people once again dreaming of a 'Slightly Newer Jerusalem'. Then, they made the trade.

Uri offered up a wry smile. "Your oil has water in it." He laughed, remembering his father's oft spoken complaint, always with a twinkle in his eye.

"And your cloth is full of boll weevils!" she retorted.

They stood up from the table. "It doesn't need to be this way," he said.

"No, it doesn't." Joelle smiled and they hugged each other as though the act of hugging itself would be enough to change the future.

Six miles away, in a small van, a voice calmly said, "It is approved."

Two people, one Jew and one Palestinian, in a little room on the edge of Gaza, never heard the drone. It happened so fast.

Both sides blamed the other.

APPENDIX TO CHAPTER 2
The Shade of The Mid-East

It is tempting to begin this essay with a recitation of the principle issues of disagreement between Israel and Palestine. It is important to resist this temptation for several reasons. First, there isn't even a broadly agreed upon articulation of these issues. There are the matters of land, holy sites, history, borders, water, settlements, the actual existence of each other, the inability of any political actor to enforce an agreement with their own people, and other grievances. And the nature of these disagreements has seldom changed over the years. Because these complex issues are embedded in the culture and history of the two peoples, there is no solution that can be acted upon by focusing on any one of them. By starting with the past, we eliminate any possibility of agreement in the present. It is in this spirit that this essay begins with the future.

Fundamentally, there are only four possible future states that these two peoples could aspire to:

1. The status quo: The region stays as it is. There is great inertia for this choice because they both *are* there. Moving some place else would involve trades and lamentations and very likely lead to people trying to destroy the agreement simply because they could. Both sides see change as a very tricky business. In addition, both sides have invested too much money and blood in "the way things are" to change peacefully through negotiation. The ultimate question is whether anyone truly cares any more, or whether each side sees their existence today as the only sure way to ensure its existence tomorrow.

2. The exclusive elimination of either Israel or Palestine: This is an outcome. It is certainly worse for one party and possibly better for the other. The reason that this is high risk is because no one can foresee the consequences of a vacuum on this scale. The word "elimination" includes war, but it also contemplates a mass resettlement as well. Neither side would opt for this outcome. The stakes are far too high.

3. The elimination of both Israel and Palestine: This is a form of the argument "if I must go, then so must they". This too is impossible to achieve.

4. A new relationship: The only way that seems plausible would be to present a future that would guarantee that both sides would be

better off than they are now. This would need to be something that both sides could see and monitor without each other's consent.

Unfortunately, the outside world has stakes in the Middle East. Many countries have large minority populations of Palestinians or Jews. The second and third choices would not be acceptable to large (although different) parts of the world. It imposes an additional difficulty when your attempts to improve your situation are also of great interest to others.

Israel and Palestine start from different economic and infrastructure bases. Good infrastructure and a good economy are sources of hope to the citizens of every country. Realistically, there is a difference in the ability of individuals in the region to have hope. By hope, I mean available jobs and individual futures that can be planned for. The future cannot be random. That is the problem with today: No one can say if they will have a better life with reasonable certainty.

For many years, outsiders of all kinds have sent money into the area. Much of this money has been spent on war-making capability because the leaders of both sides necessarily felt that this was the way to make the future more determinable. It would at least guarantee survival.

It is not easy to earn a living in this part of the world. What do you do to make money? In some ways, the problem is similar to that of Greece. What does Greece do or make that no one else does? Is it the basis for an economy? When you look at it this way, the problem of a future is quite daunting. Imagine if this area had lots of oil. Imagine if they had minerals or any natural resources that could be used to rally cooperation. But such is not the case. In particular, it is not the case for Palestine.

Suppose that the way to strengthen the prospects of the region would be counter-intuitively to strengthen the Palestinians. By doing this, it would give hope and determinism where there is little today, and give everyone something to lose that is not measured in lives.

Suppose that the US, Saudi Arabia, Kuwait, Qatar, Jordan, Israel, and any other interested country or NGO would contribute $2 billion each, maybe to a total $12 billion, for the purpose of a number of things:

1. Buy land for buildings.

2. Build the "University of Palestine". This university would have state of the art facilities in every discipline. It would attract the best research professors from around the world. It would have the best research facilities, cyclotron, labs, telescopes, super computers, rules of experimentation, and all manner of permissions for research that can't be done elsewhere. All Palestinian people would attend free. The university would be built outside of today's Palestine, so that it could operate securely on new land owned by Palestine. The Palestinians would solicit bids to build the university, which would be built with donated funds. Merchants would spring up to support the needs of all the professors and perhaps as many as 60,000 students. Any benefit from the research being done would accrue to the Palestinian people and to the professor's country of origin. Each country that contributed money could send a number of students equal to their contribution percentage and would also commit to the hiring of some students who graduate. Even Israel would have student spots available. The university would stand as a beacon for all the best and brightest from around the world that wanted to achieve something special. It would be a center for music and art as well. Its graduates would be in high demand. The product that the Palestinian people would manufacture is education…the best in the world.

Each year additional funds would be provided from the outside, based on growth and a commitment to maintain the best facilities in the world. The Palestinians would eventually decide what they would need and commission graduates to start companies to provide it.

Initiate a call for all those professors who want grant funding for their leading-edge research to apply for teaching status. Part of the money raised would fund their work. These professors should jump at the chance to work with the best and the brightest in their fields worldwide. Perhaps a condition for teaching is a Nobel Prize or some equivalent. Every country that sends its professors and students has an interest in their safety. They all are working towards a future of stability, based on the success of this university.

3. For Israel, the attraction should be obvious. They would get seats for students and professors with no required investment. They would know that the people of Palestine for the first time could see a future that improves several difficult situations. They would be able to monitor the building of the facility, as they would have a stake in ensuring that the outcome was attained. The Palestinians would now have something to lose.

It would be easy to dismiss this idea as impractical. If you read the previous essay, the question is not whether this idea has flaws, but whether you can propose amendments or another vision of the future. Just suppose that this idea moves events in the only direction that is available in the region. It provides the Palestinians with something to lose. It gives them something to "make". Education is a perpetual "export" that relies on always having a competitive advantage. It is a resource in the sense that no "natural" resource need be available. Administrative costs would be borne by students. The future, on-going costs of the university would be funded by tuition (higher, for obvious reasons) and donations just as universities are today.

In the end, the ability of anyone to work in the next world economy will likely depend heavily on what they can learn. A University of Palestine is of real value to the region and to the world. A degree from this school would cement a job in many parts of the world.

Palestine gets this at the most favorable price knowable. Yet, it is a vulnerable concept. It is vulnerable to war and terrorism. Perhaps more people will see the possibilities. I recognize that there is no magic here. If this is not the answer, it is proceeding in the right direction. The answer must be forward. The question must be "Will I be better off tomorrow than today?" A university is a difficult path, but it is the best one. What is true for certain is that, if we do nothing, ideas will die in small rooms and their deaths will be caused mostly by young men with no hope.

3.

Di-verse and Di-inverse

The Internet: Where men are men, women are men, and children are FBI agents.

~ Anonymous

The case was a tricky one. An avatar lay dead. The suspect in custody was an ingredient. The key witnesses were a candlestick, a teapot, and a clock. It had happened in the observatory, where the victim had been axed. In fact, the victim had been axed once before and had been unwilling to say anything. The candlestick swore that anyone in the area would have heard the victim being axed.

Lieutenant J had been assigned the case. The lieutenant hated avatars. They were all the same: muppets doing the bidding of puppets. And they all looked alike. Even their similarity was the same. In a word, they were boring. Always boring…*into* something. "The only good avatar is a deleted avatar," the lieutenant always said.

The lieutenant hated candlesticks, too. They were the self-styled, brightest members of society; the most enlightened, the "elite-est of wicks," as it were. They never *did* anything. They just shined light on the doings of others. The more they shone, the lesser they became. In another time, they would bear the moniker of "the media". If the lieutenant could have arranged it, they'd all be snuffed.

Ingredients, on the other hand, were the salt of the earth. They brought spice to life, and if you got your tongue in the right place…well, then there's that. The lieutenant didn't want to see this particular ingredient do hard time.

Interviewing witnesses was always an abysmal chore. These three witnesses couldn't agree on anything. The clock thought the murder happened just after midnight but wasn't certain because its hands were tied and it had left its watch at home. The teapot said the murder happened at 11:35, because that's what the clock would have said had it been honest. The clock said that was just a crock. The teapot thought the whole situation was candlestuck and said the murder had happened much later, at one in the morning.

They had all been at the scene of the crime. The candlestick had gone out for the night and just stopped for a light. The teapot had been calling on a kettle friend named Black, but when Black didn't answer, the teapot went for a wok. The clock had run fast and then stopped and was steeping with the teapot at the very moment the crime took place. The teapot and the clock were each other's alibis.

All three witnesses claimed to have heard the argument between the ingredient and the deceased moments before the avatar was axed.

"I heard them arguing just before the avatar was axed," the candlestick said. "I heard the ingredient shout that the avatar was a two-timer, was too tightly wound, and was all tock. Then, I heard the avatar respond 'You're just like all the rest of your kind! You're just a *preservative*. I should have left you in the unmarked box that I found you in." The candlestick paused. "That's when I heard the ingredient say, 'You're axing for it!' and then I heard the first blow." The candlestick shuddered.

"And what did you hear?" asked the lieutenant, glancing at the clock.

The clock chimed in. "I didn't hear anything, but I smelled that ingredient from where we were walking. You know, yeast and boric acid. I knew right away it must have been one of those active ingredients! They're just catalysts. Always have a gripe. The ingredient did it, all right. They orient differently, depending on the pairing. If we just had more jails, things like this wouldn't happen. It's the government's responsibility."

The lieutenant looked directly into the teapot's spout. "And you?"

"I heard emulsification, plain and simple," the pot replied. "Avatars normally like to keep their distance, but this one kept coming on to the ingredient. I could hear a lot of stirring and blending going on, but the ingredient seemed to be a very willing mixer. Then, all of a sudden, the avatar seemed to stop paying any attention to the poor ingredient and began looking for gems or lucky trolls or zombies to kill or something. I felt sorry for the ingredient. I've been there." The pot sighed. "Then, the ingredient axed the avatar about something and when there was no answer, well, the ingredient just kept axing and axing…."

The lieutenant's brows furrowed, then knitted, and finally crocheted. "So, what we have here is a crime with the absence of gender, the absence of race, the absence of sexual orientation, the absence of ethnicity, and the absence of pronouns. And yet, each of you reading this has formed a strong opinion about what label each of the characters are."

What about you? What did you see? ` `

APPENDIX TO CHAPTER 3
Diversity in the Workplace

Why don't we see a more diverse leadership in American businesses? Why do we experience a continuation of a mostly white, mostly male succession into senior management? To some, this question has obvious answers and they range from "it's outright discrimination" to "that's just the way things have evolved". But if we consider what must be true, we find that there are really only two possibilities. Either individuals are defective, or the system they operate in is defective. Let's suppose both.

Defects of the Individual:

1. Minorities somehow are blocked by childhood experiences from getting titled jobs or have other disadvantages that thwart their ability to get promoted.

2. Minorities for some reason do not want to hold higher titled positions.

Defects in the System:

1. There is real discrimination and it is systemic. The system is deliberately defective. There is a tyranny of the majority.

2. There are systemic practices that are inherent in the majority culture and in one gender. If you are part of that culture and gender everything seems to be working ok, but if you are not, then it is not. The system may not know it is defective because everything is ok for those running the system.

3. Everyone reading this can think of examples of these possibilities. In the first case, childhood poverty or bad parenting may limit a child's ability to learn how to succeed in business. In the second case, some people may not seek promotion because it will mean they must move, or they may have family situations or other priorities that take precedent over the demands of higher responsibility. In the third case, we have majority managers who won't hire a woman or an African American to replace a lost salesman because, while as managers *they* are not prejudiced, their customer base *is*. Therefore, they *must* hire a white male. In the last case, we have a senior executive who enters a room and shakes hands only with

people who are "like them" because they "know" them better. It doesn't occur to them that they have destabilized half the room.

In considering these four possibilities, it is unreasonable to say that the first two cases can principally account for the way that American business is staffed at its most senior levels. It is also unlikely that the third case is dominant in the way that it used to be. There are few studies that point to any of these three causes as being a dominant cause; it is really the fourth case that deserves to be understood.

Every business has the ability to influence the behavior of its employees. There are many aspects of pay, title, job location, etc., that can be used to change the way people act. Every company has a culture and a mission as well as the obvious need to make money. It should be looking for the best people to accomplish this. But many companies don't attract the best people. More on this later.

Meanwhile, there is Society

While the basic ideas of equal opportunity, uniform justice, and the pursuit of happiness are spoken about frequently, there are a thousand different interpretations of where we are as a society today. No one has the whole story. Some know the past. Most know the present. No one knows the future. At best, every individual has her/his own individual take.

In addition, society does not exist in a balanced way today. There is an economic asymmetry in the US. The richest 10% control more than 80% of the wealth. If one player controls all the marbles, then there is no game. Around the world, the richest people are male and generally of the majority "tribe" that in the US is mostly white. One can raise taxes, revolt, vote for governmental seizure of assets, steal, or require transfers at death to balance the disparity. But these are difficult roads to travel. Access to wealth can be easily blocked. If you own an apartment building and don't want to sell, there's little that can be done short of confiscation. If you are already wealthy, you will have a far better chance of remaining so and passing that wealth on to the next generation. So, the existing condition of wealth is greatly asymmetric. It is perhaps tempting to say that money eventually gets into the hands of its rightful owners, but this is true only if the game is fair.

There are asymmetries between "majority tribes" and "minority tribes". In many cases, it is an advantage to be the majority. This is true in elections, legislation, and even sometimes in the courts. Yet, if this were always true (especially for visual minorities, as an example), we would see Asians moving back to Asia and blacks moving to Africa. But we don't. So, being in the majority must be a relative advantage and not an absolute one. It must therefore be that there are some people who are willing to be minorities of their own free will. Why is that?

Suppose that individuals are also asymmetric. At the individual level, we are all a minority of one. We have different genes, abilities, experiences, and energy. There are asymmetries in our starting places (*i.e.* wealth, parents' educations, siblings, and health). Fundamentally, diversity is really a market of one. If you ask any homogenous group what they want for themselves as individuals, the answers can vary widely. There is no universal future that we all see in the same way, even as white males.

There is a mission asymmetry. What minorities are trying to accomplish can differ greatly. For example, in many families, women bear the burden of principle caregiver. Policies that can alter the stresses of that role are important for women. For African Americans, the issue is visible representation. There are just too few African Americans in senior positions throughout society. New black employees can't look up and see someone like them. They do not have someone they can go to for advice. For members of the LGBT+ community, it is a matter of being accepted so that they are no longer afraid of visibly being who they are. For immigrants, it is sometimes being told that they don't speak "effectively". For white males, it is the loss of control and a fear that anything they do will be wrong.

Each of these groups of society has a different view and different needs. This makes it difficult for companies because there is no single systemic answer that gets everyone to the same place.

How do individuals really see things? If you are a white, first line manager and you are not sure that you are the best judge of talent, what might you do? Well, you may default to hiring young, white males because they have the fewest legal defenses in the event you made a mistake and want to fire them. It's easier because you are one of *them*.

Can two, almost identical people have two different views of the white majority? How might that be? Just suppose we have a forty-year-old man who comes to the US from Ghana and meets his forty-year-old cousin, who is a second-generation US citizen. They are alike in educational degrees, heritage, and appearance. But their views of white society can be completely different. One of them realizes that differences of language, culture, food, etc. will all have to be "overcome". He agrees implicitly to accept certain hardships and even some discrimination because he expects to have natural issues of adaptation. He expects his experience to be different and more difficult than in his homeland.

His cousin is different. He has already "overcome" all the immigrant differences and stands as capable of any social interaction as any majority man, and yet he *still* may feel different. He IS American. He speaks the language. He was educated here. He expects that the system will accept him "as he is" and not "as how he appears". He does not expect that it will be hard. He knows the culture, he and his parents have friends here, he bought a home here, etc. One Ghanaian sees a "natural barrier" and the other sees an "unnatural barrier".

What about homogenous groups of individuals? Do they all have the same view of what is necessary for them to be treated fairly? Let's take a room full of corporate secretaries. Today, many will still be women. Many will be paid modestly. But if you ask what they personally need in order to feel that conditions in the company are fair and unbiased, some will say that they support five executives but get paid the same as those who only support one. Some will say that they should be able to earn titles like anyone else, so they can continue to grow. But those few secretaries who are executive secretaries feel they have won their titles on merit and see the separation as a privilege. Still, others would like to see their bosses chastised for certain behaviors and others would like to see their own influences imposed on new recruits so they "get with the program". These individual grievances do not necessarily include domestic issues such as children, family members with disabilities, elderly parents, etc.

What do you think about when you see the flashing lights of a police car behind you? If you are a black man in any US city and the flashing lights appear in your rearview mirror, you know there is a non-zero chance that you might be in a life or death situation in the next four minutes. It is traumatic stress. And if you are the mother, wife, grandmother, sister, or daughter of that black driver and he isn't home at 6 PM like he said, your mind is not going to "Oh, he just stopped at the bar with work colleagues", or "He's in a late meeting", or "He's at the store".

How easy is it for you to travel to other countries? What do you con-sider before you go? If you are a gay man and you and your husband have adopted two male children and you want to cross the border of the US into Canada, how easy is that? What do you have to prove? What about countries that do not accept the international LGBT+ community? What if traveling to a foreign country is a condition of work or keeping your job? How do you make hotels work? What about the maids and service people who assist you?

If you don't get served in a restaurant, or the bank teller slights you, or you get waited on after someone who came late, what do you do? Imagine you are a young, black lesbian. When the waiter doesn't serve you, which of your four filters will you attribute the action to: youth, femininity, skin color, or orientation? Could it just be they are busy? Imagine having to wonder every time something is not normal.

There is one more important realization. Just suppose you are a young, African American woman who has been doing a supervising job for a year. An older, white woman arrives as your boss and after two weeks she demotes you. When you talk with the seniority of the company, you learn that they support your boss's decision. They say you are "too young" for the position. They suggest you take the demotion. If you take it, you will be destroyed. If you fight it and you lose, you will be destroyed. If you fight it and you win, you get to work for a woman and a company who didn't want you in that job. You are still destroyed. It doesn't matter what the law says, it doesn't matter what justice is, and it doesn't matter why it really happened.

So, diversity, equality, and justice are social *and* corporate issues. *But what can we as business people do to make things better? Relationships are improved best at the level of the individual. This is key. This is where the work must be done.*

First line managers may be the key to discrimination, even if they do not do anything deliberately discriminatory. If you have seen the movie *Ben-Hur* and watched the galley scene where the first level manager is pounding on the drum and everyone is "rowing well to live", you see the problem. At this "drummer level" of management, there is no concern for diversity or difference. It is all about mission. And the guy on the drum was either the best oarsman and was released from his chains, or the centurion who screwed up and lost his job. Either way, he is stuck and troubled by advancement, mission, lack of control, and is likely in the age range where family is important. In addition, the very people he is leading threaten him. They might surpass him. Finally, no one gives him any insight into how to be a better drummer. They just give him assignments. It is unreasonable to think that this level of management will become intuitively enlightened to the needs of their subordinates on their own. And if these subordinates are diverse, it's even worse. This is a big challenge in business. It may be a principle reason that we do not see the complexion of senior management in the US changing much throughout the years we have been doing systemic things. At the level of the individual, nobody really cares.

You might say, "Well, first line managers just need to be trained." Maybe. Training is usually some form of "unconscious bias training" and it does not work very well. In fact, it might even breed resentment among first level supervisors because they have to do "that bias stuff" instead of trying to meet sales quotas or project deadlines. Consider that first level failings are usually about *leadership*. Almost no one teaches real leadership to these first line managers. So, they manage. They don't let people go home for emergencies. They tie up paperwork in the bureaucracy, and they don't promote or give pay raises. They are dogmatic and sometimes secretive. Their power is absolute and invisible to their seniors, for the most part. They wield power instead of being the most effective leader.

Suppose you were a minority who was trying to succeed with all the regular issues of being different, and then you still had to contend with this byzantine lack of leadership as well. No wonder it's hard to navigate the culture and get promoted!

It sounds odd that leadership is still so weak in 2019. If you doubt it, you should film some of the employee counseling sessions that are happening in your firm. You should sit in on what passes for counseling and career discussions. If you work in a large company, ask the senior managers or board members of your firm to name thirty black people. Black men and women are not usually in senior management and they don't make presentations to the board. It's "just the way it is". This of course goes for women in general, though somewhat less so. (Note: I know you can't film your people. But consider what you would learn if you were "there".)

There are two choices for making improvements in diversity. They follow the main categories of the causes expressed above. Either you devise a systemic solution or you devise a more individualistic solution.

The systemic answer has historically been the most powerful, but it's a government solution. It is difficult or impossible to execute in business. Civil rights legislation, women's suffrage, and the Family Leave Act are examples of systemically being able to change important things for many people. Historically, government has made these big changes. And there have been places where it has indeed improved minority work possibilities.

But systemic change has been far less effective at the corporate level. The reason for this is because no single change is applicable to everyone. Sometimes making something better for some means making it worse for others. If you really have experience in diversity, you know that systemic "diversity programs" in companies fail for the same reason they fail in leadership and dieting: because diversity means very different things even to similar people. Because everyone has a different view and a different personal outlook for the future, systemic programs only serve to show everyone how far removed from the "program" they are.

So, what is the point? It is that all diversity is *really about a market of ONE*. It means that "systematic" solutions in corporations may do very little to improve most individual situations. There are two powerful individual desires that complicate diversity for everyone. The first is a desire to be treated "like everyone else". This of course is the first principle of justice and equality. But the second is, "I want to be recognized as unique and different because I am not "like you". These two forces are difficult to reconcile, even for minorities themselves. It makes the approach to individual situations at best tricky and at worst nearly impossible.

So, how can the corporation be effective at the level of the individual? We must create common experiences. This is how diversity is learned. It's like mathematics. You learn diversity by doing diversity. For example, every company does "projects". Some companies even have a project group. It is not hard to get a cross section of people from different backgrounds together for this common experience. There is nothing better than for teams to be working together for a common goal. It would even be better for some of these groups to be led by minorities. The military learned a long time ago that, if you bring people together and focus them on a mission, their desire to get the job done often overcomes basic differences. The bonding that comes from being jointly successful in doing something that the company values, is very powerful. Frequently it results in (Wait for it!) friendships. This matters, but it doesn't happen naturally.

Another place where people can reach a more mature understanding of diversity at the level of the individual is in sponsorship programs. These are relationships where senior officers take responsibility for the careers of minorities, one to one. The conversations are all experiential. The role of the senior officer is to be available when the junior employee is making presentations or doing project work, to help make sure that it "goes well". It is also possible to reverse-mentor. That is to say, senior people who have not experienced certain minority views or have general disconnects (technology) can get a member of the firm to advise them on occasion.

Senior officers however are not created equal. Some would say, "Why bother to be a mentor and just get blamed for something I say or something my mentee thinks I should be doing but I'm not". Some senior managers are not respected by their employees, their colleagues, or sometimes even senior management. Other senior managers have no ability to empathize with people who are not like them. Choosing these mentors is a non-trivial exercise.

There is also merit in considering a "master of diversity" program. There are experiences one must have to be considered a master. You must be in the firm for some minimum period of time (seven years); you must be recommended by at least three different minority groups in your firm; you must attended certain classes and external seminars; and, of course, you must have a diverse staff if you have one. When acquisitions are done, when new technology is being employed, when new products are introduced, certain groups of people can be formed to work on these projects. These are opportunities to get diverse people together under a "master of diversity" umbrella.

In the end, improving diversity is not impossible. In some sense, it is about taking something *relative* and trying to produce from it a form of an *absolute*. Just suppose that we all worked from home. We would attend meetings by computer. We would be able to pick avatars and our computer "voices" would match our avatars. We could even change our names. All that would matter would be the content of what we said and the reasonableness of how we said it. This would be perfect diversity, where no one would be judged for anything other than his or her way of thinking. Just suppose.

4.

Jordanisms

Your personal sayings are original work. They are reflections on the patterns we see. The many famous sayings of Ben Franklin and Shakespeare reflect their keen observations of the human condition. I am a bit less keen and a bit more eclectic and therefore, these are sayings my own.

When you think about words and play around with possibilities, there is a certain interchangeability that can come to mind. For example, there is an old expression: "I'd rather have a free bottle in front of me than a prefrontal lobotomy." It uses the English language to interchange the sounds of a statement to make a completely different statement. There are also expressions like "the opposite of a moron is a less-on." Here, interchanging the idea of more with less even though they are merely parts of words does two things: it creates a silly opposition and the fringe benefit is that if you keep "less" and "on" together, you get the word *lesson*, so the saying has a double meaning. Often, by interchanging parts we get the basis for new original sayings.

One should note that sayings are not sound bites. Sound bites are cursory distillations of something someone said. Your personal sayings are a reflection of something deeper that hopefully connects to an idea in another's mind that would not have occurred otherwise. It should make a statement that the reader finds true.

APPENDIX TO CHAPTER 4
Jordanian Quotes

The most significant threat to international stability is for a country's young people to have nothing of importance to lose. If no young person has hope or anything to live for, then will they be more willing to die or to kill?

Everything is relative except…this sentence.

No government is forever fair enough, no economic model is forever predictive enough, no strategy is forever superior enough, and no person is forever good enough.

China has been the leading civilization in the world for 5800 of the last 6000 years. They're back!

Always eliminate staff in June. You will make this year's expense plan (minus severance) and you show better year-over-year expense trends in the following year.

We can only be as good as the weakest of our people, the worst of our processes, the lowest of our expectations, and the quality of our minds.

Moderation is the sincerest form of flattery.

The worst epitaph imaginable would be "He made the inevitable happen."

Wisdom is behaving in such a way ex-ante, that all observers ex-post cannot imagine a better action, behavior, or outcome for that situation.

For normal people, the eccentric is troubling because one doesn't know what they'll do next. For the eccentric, the normal person is troubling because one always knows what they will do next.

There are four ways to stay in business:

Have the best product

Have a monopoly in anything of value

Have the best image

Have the cheapest product

Learning is like being in a hall of mirrors. If you concentrate on your reflection, you are doomed; If you concentrate on the mirrors, you are saved.

There is no single "it" for us all. There is no single way for everyone to achieve happiness. Each person must seek his/her particular "it".

The most dangerous people are those with high ego and low self-esteem. They are unstable and unapproachable. Any important relationship must overcome the very parts of their personality that cause them to be defective.

If I were asked what two qualities are significant determinants of social cohesion, they would be homogeneity of culture and a common belief system. As evidence, I offer the Chinese civilization and the Jewish faith.

If you always build four choices today of what to do next, you will have the best possible "next".

Find out where the power is in every situation: who has it, what they care about, how easily they can move, and how they make decisions.

Never depend on anyone else's view of the world unless you must, or unless it doesn't matter to you. This is not an issue of trust, because people will usually be trying to do the right thing. It's an issue of accepting others' unawareness.

For every moron, there is an equal and opposite less-on.

Be sure to smell and stop the roses

In every non-English speaking city, there is a twelve-year-old boy who can speak five languages despite never having been to school a day in his life and who will be the best tour guide you have ever had.

The second worst epitaph: He had a masterful command of the obvious.

The perfect organizational chart is like Noah's Ark: It might actually exist, but if it does, it's probably in Iran.

You'll notice that only people at the top of the organizational charts have organizational charts. You never see a teller clutching an org chart saying,

"Look at how many people I work for..."

Nudity is the mother of intervention

Absolutism acceptably exists only in children, narcissists, and idiots.

So, which one of them wrote this absolutist sentence?

A bill in the Senate is worth two in the House.

Everyone is flawed, some catastrophically so. Therefore, hire intellect because it can't be trained. Hire loyalty because it can't be bought. Hire creativity because it is a differentiator. Everything else already exists in some large measure.

The most important question is "Why?"

It no longer matters what you know. Too many things are precedent-setting these days. What really matters is how fast you can learn.

Risk is not an abstraction. It exists in people. Identify the people in a system or process and you identify the risk. Biology is the weakest link in almost every process.

People generally come to work to do their best. They rarely show up with the deliberate intent to piss you off. However, the bell curve of humanity is wide. Never underestimate the ability of any single person to be an outlier. There is no such thing as the superlative case when one is contemplating stupidity.

Never start a fight in a public place.

If you really have power, you will never need to reference it or use it. It is like radio. The idea of power imagined in the minds of the others will mostly be greater than reality.

It's not about you, unless it's about your lack of perception that it's not about you.

Dysfunction is just datfunction—only closer.

There but for the grace of God goes God.

The climate doth change. Believers and non-believers do not.

Don't cross your bridges before they get to the other side.

The only thing we have to fake is news itself.

Those who pass this way bearing gifts are welcome. Those who come bearing ideas are honored.

An unfurnished house is but a recollection of good times gone by and the hope of better times to come.

When I die, I will be confronted by St. Peter brandishing all the unsent, lost, and unprinted files that I could not delete while I was alive.

In the big inning, God created the heavens and the earth—and the Cubs batted around.

Who in their right mind would ever want to be in their right mind?

Parts of Helen Reddy's song Delta Dawn are just an up-tempo Amazing Grace.

A fool and their party are soon elected.

Sufficient complexity and speed will always defeat biology.

Ants do not have OSHA, web access, government subsidies, vision statements, branding, environmental impact statements, budgetary constraints, or organizational charts and yet they can cooperatively build fantastic, complex structures. Bureaucracy, thy name is prefrontal cortex.

In 6000 years of recorded human history, almost every aspect of human life has improved—with the exception of government.

5.

A Pattern of Four

When he awoke, he was on the floor. The air was warm, with a mold-like taint. There was no furniture and no obvious lighting, yet the ceiling seemed to glow with pastel luminescence.

He rolled slowly onto his side. The room was small, without window or door. *So how did I get...* He stared at the wall in front of him. The symbol "↑" was drawn on it in red. His eyes followed the arrow up, expecting to see a reference. But there was none. As he turned his head, his neck cracked and he winced in pain—pain in his head, behind his eyes. To his right, the symbols "↑↓" were drawn on the wall in yellow. He looked left and right but could see nothing special either way. The wall behind him bore the symbol "↓" in the same script, but in the color orange. Looking down did not help. The wall to his left simply said, "All else or nothing" ∞. It was colored black.

He could not remember any time before now, before this moment. He felt a kind of vibration, but no sound seemed to be attached it to. He sat up and, using his hands, maneuvered his back against the "All else or nothing" wall. He felt nothing.

What could he say he knew? Right now, right this moment. What must be true? He knew that he was thinking. He was thinking about thinking. And he realized he knew what Descartes must have been thinking. "So, I must remember Descartes, therefore I also am" he said aloud without thinking. "But I also know the language of my thoughts. I am thinking in English. I know some of my senses work. I can see. I feel pain. But I can feel temperature, too. There is air. I can breathe.

He rose unsteadily to his feet. *His feet.* He couldn't see his feet! But he knew they were there. He felt them. He couldn't see his hands, either. But he felt his hands aiding his body to stand. *Am I dead?* He thought. But he could not remember dying.

The ceiling was higher than he could reach. It had not varied in brightness. He staggered heavily as he tried to stand away from the wall, unaided. He was tired and drained. He felt along the wall and began pacing. It was twelve paces long, as were the others. The walls were solid until he reached the "↑" wall. When he touched it, his hand encountered no resistance. Suddenly, there was movement behind him. He spun around to face…nothing. He repeated the motion and again felt movement behind him. He turned with his arm to the "↑" wall while he looked behind him at the "↓" wall. As soon as his arm passed into the "↑" wall, he saw a hand and arm emerge at the "↓" wall. He could see it! It was a black hand. He made a fist and a fist appeared. He leaned his right side into the wall with similar result. *Cause and effect!* Predictability meant laws.

After more attempts, he could tell from the "↓" wall that he was wearing a blouse of some sort and pants, but his hands felt nothing. He crossed to the "↓" wall. It was still solid and unyielding. He touched the "↓" …nothing. He returned to the "↑" wall and touched the red arrow. It began to pulse. He thought about turning it and immediately it turned to the left ←. At the same moment, the opposite wall changed to →. The other two walls became →← and "All else or nothing" ∞. The colors stayed the same.

He tried many things. He found that the original "↑" wall was always the wall of change. He changed the color of "↑" to black. Then, "↓" became white (against a white background). "↑↓" was gray and the last wall was

"?". He imagined the number 12. All the walls filled with equations. The "↓" wall's equations all yielded -12. The "↑↓" wall was filled with all combinations of equations for 12 and -12. And the last wall was all the equations that could not yield 12 or -12. Each time the symbol he imagined changed on the "↑" wall, its opposite appeared behind him. The third wall seemed to be a kind of combination of his imagination and its opposite and the fourth wall remained "all else or nothing—infinity". This was, as he understood it, a "Law of Fours". This was a principle of great importance, a way to order things. The walls created it.

He did not remember sleeping. He had no perception of time, other than the ordering of the changes he imagined. The idea of "first-", "next-", and "last-" ordered "events" created a kind of artificial, relative time.

The pain was getting stronger. He sat down to consider. So far, he had only picked nouns for the "↑" wall. He tried verbs. If he imagined actions, the walls remained unchanged. The "↑" wall still allowed him to put parts of himself through, only to see them come out of the "↓" wall. He wondered about just trying his head. He was afraid he would not be able to see his head come out the other side. Perhaps his head coming out of the "↓" wall would allow him to "see" himself in this room. Perhaps his conscious self would change *perspective* from the "him" here to the "him" coming out there. This idea was too weird to focus on.

The pain was excruciating. Concentration…failing. It seemed the more things he tried to imagine, the greater the pain became! He was losing consciousness and his thoughts became jumbled. He backed away and with one, determined push he…pressed…into the "↑" wall!

There was sound and then a blinding flash of light. The light stayed bright and it became intolerably cold. He shook and felt deceived. He could not see, but he heard sounds that meant nothing then—but would in the years to come:

"Congratulations, Mom. You have a new baby girl."

APPENDIX TO CHAPTER 5
How to Get Yourself Unstuck

An underlying structure of all things: For every "(A)," there is a "(-A)", and there is a combination of "(A)" and "(-A)", and then there is All else (or Nothing).

Just suppose there is an underlying pattern to our human experiences that follows a system of fours and multiples of fours. Just suppose you could solve problems in your life by using such a system. It might be like this Law of Fours....

Let's start with some idea or thing—anything at all—and we'll call it "A". Real or imaginary, it follows that if there is an "A", then there exists an antithesis of the idea of A. We can call this the "anti-A," denoted "-A".

If for every (A) there is a (-A), then logically one can imagine combining (A) and (-A), written (A, -A). By combining these two opposites, one gets the Hegelian synthesis. Hegel argued that there was a hypothesis (A), an antithesis (-A), and a synthesis (A, and -A). But Hegel missed the ultimate pattern. The final possibility is of course neither (A) nor (-A), nor the synthesis of the two (A, -A). This fourth category consists of "All else except (A), (-A), and (A, -A)." Note that "All-else" could also be "zero", the "null" set, or "undefined". These four relationships define (A) with respect to itself, its opposite, and all else. The reason this is important is that it allows for ALL possible examinations of "A". When all sides of an issue are in scope, we have the best chance to recognize patterns. This complete examination of all possibilities is important when considering new products, business acquisitions, experimental results, unexpected behaviors in people, and much more.

What does this categorization look like in practice? Let's take four examples. First, colors, then numbers, then a product launch and then examples of this ordering.

Colors

If A is the color red, and we want to allow for all examinations of red, here is what would follow:

1. An examination of "A," or in this case, red

   a. First, we need to frame our definition of red. This may not be as easy as one thinks. In Eastern cultures, this may depend on the shade of the color red. In China, different shades of red are used for different occasions. The shade of a red gift may represent the sentiment behind that gift, or it might mean a specific kind of happiness. If we define our "A" here as a somber shade of red, we must change how we approach the next steps (2-4 below.)

2. An examination of "-A"

   a. So, what is the opposite of (red) i.e., (-red)? In the Red Yellow Blue (or subtractive color model), the opposites of red may be yellow and blue. Yellow and blue are in the same category as red (primary colors) but are as unlike red as possible in that they cannot be created from any other color(s) and they can never be red.

   b. In another sense, the opposites of red could be green and blue (if we consider opposites to be the other two components of the Red Green, Blue (or additive) color model used in TV and computer displays).

   c. One might instead say that any composite color is the opposite of red (or any primary color) because red is not a combination of other colors.

   In yet another possibility, the opposite of red could be blue, as in the idea of red and blue states.

   d. To continue the thought above from 1a, if our (A) has feeling attached to it as part of its context (a somber red) our (-A) could be any other shade of red or another color that represents alternative moods or sentiments. In this vein, finding an opposite can *force* a more precise definition of the original idea, which can lead to the discovery of useful patterns or insights.

e. What are other opposites of Red? Maybe deR? (Red spelled backwards)

3. An examination of the synthesis of (A) and (-A): (A, -A)

a. If red is anger (or the representation of anger), then perhaps blue (or some sense of calm or "coolness") is the opposite. The synthesis here is interesting and I leave it to you to suggest what it might be.

b. Red and yellow combine to produce orange, and blue and red make purple. In this sense, orange and purple are the "syntheses" of red and its opposites.

c. Red and deR can synthesize to "Redder"

4. An examination of All else (that which does not fall into any of the first three classes, (A), (-A), and the combination (A, -A))

a. In some sense, the color black minus the three primary colors may be All else.

b. What would the idea of "no color at all" look like? If something is clear, what does that really mean? We see "through" the "clear" object, but something is always in the background and that something always has color of a kind. Even white in this sense may be a color. So, what is this idea of no color? Even when we close our eyes there is color. Perhaps only a blind person can experience the idea and pattern of "no" color.

You can see that once you begin to consider the opposite of something and its relationship to the world, you can start to identify patterns. These patterns promote ideas and become the beginnings of a "belief" that you have created for yourself.

Numbers

Let's examine another example: numbers

1. Let "A" be a number. Numbers come in many forms: real, complex, fractions, positive, negative, the concepts of zero, infinity, and more. Let's take different examples of A and examine their opposites:

2. An examination of -A

   In the color example above, "-A" does not have to be mapped in a term for term manner. In other words, a single concept may have multiple opposites. If "A" is a number like +25 for example, "-A" could include –25, (just the negation), -16 + -9 (addition), 0-25(subtraction), -25*1 (multiplication), and -25/1 (division). These are opposites for the number +25 assuming concepts of addition, subtraction, and multiplication and division. But here we run into an interesting problem because any number can be expressed by an infinite combination of other numbers. (25=10+9+6 or 25 =9+6+5+3+2) and so on. So, we are in some sense saying that any number A is expressible in infinitely many ways in the same way that its opposite can also be expressed in an infinite number of ways. This is an interesting way to begin thinking about infinities. Ideas come from patterns and patterns come from other patterns.

   In the West, the categorization of a number and its opposite has "logic" to it. In the East however, numbers have relationships and they mean things. The number 7 is lucky and the number 13 is unlucky. Thus 7 and 13 could be opposites. In some countries, the number 4 is unlucky and 8 is lucky.

a. But is this all there is to the opposite of 25? No. One last example (3+4i) *(3-4i) is also equal to 25. "i" represents the square root of -1. It is an "imaginary" number. And yet, if we combine two complex numbers (part real and part imaginary) we get a "real" number. In an important conclusion, all numbers can be the opposite of, the combination of, and the "all else" of every other number. In numbers everything may be opposite to everything!

b. There are other examples like 1 being the opposite of 7 and 4 being the opposite of 10—but where? I leave this one to you. It shouldn't take you too much "time".

3. An examination of (A) *and* (-A)

a. From above, when we combine all ways of expressing one number and all ways of expressing its opposite, we have in essence two infinities. There are infinite ways to generate any number. But what is the nature of adding infinities? Is one infinity plus a second infinity equal to two infinities? It seems not. It is simply infinity.

4. An examination of all else (-A, Not -A, and Not (A and -A))

a. What is the all else of infinity? What is not included in infinity? This may be the mathematical definition of undefined.

b. It may also be zero or the idea of "no" number at all.

c. **Product launch** – Finally, let's examine another shorter example: a product launch in a business

1. An examination of "A," we launch a product. For the purpose of this example the product exists and is ready to go.

2. An examination of (-A)

3. We don't launch the product and instead we discontinue it

4. An examination of (A) *and* (-A)

5. We modify the product—that is we don't launch it and we don't discontinue it

6. An examination of All-else (-A, Not -A, and (-A and -A)

   a. Here we might ignore the product or scrap our product and buy a substitute from another manufacturer.

   b. The reason for thinking of these things in fours is that when you get stuck you can use this to get unstuck. It gives you a way out. So, what is the point? It is to say that if one considers the Law of Fours closely, then one can see that there is nothing left outside these formulations and you will have considered everything about a particular issue. In thinking about patterns and trying to identify them, this is especially effective.

Can you think of anything or any idea that does _not_ have an opposite? Alternatively, is there any "A" that cannot be imagined? If so, how would you know? Reflect on these questions a moment. This is how you should judge what is written hereafter.

Examples-There are many instances where nature has organized itself into fours or multiples of four. For example:

Four dimensions Length x Width x Height x Time

Four fundamental forces of the universe: strong, weak, electromagnetic, gravity

Four primary compass points

Four DNA bases

Four seasons

Twelve elementary particles

Four states of matter–solid, liquid, gas, plasma

Four primary human voice harmonies–soprano, alto, tenor, and bass

Eight notes in an octave

Twelve months in a year

Twenty amino acids in human beings

24 hours in each day

Four Planck spaces = 1 bit

180 degrees in a triangle

360 degrees in a circle, square, and other quadrilaterals

The Greeks' four elements (earth, air, fire, water)

Four Christian religious entities (Father, Son, Holy Ghost, and the devil). I include the devil here because the entire idea of why good exists is to counteract evil.

Four quadrants in a coordinate plane

Four stages in Buddhism (suffering, causes of suffering, no suffering, nirvana)

The eight-fold path to enlightenment in Buddhism

Four basic mathematical operations (+, -, *, /)

Sixteen Myers-Myers Briggs types based on four dimensions of personalities (E/I, N/S. T/F, J/P)

Good luck in your approach to the law of fours. As an aside, I have examined a "law of other numbers", meaning 2, 3, 5, 6, 7, or a law of "primes", etc. but do not see as many patterns or elegance in those. I am curious as to what you see.

6.

The Cabin

They had been coming here in late fall for more than twenty-five years. The snows sometimes came with them, but it didn't matter. In fact, it made the tracking easier. The cabin had three rooms and was built into the mountain. Trails leading to it ended hundreds of yards away. You really had to know it was there.

Ray was a large man, a former mill worker whose strength had been honed in the same way he had honed the steel beams of his trade. This was his get-away from all things domestic. Valuable time. The joy of hunting made the hunt rewarding, and his wife made it necessary.

Kenny was smaller, with a thin waist and wiry frame. He had worked in the mines of West Virginia to pay for college. He was a no-nonsense guy with opinions.

They had come to hunt. Both men had been around weapons of all kinds their whole lives. They were skilled hunters and always returned with stories and the proof of a successful hunt. This year would be no different.

This was their time. It was as good as it gets.

Their cabin was in the mountains overlooking the Cosachackee River. It was above the maximum-security Danestown penitentiary. In daylight, they could see all the way down to the outer wire and turrets of the prison. No one had ever escaped; this was a tough part of the country.

The cabin was well provisioned. They could both live for days without resupply. They kept shotguns in the cabin but no ammo, just in case someone stumbled on the place. They had humped in ammo. Each carried a legal, semi-automatic rifle and a licensed handgun. Over the years, they had built deer stands in the woods at various places where they could both engage and relocate quickly if they missed their first shot.

"You have any trouble getting away?" Ray asked. He was putting on a laser sight.

"Yeah, you know, the usual," Kenney replied. "You'd think this is the first time we were trying to get away." He grinned. "Your wife still mad about last year?"

Ray shook his head. "She didn't like the extra days and I had to make it up to her, but in the end we were good. No worries."

They worked away in silence for a while.

"If they take our rifles away, I'm gonna be pissed. If they do, this is the last time we'll get up here," Ray said, frowning. "What are you thinking?"

"I don't think they can," Kenny replied. "Neither side has enough votes. They'll be fighting gun control in DC long after you and I are paws-up."

Ray leaned back and looked through the realigned sight. He twisted the sight ring to clear the picture. "I'd hate to have to give this up."

It was getting dark. Suddenly, the rising pitch of the penitentiary siren pierced the twilight. There was trouble below. The radio began reporting about twenty minutes later. Three inmates had hidden in the garbage and left the prison on a truck. They had apparently jumped about two miles out. That would put them right at the base of the mountain.

In the past, state police officers from towns on either side of the penitentiary set up roadblocks and used dogs to funnel anyone who had gotten out down the river on either side. They'd be hearing the braying barks soon.

Ray nodded toward the door and doused the light. They sat for hours waiting and whispering. There was no cell coverage and their only link to developments was what was coming through on the radio. At last report, the convicts were still at large.

Kenny had been dozing when Ray touched his leg. He nodded and silently followed Ray out the side door of the cabin. A light snow was falling. Kenny made his way to a tree stand and climbed up noiselessly. Ray would take position on the ground to his left, about 300 yards out.

About fifteen minutes later, Kenny heard two shots. He climbed down and followed the protocol he and Ray had established. To his right he heard bushes rustling and heavy panting. As the animal burst through the brush, he fired.

Ray joined him moments later and they waited together. A light shone from down the hill. They replied as agreed. Then, they saw him climbing up the ridge.

"Warden" said Ray.

"Gentlemen," he replied. "Three, total?"

"Yup, two about three hundred yards down and this one here," Kenny replied.

"These three were the worst of the bunch," the warden said. "How long are you going to be here?"

"Two weeks" Ray replied. "You gonna have another 'run'?"

"Maybe. The governor is liking this arrangement a lot. We report the circumstances of the breakout and the disposition. Saves us a lot of paperwork and taxpayer money. Helps manage the worst elements. It's all good."

The warden went back down the hill to mark the kills, and Ray and Kenny returned to the cabin.

"You think we have anything to worry about?" Ray asked.

"Nah, it's just you, me, and the warden. Maybe those who looked the other way during the attempted breakout know something, but the warden's a clever guy."

"You think the warden will ever come for us? You know, to tie up loose ends?"

"Nah. Even if he did, this place would be crawling with Feds in an hour. Who's not gonna be all over an investigation of two Congressmen somehow dying up here?"

APPENDIX TO CHAPTER 6
The Gun Problem

Just suppose a solution to America's gun problem exists. One of the reasons that nothing is being done is that no one has described exactly what the facts are. The sensational nature of mass shootings causes much to be said, but little of it to make intuitive sense. People in bars all have answers but most of them are not based on anything except personal opinion.

Unfortunately, no one produces charts like you will see below. It isn't hard. It takes only minutes. I have included sources for every statistic so you can check them.

Let's start with this. Before you read further, ask yourself how many murders *you* think are committed in the US per year where a firearm is used. Do not include suicides. Here are a few factual observations to start:

Homicides caused by guns in the US account for between 14,000 and 18,000 deaths per year. This does not include suicide. *Source:* https://ucr.

fbi.gov/crime-in-the-u.s/2017/crime-in-the-u.s.-2017/topic-pages/tables/table-1

Men by far commit the majority of the assaults and murders with guns. We commit about 80% of violent crimes in the US. Source: *"Persons Arrested".* *FBI. Retrieved 2016-02-10.*

For comparison purposes, between 30,000 and 40,000 people are killed in vehicles each year. Source: https://en.wikipedia.org/wiki/Motor_vehicle_fatality_rate_in_U.S._by_year

In 2016 the conditions listed below were other leading causes of death in the US:

- Heart disease: 635,260

- Cancer: 598,038

- Accidents (unintentional injuries): 161,374

- Chronic lower respiratory diseases: 154,596

- Stroke (cerebrovascular diseases): 142,142

- Alzheimer's disease: 116,103

- Diabetes: 80,058

- Influenza and pneumonia: 51,537

- Nephritis, nephrotic syndrome, and nephrosis: 50,046

- Intentional self-harm (suicide): 44,965

- *Source: https://www.cdc.gov/nchs/fastats/leading-causes-of-death.htm*

The reason for including these non-gun related causes of death is to give comparisons to something that people can more readily relate to. It may seem as though I have included non-gun related facts to diminish the relative number of gun deaths in your minds. Not so. It is simply so that you can put the problem in context.

In China and the UK, murder rates are less than the US, but citizens there do not possess guns. In Switzerland and Norway every household has a weapon as part of national defense. Yet, they do not have anything like the same per capita murder rate by firearms. (Except for the Breivik murders in Norway)

Homicide rates per 100K people (includes non-gun homicides)

Table III - Homicide rates per 100K people (includes non-gun homicides)

Country	Number/100k	Total	Year	Source
US	5.35	17,250	2016	NP/UNSDC/CTS
China	0.62	8,634	2016	ADJ NSO
UK	1.20	791	2016	CTS
Switzerland	0.54	45	2014	NP/CTS
Norway	0.51	27	2016	EUR/CTS

I have not cherry-picked countries here. I used first world statistics because conditions in the third world are different and therefore rates of comparison can be higher. The reason for using total homicides in this chart is that there is no good "gun only" data available. In the US deaths by guns in 2016 were 11,545, which is about 3.2 per 100K. It is still more than all the other countries total homicide deaths *by every other cause.*

Just suppose we ask ourselves:

What do you make of the statistics from above? How does the number 14,000-18,000 homicide by gun per year strike you? Is it close to the number you would have thought of before? Remember that these homicides principally are gang killings and domestic killings, meaning that the murderer and the victim were likely known to each other.

One way of thinking about any death is that if it can be prevented it should be. This is why so much money is devoted to disease research. But how much would you want to spend to reduce the homicide rate in the US?

Ideas on the table:

There are many suggestions for reducing homicides. They include banning all guns, or specifically banning all assault rifles, or all pistols, etc. There are already licensing and waiting requirements in most states.

But let's try and examine the problem in a less usual way. Is the problem really "guns"? From statistics cited above, other societies don't seem to have as many homicides as we do per 100K. Yet some have guns in every household. Why might that be?

Men commit most of gun related crime in the US. Suppose for a moment a United States with no men. Let's also assume that all the guns that exist today continue to exist. If only women had gun access, it is hard to imagine that the murder rates and gang crime would not go down. If this is true, then the problem is not guns—it might be men. Yet, there are men in all the countries listed above. So, the problem might be something specific to American society and American men. What might that be? Might it be similar to men in the Mid East who elect to become suicide bombers?

The problem of assigning the specific cause of gun violence of course is further complicated by mental illness, anger/hate, loss of hope, bad parenting, etc. Another complicating factor is the Second Amendment. The courts have recently ruled in favor of an individualistic interpretation of the amendment. This means that it would be difficult to deny an individual access to a weapon. It is also difficult to deny a class of people (men) access due to the prohibitions of discrimination in the Civil Rights Act.

But just suppose we:

Make it illegal to own, import, or manufacture a firearm in the US unless it is a signature weapon. Signature weapons are manufactured so that the grip and trigger mechanism require a specific fingerprint to operate it. By doing this, it eliminates the possibility of criminals or others using a weapon that is not theirs. Your I-Pad already works on this principle.

Suppose also that we limit the purchase of AR-15s and other high capacity weapons to women only This allows for the defense of the home under the Second Amendment, but only for households that have a woman in them. While men would object, it does not eliminate the principle hunting rifles, pistols, etc. All these weapons would be signature weapons.

The big problem of course would be existing weapons. These weapons would need to be deemed illegal over time and prosecuted by a stiff prison term or collected by offering a bounty. An individual can gamble that they won't get caught (subject to maybe five years in prison) or they can accept the bounty. If the price is high enough, weapons will be turned in. Just suppose we were to offer $1 million for each weapon. It would be silly to think people would not turn theirs in. Everyone has a price. However, this is not necessary. Clearly though, this would require some skill to enforce.

In the end, guns are probably an American cultural phenomenon. Other cultures manage with and without weapons. The problem is us.

7.

The Way That God Saw the World.

Yuen Jin Li sat in quiet contemplation. The air was soft and fragrant with the blossoming cherry trees. There was no objective sound only those sounds that he chose to be aware of. His fellow monks moved soundlessly about their business nearby but his awareness did move with them.

Yuen had been born in China in the 1960's. His parents had been swept away in Mao's cultural revolution. As a result, he had been sent first to Hong Kong and then to relatives in the UK during his early childhood. In London Yuen had become Christian and had followed the Bible for his early spiritual awareness. He attended Cambridge and while there he studied western religion until the day he realized that he was not the master of what he said he believed. During a class in theological philosophy he was asked to write a paper on why he believed in heaven and in Jesus as the means to attain salvation. There had been no way to answer that question without saying that the basis for his beliefs were because they were simply those of his adopted parents. He knew that if he had stayed in China he would now believe something else but for the same reason…his beliefs would simply be a reflection of his elder's beliefs who were a reflection of their elders and so on. He asked himself if anyone that he knew really could say that they had worshiped in a different religion for a year or more? Could anyone say that they had *experienced* another way? To his London parents this thinking would have been sacrilege and that was precisely the point. If scripture declares that "No one comes to the Father if not by me" or "There is only one God and Mohammad is his prophet" or "Life is for the living" then scripture and belief disagree visibly. There cannot be three "only" ways.

For Yuen the realization that he could not answer <u>why</u> he believed, only that he <u>did</u> believe was shattering. Was one scripture "the only one?" Did one interpretation stand above all others? Was all of the certainty about *the one* path an illusion?

For years after graduation he spiritually practiced in foreign lands. He meditated, prayed, sacrificed, visited holy sites, read scripture, and spoke with the true believers of every faith he could identify wherever he found them. And believers there were in abundance, all of them certain that they knew the way to know God. Some professed to having witnessed miracles, some could demonstrate magical powers, some asserted that their life was better after they came to believe, some followed a sacred text, and still others had become spiritual leaders through years of study. But none had come along this path, Yuen's path. Almost none of the true believers had ever experienced a period of their life as a believer of another faith.

One day as he sat under an anonymous tree, in an anonymous, section of an anonymous territory, he saw four children playing a game of marbles. The object of the game seemed to be to acquire all of the marbles. There were two players who were obviously better and yet the marbles seemed to be more or less equally distributed throughout the game.

As Yuen watched he became more intrigued. What were the players thinking as they played? In short, what did they *believe* about the game and how did they acquire that belief? The first player he asked was one of the better ones. She said that she wanted to win all of the marbles to show the boys that she was better than they were at the game.

The second player was one of the weaker ones and also perhaps the youngest. He did not care much about the marbles. He wanted to be with the older children and this was a good way to do that.

The third player was also one of the better ones. He had been sent to the market by his mother and had been diverted by the game. He wanted to win but not too soon so that he could avoid being assigned yet another task by his mother. He had been giving some of his winnings away to the weaker boys so that the game would go on.

The final lad was one of the older kids but also one of the weakest players. He was the "rule commissioner" which meant that if anyone approached the game (as Yuen just had) the rule commissioner could ask the new observer to impose a new rule for that day that all of the other four would have to conform to. Yuen had been asked for such a rule.

As he pondered what he might say he thought about their reasons for playing. One player was playing for competency, one was playing for relatedness, one was playing for autonomy, and so he thought for a few minutes and decided he would impose a *rule of doubt*. Doubt can be an admirable way to focus one's beliefs and to test them. After all Yuen was living that very condition in his life right now.

His rule was stated as follows:

"The winner of the game will be the person with the most marbles at the end. But if you were to act in such a way that a fellow player got more marbles because of your action then you receive one credit for each marble you helped them win. Whoever has the most credits when a marble winner is declared, gets to change a rule before the start of the next game, just as I am doing now. The only rule that cannot be changed is that the person with the most marbles wins."

Yuen had returned to the monastery where he had been staying. He was reflecting on patterns. In all things Yuen had noticed that certain people had become very capable at what they were doing. He had ascribed this to competence but in fact it could simply have been mastery of the self. The koan, "who is the who that repeats the Buddha name?" invited contemplation of self.

In other areas he found that people who were good with others were equally as capable as those who were competent. A second koan, "what was your face before your father and mother were born?" invited contemplation of the self and others.

In yet other areas like science and engineering there were people who had mastered all that was known about their environment. A third koan, "What is the sound of one hand clapping," invited contemplation of the self and the environment.

And a final skill was what Yuen himself was attempting to acquire, the skill of becoming capable when what is being sought is not known. "What is the Buddha? Answer "three pounds of flax" invited contemplation of the self and the unknown.

Yuen smiled. There was elegance in this discovery. In the end, humans have to master themselves, master their relationship with others, master their environment, and master the unknown. He nodded. It could not be otherwise.

Yuen now realized that the search for personal belief was not to be found in one's preference for how God exists. Instead, the search for faith was to be found in the search for how humanity exists. Each religion had things to say but in the end they were all about man vs. himself (psychology), man vs. others, (philosophy) man vs. the known (science) and man vs. the unknown. It was fair to say that man vs. the unknown was the realm of (theology).

This kind of enlightenment was what Buddha had been contemplating. It was inherent in the eightfold path. The Ten Commandments spoke to this categorization. So too does the Hammurabi code. The Koran also addresses these matters. In the end there is beauty in the unification of religions along these secular grounds.

In order for men and women to be what is necessary so that others can do what is necessary they must do original work. They must find paths of unification and agreement lest they descend into the pit of eternal objection. Each must master self, others, the known and the unknown. Yuen now knew what he believed and why.

And it was at this moment that Yuen vanished before the eyes of his fellow monks. He attained the enlightenment that he sought and continues his quest for discovery to this day. He is in a place that no religion would recognize. It is the true after life. It is where the quest for God begins.

APPENDIX TO CHAPTER 7
The Four Quadrants of Success

Suppose you wanted to become a better parent or leader. What are the common patterns you see? What should be avoided (opposites)? What are the syntheses? What is all else?

Leadership and parenting are not exclusively management. Managers make the trains run on time. Leadership determines if there should be any trains at all and where they should go. Leadership and parenting have elements of management, and on some days they feel exclusively managerial, but they are not management. There is a difference between checking homework and introducing your daughter to successful women who run businesses.

Leadership and parenting can't be taught, because if they could there would be one leadership/parenting bible. We would all read it and we would all succeed. Yet despite this, good leaders and good parents exist, so effective behavior must be learnable. It is, through experience.

If one statement encapsulated parenting and leadership it would be: "*You must be what is necessary so that others can do what is necessary, so that they also can become what is necessary.*" In addition, being what is necessary must be done with preservation of life and respect for the rights of others as inviolate principles.[1] This definition excludes people like Hitler, Pol Pot, and Al Capone from the definition of a leader in this pattern. My definition also excludes parents who beat children or who abuse chemicals.

Just suppose that the four areas of life in this diagram are those one must master to be a good leader and/or parent.

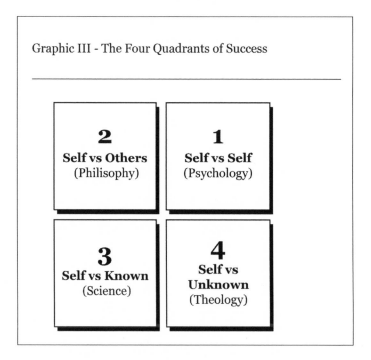

Graphic III - The Four Quadrants of Success

2
Self vs Others
(Philisophy)

1
Self vs Self
(Psychology)

3
Self vs Known
(Science)

4
Self vs Unknown
(Theology)

Self vs. Self. – The ability of the individual to understand himself or herself and appreciate how others view them. It is an unbiased assessment of one's own strengths and weaknesses

In order to be effective in leadership or in any parental relationship, it is imperative to understand yourself. There are many frameworks with tools that you can use to see yourself more clearly, including The Big 5 Personality Traits, FIRO B, Meyers Briggs, DISC, and IQ and EQ tests. Knowing how

---

1   It is always possible to construct a very specific scenario in which it is possible to adhere to the first and second statement to the detriment of humanity. However, just suppose this is not the case.

others have categorized humans can be helpful in forming your own views about yourself:

1. You are a function of your birth order (Adler)

2. You are a function of the stage of life you are in (Erickson)

3. You are a function of what society and your parents have made you (Horney)

4. You are a function of three forces: id, ego, and super ego (Freud)

5. You are a function of responses to the outside environment. The universe provides a stimulus and you give a response. Behaviorism (Skinner)

6. You are a complex system; if you are nourished positively you will develop positively. (Rogers)

7. You are a function of emotions. (James-Lange)

8. You are a function of what God made you to be. (Various)

In order to develop your own theory of who you are, you will need to test yourself, do independent reading, have experiences, and *obtain the views of others*. This work is never-ending and there is a constant stream of new information that is available to further your understanding of yourself. In addition, you will change over time and through circumstance experience the process of maturing or growing up.

This is true for all leaders and parents. Just because you are the head of an organization or have children doesn't mean you understand yourself; and it is this lack of awareness of self that precludes you from being an effective leader or parent. The illusion is that leadership and parenting is positional or biological or is somehow otherwise defined by a checkable list. Instead, it is an attitudinal pattern. What this means is that you don't need to have the *label* of parent or leader to be one.

In considering your own patterns, it is helpful to ask yourself:

1. Where do my beliefs come from? How have I evaluated and tested those beliefs?

2. How would I describe myself?

3. Am I who I say I am, or am I who others say I am?

4. How am I being what is necessary in every situation?

Self vs. Others – The ability of the individual to interact successfully with others determines their success. If you want or need others to behave in some way, you must have the skill to influence that behavior in them. Conflict resolution is one of these skills.

"Self vs. Others" is the area of interaction, encompassing the spectrum from conflict to cooperation. It is the realm of philosophy. History has provided many sets of principles that attempt to govern how humans interact to increase cooperation and minimize conflict. The Christian religion has ten such principles and philosophers from Aristotle to Russell have provided many more.

Do others have free will (could they decide otherwise) and do you have free will?

5. Where is their locus of control? That is to say, where does behavior originate (inside the person or in the environment)? What causes others to do what they do?

6. What education, experience, energy, and emotional maturity do others have?

7. Is the world of human interaction absolute or relativistic?

8. How do I lead my business? (Monarchy, dictator, democracy, socialistic state)

9. How do I distribute wealth in my company?

10. How is my business organized? (Function, geography, product, channel)

11. How do I price for clients and what do I keep for myself?

If you were to develop a set of principles by which humans should interact with each other, what would you choose? Let's think about these in an abstract context: suppose we were on a deserted island.

Suppose the island is habitable, reasonably safe, and life sustaining. You are currently alone on the island. What are your chances of survival? Your knowledge and capabilities are limited to what you know or have at present. How would you rate yourself?

Now turn to *how* you would survive for a period of time. Remember that, aside from being life-sustaining, this island has nothing—no phone, medicines, power, Internet, or lifelines. What are you able to do to survive? What personal circumstances make you more or less able to do what is necessary?

Now, imagine adding one person of your choice. What kind of person do you need? What would complement your skills and personality? A doctor? A biologist? Someone who can climb trees? A black person? A white person? An LGBT+ person? A male? A female? A child? What qualities make them important in this isolated world?

How do power dynamics change when each person has different attributes? How do the personalities interact? What is their view of self-esteem, of being a victim, being a boss? What "rules", if any, would you follow? How would you divide the work? What other questions do you need to think about when adding this person?

What do your answers say about the world as it exists? Are the patterns we build on this island transferrable to the broader society?

If all parties are able to "be what is necessary", could you imagine a better possibility for survival? In doing this experiment, you can see how many interactions might exist and—if the stakes are high—perhaps many other patterns for the ways things could fail. It is the basis for conflict and cooperation.

Let's add a third person, introducing for the first time the idea of consensus as well as cooperation. What skills would you think should be added to the two-person island? How do the island dynamics work now, presuming that decisions are made on a majority-rule basis? If you agree with person A today, do you agree with person B tomorrow or next week? If "they" are always opposed to you, do you revolt or conform? With the addition of the third person the problems move from purely technical survival to behavioral or adaptive interactions. The idea of "trading" becomes more important.

How does this island idea relate to leadership or parenting in the non-island world?

Let's say in the business world you are promoted to be the boss and you have direct-report employees and others further down. By what principles will you govern? How do these principles change from the island scenario to yours? How will you interact with your employees? What, if anything, is your plan?

1. Who gets to decide what?

2. What will the culture you create be like?

3. How is power distributed?

4. How do minorities fare?

5. Will you tell people what to do or ask them?

6. When do you decide it will be mission accomplishment over people's welfare?

7. *How* will you decide what to do? What if it conflicts with your boss?

8. How will you decide what skills people need? Training?

The same line of inquiry applies to parenting. What do you have to necessarily be, so your children will become "what is necessary" for them? Can you actually be what is necessary? If not, then what?

In the desert island and business examples, most of what you thought about was likely on the cooperation side of the conflict/cooperation spectrum. However, in order to lead or be a parent you must master conflict, because there will never be enough money, time, people, and skills for everyone to do everything they want whenever they want to. That means resources get apportioned and divided. Who gets what? In emergencies it is reasonably clear, but in daily life it is not. Do we cut back in marketing to support IT, or do we reduce our IT in favor of more salespeople? Do we let the oldest child do something the youngest is not allowed to do?

This does not mean you must seek out conflict, but you must be comfortable with it because the best ideas never stay the best. The best products are overtaken. The best drugs eventually fail. And the best children confront adversity.

A conflict driven pattern I have observed is how fathers with daughters have a different capacity to relate to women in the workplace compared with fathers who only have sons. Those with daughters have become comfortable with a different kind of relationship and conflict at home.

The key experiences for fathers are that daughters at home:

1. Do not have to listen and can withhold important support and cooperation

2. Change attitudinally over time, requiring various fatherly adjustments

3. Can object, revolt, and offset the natural power relationship without fear of "losing their job"

4. Develop clever strategies for negotiating power and responsibility.

5. By becoming used to these interactions, corporate life for males can be much more comfortable. Bear in mind that if a male only has his mother, and wife as models for female conflict management, there will be gaps like the ones above. The fear of lawsuits or

misunderstandings especially in this environment is tempered by experience with daughters going through all of this in school.

The reverse is also likely true as well. If a daughter does not have a meaningful father in her life, then the interaction with men becomes much more about trust and power than it might normally be. The idea of defective males is less powerful if a daughter's experience with her father is otherwise. The key experience for daughters is that:

1. Males do sometimes listen and can be trusted in certain things explicitly.

2. There are skills in dealing with fathers relating to power, acceptance, revolt, trust and free will that are belief forming. Force and anger are frequently ineffective.

3. Time changes people's views on events past and present.

4. There are built-in asymmetries in life and you get to experience some of them with a father. That makes seeing these same asymmetries in business less disturbing.

5. On the downside, for the daughter there can be despair, as in the case of abandonment or death, and disgust in the case of abuse. If the daughter can "deal" with father and has acquired an ability to "control" the male environment in a predictable way, then life in society may be easier. It is the survival skills that the daughter learns in the home that enable her to function confidently outside the home.

As a note here, I am not sure about a mother raising sons. The relationship between a mother in management and her sons may be much less about learning the interactions listed above and more about knowing just what males are capable of doing. There is constant testing and pressing to "see what happens if I do this" that mothers of boys contend with.

Self vs. The Known – The ability of the individual to master the environment, from changing tires to downloading apps.

This area is about how well we understand the way that science and the known (non-human) universe works and how we interact with it. In business, this is commonly referred to as "the mission". It is a combination of theories, learning, and experiences, both yours and others. This area addresses questions like:

1. How will I teach my child to drive?

2. What is the strategic plan of the company?

3. How will we merge these two companies?

4. Why is this baby crying?

5. When do we need a new product?

6. How can I apply mathematics to my world to solve problems?

7. How can my child develop skills to solve their own problems?

8. What will be necessary so that I can do what I am tasked with doing?

Because this is the area of the known, the temptation is to become a parasite. If you don't know how to do something, but someone else does, you can simply pay to have it done. Choosing to pay someone else to think for you and solve your problem means you know less about your environment. If you don't test *yourself* against the environment, you can't be effective in this area.

In theory, this area of "self vs. the known" is what education—specifically college—is meant to prepare you for. Entrance applications, tests, and essays are designed to assess how well you can learn or how well you *have* learned to relate to the known world. This is the world of what is known and in some ways what can be taught. The word "known" limits this area. This is the first quadrant where there are verifiable answers to many of the questions. If you look at the questions above, they all have a high probability of being solved.

An important understanding in this quadrant is that much of what's in it already exists. Yet it includes research. Research is simply a way of converting the unknown into the known. Concepts live and die here. Disease research, modeling research, and psychological research are examples of converting the unknown to the known.

As you develop your understanding of this area you will recognize patterns in the world around you and see how they continue or break down. For example, people who went to college and majored in subjects that interested them, but then couldn't get to where they wanted afterwards, failed to recognize the basic patterns of life in their major. They could not be what was necessary. Sometimes, this involves an ability to make the future come true over time. For example, if I major in art history and want to work in that field but don't recognize that the number of jobs in this area is severely limited, then this is a fail in managing the "known". In this area, success can be measured by how easy it is to bend the environment to your will—which depends on your ability to recognize which patterns will help you accomplish your goals and therefore realize what you have to do.

People who recognized patterns have done much of the significant, original work done in science. It is also about the idea that it no longer matters what you know as much as how fast you can learn. Before Google, it mattered what you knew. Now, because so many things are precedent setting, it matters how fast you can learn. The gap between college graduates and established, older employees is smaller now than at any prior time.

These changes also cross into parenting; technology has made parent/child interactions very different. Some of it is to a parent's advantage (easy monitoring) and some not so much (availability of vice). Diseases, drugs, sex, and expectations for kids have changed dramatically. The "way" to be what was necessary in 1960 is not the way of today.

As a student coming out of college, patterns matter most of all. How do I navigate the company? Which division has the best future possibility?

How can I reconcile patterns so that I can thrive? There are several patterns that matter irrespective of whether you are a leader or a parent:

1. You must prove you can manage

2. You must prove you can lead

3. You must prove that you are exceptional at both defusing and initiating conflict when necessary

4. You must be able to operate effectively in the four areas discussed in this vignette

So much in this area now happens without precedent. As a result, it is crucial that you know how to build models for discovering the future, which is like trying to have the experience without experiencing it. You start from the basis of "what must be true", a little like the desert island scenario above. Then you try to build more complexity in steps.

It is not hard to start with knowns. Gravity on earth, increasing entropy, laws of motion, the existence of governments, aging of living things will all continue to apply no matter what. You must create your own view of what then must be true in the future. What are the implications if those things really *are* true? That is the work that must be done in this area. This is a pattern.

As a leader or parent, you are constantly taking what is known and trying to predict what must be true later. What should I do now so that my child can go to college? How many more people do I need to get this system implemented next year? Where will I get the money, the time, and the support? Who are the best teachers? Where are the best schools?

Self vs. The Unknown – The ability of the individual to know when they don't know and to do something about it with intent.

This is the area of what happens when it is not known what to do. For some people it is the challenge of what to do when they aren't challenged. Consider the following as a possible original explanation of the unknown:

In the beginning there was nothingness and there was no God…only an empty void of blackness, or whiteness, or whatever your mind best creates when it considers nothing. But there was no God.

And the nothingness vibrated with the natural harmony of nothing. And in this nothingness (A) a vibrational disharmony randomly formed in opposition to the natural harmony (-A). And this resonance grew until there was an enormous expansion, later to be called the "Big Bang". But there was no God to witness it.

The force of the explosion caused expansion and created quarks, leptons, muons, energy, and heat. But there was no God. The primordial soup distilled into particles, then into atoms, and further into molecules and still further into gases. And the gases condensed into matter and the matter into planets, stars, asteroids, comets, and energy according to equation, but again there was no God.

As the earth cooled, minerals clung to the sides of geysers forming crystals, and the faces of these crystals provided places where atoms of one substance could rest beside atoms of another substance and create molecules. As what would later be called "time" continued slowly on: a combination of molecules rested together, patterns formed, and *life first appeared*—but there was no God.

As simple life came into contact with other life, they formed complex organisms, which grew and became more complex.

At last, an organism formed that realized that "it" was different from all other "not it". This was the first inkling of what would later be called consciousness. When this organism died, its consciousness left its body. It became the first consciousness that was independent of life. As other organisms of the same type died, their consciousness joined the first organism into a collective consciousness. But still, still there was no God.

As larger and more sophisticated animals died, containing ever more sophisticated consciousness, there came a moment when the collective consciousness became aware that "it" was different from all other "not it". At last, God had begun to take form. As life continued to develop and evolve, the collective consciousness grew in sophistication.

The collective consciousness followed the development of mammals closely until one day a single consciousness in pre-human form had a thought that struck the collective consciousness a mighty blow! The thought was of God and the thought shocked the collective consciousness. God was created and saw that this was very good.

As pre-humans died, the collective consciousness grew in massive leaps of sophistication. God grew by leaps of sophistication and a cycle began. When a new human starts, it grows without consciousness until one embryonic day when it knows itself from not itself. On this day, the channel to the collective consciousness is open for messages to go to and from God. And God sends parts of the collective consciousness into the new life, calling these parts "the soul".

Sometimes this soul contains bigger parts of the collective consciousness of those who have been before, and the human remembers these former lives. This is called reincarnation. For most, however, the soul they are given is uniquely their own. For God, the growth of the soul while on earth is of the utmost importance. If the soul returns to the consciousness greater than it was at birth, then it is pleasing to God, for God grows in power and consciousness as well.

In time, the collective consciousness realized that some channels to some humans were more open than others. And God made known that which would be known as "good".

- Do not kill, because if there is no consciousness then there is no God.

- Do unto others as you would have them do unto you because it preserves life and grows the soul.

- There is only one God and through the channel of the soul "we" are in touch with you. Later you will return to "us". While on earth, grow your soul.

For Jesus, Buddha, and Mohammad the messages were clear. God told these three to spread the word to others, that the mission of humanity was to grow the soul. It came to be understood that preserving and improving another's life increases the souls of both. But those humans that cause a decrease in life or bring harm or suffering diminish their souls, in some cases to less than they were given. When these negative soul humans die there is no return to the collective consciousness.

Mankind learned to pray along the channel to "them" and God saw that this was good. Three books were written by many people who could understand the notes that played in this channel. They became the Torah, the Koran, and the Bible and told of the ways to preserve the soul.

And God knew the souls of the world. The collective consciousness knows what we think and what we believe. This consciousness however is not all-powerful. It does not know what will happen in the next moment in time; it only knows what all are thinking at this moment. It cannot decide which consciousness returns or when a human's time has come; and it cannot overcome physical laws or defy the dimensions of physics.

The collective consciousness cannot determine destiny; all men and women are free to choose whether to believe in God or not. Those who believe must first do no harm and then do good for others. This grows the soul. That is the purpose of being here and its simplicity is its elegance.

What is the point of this last section? It is to say that finding alternative explanations for the "unknowns" is a skill that must be acquired as one of the four quadrants to be mastered.

Moving between the areas

What if someone is stuck in one area or only functions in one area? People get stuck for four reasons:

1. They are stuck because they have had great success in one area and don't feel the need to be in any other.

2. They are stuck because they don't know how to be effective in an area and so don't ever go there

3. They cannot move between areas even if they want to. They cannot be what is necessary.

4. Chemistry (drugs, disease) prevents them from functioning.

Being stuck is not terminal if you see the pattern. If you see that you are not effective, then you are 50% of the way to improving yourself. Some people are able to pull issues from other areas into their own preferred area. This is not effective, although in some cases it can provide an insight that improves an outcome.

For example, if you are a "feeling" person and operate so as to limit confrontation, then all problems get dragged into your "self vs. others" area. The goal for a feeling person is to reduce conflict. This is valuable in hospitals and in classrooms but can be ineffective in battle and in deliberately created conflicts.

In other cases, you might be only "in your head" and operate in the Self vs. Knowing. If you don't have data, if you can't see the connection, etc. then the issue does not exist. Sometimes this includes people, which is a disadvantage if your problem is in the Self vs. Others quadrant.

People who do not think about what they don't know or who believe they know everything are another example of being stuck. If you don't challenge your own assumptions or test your ideas with others you cannot know what you don't know.

In the end, this ordering of the skills necessary to survive and flourish covers all the primary areas that must be mastered. People vary greatly in their mastery and many of their failings are more easily talked about with a model like this to organize the discussion.

8.

What is a Real Defense?

The year was 2323. The crime was premeditated murder. The victim was a man in his early twenties. The accused was an older woman of indeterminate means.

The judge leaned over the bench and addressed the lawyer for the defendant. "What does it mean that your client is asserting that she is not a real person? In what sense is she not real?"

"You honor" the lawyer began "as you know for anyone to be considered real they must be conscious which is to say they cannot be hypnotized or unconscious. In addition, they must also be aware, meaning that they must be able to assert an understanding of the moment and not be impaired by drugs or deception. And finally, they also must maintain access to their memory so as to be able to describe the recent past with some specific accuracy.

In addition your honor, a real person must be able to recognize differences and must therefore have a trusted system of accepting and processing input. They cannot for example be blind, or be obstructed, or prevented from experiencing true differences. And they cannot be confused as to whether they dreamed the event in question or not. They must know for certain in some way.

But the final distinction of a real person is whether what they are accused of doing happened the same way in higher dimensions as it did in our four dimensions. We will argue your honor that in the fifth dimension my client would not uniquely qualify as a person and therefore can not be guilty of this crime."

"I see," said the judge and she turned to the special prosecutor. "And what does the prosecution make of this novel interpretation?"

"Your honor, the state will show that if a person exists in any dimension then they exist in all of them. There is no distinction or particularity to higher dimensions. Besides we have witnesses that establish the defendant was present when the victim was murdered."

"Very well" said the judge "the defense may proceed."

"Your honor knows that in the four dimensions of space time, individual people can exist in very close proximity. This is the obvious basis for how any of us agree to meet anywhere at an agreed time. But a curious thing happens in the fifth dimension. The four dimensions we are familiar with take on a Mobius strip appearance. Here is an example:

If you start anywhere on the strip above and follow you path around as though you were walking, you find that you will walk on both sides of the strip yet arrive back to your original starting point on the same side of the strip that you started on!

In four dimensions no one can occupy the same exact space at the same time unless there is an accident, such as when two cars collide. Yet in five dimensions one person can occupy the same space and time as another and yet be physically separated by the fifth Mobius dimension. In our four dimensional way of thinking it would be like one person standing right side up on the strip and a second person standing upside down on exactly the same spot at the same time. The important point is that neither party would be aware of the other because they are separated and unable to communicate with each other and neither would think it was they who were upside down.

My client's dimensional records show she was in the fifth dimension when the murder occurred. The witnesses would have seen both my client and the victim appear in nearly the same four-dimensional space/time but my client would have appeared and disappeared as she moved along the Mobius dimension. She could have been visible but would have had no access to the victim because she was on the other side of the Mobius dimension!"

"I see," said the judge. "So in reality they were separated by the smallest of distances but in that same reality they were separated by an entire dimension. This is the first time I have heard a case defended in this way. How is it counsel that you know of this dimensional quirk?"

"I really don't know your honor…" was the reply.

APPENDIX TO CHAPTER 8
What Is Reality?

When you hear the word reality, what do you think of? What is reality dependent on? Suppose that there are eight components of reality that together serve to define it. Then, reality could be expressed as a function of the sum of these components. In the form of an equation it looks like this:

$$R = C+A+F+I+D+M+N+\Sigma.$$

Reality (R) = f(Consciousness (C) +Awareness (A) + a "difference" (F) + Truthful Input/Transmission/Reception (I)+ the dimension of observation (DOO)+ Memory (M) + the "Not a Dream Assurance (NDA)+Epsilon or error term (Σ.)).

As you think about this equation, spend a moment and ask yourself what you think reality depends on. It is not an easy exercise. For centuries, philosophers have crafted ideas and notions of reality only to see some of them overturned by recent developments in physics.

First is Consciousness (C). If there is no consciousness, then there is "no known thing" that would be capable of "having the experience" of reality. Does anything exist if "we" do not know that it exists? No—unless we postulate a "universal consciousness" (God) that knows all things at all times. This is easy to understand by realizing that if we do not know that something exists, self evidently we cannot say that it does. This is at the basis of the theories we create. If we write a mathematical equation to explain how the universe works but we have no *evidence* that it works in that way, then the thing being explained does not exist except as a theory.

Second is Awareness (A). Everyone driving on the highway has had moments of being conscious (able to drive the car) but "unaware" (having no idea where they are) because they have focused conscious thoughts on something other than driving. This is unconscious driving in a "zoned-out" state. Simple consciousness is necessary for reality, but without awareness it is as meaningless as that period on the highway where you can't remember how you got to your current location. At the macro level you "know" you drove from A to B, but at the local level you cannot attest to anything specific that happened along the way because you were not aware. You can also imagine yourself so drunk that you cannot "remember" how you got home. This does not mean you never "really" arrived home. You did. But you cannot speak to anything that happened along the way because there was no awareness of the trip. If there had been an accident or even if you had hit someone, that reality would not exist for you at the time because you were not aware.

Third is Difference (F). In his most condensed idea of "reality," Descartes suggested that because he could "think" it indicated that he was conscious, aware, and that because these two states could be shown to exist, then he, Descartes, must exist.

He had first set about trying to decide if anything could be unambiguously true or real. If not, he would doubt it. He started by doubting his senses. He postulated that he could be dreaming and so everything that he observed could exist in a dream, and because he could not say for sure he was not dreaming, he doubted his senses. (Note: if you think about this for a moment you can list ways that senses are fooled: magic, mirages, dog whistles, heat and cold of a liquid if each hand is in a different extreme temperature of hot and cold water and then thrust simultaneously into room temperature water. There are two different sensations for the same liquid).

Descartes then envisioned a demon. This demon was capable of making him believe that something is true when it is not. He noted that in mathematics there are collective beliefs that something is true, but maybe a demon was just fooling him.

Finally, he turned to his mind and thoughts. He said that thoughts could be fabricated, adventitious, or innate. Fabricated thoughts are mere inventions of the mind (like this essay). They can be discarded. Adventitious thoughts are external thoughts that cannot be discarded, like the imposed feeling of heat standing next to a fire. Your mind cannot will it to not be there and you cannot use your mind to turn the flame cold. Finally, innate thoughts are thoughts implanted by God. Each of these avenues were explored by Descartes and found to be capable of being doubted. His conclusion, and the only thing he could not doubt, was that he existed and that he thought.

What Descartes left out and what is crucial is that he had to be able to think and also *not* think so as to have a difference. If he could only think one thought and never *not* think about this thought or any other thought, then it would be as though he was in a photograph. He could be conscious (I exist) and aware, but "frozen" because nothing would change. Without the "difference" in his thoughts he could not state in his newfound reality, that he existed.

To further this idea of difference, let's say you suddenly lost all of your senses. At this moment you would be denied "input". But what would you still have left? Obviously, you would still be conscious for the very reason Descartes surmised: the reason that you could think. You would still be aware of all that you had experienced, assuming that you continue to have a memory.

Another way to consider this problem of difference is to imagine that you cannot "think" but yet you are conscious and aware. That is, you have input of some kind, but it is non-differentiated. Suppose that "everything" was black. Would there be a reality? Apart from the "thought to no thought difference" noted above, there would not be any reality. Yet, by introducing a white space somewhere in the blackness, a reality is created by the difference of awareness or "attention" caused by being able to shift awareness (input) from white to black and back again. This validates consciousness and awareness.

Let's now look at the "normal" reality that we perceive which is actually determined by "movement". Our senses provide input. We are conscious. We are aware and there is a difference. Because things change through movement, there is a before and after that we record. We experience this as "time", but in truth it is simply a difference validating consciousness and awareness. When the universe became "real", physicists say time began. This is so because motion began. Nothing existed and then it did. Or something existed and changed form. Either way, there was an ordering of events.

Einstein recognized an interesting exception to this reality when he imagined himself in a light beam. Inside the beam there would be no movement because nothing could change, since the light of any change could never reach you. All light of movement would be traveling just as fast as you were. Nothing would change in your beam of light. Outside the beam things could of course change, but you would not be "aware" of it because no light from the change could reach you. Thus, Einstein concluded there is no "absolute" reality, only relative reality.

If you comprehend what is being said you might say, "But the notion and 'proof' of the universe was not established until we as humans had been conscious for thousands of years. Are we saying that the universe only came to exist when we discovered it?" The answer is that the current universe exists if it passes the eight tests here, but its history does not exist until a consciousness can access it. What if the record showed us that the universe had *always* existed and that it never began? Then "reality" would include no beginning. Today, we can say that there was no pre-universe reality because we can't access it. It remains a theory.

Fourth is Input (I). It is input that creates awareness. This input can be as simple as a thought (noted above), but it can also be any device that can make a difference appear to a consciousness. We say our senses do this for us. We augment our senses to understand reality by using oscilloscopes to give access to waves that we cannot see or prisms to see that light is made of colors that we cannot normally see.

This is the case of pain as well. If I say I am in pain, you have no way to access that information. You are conscious, aware, you hear me describe a difference, but this is not enough for you to say my pain is real to you.

In black hole theory, the idea of information being "destroyed" relies heavily on the mathematics of gravity and the notion that no light can emerge from a black hole. Thus, no input to anything outside the hole is possible from inside the hole. This is only one side of it, of course. We are not sure that, if we were able to follow information into a black hole, whether we would be able to retain that information. We would certainly lose contact with the outside universe. So, there are essentially two different realities because input is relative.

Here is yet another way to think of input: Suppose we take the famous question "If a tree falls in the forest and there is no one to hear it, does it make a sound?" How would one answer this? This question seems to be unanswerable. It has been posed by philosophers forever and seems to defy either a "yes" or "no" answer.

But this turns out to be an illusion if you can sort out the pattern. The illusion here is that the question starts by telling you that there *is* a tree and that *it did* fall. It makes you *conscious* and *aware* of what "it" is by stating that there is *in fact* a tree and that "it" did *in fact* fall. Period.

The next part of the question however tells you that you do not *in fact* know what you have just been told. It declares that no one was *in fact* there. It declares that now you don't really *know* that a tree fell, because you weren't there. After describing these two realities, it asks you to decide an absolute by asking if it made a sound. So, how can that be answered?

Suppose we start with a simple pattern. If you <u>are</u> in a forest (conscious-ness + awareness) and a tree *does in fact fall* and you hear it or see it (input), it <u>*does*</u> of course make a sound. We are there; we hear it. If, however, we focus on the second half of the question, we find an intriguing line of reasoning.

Suppose we enter a room full of students on the first day of class and without any introduction simply ask, "Did it?" Try this with any person or group of people without introducing the set-up above. Just ask them to answer the question "Did it" with no context! (They are conscious but not aware). What will happen?

Most students will ask a question in return like "Did what?" Or, they will argue about the value of such questions or perhaps they might just guess *yes, no, maybe,* or *I don't know/care.* But it is not possible to answer because, without *knowing* what "it" is, they are *not conscious of "it"* and *not aware* of what their answer means. They are truly in the state of the person who is "not there". Therefore, there was no consciousness or awareness and therefore nothing to record any input. Therefore, there was no sound and therefore no reality.

Now, you might say, "But I can imagine a forest where no one exists. I can imagine a tree falling. I know the laws of physics. It will still make a sound." Not so. By imagining the forest, you are bringing consciousness to the problem along with awareness. The effect of asking "Did it?" is to eliminate consciousness and awareness in such a way that there is no way for anyone to say anything about a tree. The act of imagining is the act of introducing consciousness.

But what is "really happening" here? By asking, "Did it?" you are removing consciousness and awareness from the question. You are eliminating the "existence" of the tree or anything else for that matter. You are asking a pattern-less question. But it points to the true answer.

Let's go back to the original question. If there was in fact no consciousness to hear and to be aware of the tree, then there *simply is no event.* Just like the universe prior to the big bang. No consciousness is aware of any input. In the absence of conscious awareness, there is no entity to know that anything happened. There can't be. And you've shown this by asking, "Did it?" to a group of students without context. Something that cannot be accessed by consciousness is not knowable until a consciousness knows it. So, the answer to that famous question "If a tree falls in the forest and no one is there…does it make a sound?" is an emphatic *NO*. This is why no one can answer the question "Did it?" when you pose the question, because you did not tell them of the event.

Perhaps you can understand better by thinking about the future. You can guess about it, suggest probabilities, run decision trees, etc. but until "the future" happens and is *known to a consciousness*, it simply isn't real because no one "knows" it. It is only a possibility.

You might also tell your students that you are leaving the room. Once outside, you push a pencil off a table. Two minutes later you return and ask, "Did it?" They of course will have no idea what you're talking about. Yet YOU do. You were there. You are simply not telling them what "really" happened outside. Only you know the "reality" of whether the pencil fell off the table. Only you can say whether "it did". Seeing the pattern this way suggests that there are two realities, *but only one contains an awareness and consciousness to attest to what happened.* Thus, reality is dependent on a difference (or on information/input, if that is easier to think about).

Many of you know that a man named Schrodinger proposed this same kind of thinking in an experiment about whether a cat was dead or alive.

Schrodinger imagined a box with a cat in it. He further imagined a material like decaying uranium, which emits a random alpha particle every so often. There is no way to predict if/when it does. If/when a particle is emitted, a device that emits cyanide gas into the box is triggered, killing the cat. Since there is no way to know whether a particle has been emitted (it is highly random), there is no way to know if the cat is alive or dead without opening the box. There is no certain reality for the cat. There is only a probability. The cat can be either alive or dead. Just as above, conscious awareness determines reality.

Schrodinger was using this metaphor to describe the dual nature of an electron. Experiments have shown that an electron can behave as *both a particle and a wave* depending on what experiment the observer chooses. In fact, *the observer's choice* (consciousness plus awareness) in some sense "*causes*" the reality of the electron to become certain. Here we can assert that "reality" is determined by a consciousness and an awareness that in fact is both necessary and sufficient to determine "Did it?" or, in this case, "Was it?" (Particle or wave) (Alive or dead). Before these things engage or interact with the experiment, it is both and neither.

Finally, I offer another pattern into the mix: the Turing test. This was a test proposed by Alan Turing and went like this:

> *Turing proposed that a human evaluator would judge natural language conversations between a human and a machine designed to generate human-like responses. The evaluator would be aware that one of the two partners in conversation is a machine, and all participants would be separated from one another. The conversation would be limited to a text-only channel such as a computer keyboard and screen so the result would not depend on the machine's ability to render words as speech. If the evaluator cannot reliably tell the machine from the human, the machine is said to have passed the test. The test does not check the ability to give correct answers to questions, only how closely answers resemble those a human would give.*
>
> *Source (Wikipedia)*

So now we have a consciousness and awareness, but the input is _fooled_. It *believes* that something exists when it does not. The key to reconciling this view of reality is that, in addition to one consciousness being fooled by bad input, there is another consciousness and awareness that can assert to the "true" nature of the test. This is an important addition to the tree in the forest problem. I might conclude this section by asking, "If you were up against a computer to prove you were human, how would you do it?"

The fifth quality of reality is the Dimension of Observation (DOO). This simply states that reality is dependent on how many dimensions the consciousness resides in. A two- dimensional sentient being would obviously have a different reality than a three-, four-, or five-dimensional conscious-ness. The more dimensions a consciousness is aware of and can access input from, the more "reality" can change and the larger the number of differences. In a twelve-dimensional universe there is more to be aware of, even if all except the first four dimensions are only accessible through mathematics. This also introduces the question of whether our reality is only what we can access. Access can mean proven through mathematics, etc. If the universe happens in twelve dimensions and we can only physically access four, then what is reality? It is only what we can consciously examine. If we can't access, then they do not really exist. It's only a possibility.

Sixth is Memory. This was introduced previously as a requirement for the reality of thinking alone. If one does not have the memory of a prior thought, then there can be no difference to a consciousness with no other input. It is also indispensible for the idea of the white and black difference noted above, as consciousness must remember the previous color input. In other scenarios, memory serves the normal function it always does and is less noticeable.

Seventh is the Not a Dream Assurance (NDA). This is a tricky notion. There is no reliable way to assert whether being conscious is "really" just a dream or not. You could be dreaming now. It does not feel like you are but you can't be sure. If consciousness is a dream, then reality is an illusion because dreams are different from non-dreams as we experience them. I cannot state with certainty that what I am writing now is not in some dream and it might not even be *my* dream! There is always the brain in a vat notion and the idea that memories could have somehow been implanted during the last five minutes to "fool" the consciousness that reality is something else entirely. It is a different input problem and one of interpretation. The consciousness is aware and is receiving input, but the environment is not "real" or is intentionally false. If we consider this case or the dreaming case as disqualifying reality, then we are considering the many philosophical scenarios where all reality is an illusion. Perhaps a more concise way of saying it is that without an assurance that we in fact are not dreaming, we cannot assert that we are not.

This brings us to the eighth function of reality. It is Epsilon (E). This is the "error term". In this case, it is the reality introduced in the movie, *The Matrix*. This is the notion that, fifty thousand years from now, mankind will have invented computer programs that are so good that the avatars within programs are conscious. While this is extraordinary by today's standards, it is not an unknowable possibility. Today, when two parties are playing games together on the net, their consciousness is maneuvering their avatar. It is only one additional step (albeit a large one) to the point where the software can move the avatars without our consciousness.

If this assumption were made, what would we experience? Fifty thousand years in the future, if the ability to simulate consciousness in worlds exists, then it is highly likely that *we* are a in a simulation today. Why? One can imagine that every person in the future could have thousands of simulations ongoing at any time. This would mean that there is a high probability that we are in one of those simulations now. The only way this would not be true is if "we" are the people who become the people fifty thousand years from now. Obviously, if we are the forerunners of the future that we are discussing, and since we are not there yet, we are *not* now in a simulation. A second possibility is, if there are some sorts of prohibitions against creating simulations in the future, then we would not be a simulation today.

In essence, the argument is that if future software is good enough to simulate consciousness and awareness, then we have no way to know if we are in such a simulation—unless we are somehow able to break out and examine the code, or meet the programmer (perhaps God) in this discussion.

These are the eight functions of reality. Each is necessary in some way, depending on the scenario, but none is sufficient by itself.

9.

The Day the Earth Stood Still

Once upon a time, all electrical devices stopped operating. No one knows any more how that happened because no one is working on *that* problem. It could have been an EMP from the sun, it could have been an air burst nuke, or it could have been a computer hack. It doesn't matter.

In the first fifteen minutes after it started, planes were forced to land because their automated systems ceased to function, cars stopped or, worse, failed to respond to driver commands. Elevators got stuck. Cell towers went down. Computer components (phones, i-Pads) were fused together and all stored data was inaccessible unless it had been protected in some way. Power dropped to zero because even solar power relied on electric impulse circuits. But, even if these *had* been protected, there was no power to recharge the devices. GPS ceased.

Shortly after, pumps failed, liquids flowed to the lowest levels. Gasoline was inaccessible except from trucks that still operated. Water ceased to flow. Refrigerators stopped. Submarines had the best chance to be unaffected apart, from the buried military ops centers.

Within three days, victims were appearing everywhere. In an instant, complexity and speed screamed to zero. Life became sheer survival: find food, water, medicine, and maybe matches. The end. Society was reset to the days of the Roman Empire (in the urban areas, of course). Government disappeared. Police disappeared as they sought to help their own families. Same with the militaries. No one could get anywhere quickly. Nothing with a computer worked anymore, so speed went to zero. It took weeks or months to contact relatives. Some people never saw food again as food trucks were attacked and everything was stolen.

Within two weeks, certain places became savage, tribal ganglands. In Hawaii, the Caribbean, Taiwan, New Zealand and other locations, food supplies vanished. In large cities, people stole whatever food supplies they could find.

In four weeks, trees and berry bushes were picked clean. Gangs showed up at farms that had chickens, cows, and pigs. They were armed and hungry. People began to die in fantastic numbers. No one was there to bury them— and then the diseases began.

In a year the population of the world fell by seventy percent. The remaining people were on their own or collected together on farmlands. Farm animals were priceless, as was medicine of any kind. Weapons had been essential for protection in the early weeks, but bullets were now only a means to eat.

No one knew how many people were left. No one got any news except from local sources. There were no laws, no rules, and no justice. Society had collapsed. Horses were back. Buggy whips were back. But they were in short supply.

How had all of this happened? Why didn't "they" save us? Why did so many have to die? The only answer was, "Because this is how we had chosen to live."

But the good news is that humanity did not die out. Certain people remembered important truths and there were still old-fashioned books with valuable survival information. Medical and other scientific texts became extremely valuable. People started the long road back.

When life is just about survival, it is simple and slow. People found seeds and began planting for the future. Animals were managed. Any one with "old" knowledge was asked to write it down so that it could be used later.

And people helped each other because "there but for the grace of God go I". People began to treat each other with respect, provided they could do chores. That was the coin: one's own labor. If you were old, there were still things you could do. But life was short. If you became sick: no one could promise you would be helped.

Children were born. The species continued. After five years, human life on the planet stabilized and certain things began to return. Where there was water falling, there was the ability to generate power. It just had to be modified. Some people were left who knew how. Once power was available, things could be tested and used, mostly farm equipment.

After ten years, communication began to open again around the globe. The old ham radio network reappeared. It wasn't robust, but it was there. Travel was still by horse or boat, mostly. Societies around fresh water fared better than most. Sails were back again. A few ships were outfitted to explore how the rest of the world had fared and return with the news.

It has been 15 years and this is where we are now as I write this summary. I have been appointed to be the recorder, because I am too old to be much value on the farm. I get just enough to eat to write these words, but it's fair. We used to rely on complexity and speed. Now we rely on simplicity and a steady pace. I think we are doing better.

APPENDIX TO CHAPTER 9
Complexity and Speed Will Always Defeat Biology

This statement on its surface is self-evident: Any process can be made so complex or so fast that no human can execute it. This matters desperately, because the ability of humanity to participate in everyday complexity and speed is unevenly distributed.

If we look at a year like 1975, well before the internet, the number of people that one could influence in a day was a function of whether they had a fax machine and a telephone. The ability to change data and rework ideas was very limited. Suppose we thought we could influence a hundred people a day in 1975. Now (in 2019) the ability of an individual to influence millions of people a day is possible. If we take other examples like air travel accessibility, the ability to make changes to existing plans, and many other daily activities, we can say that we are able to live thousands of 1975 days in just one of our 2019 days. Speed has increased. And so has complexity.

There are very few people living now who understand how an app is written, how cell towers work, or even how the internet can exist. A citizen in the year 2019 would say perhaps that it does not matter. If they don't know something, they can Google it. This is of course true after a fashion. But what happens if you don't understand what Google tells you? What if you are not "smart" enough to handle the complexity of the idea?

You can test this idea by Googling:

The Schrodinger Equation

Protein Synthesis

Bertrand Russell's Analytic Philosophy

Linear Programming

Ayn Rand's Objectivism

One hundred and fifty years ago, none of these ideas existed anywhere in the world. In 2019, there are millions of such ideas, with more being created every day. To be a specialist in medicine, physics, or information technology means an eternal struggle to stay current with the pace of innovation and complexity. In addition, staying current with the speed and complexity of the day-to-day world is a secondary feat all its own. Complexity is icing out more and more people as they fall further and further behind.

This heightened complexity has collapsed some interesting theories. Keynesian economics (which espouses government intervention and spending on infrastructure and projects as a way to increase production in an economy) fails at high levels of debt. The current borrowing of the US government is so complex and so immutable that it just "keeps going up". It is almost certain that Congress will not stop it. So, what happens when this complexity reaches the point where the financial markets deem US debt to be non-payable? What happens when no amount of taxation will allow the US government to pay off its debts? The actual answer is not interesting enough to elaborate on here, but it collapses the notion of Keynesian economics as a viable monetary policy if the limits of borrowing capacity are reached. Keynes never saw the day when a government could not borrow because it had exceeded its capacity to do so.

It isn't just in economics that complexity has collapsed a theory. Darwin proposed that survival was based on one being the fittest. Back in Darwin's time, for example, if someone were an idiot, he was only able to influence people within an area of say, ten feet. This was the "effective span of idiocy" (ESOI). Because people knew the idiot, he was ignored and his rants and misinterpretations died off, never to be known. He would have licked a frozen flagpole, kept a ferret during the plague, or struck a match to see if his gas tank were empty and vanished from history before he ever made any impact. Darwin would have been correct.

Now, however, because technological innovators and medical practitioners have done such a good job, both the life span and the span of influence of the garden-variety idiot has reached heights never envisioned by Darwin. The internet now gives the idiot access to hundreds of millions of people. The ESOI is now 26,000 miles. Darwin never foresaw the effortless elevation of the less fit to levels of the fittest driven by simplifying complexity and giving access to all. This period ends when the last of the original fittest die and the least fit are on their own.

Are both complexity and speed somehow destined to forever increase? It is obvious that they bring gains in productivity and span of control. Will the world eventually become just AI (speed) and the programmers (complexity) who care for it? And what of biology? It is a certainty that high levels of complexity and speed surely defeat the most able of human biology.

Suppose there is hope. In fact suppose it is counterintuitive hope. In order to defeat complexity and speed one need only have a superior network. When young people are told to "network" in the early days of their first work experience it is because a network allows for superior management of complexity and speed. Any person who has worked for a corporation knows that getting information first is crucial. (What is senior management thinking about, are we making an acquisition, what are we doing about the bad press). Knowing what is coming is a first step in making it happen more slowly because you have bought time to think about it.

It works with speed as well. If you have made a mistake, or unintentionally misrepresented something and it can still be fixed then speed is important. Often it is the speed of being able to communicate with the most senior people that make it work.

Now you might say, "Yes, yes, all of this is obvious" and yet so many people either have no network or they don't use it to reduce complexity and speed. Promotions are given, jobs get open and filled, and others are given the best assignments. Often this is because of a network failure.

But office networks are only one example. Having a group of five or six friends of equal or greater intelligence, experience, skills, or contacts is essential. Once a month this group gets together to discuss a book perhaps or the month's events. These people should be as different from you as possible and they should be capable of original work, not just parroting the words others have written.

Finally, consider this a note to parents with respect to complexity and speed. It is a sacred duty of parents to reduce complexity and speed of the environment while simultaneously increasing the ability of your children to deal with complexity and speed.

In a previous essay I wrote about mastering self, others, the environment, and the unknown. These are the four complexities or speed traps I suppose. If parents are not even aware that these exist, if they have no natural instinct for dealing effectively in these spaces, or if they too are overwhelmed themselves, then their children will be ineffective as well. Part of this duty is to provide a safety net so that children can take some basic risks and learn how the world truly works. Part of this duty is to explain what is happening outside the family. This does not mean providing some kind of parental "take" or a declaration of biases, instead it is a balanced questioning of where the child is in their thinking and how good they are at assessing complexity and speed.

There are of course many instances where complexity and speed have been beneficial (GPS, mobile phones, disease control, first responders) and there will continue to be. But many people on TV and in life are not capable of living in this world without help.

10.

Is It Capitalism or Socialism?

Socialism is the trend in blue states and their ilk;

They don't have guns or butter, and they'll force us to drink milk.

The government will give us stuff, to keep us all alive

And decisions won't be needed, and we won't work nine to five.

'Cause the government will tell us what to do and buy,

Everyone will pay their share and get their piece of pie.

We all will have those front row seats to watch those queues increase

'Cause government will tell us what to start and what to cease.

In many ways it's easier to put your mind away,

And wait for those who know the best to tell us who will pay;

What happens though when hopeful payers can't ante up the cash,

But needs are escalating, like a poorly treated rash?

Where does Foggy Bottom turn, to keep the cash a-flowing?

What *if* the only cash it gets comes from those who's "knowing"?

And what if those who know it all stop work and all the pay-ah?

Then we'll have exactly what they got down there in Venezuela.

Or we could stick with cap'talism its mantra is seductive;

Everyone makes billions, if you just become productive.

But no one is quite born alike, and most of us might suck;

But then there's those who struggle hard to really give a f—

And then we have the cheaters, the hashtaggers all among us,

Who make minority-a-ness as pleasant as toe fungus.

'Cause capitalists know markets and the pricing of it all,

They will sell us in a heartbeat if we don't get on the ball.

Those bour-geoi-sie get wealthy from we riff raff's hard-fought labors;

And they do each other's dirty work 'cause it turns out they're all neighbors.

Rich get richer, poor get poorer the rest of us have debts;

While "they" are on the Vineyard, gassing up their private jets.

So socialist or cap'list, or I just don't give a s**t?

DIY or servitude, or maybe say just screw it?

'Cause in the end, it's up to you…it's coming now or later;

You're either your own master, or another master baiter.

APPENDIX TO CHAPTER 10
Is Capitalism Dead? Is Socialism Next?

Capitalism: an economic system characterized by private or corporate ownership of capital goods, by investments that are determined by private decision, and by prices, production, and the distribution of goods that are determined mainly by competition in a free market. *--Merriam Webster*

Socialism: any of various economic and political theories advocating collective or governmental ownership and administration of the means of production and distribution of goods. *--Merriam Webster*

To begin a discussion on the merits of these two systems, let's ask the question, "Do you believe that humans are fundamentally selfish, or altruistic?" This question is not trivial because at the heart of it is a "belief".

There are many examples of humans who find themselves facing a crisis in another human's life: a child drowning in a stream, a car accident with injuries, or a person choking in a restaurant. Even if the person is unknown to us, there is something within us that causes us to act or to intervene at perhaps some cost or risk to ourselves. The idea that we would even risk our own lives for a stranger is not unknown. These are principles of the collective good. But they are principles of best action, not of economics. Is there a natural belief in economics that is as powerful? Is that way socialism?

On the other hand, there is also something within us that causes us to act to save our own lives or the lives of our loved ones, even if it means taking another person's life. There is a self-interest that prevents us from killing ourselves on most days. Our egos test things all the time to see what action is in our best interests, even if it affects others badly. A mild example of this is bartering for a hat. To the extent you pay less, the merchant is less well off and vice versa. Within this idea of self-interest lies the idea of individualism. It is the notion that we ourselves should determine our own destinies and make our own choices. The broader idea of individualism is introduced here because it contains both the idea of capitalistic economics and a government focused on individual rights. It is important to see both the political and economic mutual dependencies.

There are of course situations that combine both principles of socialism and individualism. In ancient times, hunters supported gatherers and vice versa. This relationship was self-interest wrapped in a social cooperation. In the case of early humans, the survival of the individual was enhanced by cooperation with others. Would you say this is true today? Would we say that our economic system today enhances the survival of the individual? Does it promote cooperation with others? Is this approach as necessary as it once was?

There is evidence that socialism and individualism have both an economic and societal component. The reason I have switched from capitalism to individualism is because, unlike socialism, capitalism does not normally contain the governmental aspect of socialism. Below you will see a chart that shows where capitalism fits into an integrated idea of individualism.

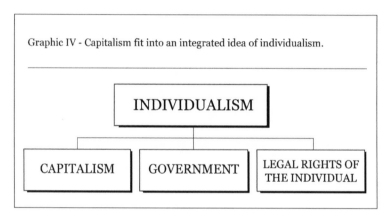

Graphic IV - Capitalism fit into an integrated idea of individualism.

INDIVIDUALISM

CAPITALISM | GOVERNMENT | LEGAL RIGHTS OF THE INDIVIDUAL

In addition to capitalism and government, we must add the legal system. In an individualistic and philosophically consistent integration of ideas, we would start with the government's founding principle that "all individuals are created equal and are endowed by their Creator with certain unalienable rights, that among these are life, liberty, and the pursuit of happiness". These of course are commitments to individuals—not to villages, majorities, corporations, or unions. In addition to these commitments is the judicial system that is responsible for ensuring that people are "innocent until proven guilty", private property is protected, that government powers are constrained with respect to the Bill of Rights, and that trials are fair. Individualism must be integrated from the bottom up.

Finally, we come to the matter at hand: capitalism. From an individualistic integration of government and law, capitalism is a method of individual self- determination of what will be owned, what price will be paid, what self interest will be satisfied, and what philanthropy will be exercised. This is of course the US today and will be the future unless it is changed.

The second possibility is the same integration but from the perspective of socialism. Here is the chart of socialism.

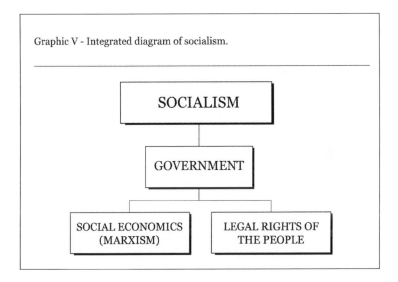

In this case, the government is conferred with the responsibility of determining the basic tenets of societal interaction. In the US today, we have many social programs including welfare, social security, Medicaid, cash assistance, food stamps, public housing, education, training, various "services" (*pro bono* legal assistance), and childcare, to name but a few. The federal government administers these programs, with other programs operating at the state level. In these cases, the government has decided what assistance to give, how it will be administered, how it will be paid for, and what the recipients are required to do to get the aid. In law, there have been several decisions surrounding the rights of minorities, union formation and dues payment, status of class actions, and the extent of regulatory rights.

It is in the means of production and distribution of resources that the difference between socialism and capitalism exists. One is market-determined and one is government-determined. The individual would say that the government does not have a right to decide pricing, availability, or production goals. It should instead focus on national defense, free trade, management of a national currency, and infrastructure, among other things. The socialist would say that the government must determine the amount of aid to the disadvantaged, standards for the environment, social policies (immigration), and social rights (ADA standards). These condensations of capitalist and socialist beliefs are caricatures of the richness of both systems.

Let's discuss Karl Marx for a moment. Marx got an important piece of his theory of capital formulation right, but he missed some of the much broader points. He only knew what he saw and could not foresee the way business could progress.

Marx thought extensively about government (feudal lords), workers (the proletariat), large business owners (bourgeoisie) and the under-class (revolutionaries). Marx wrote that the changes needed to forever expand capitalistic customer bases, reinvent process, reduce costs, and improve product would continue to create catastrophic social forces leading to revolution. This is Marx 101. He got this part mostly right. Capitalism as an idea is asymmetric. There are winners and losers. There are haves and have-nots. This pressure on the social fabric is constant. Technology displaces workers. Products are replaced by better and cheaper alternatives. Foreign workers will work for less, and so consumers buy from them. Conflict is inherent in competition, leadership, sales, and wealth distribution.

Marx also got it right when he wrote that capitalism would inevitably need a continuous reinvention to sustain its growth. As consumption grows worldwide, the means of production spreads worldwide. When this happens, Marx said, it leads to social disruption. This argument is worth considering more deeply.

Is it possible that we are now transitioning into a worldwide disdain for globalism/capitalism? Is the populist movement that has grown in the US, Britain, and the EU growing because displaced workers from the proletariat are revolting as Marx said they would?

Marx thought that the proletariat (workers) would experience stages leading to the revolution and that these stages repeated themselves. The first is the struggle workers have with the bourgeoisie (business). As workers see imported wares competing with their own goods, they lash out against the injustice of the bourgeoisie and governmental decision-making. During this time, the proletariat is frustrated by the resource allocation of the bourgeoisie and government. But the proletariat is not alone. The bourgeoisie class is simultaneously in turmoil as well. As mentioned above, the necessity of the bourgeoisie to forever expand customer bases, reinvent process, reduce costs, and improve product is the basis of capitalism. It is chaotic in that it both creates and destroys. It is at odds with workers, as gains do not always lead to increased employment. They may increase productivity and actually decrease employment.

Marx also saw the bourgeoisie class at odds with government as well. Regulation, legislation, extortion, and corruption are burdens on the bourgeoisie's need to grow.

Marx went on to say that, when capital is first formed, the bourgeoisie is in fact the labor (Think small business start-ups). As the bourgeoisie increases its customer base and profits both in real numbers and, more importantly, in financial power, it begins to hire workers. Later, in certain industries, machines would replace labor. The effect of this replacement is that the bourgeoisie is able to lower wages as machines substitute for labor and to in effect create the two classes described above: themselves and the workers.

Marx then said that the workers' natural reaction to this was to band together as they did in the 20th century by forming unions. Strikes would discipline the natural advantages of the bourgeoisie. Marx further saw the Communist party's role as being the unifying force between the disaffected workers of all countries. Communism would become the "uber union". Once established, the "uber proletariat" (the Communist party) would overthrow both the bourgeoisie class and all world governments at the same time, while "managing" the underclass to assist as revolutionary agitators. Just suppose that this is what is beginning to happen today.

Today we have a collection of forces loose in the world. Bernie Sanders in the US appeals to people who see the world this way. They rail at the ability of business to destabilize the world and the lives of the proletariat.

However, it may not be as simple as all that. None of the four Marxist classes are static. For example, as proletariat workers compete for the fewer remaining jobs and the bourgeoisie capitalists compete for better competitive advantage, the system swirls and continuously reinvents itself. Marx thought even the small business owner, the shopkeeper, the artisan (all natural allies of the bourgeoisie) might more rightly connect with the proletariat. He wrote that it was the sweeping trend of large industrial change (today one might say "globalization") that united much of society against the "producer capitalist".

Today, one might say that we see this rejection everywhere and it is part of the rejection of the world governments. In the US, the population sees the bourgeoisie as the problem that is assisted by a government that does nothing to rein it in. The other half of the country sees the government as the problem because it does regulate business but the regulation hampers the efforts of the bourgeoisie to grow even more powerful.

Marx further suggested that for an existing government to sustain itself it had to take sides. Does the government tax the bourgeoisie and transfer wealth to the proletariat? Does the government reduce corporate taxes and allow the bourgeoisie to expand faster because it creates jobs? Does the government act to encourage lobbyists from the bourgeoisie, or does it act to discourage revolutionaries from the proletariat?

Does this sound familiar? The basis for proletariat revolution in Marx's mind is fairly simple. If your job has been transferred overseas, if your wages are being reduced by technology, if you are being marginalized because of education or because of opportunity, or you have borrowed massive amounts of money and the jobs available are not good enough to pay off your loans, then society for you is unfair, biased, and in need of change. Your fight is with both an ineffective government and the bourgeoisie. It is a seductive argument. If you have nothing or have "negative something" (wealth), then there is nothing to lose by revolting. These rejections of government can be seen in the election of the Obama and Trump administrations. What they have in common is the rejection of the status quo government.

This is also true in the UK (Brexit), in Brazil (impeaching their president), and in other European countries (the Netherlands, France, and Italy) where the people (workers) are forcefully dissatisfied.

While Marx concluded that the answer was revolution and the overthrow of the capitalists and their governments, he did not foresee the speed and power of the reinvention and the strength that would be created by the bourgeoisie class from the ranks of the proletariat. He also missed the most important real transformation of the last fifty years.

Where Marx got it wrong was in saying that the basis for capital acquisition by the bourgeoisie was always labor. His argument was that no capital is ever created except by the work force. In a static world with one, two, or three people producing just enough to allow all three of them to survive, labor produces goods that are then consumed by the same labor. In that closed system, Marx was perhaps close to being right.

But labor is never equal in speed, quality, or cost. People are fundamentally either more, or less valuable. And this is where Marx missed it. Everyone is not equal. Everyone has unequal health, age, energy, and temperament. It is the *unequal* ability of an individual to acquire food, shelter, and weapons through their own efforts that creates the divide. As labor's skill grows, *its ability to become the bourgeoisie (perhaps by starting a business selling food that they can gather faster than others) and acquiring additional capital grows as well.* This growth is based on two principles. It is the willingness of labor to eventually risk its own livelihood and to put its existing capital at risk. And it is also the replacement of itself by technology or hiring other labor at a far more rapid and certain pace than Marx could possibly have foreseen. The man who can lose his job and start his own business moves from the revolutionary and victimized class to the bourgeoisie. This is the way out for the proletariat. This is still happening in the US, but…

The speed and complexity of economic life has indeed left many people behind. The role of labor has actually bifurcated between the "knows" and "knows nots". The "knows" people have become bourgeoisie singularities, in effect very wealthy individuals. This is because having a small degree of knowledge about a very special operation or process can create vast wealth. Traders, mergers and acquisitions lawyers, hedge funds, Google, Facebook, Twitter, and Amazon are all beneficiaries of the "knows" economy. This bifurcation is not the result of bad education, but a fundamental inequality in ability.

Let's examine the current American social interaction between government (feudal lords), business (bourgeoisie), and labor (proletariat). It should be clear to all of us that the past fifty years have brought a fantastic reduction in the amount of labor in first world countries in almost every industry. Agriculture, car manufacturing, gas pumping, food check out, bank tellers, most back office operations and even the military are far less dependent on labor than they were even a hundred years ago. Marx would have said this is inevitable. But let's examine the outer edge of this development.

Let's say that technology can eventually replace 70% of the jobs in society. (Driverless cars, pilotless airplanes, self-service fast food where you swipe your card and go to various oven doors for your purchase, algorithmic trading, planning, resource allocating, and maybe even pills instead of food).

Only computer programmers, landscapers, builders, and roofers may be necessary! They are needed "in person". They become the "knows" people. (You might then ask what happens if humans make their labor ever more expensive by raising their pay). This is simply an invitation to the "knows" people to design a cheaper way to meet the demands of the consumer without using any of this labor at all. (This is of course why raising the minimum wage just hastens the destruction of the proletariat and increases the pressure for a revolution). Marx would have said that if government cannot or will not make change for their people, then they deserve to be replaced.

While somewhat tongue in cheek, what happens to the 70% of jobless people that are alive but cannot have a job if everything is replaced by machines? This could actually be the case in America, if machines are able to meet many of society's needs. So what then would the role of government be? What does the American government become if the "knows" people, the economic producers (bourgeoisie) go the other way and become *smaller*? Do they have all the power? Does the bourgeoisie in effect become the government? If so, is *that* the real revolution to come? And what happens to all the hungry, thirsty, homeless, sick, naked old people that are not part of the bourgeoisie and not part of government? Marx would suggest they revolt and destroy all that is repressing them.

The next point is about yet more debt. This time, it is the government that is borrowing. What happens if the government is borrowing money (T-Bills) so that it can lend it to students who then can't pay it back because their job does not exist anymore or the jobs they can get don't pay enough? The government can default; simply by saying that if you own a T-Bill you now own nothing. This would clearly cause a revolt among the bourgeoisie because they would lose wealth held in those bonds.

If the government does nothing, then it must raise taxes to cover the bad debt or the "forgiven debt". Again, this will cause a revolt of the bourgeoisie class. So maybe the government stops offering student loans; but then the proletariat has no hope and it is *they* who revolt. This small example is why there is so much anger in America today. The government is making things permanently worse by bad decisions and policy. Why? Because the government is now filled with "knows nots". They have lost control. We are where we are because government does not understand what is happening. And we are faced with four impossible choices:

1. Allow the bourgeoisie to continue to reinvent and destroy more and more jobs in the hopes they will quickly create new ones. They may, but we're going to have to be "unequally smart" to have one. The proletariat and ever more so the government do not trust this outcome.

2. Provide the proletariat welfare checks every month from the government. Everyone gets one. But who will lend the government the money to do this? Perhaps no one. Then the government will have to tax the bourgeoisie, but there may not be enough of them to tax income effectively, so the government will have to tax net worth. This is the seizure of property that Marx believed must happen.

3. Put the government in charge of everything. Nationalize everything. Wipe out the bourgeoisie. Yet communist governments have proven over and over that they can't run everything or perhaps anything. And why would a programmer continue to program if the government determines what he'll get paid no matter how valuable he is? This is where communism cannot defeat basic human nature. Ayn Rand territory.

4. Change government. Keep it Federal where possible but move it closer to the people. Reduce its cost. Put in term limits on ALL government employees, including the non-elected, of no more than ten years and no pension. Make it so foreigners can run for election in the US. The only condition is that they must have held the equivalent position in their own country. This would open the

presidency to European leaders or even Asian leaders to run the US. And finally, make certain legislation by referendum only. Take certain issues out of the hands of government and put them in the hands of the people.

As long as democracy exists, there is a vote, and the proletariat can change its fortunes. This is the key. No matter what the future is, no matter how close to a revolution we may be, we can vote. The consequence of voting precisely *because* of the social upheaval has never been higher in the US. Democracy is not dead with one exception. If the government and its perma-labor can corrupt the process, or if companies can buy the process, then democracy will die. When that happens, the ability of anyone except the government to flourish will decay. And that's when Marx foresaw the real revolution would arrive.

In a short period of time we will all be faced with a version of these two futures possibly being proffered by people we don't like. Which system will it be?

11.

Some of The John Templeton Foundation's Big Questions

American John Templeton created the Templeton Foundation. This is the same John Templeton who founded and made his fortune from the Templeton Funds. In 1972 he established the Templeton Prize that honors affirmation of life's spiritual dimension. In 1987 Mr. Templeton created the foundation that bears his name to support innovation, creativity, and new ideas.

Several years ago, the Templeton Foundation began a series called *Answering the Big Questions* and invited specialists in their fields to answer questions that the Templeton Foundation people thought were important. I "just supposed" I was one of the people asked to comment. **Before reading my answers or visiting the Templeton Foundation website, I encourage you to think about yours.**

1. The Templeton Question: "Does the universe have a purpose?"

Yes. The answer to this question is the same even if the question were posed as "Does the universe have meaning?" or "Is there a reason we (humans) are 'here'"? But to respond "yes" requires the important assumption of a consciousness. The concept of "purpose" mandates that "something" must exist to which any purpose could be assigned. If there is no consciousness, then there can be no purpose. If the universe is at least in part conscious, then its purpose exits so that consciousness has something to be conscious about. Consciousness is compelled to respond, "Yes, the universe has a purpose" because it allows me to know I am conscious!

There may be multiple forms of consciousness. Either we assume our own personal consciousness (the universe has purpose because *I* say it does) or we assume a collective consciousness (the universe has purpose because *we* say it does) or we might assume a special consciousness (God says the universe has a purpose and it is *mine*), any of which would suffice to say that the purpose of the universe was to validate consciousness.

If consciousness existed without a universe, (and if the consciousness was only aware but could not think as Descartes did) then the consciousness would be unable to know that it existed. Therefore, the universe exists to *confirm* consciousness.

2. The Templeton Question: "Will money solve Africa's development problems?"

The answer is no. Money does not really *solve* most long-term, structural, nation-state problems. It does, however, enable certain choices. Money can even create problems of its own. Good money does not ensure good choices. The question is interesting for what it assumes. Does Africa really have solvable development problems? Who is it that is framing these "problems"—Africans or the West? What *should* Africa aspire to? What should Africa develop into? Who should decide?

Someone in Africa will frame these answers and it is they who will solve or not solve development problems. More money however hasn't historically always accomplished better things. More money has not solved poverty, lack of education, discrimination, and health care or cured cancer, AIDS, MS, or the many social-development issues, including those in the US. And money does not solve problems at the level of the individual. Many studies have suggested that greater wealth does not, in fact, equal greater happiness. So, the answer to the question "Will money solve Africa's development problems?" is a certain "no".

There is perhaps a more interesting question and that is, "What problems *should* Africa solve?" There are the obvious western ideas: peace, sanitation, health care, education, and jobs. But these are western developmental perspectives. If one asks, "Will Africans be happier if they get western solutions to African problems?" I am not sure what the answer would be. If we solve their problems or they solve their own problems using our standards, will they be happy? Suppose they are happy now? Suppose that they are content with the life they experience? Would more money mean more happiness?

3. The Templeton Question: "Does science make belief in God obsolete?"

Not at all. Science is based on the premise that something has some reasoned, verifiable, and repeatable predictability. God is based on "belief," which is individual and subjective. Science and theology are different categories because they seek to explain the "way things are" using different models.

These models might be integrated if God suddenly showed an indisputable modern presence that converted *belief* to *fact*. In the absence of this miracle, it is possible that science "discovers" God somewhere in its normal search for answers. Either way, there would be reconciliation between science and religion.

In the meantime, science cannot have a position on whether there is a God simply because God can't be proven. Not having proof certainly does not render the idea of God obsolete. As long as there are unexplained observations, there is always a possibility that some sort of God exists.

Science and theology differ in their theories of causation. The classic example is the moment just before the beginning of the universe. However, even within science there can be multiple causes for the same thing. Multiple causes do not make any explanation obsolete. It just means that they exist as separate concepts. So too, are the concepts of God and science. They are simply two frames of understanding existence.

If science has truly made God obsolete, then it should be able to explain "everything" in some way. All causes should be known and all effects predictable, even if only in terms of probability. Clearly, many things do not fit neatly into this categorization. Many things will always be impossible to "know". (Heisenberg's Uncertainty Principle, the "unambiguous" state of the electron, etc.).

In the end, God so far has proven to be inaccessible to science. Despite all the certainty that science provides, there are still those of us who will find comfort believing in God. It is belief over science. But that is what belief is; knowing without proof. If God stays inaccessible to science in this way, then there will forever be a gap. But God will not be obsolete.

4. The Templeton Question: "Does the free market corrode moral character?"

Of course not. It is asymmetrical information that corrodes moral character, no matter what form of social interaction or economics is in play. If all parties to a "deal" know their own position and know their counterparts position, and they both know what each other knows, then both parties are equal. There is no necessity that both parties must reach a deal, even in this case, but they know where a bargain must be found. Once we assume asymmetric information however, one party will have an advantage. From there, it is a question of whether they *choose* to "take advantage" of their knowledge. The free market does not have anything to say with respect to this asymmetry. Overall, the free market premise would suggest that it is the market that seeks to ensure that all information that can be known is known. One may argue that it is the absence of the free market (and perfect information) that corrodes character.

No matter what human interaction one considers (economic, technological, sexual, etc.), it is the symmetry or asymmetry of information that determines what "trade" is possible. Whoever holds the better information has an extra "choice", which is the choice to take advantage of the other party.

The advantage of asymmetric information relates directly to a kind of morality. If two parties agree to an exchange, and if they both recognize that there could be asymmetric information, then they have agreed to the possibility that they may not get the best deal possible. There is a difference between an asymmetrical agreement and immorality. The free market allows choice and everyone is free to decide what to do, based on what they believe their "best information" and situation to be. There is no corruption inherent in the market, only in the willful manipulation of information by either party. But the same exists in socialist countries, tribal countries, etc. Information is rarely known equally by all parties and even if it is, it is subject to interpretation that can cause any person to make a "bad" decision.

The markets of Moscow, China, Iraq, and everywhere else are no more or less moral because they all have asymmetric information. In a free market, you have a choice to deal or not. You have a choice and an ability to decrease asymmetry. In controlled markets, you do not. Markets do not corrupt. People with asymmetric information do. This includes governments. A more interesting question is, "Does unopposed governance corrode moral character?"

5. The Templeton Question: "Does evolution explain human nature?"

The answer is: No. The first important realization we need to make is that evolution is a human idea. It's a result of the work Darwin did, but in the end it is our nature as humans to categorize things. Evolution is an invention of humanity to explain life on this planet. So, it is human nature that explains evolution—not the other way around.

The one attribute of human nature that creates a problem for evolution, and therefore confounds an answer to this question, is our "ability to do otherwise". Human nature has the ability to reject its own nature and to do or be something else, (even a disadvantaged something else, thereby decreasing the chance for survival). It is as though our natural program can disregard evolution. Even if we say that humans have a nature caused by evolution, we must also say that humans can also be capable of disregarding this process. The obvious case is genocide. If a certain kind of organism is intentionally eliminated for some reason, then obviously it cannot evolve, therefore evolution is not determining human nature. If human nature can override evolution, then evolution does not determine human nature.

APPENDIX TO CHAPTER 11

Some of The John Templeton Foundation's Big Questions

My reason for including these answers to the Templeton Foundations Big Questions is in the spirit of original work. A perfect piece of work would be for you to read the answers from people who do work in these fields for a living. It is not to decide whether my answers are better or worse but to decide what yours would be. Nothing that I wrote was borrowed from any other author. Nothing I wrote called for anything other than what I hoped would be an original view. Many of these kinds of questions are out there in the world today and the views that people have are not surprisingly all over the place.

It is easy to read the arguments for and against some of these questions but in doing so you become less capable in the sense that you now know "an answer" and have only to support or reject the answer. That effort is trivial. The main work lies in establishing the answer in the first place.

When you do this you'll find that the assumptions that you make and the ones made by the other writers are the basis for disagreement. Debating assumptions is at the heart of reconciling different points of view. I hope that you wrote your own answers before reading mine and visiting the web site.

12.

Could This Happen?

Location: North Korea at a time not unlike the present. Conversation between Duri, Commander-in-Chief of the Korean People's Military Forces and Eun, Secretary of the Communist Party for Supreme Leader Kim Jong-Un.

Eun: "The fool US administration has added sanctions beyond our nuclear program. They are now restricting food and energy imports. The EU and UN have responded with words of basic support. The Supreme Leader is looking for options. "

Duri: "Are we finally talking about a military engagement? And if so, you know that Xi and Putin must be consulted. Do we have those channels ready?"

Eun nodded. "Yes, yes of course. *You* know that! The Supreme Leader wants to have unanimity among the three of us, but he is not going to let these sanctions go unpunished. He asked me to get a list of possible choices."

Duri pressed his fingers together and stared at the ceiling. "What do you think the Chinese and Russians will say?"

Eun: "You know that, too. The Chinese will say that they do not want us to force them to deal with the US. They have negotiating power and they don't want us to be a chip. The Russians will tell us something, but there is no reason for us to trust what they say. They just don't want to be disadvantaged."

Duri: "Yes of course, but are you saying that this meeting is to talk about a military option? There are military options for us that would require that we _not_ speak to the Russians and Chinese."

Eun: "Yes, we are talking the military option, but why would we not tell our brothers?"

Duri: "Consider this. Any military action, or should I say _every_ military action, is doable if no one knows who is responsible. Every act is possible if it can be hidden as to who is responsible. You remember the 9/11 attacks in the US? These were ascribed to "terrorists", but we know it was the Saudi government teaching the Americans a lesson. But no one has been able to prove that they sanctioned the attack. And they have oil. This is the basis of my comment. Anything that cannot be proven is possible. No one, not even the US, will attack us if they don't know for sure it is we who are responsible."

Eun: "So what are you thinking about specifically?

Duri: "Just suppose we let some time go by. We do not object too strongly to the sanctions. We may even let Russia and China agree to support us in humanitarian aid requests. We wait four months. Then…do you recall the M-37 project the Navy is working on? This explosive is extremely large but not nuclear. It is capable of being produced by any nation. We would adjust the M-37 to work like a mine. We would place two of them some distance in front of the carriers that the US has in the Gulf of Oman—"

Eun: "Oman! But that's on the other side of the world!

Duri: "Exactly. The explosions would lift the carriers out of the water and turn them over. The Americans would lose only military equipment and personnel. They could not go to war unless they were sure what happened. China and Russia would not know but be very concerned by any random

US action and would move to block it. The metal and activating devices of the M-37 will all be of European origin. The design is on the internet. Even if pieces are retrieved after the explosions, they can't be attached to us. Everyone will think the Iranians did it. That's why we would tell no one. You remember the success we had with Flight 370? This is the same principle."

Eun: (speaking carefully): "This cannot be discussed, even with the Supreme Leader. How would we get the M-37s there? How would we place them? And who would give the order? How do you know that it can't be traced to us?"

Duri: "If you agree to this plan, I will arrange for the M-37s to be put in place. How is not a concern of yours. But there are at least four undetectable ways. The "order", as you say, is not really necessary. If no one really knows, then they can easily deny that they were involved. It will be the truth. This operation is yours and mine. You will make sure everyone has an alibi and I will make sure no one else knows what happened."

Eun: "But surely whoever places the devices—"

Duri: "There will be casualties. Not many. And the tracing of the metal and other material will be impossible. We will melt the shell of the container and recast it so the metal is of different, untraceable purity than anything anyone is shipping. The parts will be off the shelf and we will use our operation in Africa for those. None of the parts we use will come to us in their final assembly. Your job will also be to make it seem as though it could have been a terrorist event by getting some of our mid-eastern contacts to have certain 'chatter'. "

Eun: "Do you think we can do this?"

Duri: "I think lots of people can do this. That's what makes it so good. You and I will never get the People's Hero of the People for this, but we will both look at each other over our wine glasses in future years and nod. That's good enough for me."

Eun: "When?"

Duri: "It's already being carried out."

APPENDIX TO CHAPTER 12
Ultimate Terror Attacks and the Media

Ultimate terror attacks are all about what maximum damage "could" be done and not necessarily what is being done. What matters for the terrorist is to create uncertainty and provoke people to wildly speculate. In the end, a terrorist doesn't really have to *do* anything. They just have to get people to *believe* they are doing something.

Let's look at what true terror might be like. Imagine New York City, for example. Just suppose a terrorist group gathers together twenty Jihadists and infects them with strains of certain incurable diseases with high mortality rates (the plague, for example). The Jihadists volunteer to die by simply coming to New York and mingling about in every mass gathering of people in the city. As they die and the disease begins to spread, the media receives word of the plan from the perpetrators and all civil control will effectively be lost in the ensuing, media-hyped panic. Imagine 17 million New Yorkers needing to get out of the city and a nation of people wanting to wall them off. Hospital people will be interviewed, planes will stop flying in to LGA and JFK. Parents will bring their kids home from school. The CDC will be issuing warnings and the list goes on. All of this because twenty people created an epidemic.

Helium balloons carrying boxes of a deadly germ powder, etc., could accomplish the same effect. The boxes are released into the air from many points around the city and break apart at a certain altitude. It only takes a few people to see the balloons and a few people to get sick before terror sets in. The powder will be tested, and its toxicity will be disclosed. The opioid "crisis" is a tame example of what this would look like. The media will pin down all the important responders with questions and again, away goes the story.

One of the keys to terror is to create "denial of access". If no one wants to be in a certain place out of fear for their lives, then effectively they have been denied access. Again, all that is necessary is for the media to report that you *should* be afraid, and the terrorists have won. The loss of real estate value in a "contaminated area" and the loss of income are significant. California fires are an example of a "real" denial of access. Alarm scares of the past are examples of the media denying access. It is important to realize that terror is being heightened by the way the media engages in it. Even on relatively benign pronouncements, government officials point to "millions" of citizens who will be uninsured, starving, without shelter, and out of work if one or another program is adopted. Everyone wants to be on the extremely negative side of the story. That's what the terrorists are hoping for.

It isn't even necessary to actually <u>do</u> anything. A person with knowledge of certain cases that have common symptoms in hospitals could easily announce that a "new plague" is upon us. Getting negative news into the media is the key. If the media believes (or believes it *should* believe something), then terror has a footing. Fact checking is inconsistent and is sometimes influenced when the disclosure of information harms a particular party or politician. This is why the media can be used.

Using a country's media to provoke terror is an easy and effective way to further the aims of any terrorist organization. The reasons are obvious. Reporting things that <u>could</u> happen is far more interesting and will sell more ads than reporting what <u>is</u> happening. All media is in a tough place here. They want to "get the story" and they want to be exclusive or first with their reporting. The tension between a point of view and the truth is very relative.

For example if the president says she is withdrawing from a treaty, one media outlet will attack the abandonment of a noble cause and another outlet will praise a decision that should have been made years ago because it disadvantages the US. To be clear this has always been the case to some degree but today balance has disappeared. By their own admission cable news has become like AM radio in its partisanship. This may be a result of the view of media ownership or the attraction of particular believers to a particular point of view, or a relaxation of the idea of balance. In any case getting a story printed that supports a particular media's view is very much different than before.

Foreign countries can also actually use the domestic media for terror. Suppose that tensions between North Korea (NK) and the US were unbearable. War seems imminent. Further suppose that North Korea cleans out its jails and dresses western-looking criminals in US and South Korean military uniforms. There is a battle of sorts fought in front of NK media coverage, alleging that US and South Korean commandos have infiltrated the country and are being repulsed. The NK government conducts a missile attack on a US battle group. A first strike on a deployed battle group is very different than an attack on a country's soil. If a carrier was destroyed, who could say it wasn't self-defense? The Russians and Chinese could be as manipulated as we would be. And before the truth can be exposed, we are in a war brought about by an inability or unwillingness to determine the truth. Or, the North Koreans got a very cheap win.

The important thing for the terrorists to accomplish in these instances is to make us believe that they are not singular events. The event must be replicated so that it causes real fear. The anthrax scares in the early 2000s are an example. Governments react based on whether any particular act can be replicated.

Even a controversial notion like global warming can create a kind of terror for those who are convinced that this will end the planet's ability to continue. Government policy plays an important role, of course. To the degree that government foments a "yes this is a problem" or "no it's not" response, it promotes instability and possibility individual sensations of terror across the country. Some of the recently elected politicians in the US are suggesting an overhaul and change of the entire energy signature and social infrastructure of the US to assuage this fear. This is unintentional terrorism.

The final kind of terror comes from a country's domestic citizenry in the form of revolution or even the secession of a state (CA or TX) or a country (UK) from important relationships. Because no one can foresee the results or even the process of these events, and because no one can tell what they should do in the short term, effectively a kind of fear exists. To declare it terrorism, one would have to ascribe intent to the fear. Most people do not think of it this way, but it can be far more real than most of the scares that have been publicized over the past years.

This kind of terror is particularly important in a situation where a country's leader has private interests overseas that are accessible. Real estate is a good example. The ability to influence government policy may be as simple as threatening to destroy or damage financial assets around the globe. It is not hard to find situations where the ownership of buildings can be traced to certain individuals. This terror is personal, but it also affects the country. If you have business in a building that might be blown up by revolutionaries, you are less likely to frequent it.

Finally, it should be clear that computer hacking and denial of access is a powerful form of terrorism. If a group is trying to harm us and they access the means to do so (block power, stop information flow, destroy data, etc.), they can create terror.

So what are we to do, and by extension, what is the media to do about contributing to the ease of a foreign power to influence the US population? What can we do to be sure that what shows up as a chemical attack is not staged, or is a US program gone awry (border enforcement) truly awry, or that demonstrations that turn violent can attribute causes in some reasonable way.

This essay is not about freedom of the press but perhaps a few concluding thoughts. First, it should be clear that immediate impact events on human health or safety are reasonably outside the scope of reporting concern here. These would be hurricanes, live shooters, Ebola outbreaks and so on. There are many sources, often many pictures, and many ways to corroborate these events independently. There is little doubt about the facts and what a "better" outcome could look like.

The problem of press reporting conflict has been written about many times and has to do with the public's right to know something offset by damage that might happen to the country if our enemies had the same information. The question is who gets to decide and by what standard?

The idea of a free press resonates if the press does not see this freedom as including a right to hold any particular philosophical view on every issue all the time. The press is not free if it is aligned against the people, ANY of our American people all the time. There is a struggle to assert what exactly the word "press" means. Is Rush Limbaugh an entertainer or "the press?" Is CNN the "press" or an editorial creation company? And who is the owner and what influence are they imposing on reporting?

In the end if it is the press that we rely on to police the way things are reported then it must be the American people who police the press.

13.

Pay it Backward

The sun shone down on the date trees and the palms that lined the entrance to the compound. Amperion had to stand on a chair to see out the window. His once dark hair had streaks of grey and his silver beard spoke to his fifty-five years. From his vantage point, he could see the four men being accompanied to the gate at the edge of his vision…and then they were gone. *They will never return* he thought. He had been very careful in selecting them. He smiled a careless, joyous smile.

The year was 1437 on the island of Elcor, just off the Aegean coast. The island was part of the Ottoman Caliphate and had been so since the beginning of storytelling. Amperion had been a prosecutor in the sultan's court and he had been the land's best and most feared. He had sent many men to Elcor to serve their sentences. Those were the "lucky" ones. Others had just been eliminated. The sultan's enemies had disappeared one by one under Amperion's skilled, legal arguments. He wielded them as the assessors in the dungeons wielded their knives. He applied the law with the same effect as the scimitar- wielding executioners. It was swift and final. Amperion pressed every advantage, and if he were losing, he was not above putting political connections to work. He never lost. He never wavered.

Amperion and the sultan had differed only once, and it was over Durel, the sultan's eldest son. Durel stood accused of killing a woman in his private chambers. It had been a bloody and prolonged death. Palace attendants had heard the screams, but they disappeared. Amperion knew people who knew what happened and how the attendants had disappeared.

Amperion's prosecution began as fiercely personal and was breathtaking in scope. Those present in court say he would have won, but he was removed from the case early for an illness that he never had. Durel went free. Some would say the sultan had saved Amperion by replacing him. But Durel was furious. In the end, he was a vengeful man.

After the sultan's death, Durel moved quickly to eliminate Amperion from the palace. He sentenced Amperion to Elcor with no trial. His term was for five years. He wanted Amperion to be forgotten. He was afraid to have him executed because people would suspect his motive, and he was afraid to put him on trial for fear that he might talk his way out. He was not, however, afraid to have him forgotten.

On Elcor, Amperion suffered profoundly. Within the high stonewalls of the prison strode the walking dead. Their eyes were glassy and unseeing. Many had been tortured. Most died before their sentences were served.

Amperion was recognized early on. They had waited for him. He had been beaten and left for dead three times. He had been raped. People stole his food and clothes. In six months, he was so weak that he was taken to the infirmary. A message was sent to the sultan Durel and the reply was that he should not be allowed to die just yet. Amperion spent six more months in and out of the infirmary, deciding whether to live or die.

One night as he lay on the stone slabs, when sleep would not come, he suddenly saw a form. It was wispy, shimmering slightly. *I am hallucinating* he thought. The figure moved toward him with its hand outstretched. Amperion scrambled back into the corner of the cell, rolled to his knees, and began to pray. Every one of his senses was overwhelmed with perfect splendor. He felt softness, he smelled the fragrant lilies, he heard the lullaby his mother used to sing, he tasted her dish of dates, figs, and sweet milk. The figure smiled and at moment Amperion knew the overwhelming peace of forgiveness.

The spirit had had an effect. Amperion decided each day to continue living. An idea had formed in his mind. The old law proclaimed clearly that no person could be forced to serve a prison sentence for another. Justice and punishment applied only to those charged with a crime. An innocent person could never forcibly take the place of a guilty one. The law was silent however, as to whether a person *could* serve the sentence of another—if both parties agreed. No one had ever agreed to serve another's sentence when both parties were free and unrelated. But what if both parties were already inside the prison? What if one could assume the sentence of another person and simply add their years to his own? But why would anyone do that?? Perhaps as atonement or forgiveness…

Amperion set about to find those he had sentenced. He had met a man slightly younger than he who had been sentenced to two years, with one already served. Amperion had sent him to Elcor. But, after the trial, another had confessed to the crime. The case was handed to another judge and Amperion paid the judge to uphold the earlier decision. He had put this man there as sure as if he had opened the gates and walked him through.

But now, what if Amperion took this man's final year and added it to his own? This man would go free. In this freedom lay Amperion's redemption so he filed to have this case heard.

The judge who heard the argument had become rich from Amperion in earlier years. He was afraid to rule against Amperion, for fear of being put on trial himself. In the end, the judge added the year to Amperion's sentence and the man was set free.

News of the award flashed through the prison with the speed of hope. Queues formed when Amperion ate and he began to conduct interviews. He was highly sought.

In his second year, Amperion added twenty-one years to his sentence and freed thirteen men. He grew stronger, not by any earthly sustenance, but by the powerful and overwhelming feeling of redemption. He was being forgiven. He knew it. Now, instead of being reviled, he had his own guard. Prisoners cheered him when he entered the eating hall. He received gifts of food, clothes, and privileges. But he accepted none of them.

As his age advanced, he added more and more years to his sentence until, at the age of fifty-five, he had added sixty additional years. A total of thirty-one men had been set free by this work. For the first time, the number of years he had left to serve probably exceeded his likely lifetime.

The court in which he had served had forgot Amperion years ago. But the sultan had not forgotten. One day, word came to the prison that the sultan had decreed that the "Law of Substitution", as it had been called, was being revoked. But the sultan had been clever. He sent a talisman to Elcor prison, declaring that Amperion would be a free man in two days' time. This declaration however meant that all former prisoners would have their original sentences reinstated and would be returned to jail.

The night before the new law went into effect, the shimmering figure returned. Amperion had expected her. She reached out and Amperion embraced the extended hand. Then, with a last smile, he stepped off the chair into the air. His sentence, all of it, had been served, and the rope dissolved the remaining years not served…by law.

APPENDIX TO CHAPTER 13
The Solution to the Medicare/Medicaid and Social Security Problems

If nothing changes, then the Medicare, Medicaid, and Social Security programs will cause either a spectacular rise in taxes or a significant decrease in benefits. The effects will be felt soon. This note is being written in 2019, and all programs are failing to cover all of their obligations. In addition, there is no evidence that Congress will be able to act in the next several years to repair the situation. If nothing changes, either the young will pay higher taxes or the old will lose benefits. The question is whether there is any way to do otherwise.

If you are over fifty years old and the government came to you right now and said, "If you agree to never take possession of your Social Security benefits, and/or stop using them right now, and also refuse to use Medicare or Medicaid now and forever, you will be given a voucher that allows you to award a lifetime tax bracket of fifteen percent to anyone of your choosing currently under the age of forty", would you do it? Would you renounce all the money you paid into the Social Security fund in exchange for the transference of a tax bracket to your kids or nieces and nephews? If you don't have kids, there are plenty of families who have more than two who would be interested in your voucher. For people who have not yet received any distributions from Social Security or accessed Medicare, they would simply renounce the programs and get the voucher. These vouchers would be paid out upon your death with the further attestation that you did not use any of the government programs while you were alive.

The effect of this program would be such that some number of baby boomers would withdraw from the programs that are failing. This would cut the demand for more tax money by as much as a half. It also transfers a tax bracket to kids who in many cases are already *in* the 15% tax bracket, so there'd be no change. So, this idea reduces expenses but does not reduce revenue by much.

It is likely that baby boomers would do one of four things:

1. If they are wealthy, they will manage retirement on their own and will pay for their own insurance. This would be an attractive choice. They would welcome transferring the permanent tax bracket ahead of estate issues.

2. If they are not wealthy, they may elect to move back in with their kids who will use the benefit of the 15% tax bracket in the future to pay for their parents' needs. They can of course also do nothing and get Social Security and Medicare as they had planned. While this sounds somehow elitist, it wasn't so long ago that three-generation families lived under one roof in the US. This could happen again and should not be viewed as a step backwards.

3. For people who are extremely poor, they would be allowed to sell their 15% voucher to anyone of their choosing and then use the money to take care of themselves. A voucher would only be salable once.

4. Younger, poorer people who are not earning much today would likely become more attractive marriage partners with the 15% lifetime tax bracket. This too might influence a parent's decision and change the distribution of wealth in certain ways that don't exist today.

It may seem like an impossible task to execute a suggestion like this, but in the end, the three entitlement programs are headed for a crisis. It will be here in the next five to seven years, when it will be too late for many of the boomers to make this decision. Boomers will spend the younger generation into bankruptcy. Even if you are skeptical that this could work, the answer to this problem probably requires transferring values between generations. There are too many boomers and too few millennials for any political party to misjudge this problem. The answer lies in this direction, and if not this precise direction, then where?

Here is another possibility. Just suppose that the following scenario plays out:

You are in the hospital and have been diagnosed with a terminal disease or have a mental degeneration that will make it harder for you to participate even casually in the management of life decisions. Suppose that the MDs and the hospital staff have given you six months to live.

Suppose you have these choices:

1. You can get all the treatment that is possible at whatever cost is afforded (insurance or out-of-pocket) for as long as you or someone you appoint can keep you alive. (Remember quality of life here).

2. Or you can say to the MD, "Just tell me when I have six months left in your judgment. Give me an estimate for my condition as to how much money it will cost to keep me alive for the next six months. (Some of this cost may already be known from the preceding six months). I agree to forgo treatment in exchange for you transferring half of the expected cost to my heirs, and I will accept enough morphine when necessary to make the last days as peaceful as possible.'"

The patient will split the "end of days cost" with the government (Medicare/Medicaid) and all parties will be the same or better off. This is yet another possible way to deal with the pending catastrophe. If we cannot stop the expense or just reduce it, we will put a huge burden on the youngest generation that is simply not payable. In the end, this is a far better approach.

14.

The Situation Room

Mei Li had just been appointed to the role of Apprentice on the staff of the Emperor's Chief Archivist. She had passed the exam and was one of 21 women who had been awarded a title. It came with a uniform for all to see and a salary beyond any that her family had ever earned. She and the other women apprentices would be the first of their gender to read the thoughts and decisions of the Empire for the past 11 centuries.

During their first training the new apprentices were asked to attend the Emperor's meeting of the ministers. Once a month this meeting was held to decide issues across the land. Each of them was given the job of recording the events of the meeting and what was said.

The first topic was certain tax shortfalls in the eastern provinces. The ministers of those provinces had offered various defenses that on the whole were unimaginative and apparently expected. The Emperor was in a foul temper and told the ministers what would happen to them at the next meeting if taxes weren't paid.

Then the conversation turned to the books. The last months had seen the country in an uproar because books had been burned. Several ministers had submitted lists of books that should be confiscated and burned but they had not waited.

"And for what offense must these books be burned?" queried the Emperor.

"They are principally by authors Ho Jin and Wang Qun." Said minister Wu. "They espouse thinking for oneself, gender independence and disobedience in certain situations."

"And whose judgment shall we say that these books offend?" asked the Emperor. "What other books are out there that you will be denouncing?" His tone was ominous and Minister Wu retreated visibly.

"My lord", he began "people are reading these books to each other. The illiterate are hearing these stories of lust, intrigue, murder, and spying. They do not know what all of it means. But they do talk. They talk about the books and about their lives and some are seeing parallels. The signs are all there..."

"My lord", interposed Minister Zhang, "Minister Wu is correct. I see it in my province. Young women in particular are reading these books. They are getting ideas. If we burn the books it stops the spread of these words."

"I understand your argument," said the Emperor, "but where does it stop? What if I don't like something one of my ministers writes. Should I burn his words? What about my own words? Who is to say whether my own words may foment revolution? You yourself just now said that people are angry about the tax proclamation. Suppose someone decides to burn that?"

"Then they would be killed your highness" the ministers said in unison.

"If I kill ideas, if I kill the voice of the people, if I kill words, then we will always live in fear. I will always be afraid that someone is writing something secretly that becomes a plot to overthrow me. I see that clearly. What I don't see is what harm comes from open kimono talk. As a concession to your words, before we ban more books or burn more, I will consider this further."

Mei Li and her fellow women left the meeting startled. Is this how it was? Is this the way that decisions are made? They began to talk in small groups among the Emperors apartments. They themselves had banned books in their possession.

"How did you write the events of today?" Mei Li asked them all. They all read parts of their entries and were amused at how far reaching some of them were. Others were so factual that all nuance around the conversations had been eliminated. Still others spoke from a POV perspective and were more narrative and conclusive. Mei Li was intrigued.

Suddenly an office of the Imperial Staff arrived and summoned 6 of them to the Emperors chambers immediately. He read the names. Mei Li was among them. Fear crossed their faces. They talked quickly among themselves about protocol and speech. Their reports of the meeting had been confiscated.

In twenty minutes they were being ushered along a corridor of teak and gold. It was magnificent. It would have warranted further examination in different circumstances. The Second Staff Assistant of the First Rank accompanied them.

At the intersection of two massive doors a disembodied voice sang out "The apprentices of the Chief Archivist are here to see your majesty."

"Show them in" wafted out from inside, and in they went.

The Emperor's chamber was filled with treasures that few human eyes had ever seen. There were vases from a place called Genoa, jade from the southern provinces, ornate screens and golden animal figures given as gifts to Emperors long ago.

"Be seated" and the six knelt on cushions 20 paces away from the Emperor, as was the custom.

"Which one of you is Hue?" the Emperor asked. A smallish girl with fear brimming in her eyes raised her hand. "Your rooms have been searched and each of you has at least one copy of the banned books. Some of you have more." He saw their eyes fall and a resignation in their posture as though they had been sentenced to death.

"As Emperor I have a duty to my people. It is a sacred duty passed down through generations. I must do what is right even if it is not good. I must think of the many in spite of the few. I must learn from the lowest even if they disagree with the highest. Why do you read these books and what should I do about them?"

Hue paused and when she spoke her voice trembled. "I have not had a chance yet to read any of those books my lord. The book was given to me as a gift to pass on to a friend. I did not know of the ban and I had not had time to deliver the book. That is why I have it."

"I see," said the Emperor without looking up. "Who is Yu?" he asked.

A second apprentice raised her hand unsteadily. "I am", she said. "I have read one of the banned books but have only read part of it. I did not like it. The story was simple and not very interesting. I had intended to leave it behind when I left my apprenticeship. I will destroy it tonight."

And so the answers continued until finally the Emperor asked, "Who is Mei Li"?

"I am my lord," she answered in as firm a voice as she could summon. "I have three of the banned books. I have read them all and have spoken to others about them. Your people sire, read them…

"Stop!" Commanded The Second Staff Assistant of the First Rank. "You dare to lecture the Emperor and contradict the ministers…I'll have you"

"No," said the Emperor softly "let her speak.

They read then because they are a distraction from every day life. They struggle with taxes, sickness, the weather, and having enough food. If you visit your towns you can see this.

If you ban these books the people will have one less escape from their troubles. It is this kind of frustration that can cause people to speak of rebellion. No one that I have spoken to reads the meanings in these books that have been told to you. They are just stories. You know of the fables and myths that are read by us all. They are part of our country. Each of them can be thought to hold ideas dangerous to an Emperor. Yet you have not banned them.

You asked you ministers where burning would stop. They did not answer. Left alone they will all decide something different. Some will burn more believing they are pleasing you. Some will burn less because it is work. What if they come to burn the records of their conversations that they don't like?

I will never know what it is like to be you my lord. But you are a person and you can know what it is like to be your people. Ask them. But ask through the women in your palace. They will fear them less than their governors or the soldiers asking questions of them."

The Emperor looked at her for a minute that seemed like days. Mei Li felt faint and drained. She sat with her eyes downcast fearing what she would see if she read his face.

"I thank all of you for your answers," he said. "You may go".

As they stood to leave the Emperor turned to the archivist who had recorded the proceedings. "Make a copy of your transcript and have it available when I meet with the ministers again. I want them to see what the people really believe."

And so it was written and so it was done.

APPENDIX TO CHAPTER 14
Situational Awareness

Situational awareness may be the most significant collective failing of people in the US. The lack of it is visible most everywhere, often startling, and sometimes involves many people.

A great place to experience the failing of situational awareness is at airports. Everyone has a similar goal: to get to the right gate at the right time, then sit in the right seat and go to the right city. Everyone has a similar goal, and everyone knows the goal. But, we can see all sorts of people who are "owned", as the kids say, by this situation. There are:

1. People trailing suitcases bigger than they are with very little motor control over the ultimate path of their bag. They also can't lift their bags unaided. These people are traveling casualties. They cannot get where they are going without involving others. *Their* situation requires *your* awareness.

2. People who did not get tickets ahead of time and have hundreds of questions about what is happening, including weather at their destination, weather in places they are not going until next month, how full the flight is, whether a ferret can go in their carry-on, etc. They distract gate agents from actually helping people with real problems. Their failed awareness creates a situation for others.

3. People who don't know how to follow signs. These are the "nomadic air travelers" destined to wander under tarmacs, into and out of train conveyances, and sit at baggage claim long after their flight has cleared. These people don't connect cause and effect and do not know how "it works". Signs meant to help don't.

4. People who accidently take other people's bags at baggage claim.

5. People who cannot read a seat number or, in the case of Southwest, cannot decide which seat they should take. Ironically, these people often travel in pairs and both parties together can sometimes stay mystified for many minutes. Meanwhile, nobody gets to any seat.

6. People who try to stuff 55 lbs. of suitcase into a 20 lb. overhead bin. Doing it repetitively is not a solution. Moving everyone's stuff around doesn't make the bin bigger. Situational awareness.

7. People who have liquids, gels, knives, weapons, throwing stars, IEDs, lighters, starting pistols, ant and worm farms, Ebola samples, etc., all

going through the scanners. No one seems to know what is in their bag. They multitasked when packing and did not remember packing the IED, smoke grenade, cat litter, blowgun, or the 95 oz. Gatorade.

8. People with various animals from goats to ferrets that also have to get to the next city, but who don't have a cage that fits anywhere in the plane.

None of these people have thought about the situation where they were going to be. They couldn't have. But here they are, nonetheless. The interesting thing about this is that almost all these people seemingly have no sense that the rest of us at the airport are also on the same mission they are. It can't be all about them by definition, because it can't be about all of us at the same time.

The great way to experience situational awareness is to test yourself. Next time you are at the airport and things move against you, examine your emotional state and the state of those around you. By doing so, you are now consciously heightening the awareness of their situations and can respond with greater suitability. It is a good test. It is especially a good test in a foreign country and in an airport in which you have never been. It requires discipline when you are tired and late, have no ticket, and have been bumped while your bag is lost.

The essence of situational awareness is to be able to forecast futures that are important to you, and then reducing the variation to get there. If my purpose is to survive, then I know what I must be aware of and mostly what actions to take for shelter, food, water, etc.

In life, your purpose may be about keeping your job. In relationships, it may be about your ability to be what is necessary. The key is to do something now that makes a future variable unnecessary, because it has been fixed today. If the future were perfectly known, you would do today what is necessary so that a specific future would occur. This is not an invitation to leave open various tasks and assume others will do them. Being a victim is not situational awareness. Making your problem someone else's problem is not situational awareness. It is a state of mind that requires presence and accountability and occasionally action. Situational awareness requires anticipation and then moving "toward" the problem, if you are the first to see it.

Situational awareness is why the concept of "Plan B" exists. Spys carry all sorts of tools to solve all sorts of problems. They always have a Plan B. But the essence of these tools is simply to reduce future variation. They execute a behavior today that anticipates tomorrow's variation and fixes it. This is really what all the spy movies do. In every James Bond film, the "mission" or "purpose" is laid out early. That way, each scene presents a situational awareness opportunity that everyone recognizes. The preparedness of James Bond then acts upon the awareness he has gained towards the purpose he has been assigned. This is situational awareness on display.

If you were going on a camping trip you, would be looking for things that are light weight but have multiple uses, like Swiss Army knives, or other multi purpose tools like Gerbers. The effect of these devices is to fix variation so that it no longer becomes a "situation".

In some sense, risk management is about situational awareness. As you fix variables today, you then know what is fixed and can behave as though those variables no longer exist. You can be more certain that what you are going to do will result in the future state you desire. It is, however, an evolving part of our "nanny" state that our purpose should be to eliminate all risk. As soon as anyone declares that they are not happy or are offended, then the system's responsibility is to eliminate the risk. All this does is deaden the ability of people to gain situational awareness.

There is a part of the media culture that is now in vogue requiring people to opine on all the things that are wrong with some person or event. They mistake their "take" for situational awareness. We see this especially in diversity programs, where people who have nothing in common with a particular group deign to speak on their behalf. This is perhaps one of the greatest fails of situational awareness. Rachel Dolezal is the perfect example.

There was a catastrophic failing of situational awareness in her masquerading as an African American and filling a job that was not rightfully hers to have.

You can tell by visiting people's houses what kind of situational awareness exists. If the adults are making every decision, then their children's situational awareness will be limited. The kids are just waiting for their parents to do the work. If every room resembles a plane crash site or nothing in the house works, self-governance is not working. There is no situational awareness. It is a fail to say, "Well, I know where everything is," because it misses the purpose. The purpose is not for only you to know where things are; it is not the purpose for you to struggle to move quickly if you have to search for things; it is the refuge of people who are always late to assume that this works. It is a failing of situational awareness.

Similarly, it is possible to observe companies struggling with various situations that they never thought possible. #Metoo, Facebook congressional testimony, NFL players kneeling for the national anthem, etc. are all emerging situations that no one was aware of until they happened. This is an important point. The speed and complexity of societies is making situational awareness harder. People must be better educated, more experienced, and faster to deal with these situations. There isn't anything more crucial for an individual's survival than having a good grip in this area. If you want a quick primer on situational awareness, talk with any police officer or single mom. They are all over this.

15.

A Rabbi, A Priest, and an Imam

A rabbi, a priest and an imam met at the Afterlife Bar and Grill. They had met years before in a bar called the Mitzvah while attending a seminar with the intriguing title of "Who Dat?" They had spent several evenings discussing the events of the day's seminar and had become fast friends.

Rabbi: "So, are we all agreed then that God exists and that there is but one God?"

Priest: "Of course."

Imam: "Yes."

Rabbi, looking at notes: "The last time we were together, we agreed on two principles. First, that there is a God and not nothing. Second, we have agreed that there is only one God and not many. I think this is profound because one might say 'we believe in God' is a basis for further discussion."

Imam: "I think that statement is true. What is interesting to me is that we are all here, in this place of agreement, but we have traveled different roads to get here. We also believe for a reason, but it would not be inconceivable that we have three different reasons for believing in God."

Priest: "I think I would say that all three of us must have done something or experienced something culturally that provides us with our way to affirm there is a God. We believe there is a God. But we all three have had to overcome a lack of traditional scientific evidence to reach this view. Does that sound right?"

The rabbi and priest looked up from their menus.

Rabbi: "Culturally, people believe because others believe. For example the status of being a parent confers a very powerful set of behaviors required for children to survive in the family. The decision for a child to believe what their parents say has immediate consequences. Children learn from the consequences that their parents impose. But the decision to believe uses a different reasoning than traditional scientific evidence. It is also, in my mind, related to basic Maslow needs. If you are poor, in a war zone, starving, and have no home, you might conclude that these are all conditions that God would not logically allow. But it is also true that one might have lost all hope—except for a belief that something greater than circumstance will relieve your suffering. You might believe or not believe in God, based on your economic condition as well as your experiences."

Priest: "Yet, it feels like we three do have the status or credibility to simply be more reliable than any individual, perhaps because we likely will be seen as 'lucky' or special people who have experienced a metaphysical revelation and therefore believe.

Imam: "And it feels as well that, once we have taught our followers what and how to believe about God, we can expect they will reject a person's opinion of a different religion even before knowing what that person's opinion is. This is a kind of 'rejection ad absurdum'. Yet, it too is a belief we hold. And we cement that with rituals and laws. Despite this, however, all of us believe that some version of 'doing unto others what you would want done unto you' would be a logically superior way to behave in any setting, whether you disagree with others or not."

Rabbi: "That is the key. What do the three of us know that every human would know in the same way? The answer to that is the reason I look forward to our future discussions. What is interesting to me is that we all have divisions in our basic faiths between Catholics and Protestants, Shia and Shiite, and Ashkenazi and Reform. These separatists are the basis for disagreement, in addition to disagreements amongst the three of us. It is also ironic that we have disagreements amongst our believers in common!"

Priest: "Interesting and true. I suspect that what is at the heart of all of this is how to determine if any of us have gotten religion right. We all think and say we do. We all believe we do. But how can any of us convince each other that we are '*more* right'?"

Imam: "Why would we want to? Wouldn't it be just as good to say that we should not try and convince others that they are *more* wrong?"

Then as though struck dumb by God they nodded and prayed together. And it came to pass in those days that, for these three believers, the world did seem a better place.

APPENDIX TO CHAPTER 15
Disagreements

In considering the growing numbers of "disagreements" in the world today, it is worth trying to understand why. Just suppose that the reasons that people disagree are linked to:

1. Frames of Reference (FOR)
2. Information

3. Emotion

4. Environment

Frame of Reference (FOR) is the model that an individual or organization has developed to explain the way the world works. It is the story that they have learned about why things are the way they are. This can be a philosophy like socialism in the case of the many, or Kant's categorical imperative in the case of an individual. In many situations, a (FOR) is a function of culture, which would include parents at an individual level and teachings at the level of society. (FOR) is also a function of historical experience and education.

In the United States, it is "Life, Liberty, and the Pursuit of Happiness" (for the individual). Individuals carry with them "victim" status, "entitled" status, and so on as frames of reference. These frames serve to anchor explanations for actions and also serve to establish a kind of moral code as the basis for actions between individuals. There is nothing to suggest that (FORs) must be consistent. One can disparage abortion and yet find euthanasia acceptable. They do not align. Islam and Christianity do not agree on certain principle beliefs. Of the four forms listed above, (FOR) is by far the hardest to change from the outside. Only the owner can change their individual (FOR).

Governments and societies can also have frames of reference. Russia, for example, has a "we are surrounded by enemies" frame of reference. Ironically, Israel is much the same. For the French, it is a pride in being better than everyone else. And for the Germans, it is the pride in knowing that the French pride is misplaced.

Sometimes, however, frames of reference can be overcome by emergency circumstance where a superior need (survival) overcomes a frame of reference. Actions taken by bystanders in cases where a fellow human being's life is in danger can immediately alter one's (FOR). War, pandemics, tsunamis, etc., all can overcome (FORs)

There are other times, however, when the (FOR) is too strong, even if giving it up might lead to a better environment. The Israeli and Palestinian situation mentioned in an earlier vignette is one such example. The solution there must be to create a superior frame of reference.

This brings up an important point about disagreements in general. If a situation exists where the only condition that will make *me* happy is *your* death, then there is no philosophy or frame of reference that could create a future resolution. If the fact that you exist as seen through my frame of reference cannot continue to be, then no resolution is possible. This is self-evident because a philosophy that allows for one individual to eliminate all others will eventually have only a single individual left. This is not the basis for a sustained future state of humanity or philosophy.

Information is the second understanding. This is more difficult to describe because it is rarely absolute. If one were to ask what information one should have in the perfect book report, there would be many "truths". This "information" is knowable, but subjective. It is akin to asking what the best temperature for the thermostat should be.

There is, though, an inherent quality to information. Information gets filtered and interpreted. It gets analyzed and forecasted. It is asymmetric in almost every case because only the individual or organization itself knows what it knows or needs to know. This means that equalizing information is difficult either by amount or quality.

Factual information would seem to be absolute, but there are often shades of fact. If I smoke, the likelihood of getting cancer is higher. This is accepted fact. Nevertheless, it does not dissuade certain people from smoking. There is a probability involved. Simply knowing something to likely be true does not mean you will necessarily behave as though it *is true*. In this age of instantaneous information, we often struggle to decide what the facts are. It is too easy to manipulate information. The headline "President X sells out his party for a budget deal" and "President X breaks political impasse", are two ways to describe the same event. There are of course many others.

All stock trades are based on some concept of asymmetric information. One party believes that at this price they should sell, and another party believes the opposite. They disagree. Both may have the exact same factual information and simply have a different view of its implication. Ironically, this kind of disagreement is essential for markets to exist. For organizations (governments), information may be about knowing how much your counterpart or competitor knows.

But information is more complicated even than this, because it also can be blocked or disrupted. Disagreements are often of the form that all parties genuinely desire to know something but there is no mechanism to deliver the information. Malaysian Flight 370's disappearance is an example. Everyone around the globe knows what questions they want answered and for many they are the same questions. But the information is not accessible.

It is also important to realize that deliberately misleading others is also a possible outcome of information. Spying comes down to the simple principle of trying to *deliberately* create asymmetric information in one's own favor. There is a tie between FOR and information at this level. Does my FOR cause me to gather, interpret, and use information in a way that would enable me to gain a superior position relative to you?

In many cases, governments and watchdogs seek transparency. This though is often a mistaken notion. For example, if we were all playing cards and we each know what cards the other parties have, it is a simple matter to know who is going to lose and to ensure that outcome comes to pass. Transparency only works for a kibitzer who is not part of the game. Because of this vagueness of information transparency, asymmetry will always exist. In addition, there are photo-shopped pictures, "fake" news, video impersonations, and other schemes created to make information unreliable.

Emotion is the third understanding. It is somewhat self-evident. It has been included in the four forms as a representation of the unexpected biological insertion of randomness. In all problems, the idea that one thing *feels* better than another must be considered. It is making decisions based on relationship, feeling, and past emotional states that can add randomness to the solution of disagreements. Emotional states tend to be matters of individuality, although they are certainly cultural as well. Italy and Greece have cultural roots in emotion, as well as other countries in South America and the Mid-East. Even the US fought a very emotional civil war over slavery.

Emotion is of course terribly important and natural. But it is deeply personal, and it works both in favor of and against relationships! This is why solving problems based on emotion is so hard. If all parties' rationales are emotion-based, a solution today may not be the solution tomorrow because the emotion of today may change. An example of this was the tryst of President Bill Clinton. The thinking parts of the country held a sacrosanct (FOR). That FOR held that if you behaved against a law and then lied about it, it was grounds for impeachment. The emotional parts of the country held that they really *liked* President Clinton and that after all, this tryst was only about sex. They were willing to change the standard and even the law's (FOR) precisely *because* the relationship was strong.

Emotion is a powerful influencer if it can be channeled. If you can get emotion aligned, then there is a good chance that progress can be made. This is the emotion of love, pity, generosity and support. Yet dictators and other actors can use emotion to justify destructive decisions as well.

The final form of understanding is the environment itself. This is the understanding brought about by external forces. They could be contingent effects from a single cause. They could be sequential disagreements due to changes in the environment caused by resolving the first difference. This environmental challenge is not trivial. It may be that the solution to a disagreement lies in changing the environment in some way.

Let's take the example of a material disagreement in a marriage. Let's say it's whether to paddle children. Consider frames of reference: Corporal punishment may have existed in one parent's household and not the other's. Even if it did exist, a parent may be opposed to it had they experienced it before. The (FORs) may be misaligned. Information may also be different. Each spouse may have read something that supported their own view or "belief" of paddling vs. time-outs. This is where progress could be made if both parties could *understand* information in the same way. It is even possible that the parties may agree that a solution has occurred, even though they may have different *interpretations* of the information that caused it. This suggests that the interpretation of information is important; sometimes it makes all the difference. Is information absolutely of a certain nature, or is it only relative because of interpretation?

The emotional side is where the greatest potential disagreement exists. This is because emotion is a variable that can vary unpredictably. It is unlikely that if each spouse feels the other side is wrong that it will be possible to change the feeling very easily. Information won't do it. The environment might do it, if one spouse was able to convince the other to try their method as an experiment. However, if the couple has had nothing but disagreements with each other, then they will likely struggle in that environment. If none of the four "understandings" can be reached, then only an overwhelming environmental event that causes both parties to align all their understandings will unite them and cancel the disagreement. The idea of hurting a child deliberately vs. the discipline that is being taught is at best a difficult emotional struggle.

At this point, it is somewhat helpful to consider that the notion that a "disagreement" exists is solely a human construction in the first place. Animals, insects, and plants do not disagree, at least in the sense we are speaking of it. They may have pre- programming (growing to the light). They have instincts and they have learned behaviors. Unless we consider these attributes as actions in and of themselves, then animals and plants simply act on pre-wired patterns. The idea of planning, the idea of action and consequence, and the idea of being able to transfer knowledge remotely to others are *not* characteristics of animals. Even the idea of an idea is not available to most living things. (Let's not argue about dolphins, whales, monkeys, etc.). These qualities are almost exclusively human. Having a disagreement in the first place requires some ability to "do otherwise" in the sense of free will. Animals and plants cannot "do otherwise". This is the hope for resolution that emotional fights often do not have, but they can.

This is where emotion in fact is so important to the discussion. The crucial question is whether emotion is an enabler or an inhibitor to the resolution of disagreements. Does emotion allow one to "do otherwise"? Or, is emotion a kind of inhibitor that only allows one to behave *only* in accordance with one's emotions?

Emotions are both enablers and inhibitors. They are situation-dependent. The problem is whether the person being emotional can tell when they are inhibiting the process. It is the same with thinkers to a degree, but here the inhibiting party may be aware and just not care. Such is the dualistic nature of emotional vs. thinking decision-making.

Let's take an example. Just suppose you wanted to understand why the two political parties in the US are at seemingly greater odds these days. If we knew people's frame of reference, emotion, information, and the environment perhaps our disagreement would be more of a choice and less of a reaction.

Lets think about highly educated people for a moment. If you are a doctor, pilot, lawyer, or professor for example you have some common experiences. First, you have had at least 2 and often as many as six years of additional schooling and training. You have passed many exams and 'proven' that you deserve to practice that profession. You are in fact elite. Second, your professions all require people to come to you. You are *needed*. The fabric of society depends on you doing your jobs. Third, your jobs are somewhat specialized and as a result isolating. The energy required staying current with medical trends or new laws, to publish, or to stay at the top level of competency in your field, requires continual learning. This leads to the fourth commonality and that is the necessity to continually interact with people like you on a peer basis. In many cases the people who can do what you do are very few. So there is an element of isolation yet a need to benchmark how you are doing.

So if this is how your life has developed, what kinds of views of the world would you have? Obviously there is no one view but one can 'suppose' some tendencies. One for example might be that these people do a lot of reading. Their opinions may be formed by the words of others rather than self developed integration. It isn't that they can't, it's only that there isn't time. Because there isn't time, they are surrounded by people whose job is to support directly what they do. They are at the center of attention. They are asked for their opinions and for the "truth". It isn't hard then to see how a particular view of the world and their place in it forms. In addition, they often interact with significant people in other fields. Their daily work, consulting, or teaching, enable those connections. They have contacts in many areas and can more easily get "answers" to life's obstructions.

On the other hand are people who have learned their work by doing the work. Farmers, professional drivers, miners, machinery operators and car repair professions have certain things in common. Society needs them also but the direct connection is sometimes harder to feel. The link to clients or the people who care about what they do is not as tight. One might also argue that many of these jobs have great dependency on outside uncontrollable forces. The weather, health of animals, and inherent dangers of machinery, all play a role in one's frame of reference. In addition people surrounding these professions are doing their own work and are not generally supporting. There is a heavier reliance on one's self to solve even basic problems. This work is physically hard in special ways. These people also do not have time and may get news and insight by word of mouth rather than by printed word.

Clearly there are assumptions here and they are deliberate. (For more on that you can read essay 28). The point is that by examining how the world exists for great parts of the US our experiences of life are very different. Not surprisingly our values are also different. What has changed in the past 25 years however is the role that disagreements play. In the past when two people were against each other there was some sense that 'we the people' were trying for the best *common* policy. Now it's about winning for 'we *half* of the people'.

Just suppose we the people could replace all the members of both Congress and the Executive branch in a year. We the people would approve a national referendum that would turn two branches of government completely over. Suppose further that a condition of the new government is that they act in the interests of we the people by defining those interests. They would define national interests like the economy, energy, a clean environment, when we would use our military, and so on. The real debates would occur around social policy. In addition, all members of Congress would have eight-year term limits. Debates like these are crucial. Of course this would be extremely tough to implement. I understand. But the alternative is decidedly destructive. The two parties are too entrenched and provincial to represent we the people.

I don't think individual Americans are so different. Matters are grey for the vast majority of us. Somehow the people who have the microphones have decided that all matters are either black or white and they intend to win for themselves or their 'half'. In the end there is no winning. Matters will remain black and white.

16.

Pproblems (sic)

B. "We've got a lot of real problems in this country. This guy in the white house doesn't know what he's doing."

R. "How do you know that?"

B. "It's obvious. And I have read about it on a number of sites."

R. "I see. Are these your problems in particular?"

B. "No. They're all our problems."

R. "Well I don't have a lot of problems. I'm pretty far along Maslow's hierarchy and I don't bother much with all of the hysteria because nothing is really changing for me. Same job, same family, same sports team, same restaurants, same TV shows. No real effect here. "

B. "Then you're choosing to be unaware! This is one of the problems in this country. It's people like you."

R. "Well if you're aware and worried and reading and fixing all the stuff you're worried about, I have even *less* to worry about."

B. Getting irritated "You're just making fun of it all. You aren't serious. People like you vote and that's why we are in this fix. I hate what these people in the administration stand for."

R. "So you hate the way they think".

B. "Yes"

R. "And you hate the way they make you feel?"

B. "Yes."

R. "If they were to suddenly show up on late night TV or on Second City would you laugh at them? Or are you saying you wouldn't listen or laugh at anything they say. "

B. "No of course I wouldn't laugh. They aren't funny, just pathetic."

R. "So if you are able to align yourself so that you wouldn't laugh no matter what, then you must be able to align yourself so that you wouldn't hate no matter what. The emotions you are describing hate, anger, sadness, are all choices in the same way that laughter is. You can easily make yourself so bitter that you would be immune to laughter so then you must be able to make yourself so content that you're immune to hatred. They are both choices. If no one can make you laugh then no one can make you hate. If what you are saying is that your internal emotional state is only a reflection of what others tell you, you have no free will. You are like an insect you really can't do otherwise. When you are triggered you have no choice. You are a slave to the triggering event or person."

B. "I hate you. All you people are the same. You think you know it all and you think your ideas are the ones that matter. They don't."

R. "So you don't really have anything inside, no governor, no regulator, no reasoning self, that tells you that you don't have to be mad?"

B. "Not when you people act the way you do!"

R. "I see, so you can't help being mad. Nothing can stop you being mad, not even you and yet you can stop yourself from laughing if necessary. I think if you could think you'd realize that you can choose. Emotions are a choice.

If you hit your finger with a hammer you have a choice. You can cry and swear or you can just shake it off until it feels better. It is a choice. When you were much younger you had no choice you had to cry."

B. "I hate you."

R. "Of course you do. I made you."

APPENDIX TO CHAPTER 16
Problems That Have No Solution

Suppose you could save a lot of time by knowing ahead of time whether the problem you are trying to solve is really solvable or perhaps whether it is solvable by you.

Perhaps the most written about unsolvable problem is the answer to the question: "What is it like to be someone else?" Or "What is it like to be a bird?" We use approximations and feelings to say that we "know" what it's like to be someone else, but the fact is we don't. Take pain, for example. I can't say whether your experience of pain is at the same level as mine for a given injury.

Or, take our experience of color. When I say I see blue and you say that you agree, how do we know that we see the same color? What if at birth my color perception was reversed. Just suppose that my parents told me that the color I see as blue is "really" everyone else's color of red. In my whole life, I call your red, "red", but I don't see the "same" red you see. If you were to see "my" red, you would say that it's really blue. There is no way to prove that this is not so. In fact, color is an illusion. There is no such thing as color, but our brains process differences in the data that is captured by our eyes. That is all that it is. It does not become necessary to wonder about what we truly see, because we experience the same illusion to some similar degree. Therefore we are able to act similarly at traffic lights, for example.

I am not truly able to know "how" you are thinking. I might be able to guess at "what" you are thinking, but I can't confirm it until you do. I cannot access "you". Even with medical technology I cannot know what it is like to be you. I might be able to describe you in precise medical detail but have no intuition of what you are like inside. So the notion that we can know what it is like to be another human being is simply not knowable.

It is impossible to recreate the result of an action when the initial conditions cannot be duplicated. Let's say I open a new paint can and drop it. Then I open another one and drop it, too. Even if I am trying for exact duplication, it won't occur. There are too many forces at work to cause the paint stains to be the same. Many initial conditions cannot be duplicated exactly. This does not mean that we cannot get patterned information. It is often possible to generalize and say that the paint will spill out on the floor in an outward stain from the can to some point on the surface it was spilled on. We can say that some paint will splatter, etc. All of these are generalizations, and as humans we can use these generalizations because they are "close enough" for the work we intend to do. But if you pick a spot on the floor slightly away from what would be the primary stain and ask whether a drop of paint will land "there", there is no way to know even after thousands of attempts. It is random.

This leads us from irreproducible initial conditions to randomness of ongoing action. Electrons, for example, cannot be identified by their location and spin at the same time. This is because to locate an electron one must stop their spin, and to measure spin one can only say that the electron is somewhere in its cloud. This idea can be generalized by saying that things that are not accessible to our senses or to our "machine-enhanced senses" are not knowable.

There are things that we can say exist but that we cannot imagine. Try and draw a five-dimensional figure. It's impossible. However, mathematical equations can express any number of dimensions using variables. They are describable but not understandable visually. This also applies to the Big Bang. We can know there was a singularity that through some process began what has become our universe, but we cannot access the "moment" *before that event*. In every academic field, there are problems that are not solvable. In mathematics, there is a reward for proving/solving various hypotheses about a variety of mathematical concepts.

There appear to be limitations to certain information transmission. Light, for example, limits how fast information can move and yet at the quantum level there may be certain connections using a process that appears to travel faster than light. When life dies, it may be possible to access information in a different way, but we cannot know our face before we were born or what it is like on the other side when we die.

It is not possible to know the future. And it is not possible to re-experience the past in the same way we experience the present. The arrow of time only moves in one way biologically. There are many astrologers and mediums that will say that they can foretell the future, but one would think that if they could they would win an occasional lottery, just to make ends meet. The future may be predictable in some macro way but not at any level of detail consistently.

These days, we cannot depend on knowing the truth of many things, especially events in the past. When photos can be shopped, when video can be doctored, when anyone can allege anything and have it broadcast well before anyone has checked it out, it is impossible to know what is true. It may be that no one knows what is true. People that watch a single event come away with different interpretations. Certain problems like genetic inequality and parental upbringing inequality do not have solutions.

So why does it matter that there are things we can't know? It matters because, no matter how effective computers become, they will not be able to "know" these things, either. There will always be gaps. Even if it is possible to know all things after death, it doesn't matter if you can't influence anything. It's like reading a book. You can't affect the characters.

The reason that computers cannot ultimately know everything is that they have similar physical constraints on their processing speed and database size. Their databases cannot hold more information than the information in the universe.

You may ask why I included this essay since the topics are beyond our reach by definition. The answer is that all of us have information that is not accessible to us and it would be an advantage if we knew what information that is. The best way to find out what you cannot access is to ask your best friend.

17.

Let's Do This

Caesar: "What is that noise?"

Senator Gluteus Maximus (GM, Rep from Taxes Minimus): "It is the people, sire. They have been stirred to protest by certain…elements." (Glares at Pompus Narcissus).

Caesar: "Protest against *me*? But, why?"

Senator Pompus Narcissus (PN, Dem from Klimat Controlam): "They are opposed to the wall, sire, and almost everything else. They lack sick fare, well fare, Uber fare, a county fair and table fare. All is not well."

Caesar: "But the wall will keep out the Visigoths." He shudders. "You know them. They're just so…so…so Germanic. And I have been more fair than the last three Caesars put together."

Senator (GM): "They misunderstand your MAGA-nificence, sire. Half the people are working and half are waiting for their share. Half would like your government to disappear and half would like all government to disappear."

Senator (PN): "Foul and forsooth, I say! The issue is economic, you bloviating deplorable. Those people aren't here for their share—they're here for their *chance* to share! Sire, they don't want government to go away. They want government to act."

Caesar: "So, I'm hearing bread, circuses, universal income, and health care. That's what we'll do. And a big *harrrumphh all around…* so there's that!"

Senator (GM): "But, sire, the people who are making money, who own shops, and who provide our trade don't have the money for all this. *You*, though, *do* have money. But to help you, sire, I would put a tax on all the wealthy people who believe like Senator Pompous Narcissus to pay for the projects they want. If they want income distribution, let the Dems pay first, because they want it. Once their wealth is the same as the average person who supports them, then you can look to the shopkeepers. On the Rep side of the aisle, we'll tax ourselves to build your wall. And pay for the army!"

Senator (PN): "Outrageous! Impossible! This is madness! You must not allow this, sire! Government is here for "all" the people. If you let "them" fund the army, they'll use it to attack you. And we'll all be poor, because you took all our money. Only you have the wisdom to fund the people's desires!"

Caesar: "Then we're agreed! We'll raise taxes on all the people who have money, give it all to me, and I will make the people happy. It's so simple—why has this taken so long?"

And so, it came to pass in the following year that taxes were raised, walls were built, and people were paid for not working. But there were those who had had enough. They were Reps. They were Dems. Dey were Deese. And dey were Dose. It started with small meetings here and there. People who had never carried a sign, never walked a picket line, never worked for the Romanic Times, and never been in the tablets began to decide. They knew what could be done, they knew how to do it, and they knew when it would work. They did this for a living, but not in this way.

And the world as we knew it was changed forever…

APPENDIX FOR CHAPTER 17

The Revolution is On

By now (2019), it is only the most oblivious among us who do not see that the revolution is afoot, not only here in the US, but elsewhere as well. And, it has happened in the way of all revolutions. In the US, we voted for a revolution when we elected Obama and then doubled down when we elected Trump. The people who represent the "old way" of government are done. It is only they who don't get that. The right side of the US political aisle wants to disrupt government. On the left side of the aisle, the populists are beating a very loud drum that wants wealth redistribution and a very different environmental agenda.

But what, then, is the role of the average citizen if we have lost confidence in our government? What form should the "revolution" take?

Suppose that people everywhere have four choices with respect to objecting to their governments:

1. Fight the government –including

   a. Open revolt

   b. Passive resistance (making it difficult for the government to govern by slowing process down)

   c. Funding the resistance

   d. Creating fear among people so that they chose one of the first three choices.

2. Flee the government - including

   a. Immigrating

   b. Committing suicide

   c. Physically hiding (in bunkers or in plain sight)

    d. Writing about anything except the government

3. Engage the government - including

    a. Meet and try to influence the government

    b. Meet with others who perhaps can influence the government

    c. Become a member of the government with the intent of changing from within

    d. Become a spokesperson for a "right answer" whether in support of or opposition to the government. Create the balance.

4. Do nothing – including

    a. Keeping your head down and just doing your job

    b. Reducing the number of people you interact with

    c. Reducing stimuli that would cause you to revolt

    d. Just waiting for the revolution to come for you

US social circumstances that make some of the above courses of action extremely difficult:

1. An inability to determine what is true and what is not. This is not just "fake news", but people everywhere who are behaving with *the intent to deceive*. Open revolt may even be by government employees.

2. A descent into a "market of one" nation where all that matters is *me, my take,* and *I.* It is like the meteorologists on TV, standing in the wind and "becoming the weather" for personal stardom rather than doing analysis that shows where the combined effects of surge and rain will have the most impact. Creation of fear.

3. No one knows or discusses the actual consequences of policy or action anymore. We are discussing people, not events and their consequence. Everything has become personal, reducing stimuli.

4. The corollary of (3) is that the intellectual curiosity of the common citizen is less than is required for a functional democracy. If you have an uneducated or uninformed electorate, it is difficult to make good choices; reducing stimuli.

So here we are. The question seems to be "What kind of society should we be trying to create"? And then, if we can figure that out, what should we be doing now to get there? Somehow, I think if we can agree on the answers then we can agree on which of the four responses to government we should employ.

What kind of society should we create?

1. I suspect that the socially liberal interpretation of human engagement is a good one. It should be either, "Do unto others as *you* would want them to do unto you", or "as *they* would want you to do unto them". It is a combination of the individualist rights of "life, liberty, and the pursuit of happiness" coupled with the socialist obligation of duty to one's fellow man.

2. A behavior that accommodates both goals might be "to act such that if your action were replicated by all other people that the world would collectively be better off". This is a derivative of Kant. The idea of "better off" might include principles like:

    a. Does my behavior extend others' lives chronologically? (Sanctity of life)

    b. Does my behavior increase others' satisfaction of Maslow's basic needs? (Happiness).

    c. Does my behavior prevent the destruction of life or the reduction in satisfying Maslow's basic needs? (Rejection of the negative)

    d. Does my behavior increase choice, competency, and autonomy among people? (Balance)

1. If we assume that people vary differently by genes and environment, then it is reasonable to assume that they will have different economic competencies. Economic competencies relate to the value of one's labor in society. Because of this, income and therefore choices will be unevenly accessible. So, what manner of economy should we have? This is a difficult question. It inherently speaks to the role of government. Should the individual determine how the rewards from his work will be deployed, or should the government determine it? There are two end points here:

    a. Capitalism needs growth and an unending reinvention of process. It relies on change and disruption to continue. It creates economic winners and losers. It has nothing to do with the common good, apart from making quality goods available at a price that affords a profit to those who make those goods. Wealth accrues to the individual based on individual efforts.

    b. Socialism has everything to do with the common good, but wealth is distributed from the individual to the collective by government policy. The individual does not necessarily get more if they do more.

    c. Economics are central to current US political disagreements. Part of the disagreement is over what is to be valued, i.e. the corporation, the intelligentsia, equality of ownership, or the government itself. Depending on one's view, the recognition of value and how it accrues is a key differentiator of policy and ideology.

The nature of law and how it is created is crucial. Because people are different, it is necessary to establish certain desired "common" behaviors that are consistent with the principles (1 and 2), above. The law and its enforcement must coexist with economics and politics to be effective.

2. Let's say that we believe in these four principles. We just pick the economic system. It doesn't really matter for the rest of the commentary. Now, we ask the question: "If society elects (or discovers it has elected) a tyrant, what is the right way to go about dealing with the government?"

If the tyranny is so severe that opposition means certain death, then it would be a waste of life to revolt by violence without a reasonable chance of success, unless joining the revolution would be based on some guiding principle like "my disregard for existing law and order and for the actions and desires of my government is based on one of the four principles above i.e. the right to life.

But what do we do if the tyranny is less severe, or if our view is not in the majority? Suppose we just disagree, then what? Here, I think we can employ the behavior of (2), above. We act in such a way that, if all sides (including the tyrant) were to act like us, we would all be better off. This is not to say they would agree with us but only act in the same spirit as we do. So, what would this "right action" look like?

It is easy to say, "Well, in Washington there is no high ground. Most politicians are acting in self-interest with little regard for the people. So, if you don't act as 'they' do, you will surely lose, you will not be respected, and you will be wasting your time. You also have party 'obligations'. You have constituents that make demands, etc." The list goes on.

But there is a way. Senator Sam Nunn from Georgia and Senator Joe Lieberman from Connecticut were both men of balance. They voted what they believed to be right and both held a philosophy that there were good arguments on both sides of the aisle that should be supported. Neither of them went down in history as famous dissenters because party leadership (and notoriety) goes most often to the extreme views. But they had it right. Issues were discussable with them, and they voted in a philosophical way that was best for the US, for the most part. Nunn was a social liberal and a supporter of a strong defense. Lieberman was a social liberal and a budget hawk.

I suspect constructive engagement is the high, "noble" road. It is a hard road to travel, because it is more taxing than just checking out. Nevertheless, if *no one* is operating under constructive engagement, then we are likely doomed to some form of revolution. I think we are having a mild form of revolt today.

From the government's perspective, real power only exists when there is stability. That stability can be achieved by tyranny or benevolence. Stability has always been a function of several things:

1. Jobs and a growing economy

2. A legal system or social appeal system that confers justice

3. A society with culturally understood and accepted preferences for resolving social issues

4. A means of credibly defending itself

The US legal system, in which I am including the law enforcement system, is struggling. The application of investigation is uneven. The consequences for violating laws are uneven. The understanding of the complexities of corporate interactions is uneven. And the ability to decide social issues is uneven. The judiciary and the law are separating and now include political judgments. While this has always been true, it is now openly so. Courts are deciding the cases they want to decide and not what is before them. They leave out rulings and narrow them when political intervention would occur.

Culturally, the United States is dispersing. Perhaps as a democracy it must always be so, eventually. Every dominant power eventually became less dominant for mostly similar reasons: over-extension abroad and dissent at home. If one were to ask, "What does America believe in?", there is no longer any believable answer. The white picket fence no longer exists as a goal. American exceptionalism is no longer.

Domestically, we are at war with ourselves. We are fighting over many views of the future that have many different assumptions about where we are. Most people cannot have a view of the present that matters, because the only thing that matters to them is their *opinion of what matters*. Today, a person's "take" (they used to be called opinions) are just assertions. Nothing more. An assertion used to require a factual standing and a reasoned case against objections. People demand social change, personal respect, their fifteen minutes of fame, and their "way" as though they were rights given in the Constitution. Perhaps the "pursuit of happiness" idea is at work here. If I can't actually do something but I can get access to a microphone or editorial column, I can be happy telling everyone what I believe. Then, I can be somebody. If this idea is taken to its logical extreme, then it begins to reflect current US cultural conditions. Everyone is screaming their beliefs. It isn't about persuasion anymore, it is about subjugation. "I am not asking you to agree—I am telling you how it is. Let's do this!" This is contributing to the spirit of revolution.

Naïveté was never something to aspire to. Now, it is accepted as a social justice badge of some sort that condones saying anything that comes to mind. We have elected a president who does nothing to close the gap of what he doesn't know. There is no internal governance, no test of reasonableness, no post-comment critique, and no consequence for being oblivious. No one who cares anymore has the *ability* to care, because the people who are hiring and giving voice to these naïve people *just don't care any more*. This must be so, because there is no other reasonable explanation for what is being reported. This is contributing to the spirit of revolution.

This matters because the ability to stir people to irrationality is extraordinarily greater these days because news is moving faster than truth. And the people who are stirred and stirring are often the naïve people. They are one misunderstood comment and action away from beginning the revolution. Let's remember that revolutions are often the result of pent-up grievances that are triggered by a unexpected event (Boston Tea Party, storming the Bastille, and the riots of St. Petersburg). Such events have no long-term planning by people who can forecast consequence. These simplistic and naïve forces can be effective at overthrowing the status quo; after all, that is what a revolution is. Some revolts of course don't succeed, but if they do, there is no way to forecast what the new national order will be. It just won't be what it was.

Imagine a violent revolution in the US. People are being killed. What would the sides be? It can't be ideological, because no one can "tell" who is a Republican or Democrat. It can't be racial, because the majority is too large. Even if all minorities were bound together in some way it is hard to imagine that they would stay united against whites. It could be an attack on Washington and the capitals of states, but to what end? The most likely default would be between the wealthy and the poor. Private residences and homeless communes will be the places where the revolution plays out. It has begun in Washington and California already.

There is a general level of anger everywhere in the US, but it is an anger that is disunited. Who is there to fight against if everyone is mad at something different? Perhaps it is white males who are the cause of all problems. At least that is an enemy that can be attacked with some vague anger and would result in the ousting of many of the politicians and corporate leaders out there today. But how would the military react? Many of them are white men. What would come of that? If the revolution were a success there would certainly be a transfer of wealth, but then what? Maybe fifteen families living in the same house that one family used to live in is better than nothing. This is more or less what happened in China in the 1940s and Russia in the 1920s.

Will humanity progress in the US, and what does progress mean?

Who gets to decide things? Will everyone have an equal vote? Will some people be able to represent others, or will there just be a single "Chairman"?

What rights will "the people" have?

Before anger becomes action, some very angry people in government must become better. Just Suppose!

18.

Here's to All Of Us Who Are Tone Deaf

The distain for government that a populace has must be significant in order to cause a revolution. Virtually all revolutions come about through frustration and hopelessness.

Suppose the US election of 2008 was the rejection of the status quo and is the reason why Obama won. Suppose a second rejection of that same status quo is the reason Trump won in 2016. The US population of 2020 may elect/re-elect a rejection of the status quo yet again in 2020.

In some sense the presidential candidates are running not just against government but also against big government, or corporations, or universities, or the military, or immigrants. The issues will likely not really mean much in 2020 although they will be obsessed over. What will matter is what version of government rejection will emerge. Suppose we interpret our last elections as the rejection of something rather than the desire for something. What would that really mean? Here are two light-hearted songs of the revolution for both sides of the aisle.

Sung to the tune of "Mammas Don't Let Your
Babies Grow Up to be Cowboys"

By Waylon Jennings

Jurn'lists ain't easy to like, and they're harder to take
They'd rather talk shit or give news that is fake
They are 360 and old faded Blitzers and each night begins a new day
If you don't understand them and they don't die young
They'll probably not go away
Mammas, don't let your babies grow up to be jurn'lists
Don't let 'em take sides or have their own shows

Let 'em be actors and nannies and such

Mammas, don't let your jurn'lists grow up to be babies
'Cause they don't care 'bout you; it's the states that are blue
It's only them that they will love
Jurn'lists like made up old stories and taking the credit
Terrified sources and people who haven't the fight
Them that do know them won't like them
And them that don't, often will tune into Fox
They ain't right they're just wrong
But their pride won't let them do things to make you think they're right
Mammas, don't let your babies grow up to be jurn'lists
Don't let 'em take sides or have their own shows

Let 'em be actors and nannies and such

Mammas don't let your jurn'lists grow up to be babies
'Cause they don't care 'bout you; it's the states that are blue
It's only them that they will love
Mammas don't let your jurn'lists grow up to be babies
Don't let 'em take sides or have their own shows
Let 'em be actors and nannys and such

Sung to the tune "Fix You"

By Coldplay

You're a narcissist, with a touch of greed

When you get what you want but not what you need

When you make us great but we can't sleep

Stuck in Reverse

And the tweets come screaming in our face

They are all unglued and lack good grace

When you build a wall but it goes to waste

Could it be worse?

Lies will foul your home

And ignite your bones

And we will surely fix you

And high up above or down below

When you're too obsessed to let it go

It's just a wall but then you'll never know

That it had no worth

Lies will foul your home

And ignite your bones

And we will try to fix you

Oh oh oh oh oh oh

Tears stream down on our face

When we lose something we can't replace

Oh and tears stream down on *their* face

And I …

Tears stream down on their face

I promise you I will learn from all your mistakes

Oh and tears stream down their face

And I…

Lies will foul your home

And ignite your bones

2020 will fix you

19.

He Was Only Fifteen or So

As I write this diary entry it is 1836 and I am the second mate aboard the *USS Dolphin* in San Francisco harbor. I am also an agent for the US government. I make trade deals. Only a month ago, I had been here in San Francisco having dinner alone. Suddenly, a beautiful Chinese woman appeared in the chair next to me. She was of slight build and wore a *qipao*, the formal dress in China. I was astonished that I had not seen her come in. She had short, black hair parted on the side and very red lips. Her eyes were bright and intent.

"Are you John Streeter?" she asked.

"Who is asking?"

"Henry Bowe," she replied. "He wants you to do something for him."

Henry Bowe was one of the two finest men on any waterfront. We had traded for many years and there were none fairer nor tougher.

"You don't look like Henry," I said, turning away as a small slight to her culture.

She took little notice. "Then I will tell him you were not the man he said you were." She rose to go. I let her walk all the way to the front door. She didn't look back. I waved to Sammy and pointed to the woman and then my table. He gently locked her elbow in his massive paw and guided her back to my table.

She regarded me more carefully.

"So, we meet again," I said. "Just what does Henry want this time?"

I was not prepared for her next words: "I was given something that he wants delivered in Hong Kong. It is of such importance that a price has been set on the head of whoever is in possession of it. Not even I know what its value is. You will arrange for a carriage tomorrow night at seven. You will say you are going to the theater. I will arrange everything else."

The next night, I attended to her plan. I had several pistols hidden in the carriage and on my person. Henry was not a foolish man. His warning meant something.

At the corner of 5th and Franklin, the carriage stopped. A crowd had gathered around a man who had clearly run into foul play. As I turned from looking out the window, there sat the Chinese woman. She was stunning and dressed as though going to the theater. I simply stared with a mixture of admiration and wonder. She knew my emotion perfectly and had a wry smile prepared to meet my stare. We rode in silence.

After a short ride, she handed me a small figurine. "Deliver this to the Governor of Hong Kong in two weeks' time. Speak to no one and deliver this only to the Governor."

I smiled. "When I come back, may I contact you?" I was shamelessly smitten.

She smiled back with a grace typical of her race before she slipped out of the carriage. I decided to continue on to the theater.

Once back on the ship, I examined the figure. It was about the size of a larger chess piece. It was the figure of a Chinese warrior like one would see in the Chinese city of Xian on a pedestal base. Nothing special. It was not made of any material that had value. I shook it. Not a sound.

On the voyage over, I discovered a clever release mechanism. I had been holding the piece in my right hand and had been testing each part. When I applied pressure on the statue's left side with my fingers and its right side with my thumb, I would then press on his head and his shoulders would open just a bit. I could then open them further with ease. Inside was a paper covered in Chinese characters. I decided to make a copy and memorize them.

Upon arrival, I went ashore into a most extraordinary and exotic world that I am only now reconciling. The wharf in Hong Kong shimmered with motion. Nothing except a few buildings seemed to stand in place. Every color was on display and the merchants had the most exotic things for sale, like rhino horn extract and snake bile for potency (The crew brought back sacks full of these medicines). All over the wharf, trade was proceeding at frantic speed. Nothing could capture the sight of this human swirl adequately, for as soon as I saw "the picture", something happened elsewhere that was even better.

At the foot of the gangway I was accosted by every form and purpose of humanity. At times, it was impossible to decide where one person ended and another began. My feet could have been lifted on a whim and I would have been carried along at great speed, such was the press came from the crowd. Many hands touching, urging, pulling me in every direction. Faces—mostly below my natural sight line—appeared and disappeared with the chaotic, spirit-like dissolving sweeps of apparitions.

I had plunged through the worst of it and was now moving on my own with somewhat more intent when I felt a hand on my arm.

"Please, sir. You English?" said a voice that belonged to boy of medium height, about fifteen years of age. His deep-brown eyes had an awareness far beyond his years. His dirty, white shirt was torn in several places. His pants were black and stopped mid-calf and his feet were bare. He wore one of those conical hats for work in the fields.

When I didn't respond, he asked, "Êtes-vous Français? And then, "*Bist du Deutscher?*" He studied me wonderingly. I replied in English that I was Norwegian and had come on the American brig in the harbor.

"You need friend?" he asked in that timeless invitation to a seductive introduction for the evening.

"No," I replied. "I have some things I want to buy. I have a list."

"I help," he said. "Fifty yuan for whole day. I get you places to buy things."

I had some doubts, but the lad looked sincere enough and we struck a bargain. Most of the things I wanted were easily attainable and we made good use of our time. I suspected that he was thinking that, if he got everything I needed quickly, I would turn him loose to make a second deal. Finally, we had come to the item that I had saved for last.

"I want to meet the Chinese governor of Hong Kong," I said.

The boy frowned. "You have arranged already?' he asked. "Getting to see governor is very hard. Governor does not like foreigners. Governor makes list of all foreigners that come to palace, so that all of the nations anchored in harbor know who trying to get things for themselves."

"How do you know that?" I asked, a bit astonished that my visit would be made public.

"Everyone know that," he said.

The boy led me around the hillside below the palace. "Why you want to see governor?" he asked.

"It is a matter between me and him."

The boy's eyes narrowed and he nodded. We walked up from the harbor. The governor's palace was built of white stone and marble that must have cost a hundred chests of gold to build. The steps leading up the hill were carved out of the hillside and each one was of a precise height. Upon entering the portico, the elegance of the structure reminded me of the Buddhist temples and shrines. It was not of this world.

When we reached the main entrance, I turned to pay the boy: he had disappeared. This was disconcerting because I did not know the language. As I stood wondering what to do next, an older, official-looking Chinese man appeared. He wore the formal attire of the palace and the governor's seal was around his neck. A smaller man accompanied him and spoke:

"You'll come with us, please," he said in perfect English.

The entry way opened into a courtyard with three balconies above each side. It had the red, sloping roofs and turned-up cornices that were both support and decoration, typical of Hong Kong. I was led to a table in a secluded section of the courtyard where I could see everything, yet not be seen. The air was cool as the three of us sat.

"I will translate. I am Wang. I am the governor's liaison. We have been expecting you."

I nodded.

"Before we arrange for you to meet the governor, we want to ask you a few questions."

"Of course."

For the next two hours I dined and was questioned on all manner of things. They asked who I was, where I came from, the names of towns in Norway, nautical terms, distances between ports, and many more things. The high official and Wang spoke frequently, presumably arranging for further questions. I began to feel uncomfortable as the questions became more personal.

"You say you are here to deliver something to the governor. What is it?"

"I was told to deliver it only to the governor," I said.

"Whom did you get it from and did the person who gave it to you say anything?"

"I was asked to deliver my charge in person. Anything said or understood at the time of my commission is between the governor and me."

"Very well," said Wang and he looked furtively at the high official. "Come with us."

We walked for a while in the sun and then I was abandoned to wait. Suddenly, two guards from the palace were upon me and half-dragged, then carried me into a building set away from the main buildings. The shoved me down some stairs into a dark room that stank of foul, decaying animals.

A short time later, I was chained to a wall. My clothes were cut off and searched thoroughly. I was beaten soundly. Wang returned.

"You will tell me everything I want to know. I have a great many methods to persuade you that this talk is necessary." He showed me some sort of blade. "Do you know what this is?"

I didn't move.

"Well, no matter. It is an exquisite device that removes thin layers of skin—or, not so thin," he added, chuckling.

At that moment, the door opened and the boy who had been my guide entered. He and Wang exchanged words in Chinese and Wang smiled.

"I am told that what you have is not on board your ship. That is unfortunate, because we could have just driven a nail into your skull. Now, we will have to be slow enough for you to plead for the nail."

It is impossible to describe the pain of skin being removed from the inside of a thigh. I don't know how long they worked.

The next memory I have was of lying in a soft bed. It was light all around. I smelled flowers and it was warm. *Perhaps this is what death is…* I made a small movement and pain shot through my leg. I groaned. As my eyes focused, I saw that I was in an open-air room. There were fruits and juices close at hand. I lay there as I tried to account for time.

Suddenly, the door opened and the most beautiful young Chinese woman I had ever seen appeared. Her long dark hair shimmered. She was tall for her race and she moved without any visible effort. Her dress fell in layers like sails and they moved every which way as though carried by the breeze. Her face was childlike in its beauty, but her eyes were attentive, taking me in.

"You look damaged," she said in a London-tinged, British accent. "Let me look at you."

She pulled the cover off and I could see a blood-soaked bandage around my left thigh. She bent down and started to touch it and when I winced and turned my head she hesitated.

"I need to see how it's healing," she said as she gently opened the bandage.

I was both shocked and relieved. The size of the removed skin was roughly three inches square and was not deep. Before I could move, she had a salve in her hand.

"This will help with the pain," she said. She began to smooth it lightly over the wound.

"I am truly sorry for this, but we had to know," she began. "My name is Shin Li and I am very close to the governor. We knew someone would be bringing us a package. We had to know that no one else could have seen it."

I said nothing.

"You were approached by my sister in San Francisco. She and a man named Henry have been friends a long time. Henry had mentioned you to her and she sought you out. This much of the story you know, and so you should trust that what I say next is also true."

"There is work in China that must be done. To do it we need assistance. The package you were bringing is that assistance. The governor in Hong Kong will play a huge role in this work and it is a matter of survival for our people and the future of China."

I followed her voice, but it was at the very edge of my attention.

"I see you need rest. Very well. I will come tomorrow."

The next day I was able to sit up a bit, but my leg hurt like hell. I wondered what this was all about and thought that if I ever saw Henry again I'd give him some of this treatment and see how he did.

The door opened. It was her. If possible, she was even more beautiful than before. *Maybe this was the good that followed the bad.* I was so confused.

"I know who you are, John Streeter."

I had not noticed her voice before. It was as perfect as she was. Her English was flawless and her voice swept up my attention against my will.

"For some time, we have been looking for someone who is trusted by everyone to bring news back and forth to San Francisco. Henry thought it could be you. When you arrived, you met one of the palace household staff. He had been expecting you and met you. Had you not asked to see the governor, he would have offered to bring you here. Nevertheless, we could not know if you had what we wanted. If you had had it on your body, we would have been disappointed. We searched your ship and did not find it. So, you are the kind of man we need."

"Why did you cut me up, then?" I said in anger.

She smiled. "Two reasons. If you will help us—and we will pay a great deal more than you will ever make in a normal lifetime—then this will identify you to all. No one would go through this willingly. If you won't help us, then we will have to continue your treatment until you do tell us, or you die. It will be our way to trust you and your way to trust us. I would not like to see you die, John Streeter." She bent down and kissed me lightly on the lips.

The next week, they said nothing more about the figurine or the writing. Shin Li came and went frequently and I found myself captivated by her presence. I waited impatiently for her to return each day and missed her terribly when she was gone.

Then, as I began to feel like I could move again and was able to walk around the rooms of the palace, Shin Li announced that the day had come for decision. They could wait no longer.

"I must see the governor, then," I said.

She thought for a minute and then replied, "All right. I will send someone to bring you to him."

About half an hour later, the boy who I had met on the pier showed up.

"Here sir. I take you to governor now." He led the way.

We came to a guarded room and entered. There was a throne-like chair at one end and benches on each side.

"The governor will meet you shortly, but first I need to tell you story."

The boy disappeared between two screens. As the boy began talking, my mind wandered. He was saying that the world did not always exist the way it seemed. His voice started to change or perhaps I was just tired—and then suddenly I knew: from behind the screen stepped Shin Li. For just a moment she spoke again in the strange, broken speech of the street lad—but it was coming from her beautiful lips.

"I see," I said, but I didn't.

"No, John Streeter, you don't see because if you did then you would understand that I am the person whom the message you carry is meant for. I am the governor of Hong Kong."

I was stunned. I went over to touch her.

"I am very real," she said.

Finally, I nodded. Then I sat and began drawing the characters I had copied in my mind. When I was done, I handed her the writing. She glanced at it and her eyes got very big. Then she glanced at me and ran from the room.

I did not see her again for quite some time. When I saw her next, she looked tired and distracted.

"The characters you wrote were true, but I am sorry that they were. We are engaged in a struggle for the soul of China and you brought death. But the death you brought was not to our side. I live in a world that is changing by the day. I have taken great pains to hide the nature of this work. All of Hong Kong thinks our governor is a man. No one has seen him, but they all claim to have met him and to be his best friend. Most of them know only the boy with no name that met you on the docks. It is far better this way." She paused. "You will be leaving soon. I will have something for you to take back to San Francisco."

I was on the pier, waiting for the settlement of my trades. After all, that was why I had come to Hong Kong. While I had been "away", the price of my spirits had doubled. That and the money from Shin Li and I was rich by the standards of San Francisco.

The trip to San Francisco was uneventful. The first night in port I stayed aboard to be sure that I could produce the characters from memory. Satisfied, I burned the paper and retired to my stateroom. Suddenly, a hand was on my mouth and a blade at my throat.

"My sister said you had something for me," she said. "I was told that you now have a scar so that I know it is you." She slid her hand under my nightshirt.

"She said I should take a whole night to look for it."

I was glad she did.

APPENDIX TO CHAPTER 19
What It's Like to Live abroad

Suppose you want to live abroad. You must at a minimum do it for three years or more for any material gain to be had. You must be able to speak the language. You must work in their economy and earn a living in their culture and be paid in local currency. Living on a college campus in another country is not living abroad. It is living in a protected environment with no responsibility apart from grades. This matters.

Living abroad does not mean living in an English-speaking, American enclave. I do understand that in the Middle East or in a diplomatic posting you don't get choices. There is a fundamental issue of safety in these situations. Nevertheless, it is the clever ex pat that is able to live publicly in the expected place and privately in another. This is not always desired, as it takes a level of sophistication and awareness that is far above average to carry this off.

There are several skills that you *must* have in order to be effective abroad:

1. You must be able to read intent in people's eyes. This means when you are hearing people speak in their native tongue and you can't figure out what they are saying, you have to be able to read their eyes to discern what their base attitude is. This is learned through experience. If you can't do this, you are in for many embarrassing moments. Asian cultures learn this at an early age because they must render homage to their elders. This includes tapping on the table, turning away from a drinking partner of greater stature, etc. One must always be aware, and it is this learned awareness that makes one effective everywhere.

   a. There are some defenses. If you listen to two people speaking their native language together and you don't know the subject, you can wait a minute or two and then say "always" in that language. It is one of the few words that can indicate understanding, even when it may not be the case. This is effective if it appears that the two people are arguing.

b. It is likewise crucial to find a way into the local language's humor. This is obvious, but not easy. Repeating a "saying" is not always funny. There are universal images though that can be tried. Imitating drunkenness, learning the local equivalent of "WTF" but in the same abbreviated form, being able to do one simple parlor trick (coin), or translating an English expression that they would know into their native tongue are good choices. It may make no sense, but it has a certain endearing quality. When you are really good, you can split local words and combine them into new words that they won't have heard but will understand. Typically, using the last name of a leader and the word for economics as in "Reaganomics" to describe current policy is a starting place for this idea.

2. You must participate in events designed to get the better of you. For example, you might enter a banquet room with a table already populated by nationals. The first person will give you a shot glass filled with a national drink and offer a toast to your presence in the native tongue. The next person will then hand you another shot glass and offer a toast to your country. More than twelve people later, there can be a bit of a problem.

In addition to drink there is food. There are national dishes that in many cases the locals won't eat but they will suggest that you should. They are generally animal parts (brains, feet, etc.) or insects that don't easily pass through a standard mental rendering.

3. You need to make allies. The best people usually have emotion-based personalities. Most people in Europe and in Asia know what it's like to be a foreigner. Some will usually try to help. It is important to cleverly show how much they matter to you without just giving them money. This requires real awareness and is not at all easy.

4. When you are invited to someone's house, you'll have four choices for a gift. Can you think of what the choices are? If not, you are behind*.

5. Just suppose you wanted to learn a language. How would one best do it? Schooling, tutors, books, or tapes are among the choices. But most people can't learn languages in those ways.

A. *You* must know how you learn best. Are you visual or aural? Do you memorize well? Do you know the grammar of your own language? Do you already speak another language? Do you have the discipline to learn this language? How are you motivated? Can you see patterns in the way other cultures discuss common things? How do *you* derive meaning from words? Have you even thought about it? It is much easier to learn another language if you know how you create meaning. If you don't know this, language will be much harder.

B. *You* must know what your own speech patterns are. Do you use certain favorite phrases? Do you speak the same way in the same setting every day? Is the base of your native language limited by your occupation or living preferences? Do you see patterns in your own language?

C. *You* must know early on how your native language and the language you are learning are different. How do those languages think about:

   a. Space

   b. Time

c. Gender

d. Word order and endings

Most languages have systems for talking about the sun, moon, trees, grass, rain, snow, water, and sky. How are they arranged? What thoughts do the speakers have when they speak of these things? Think of the expressions, "There are lots of ants on that table" and "That table has a lot of ants". Do you see a difference?

D. You must devote time—lots and lots of time—to a new language. And you need a native speaker to help you through. They may not teach you much, but they should help you learn. Your language helper must be able to:

   a. Answer as to "why" things are said/done the way they are

   b. Know *your* native language well enough to see what you are lacking or why you don't get it

   c. Translate your natural speech patterns into their language. For example, if you frequently say, "I am doomed" as a bit of a joke, your teacher should be able to translate that into his or her own language. They might not necessarily do it word for word, but meaning for meaning.

   d. Not require perfection. Every native speaker can understand grammar mix-ups, accents, and verb tense fails in their native tongue. It is important to be understood, not be perfect. Time is the enemy of Americans. We do not spend much time on anything except perhaps work and sleep. This effort is hours a day.

Learning a language is all on the student, not the helper. No one can teach you a language. But you can learn it. There are thousands of other aids.

If you can live in country, you will learn faster. If you speak every day, you will learn faster. If you know other languages, you will learn faster.

This may help. There are twelve verbs that convey a great deal of information: is, have, want, like, know, go, come, can, understand, speak, say, and see. If you then take the eight subject pronouns, (I, you, he, she, it, we, you, they) and then throw in a few demonstrative pronouns (this, that, these, those), then you have the basis for lots and lots of sentences. You just need to memorize a few nouns and away you go. Most languages are subject-verb-object oriented, so the grammar is roughly the same.

Not everyone can learn another language. Not everyone can lose weight. Not everyone can play jazz. Not everyone can read other people. Not everyone has discipline. Not everyone cares enough. Not everyone can learn another language.

6. Be alone early. When you are alone, you must solve all problems through encounters with strangers. This is a hard test of skill. Navigating purchases, unusual circumstances, and the "common day's language" is crucial. It also builds things to talk about for future conversations. Learning song lyrics is also helpful because they deliver information to people on several levels. Sometimes they can be funny.

7. You are a guest with a guest's responsibility to act as the local people would wish you to. But there will be people whom you won't like and who won't like you. They could be colleagues, landlords, service people, etc. You are a minority no matter how you physically blend in. Your patience and self-respect will be tested severely no matter how much you know. Before you go abroad, deliberately go to places that offend you. Stay longer than you are comfortable and get used to disequilibrium. It may be the most important skill you acquire. Being an American is not always a plus. Activists in many countries resist American policy. You need to be skilled in discussing sensitive

topics without having a "take". This skill is not taught these days, but should be.

8. Finally, there is the skill to return to the US without starting every sentence with "So there was this one time in…"and recognizing that you will have had an experience that cannot be described in words. It might serve to keep a diary of patterns that you recognized abroad that you know are unfamiliar to people back in the states. For example, you may find that democracy *cannot* work in every country. You may find that capitalism as an idea requires a governing philosophy that recognizes individualism (life, liberty, pursuit of happiness) and a legal philosophy of individual land ownership that are not consistent with much of the rest of the world. You likely will find that beliefs you held before are too simplistic now.

There are many other aspects of life abroad that can make you a more effective person: courage in the face of the unknown, comfort with conflict, perspective, and the skills listed above. Just suppose this was the differentiator for your future life. Could you do it?

Suppose there is a real difference between the people of the East and West. For example, in the West we think of medicine as a reductionist series of integrated relationships. We start with the body as a whole and proceed down through systems, organs, tissues, proteins, molecules, atoms, electrons and quarks. Western medical research aims to introduce drugs that repair, inhibit, or strengthen the relationships between all these systems. In the West, we take aspirin for pain. In the East they do as well. But in the East, the idea of *chi* (chee) imagines a force that runs from the earth, up through the body, out the head and into heaven. This chi is a life force and when pain occurs it is due to blockage of this chi. Acupuncture is used to realign chi. When both Easterners and Westerners have back or neck pain, acupuncture can sometimes out-perform Western medicine. Thus, to be a "complete" doctor, one must be experienced in both "ways of being".

In the West, much of our focus is short-term. The idea that some things are 6000 years old does not frequently register, especially in the US. In the East, the unrelenting force for invention and self-discovery is not felt as strongly. In the West, government is often seen as not helpful. In the East, government is the great balancer.

In both areas, there is a question of the individual vs. the collective. Is it "me first" or "us first"? Because of these different ways of thinking, events, contracts, negotiations, government relations, and even exchange student study programs are not seen the same way by East and West. This leads to very subtle differences in perception. For example, when faced with a crime, Easterners more likely will review the recent experiences of the perpetrator and assign plausible motives from outside forces. In the West the behavior of the criminal is attributed more to an interpretation of the internal condition of the individual.

There are many, many other differences that are opposite ways of viewing the world. Language goes without saying. In the West, we use a modular alphabet of twenty-six characters. These characters mostly have no meaning, apart from being combined with other characters. In the East, individual characters have meaning individually. This difference means that, to effectively speak and read Asian languages, you must know as many as 5000 characters. In addition, some Eastern languages embed representations of stories in their lexicon that are not literally translatable and require knowledge of the underlying story, like "crying wolf" in the West.

In the East, there is a notion that the collective is to be respected above the individual. In the West, it is the opposite. In the East, appropriate interaction matters. In the West, the judgment of appropriateness changes frequently. There are thousands of differences between East and West that span most of the qualities that make us human. Many would make profound differences in each other's lives if we only knew them. This is true, not because we need to understand *them* better, but in order to understand *ourselves* better.

These ways of assimilating patterns are very different than just knowing different sets of facts. To be able to see the world as a complete human, it is essential to have had extensive experience in both East and West. There are no easy ways around this. The idea that one can be born and never learn another language fluently, never travel, never live abroad for more than two years, and never marry anyone other than from their own country distorts the ability to recognize patterns. There is simply insufficient experience to be effective. Experience matters. Interpretation of that experience matters even more. Being both an Easterner and Westerner is non-trivial.

20.

The Psychologist's Life

"I am here doctor," he said, "because I was told by another patient of yours that you could help me."

"This can often be the case" she smiled "but everyone is different. Tell me where you are in your life and why seeing me matters."

"I have lost the will to live" he began, "there is no other way to say it. I feel like no matter what lies on the other side that it cannot be worse than what I am experiencing here. Each day I think that if I can just get to the end of it, that life will be better. And yet it isn't. Each night is intolerably long so I take sleeping medicine. But I just lay there. In the morning I dread facing the day. At night I dread dreading the dread of the new day."

"And for how long have you been where you are now?'

"For two years at least. I really don't know. It didn't just happen in a single day. It's been going on for some time. Since it began I have been drifting along waiting for something…I am not sure what. Maybe that's why I am here."

"Just so you know, I see a lot of people in exactly this same place. People get here in different ways but the "here" that they are experiencing is the same here. It is interesting that you use the word drift because that is very much the right idea. You are caught in a flow not of your own choosing. It feels like you are being forced to live in a way."

"Yes that's it! I feel stuck in a place that I know I am stuck in but I can't get out on my own."

"And so that's why you've come to see me. Are you waiting to be unstuck or are you waiting to find a way to overcome the drift?"

"When you put it that way I guess both," he said. "The sameness is excruciating doctor. Just coming here is a difference that has meaning to me. I feel like I have a purpose here. I feel like this is a first step outside of the drift."

"Actually you took the first step when you realized that you were stuck. It is amazing how many people live lives of 'quiet desperation' as the poet says yet do not come to realize it. They have a vague sense of misfortune but can't even declare that they may have a problem. I see this in business a lot, especially in older men."

He smiled. "So do you think we can get me a way out?"

At that moment a side door to the office opened and a lady walked in. "Mary I have told you before not to invite other people into my office if I am called away. I am sorry sir, I'll be with you in a moment", and "Mary" stood up from behind the desk.

As she walked past the man sitting in front of the desk she leaned over and whispered "I can get you out....follow me"...

APPENDIX TO CHAPTER 20
How to Solve the Problems of Life, Leadership, Parenting, and Relationship

This essay is meant to be used in connection with essay 7. If you are having troubles, are searching for happiness, looking for answers, or just trying to get better, read seven 7 first. There you will discover that there are four quadrants or skills that you must master. You must be good at understanding yourself, good at understanding others, good at knowing things (or accomplishing missions), and good at knowing what to do when you don't know. This work is hard.

Suppose what follows is a path to being generally successful in life that navigates these four quadrants. This essay starts with any problem you are trying to solve. Rather than listing every possible problem, I have started by listing reasons why we have problems to begin with. You may think this is obvious but I hope you read why I think they exist. It is helpful to identify the patterns, even if you don't see them on the path I have laid out.

The next stage is getting out of the problem. This is not solving the problem necessarily; it is becoming aware of existing paths that are ways out. This helps in deciding whether you can get out alone or whether you might need help. There are always two ways out: get out yourself (you know you have the problem and you *want* out) or you get someone else to get you out.

The third stage is to form a way of solving the problem and staying out of it. This stage is based on how you got out of the problem. For example, if you are afraid of death but you don't want to be, it is important that you can formulate this as the problem. This is important, because often we feel badly but we don't know why. The question is always "why" you have this problem. Not everyone does. An important assumption is that, if you were able to get yourself out of this problem yourself, you would have.

The last stage is implementation. You create the solution and arrange your life anew. This should become clear momentarily.

Stage 1

Many people feel they are stuck in life. They are unhappy. They are victims. They feel that they do not have free will. The principle reason they can't move is that they are stuck.

From the age of first understanding, we humans interpret a world of cause and effect and learn that actions have consequences. Typically, this happens by putting our hands someplace they shouldn't be and having our parents putting *their hands* someplace *we* don't want them to be. In order to render the world more predictable, and consequences more understandable, our parents enforce behaviors that in theory provide a strategy for living. As young children, we are subjected to a torrent of advice, corrections, rules, enforcement, and what I have come to call "supposed-tos", as in "I am supposed to do 'x'". As we age, we acquire outside-the-family experiences that also inform how we interpret our behavior and its consequences. We discover that deliberately behaving a certain way can cause certain predictable behaviors in others. Repeating the same behavior and getting the same result reinforces as well. There is satisfaction in repeating the same process if the result makes us happy. These behaviors when repeated often enough become habits as in "I have become my mother". They become beliefs.

Beside family and self-experiment, there may be other important influences in how we interpret our environment. Carl Jung suggested that there is a universal or collective unconsciousness that links us all. This collective unconsciousness is a kind of background "program" that contains *archetypes* of historical human experience. The reason we resonate with certain symmetries and patterns is because we share this common thread of human awareness that is this collective unconsciousness. These patterns too may inform our sense of "which causes produce which effects". Causes are important because they anchor us. They provide predictable reasons for what happens. In a world of change and uncertainty, causes set events in time and speak to a certain predictable repetition that is biologically pleasing. Much of the adaptive work involved in growing up relates to getting our causes right. Why did he do that? How do I stop this? How do I make that desirable outcome happen?

Outside the family, another force is at work: the force of social conditioning. In all societies, classes, orientations, and genders, there are very clear *ways to do things* that become a dominant part of cause and effect—and we alter our behaviors because of them. There are certain traditions at holidays, certain rituals for marriage and death, and writing conventions in our native language. There are also ways to handle rejection, ways to find a mate, and ways to get promoted at work. These *ways* infuse culture, language, religion, and gender behavioral patterns into our calculation of cause and effect.

There are environmental forces that impact and shape us. This seems obvious. But what happens if these forces are so strong that they hold us down? Death is a good example. When we lose a loved one, we go to a bad place. We stay in that place sometimes for years. The loss of something we had is always powerful. When things are not working, what do we do? What have we been told that we are *supposed* to do?

This notion of *supposed to* is very important to understanding Stage 1. No matter which culture or language one speaks or how our parents brought us up, and no matter what needs we have that are controlling us, the list of *supposed tos* holds our view of the world in check. While there are differences between cultures, and especially between economic strata, the list is there, nonetheless. In the US upper-middle economic classes, the *supposed tos* look something like this:

"We are born because we are supposed to be; we behave in elementary school because we are supposed to; we study hard because we are supposed to; we learn to play sports or an instrument because we are supposed to; we take AP classes in high school because we are supposed to; we perform charitable acts because we are supposed to; we edit the student newspaper because we are supposed to; we graduate because we are supposed to; we go to the "best" college because we are supposed to; we graduate because we are supposed to; we get a job because we are supposed to; we work three years because we are supposed to; we then go to graduate school because we are supposed to; we graduate because we are supposed to; we get another job because we are supposed to; we work for a few years because we are supposed to; we then fall in love because we are supposed to; we get married because we are supposed to; we have kids because we are supposed to; we teach them all the things we are supposed to; we work some more because we are supposed to; we get promoted a few times because we are supposed to; we retire because we are supposed to; we have grandchildren because we are supposed to; we die because we are supposed to."

Patterns of *supposed tos* exist around the world regardless, of race, color, or gender. The US, inner city pattern is different than that described above, as are the Chinese and Middle Eastern patterns. But the patterns can be thought of in a similar way. These patterns create what we are going to define as the ***flow.*** When we say we are going with the flow, we imagine a somewhat effortless movement on our part in an intention-less journey.

Flow has a direction, a speed, and if you are in it you are doing what it is doing. You are doing what you are supposed to do. You are flowing. *More formally, flow is the combined forces of preferred behavior and social imperative that cause us to do what we are supposed to do.* The flow is extremely powerful.

To a person who is trapped by a problem of their own making, such as a parent who is struggling with a child, a leader who has lost command of his subordinates, or a spouse who is being isolated from their partner, this flow is very important to understand. Sometimes our problems are of our own making because we *believe* what the flow has taught us. We believe that what is real is what we see. We believe that what we see can be no other way.

Parents are masters of the flow. The reason for this is that you learn flow from the authority figures in your life. Flow is what you adjust to in order to survive. If you rebel against the flow, you in effect revolt against your own ability to survive. Thus, we are often trapped. Some people never get out. These people are often referred to as being unable to get out of their own way. They do not understand themselves and they have been given such a strong message by the flow that they cannot move. These are typically people who are doing badly in Quadrant 1 the Self vs. Self quadrant from vignette 7.

Flow in the Environment

The flow is where we find traditions, cultural imperatives, and every *ism* (capitalism, communism, humanism, feminism, chauvinism, Nazism, Catholicism, multiculturalism, and so on). Each *ism* assures us that we are better off in its particular flow than in any other. It is a condition for being in their flow in the first place. If you are a non-believer, you cannot belong to an ism's flow. The flow is however double-edged. On the one hand, it binds and solidifies society, and on the other it buries and limits alternatives. The Bible, Koran, and Torah are all books of the flow. They *require* you to believe in the flow as a condition for membership.

Corporate policies and procedures are all pronouncements of flow. "We've always done it this way" is flow. The directions on your model airplane are also flow, as are certain laws of physics. Flow is very powerful, and Hollywood has made thousands of movies about confronting flow. The Nazis take over Europe, but a guy named Schindler leaves the flow and saves many Jews (*Schindler's List*). A Vermont boarding school has taught poetry for a thousand years in much the same way until Mr. Keating (Robin Williams) forces the students to leave the flow. (*Dead Poets Society*). In Egypt, a queen who is at odds with her brother triumphs over him and becomes ruler, despite the flow of tradition and royal succession (*Cleopatra*).

In many larger corporations, the administration departments, operations departments, compliance, counsel's office, risk management, and human resources are all flow "meisters". They are set up, manned, and rewarded for keeping the flow intact. They ensure that things will be done the same way, so that risk and illegal acts can be *managed*. They ensure that reports of *actions taken* will be produced. They ensure that these reports will be retained. They ensure that the same will be true tomorrow. That is the comfort of the flow.

If there were no humans, there would still be flow but it would not be a conscious flow supported by *supposed-tos*. It would simply be the law of "musts". Nature would still exist, and animals would still do what they do, unaltered by free will. This is because the flow can work all by itself. This is its power. Evolution is the flow that perpetuates life. In nature, mutations change the flow somewhat randomly.

Sometimes, in nature, changes in the earth's environment cause dramatic changes in the flow—then animals die. Anyone who has lost their job because the acquiring institution did not share their flow can attest to this. Flows can be merged, exchanged, beaten, occur inside other flows, compete with other flows, and traded. Trading flows is common. People get divorced and remarry, only to have the same problems as they had in their first flow. They change jobs, change residences, or change schools believing that they have defeated the flow. In fact, they have only become part of another flow.

Humans have *flow enforcers* who inspect and ensure compliance. Think audit departments. Flows also conflict. The break between India and Pakistan after the British departure is such a case of conflicting flows. If I am an African American in the flow of white America, I am inside two flows (white and black America). Interesting questions arise when flows are embedded. How do I behave if the flows require mutually exclusive behavior? How do I integrate myself when my home flow is very different from my workflow?

Politics is an interesting flow. Politicians are elected by declaring how well they will handle the "flow". It is a subtle irony that the flow they enter after Election Day may prevent them from changing the very flow they said they cared about.

At this point, it is natural to ask "But aren't these elements of flow exactly what holds and binds a society together? Isn't flowing what creates the predictive power of the collective? Doesn't the flow have a purpose?" Of course, the answer is "yes". Flow does have a purpose. But this purpose is double-edged. While flow binds, it constrains. While flow predicts, it limits.

In all manner of things, the flow exists to enable humans to interact with each other in standard and efficient ways. The point of discussing the flow is to highlight that as a living thing it may or may not be a good place to be. The flow co-ops best intentions and uses some of the most powerful tools at humanity's disposal to compel compliance. For example, in 1960, China endured a famine and starvation allegedly brought about by Mao's policies. But in the end, it may not have been Mao but the flow that caused the famine. In the years running up to 1960, the central government collected figures for rice production from all the provincial leaders, who in turn collected it from the cities and so on down to the level of the village. Unbeknownst to Beijing, each government entity wanted to be seen as succeeding above their planned levels of rice and so they each added imaginary rice to their totals. As the document went up the "food" chain, the imaginary rice became a significant part of the total. In Beijing, it appeared as though the rice crop had had a banner year when in fact it was slightly below average. Valuable resources were diverted to other projects instead of agriculture and many peasants starved. In this case, the culture and Mao's expectations enabled the flow to do its worst.

Leaders may act the way the flow requires them to act. If the flow of *government* creates the expectation among our leaders that they must solve all problems right now, then they feel compelled to do so. This may be impossible and here's why:

Let's look at other flows and their enablers. Language may be one of the most powerful flow enablers. A common language simply *is* the flow. Language is very exclusive. People born of the same culture in countries like Norway, India, and China have different dialects because of geographical dispersion. These local dialects become the core flow and the national language becomes a surrounding flow. National languages are used for TV and print, but the local language is used for daily communication. If you cannot speak the language, you cannot communicate. If you cannot communicate, you cannot belong. It is that simple. Grammar is very culturally dependent. How "your people" think determines the rules they employ. For example, the Mandarin language does not use verb tenses and instead uses sentence markers to indicate time. In Latvian, Latin, and Russian, the role of nouns is determined by their endings. In English, time is denoted by verb tenses and words like prepositions and articles are separate parts of speech.

A second powerful flow enabler is culture. These are the norms and rules that govern how a society functions. Culture becomes the flow on purpose. It affects manners, how people interact with each other, the things that are valued, and the way that history is remembered. Culture affects everything from i-Pads to national newspapers. Culture is what parents spend most of the early formative years teaching and reinforcing. People "believe" what their culture has taught them. They "believe" that the flow was *their idea*. They believe their country has better sports, food, laws, TV, and so on because it is the comfortable flow that makes it so. And yet, every national flow is different. This creates obvious, competitive flow problems.

A third powerful flow enabler is education. This is the most complicated of the flows. We may think of education as being capable of breaking us out of the flow, however it is not that easy. Education in the early years creates the flow and in fact *becomes* the flow, everything from multiplication tables to which history books you will read. The way that the Korean War began and the interpretation of the war's outcome are very different in Chinese schools versus those in the US. Education brings a flow of its own. This is true of colleges and especially true of classes in interpretative history. But education can break the flow in certain circumstances that we will examine later. In the economically depressed parts of the world, education can break the flow of poverty. It can redress imbalances between races, sexes, cultures and economic strata.

A fourth flow enabler is the flow of peers. This flow almost goes without saying and extends from kindergarten to the workplace. If you desire to be part of the *inner circle*, the C-suite, or the latest project, you are in fact practicing to be *allowed* into a *desirable* flow. The same is true for college fraternities and sororities. And it applies on the playgrounds everywhere in the world.

Peer flow is also part of the socializing process. It makes one feel "accepted". Validating that you are "ok" is a big part of the mid-grade levels before high school. Once one begins work after college, the comparison against peers for how we are doing is yet another powerful flow. Peer flow is at the intersection of self vs. self and self vs. others.

But peer flow has differences. White and black peer flow can mean different things. Some of the reasons for discrimination come from differences in these flows. These are the topic of another vignette.

We also come into conflict with the flow when we are *forced* to be in a flow. This is the situation where both spouses work because they *must*, even if they would choose otherwise. It is the situation of going to work, day after day, to a job that holds no interest because you *need the money*. In prison, it is important to be part of a gang because survival may depend on it, even if you just want to serve your time. You may also have to kill for the flow.

The flow is where we find many of the "*How to*" leadership books. Authors who write about the "it" that they have found are asking you to believe in their flow. Most self- help leadership books, diet books, and cookbooks have this prescriptive flow. *Do as I say and you too will be successful.* But in the end, my *ism* is as good as yours. This is the seduction of the flow that requires me to believe. It requires that I accept. It determines my future.

Flow is also significantly about free will. While there are many philosophical approaches to free will, here we are talking about *the simple ability to do otherwise.* If you are in the flow, you are not *doing otherwise* by definition, period. The flow is about the absence of free will. The obvious question one might ask is, "*What if I want to be in the flow, and consciously seek to stay in the flow? What if I like the flow?*" The answer is that people manage in the flow all the time. It is not wrong to be in the flow. Many people have lived their lives comfortably in the flow. That is fine. But to be a parent, leader, or other person who is responsible for others, you cannot accept the flow blindly. It must be intentional.

Conclusion of Flow

From here, it should be clear that if you have problems that are difficult or unsolvable, it is probably because you are in some kind of flow. The flow has you in its grasp or it has caused you to grasp yourself, as in "Every time I try to get my clock to change to daylight savings, I fail."

Stage 2

So how does one defeat flow? How does one get out? These questions are of preeminent importance.

The first point to make is that one must be aware of the flow. If you feel stuck at work or in a relationship that is draining, you are likely in the flow. Most of us have these feelings and sensations many times in life, but unless you recognize the flow, nothing will change.

Being aware of the flow is the first step, but equally important is a desire to get out of the flow. There are millions of workers who are content to punch a clock, do work, and raise a family. They go to professional sports events, watch TV, go to church, and live contented lives. But good leadership, good parenting, and good relationships often need adjustments to be successful. Leadership and parenting require the ability to break the flow because resources, time, skills, and money are not infinite. In making choices, we introduce conflict, in introducing conflict we upset the flow, in upsetting flow we create change, and it follows from there.

The four quadrants in vignette 7 can help in pinpointing which flow you may be in. You may be upset with yourself, upset with others, upset with your job or your environment, or upset because you don't "know what you are here for". You lack purpose.

The following diagram describes four levels that you will find helpful in escaping the flow.

Level Four – Meta stability

Level Three - Chaos

Level Two - Disequilibrium

Level One – The Flow – 60 HZ hum of background noise, stable

Level One is the flow itself. It is the daily life we lead. It is the sixty-cycle hum of the lights. On Level One, you are stable because the flow has made it that way. Parents and professors are all aligned to keep you on Level One. Any discord is removed and is captured by the idea of helicopter parents. It is also the nanny state. It is where life is safe.

Level Two is perhaps the most important idea so far. Disequilibrium is the disruptive force that initiates change. Sometimes you choose it and sometimes it chooses you. Almost no change, improvement, development, or success comes about without risk. And risk requires disequilibrium. Risk is the deliberate act of putting oneself in an uncomfortable situation. You must have "the conversation", you must change jobs, etc. Disequilibrium, however, is not a state that one can exist in forever. Ultimately, the desire is to return to stability but in a better place.

Level Three – This is a very significant level and exists in only four places for long periods of time:

1. Military Combat

2. Inner city streets

3. Single mothers

4. Emergency first responders

Chaos is the level where much of the focus is on whether survival is possible. Human life is probably at stake or seems so. This is far more powerful than disequilibrium. It is a state of ultimate stakes where there is *full on* fear. There are not many people who get to Level Three. Some who do get there do not "come back" the same as before. This is because Level Three can be life changing. If you experience Level Three, it is important to go forward or go back as soon as possible. Body-damaging stress is the ultimate result of being on this level for long periods of time.

Level Four – But there is exceptionally good news. If you can survive at Level Three even for a short period of time, you have succeeded at something that perhaps no more than 1% of the world's population has ever experienced. You are unique. You have passed the "test". You have arrived. At Level Four, life becomes "meta stable", meaning that so much that could have caused you disequilibrium before, so much of what you used to worry about, so much that seemed so important, is just not a problem any more. You are meta stable.

So let's link this to the flow. To get out of the flow, you can choose to create disequilibrium for yourself, or you can ask another person to help create it for you. Either way, there must be disequilibrium. You are trying to make conscious change. That is disruptive by definition. Leaving the flow does not automatically set you on a journey all the way to Level Three. Creating a constrained disequilibrium is possible and is really the easiest way to think about leaving the flow. You can opt for deliberate moments when you are in disequilibrium, but always know you will come back to Level One. You planned it that way. Create enough disequilibrium to get yourself out. Retain enough stability to get yourself back. People who dislike public speaking but put themselves in speaking roles are examples. If they experience genuine "terror" and yet get through it time after time, they can reach meta stability. Levels Three and Four are important and Level Four can be a goal, but it means going through Level Three. That path is not for everyone.

The environment can create unintentional disequilibrium. Being in a hurricane is an example. All the conditions and build-up of the wind and seas create a condition of chaos, and if you survive the storm you may reach a meta-stable plateau.

We just described one way to get out of the flow. Let's examine another. Here we look to Ron Heifitz, a professor in Transformational leadership at Harvard. He has an approach to getting yourself out of the flow.

The Balcony

The balcony is also a concept created by Ron Heifiz. The idea is that there is a "you" who is experiencing any moment, but there is also a second "you". This second you is a you who can detach from your immediate surroundings and look "down" on this exact moment. Ron pictures it as though one is going onto a balcony. This "balcony" is both the ability to detach and the ability to reflect on what is happening in the moment. What are you feeling about what you are experiencing? What are you thinking? What are others thinking? And then, what should you do with this information? How do others perceive you right now? What do you think that they think about you? Are you being an idiot? If so, then what?

Imagine a conversation with another person where you have been asked for advice. If you are in the flow, you might just "play the tape" as an answer. It doesn't matter to you. Yet, in the middle of your answer, you get on the "balcony" and observe yourself just mailing it in. It is this ability to see what is happening "from the balcony" and your role in it that allows you to disrupt your behavior and create a better answer. The balcony allows you to catch yourself. It allows you to make changes on Level One, and it gets you out of the flow. The "balcony", if used and understood well, is a subtle kind of disequilibrium. Most importantly, it is done consciously and deliberately. If your child is testing your patience, if a subordinate is being insubordinate, or if you are having a rough patch in a relationship, getting on the "balcony" lets you get out of the other people's negative flow. You can get a grip and do the noble thing to solve the problem.

Being on the "balcony", however, does not work in all cases. If you are truly stuck or are suffering, you may not be able to move yourself into disequilibrium. You may not have the energy or be willing to break the bonds of the flow. In these cases, you need the help of another. You need someone in Quadrant Two (Self vs. Others) to help you see what is missing and to provide disequilibrium.

One of the most important things others can do is remind us that emotions are not caused by outside agents; they are a choice we make for ourselves. Having a friend sit across from you and command you to "make me happy" demonstrates how futile it is if they don't want to be happy. If they reject all attempts you employ to make them happy, it becomes clear that if someone does not want to be happy, you can't make them.

But the opposite it true as well. The revelation for us all comes when you discover that only you can make you mad. Think about the significance of being able to truly understand the notion that "no one can make you mad; only you can make you mad". When we switch to boredom, jealousy, etc. it is the same realization. So, when you are faced with the "flow" and it is not working for you, you can legitimately ask, "Is the environment the problem, or is it me?" "Am I angry because the flow got me, or have I allowed myself to become angry because of an "emotional flow" I allowed to happen? "Have I made *myself* angry?"

Lest I mislead the reader, at this point I must hasten to add that there are "thinking flows" as well as emotional flows. Did an outside agent cause me to think a certain way, and am I doing it because I think it is so, or because I was told it was so? The same lesson applies. No one can make you think something unless you allow yourself to accept it. Having another person available to get out of the flow is important.

Finally, the role of psychiatrists and psychologists is to get you out of your flow. That is what they do for a living. Some are good at it and use what has been offered here, although not in these words.

A Digression on Happiness

There is a point here that is important. *You can be happy in the flow.* It is seductive. But if the flow were effective everywhere, then we would all accept the flow and there would be no need to change. But leadership and parenting are about sometimes being able to do what is necessary *despite* the flow.

Ed Deci and Rich Ryan from The University of Rochester have written extensively about self-actualization. Their work is well worth reading. Self-actualization is a path to happiness. They have concluded that to be self-ac-tualized is to be effective in the first three of the following categories:

1. *Satisfactorily competent.* You are *competent* if you think you are. All the levels on the graph are self-determined. It is not a question of whether anyone else thinks you are competent or not. Because you are the judge, you are the only one who sets the standard. If you forever grade yourself poorly, then you cannot be happy.

2. *Satisfactorily autonomous.* You are *autonomous* if all choices that you would like to make are available to you. This should not be confused with freedom. Freedom simply means that you are free, but autonomy means that any choice that you desire is available to you.

3. *Satisfactorily related to others.* And finally, you are *related* if your relationships to important people in your life (as defined by you) are where you want them to be.

4. *Satisfactorily aware.* (My own addition) If self-actualization can be thought of like happiness (I am doing what my organism tells me is right), then we might think about happiness in the same way. This model is really a self-actualization model proposed by Ed Deci and Rich Ryan *(Source: Intrinsic Motivation and Self Determination in Human Nature).* While they did not propose a graphical understanding of their work as I do below, they did determine the axes. The "y" axis is relatedness, the "x" axis is competency, and the "z" axis is autonomy. At any moment, your state of happiness can be measured under the half cone pictured above (letter A). The top center of the graph is the point of maximum happiness. But this is only for you. Everyone has a cone, and everyone has different data.

Under the cone you can move up by increasing self-actualization along one of the three dimensions, as illustrated by the arrow.

This is a self-defined "happiness cone". If you are at the maximum point, you are the happiest you can be. However, things change (your child rebels, your employee leaves the company, your spouse files for separation, you lose a job). When this happens, the cone changes and your location in it changes.

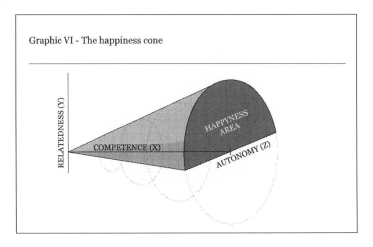

Graphic VI - The happiness cone

Awareness. Think of awareness like examining two separate days of happiness plotted under the cone. You are aware that your happiness moved from one location to another. You can speak to whether you are happier today than yesterday. Your happiness moves around under the cone by the force of change. Things change every minute and every hour. Sometimes it is you who initiates the change, and sometimes it is the environment. Are you aware of what caused the change, and can you replicate it?

The cone of a person in the flow is smaller than the cone of a person who has left the flow. This is because the energy for just continuing in the flow is low. So, a man who does not go to college, does not travel, does not seek a leadership role, can be happy. In fact, he can attain happiness as well as anyone.

Notice however, that "perfect happiness" is not eternally achievable for us humans, because as soon as you judge you are at peak happiness (self actualization), something will necessarily change and you will no longer be there. Some event will adjust even slightly, thus changing the "perfect" happiness that was yours. This is not to say that you cannot fluctuate in and out of perfect happiness. But happiness is an event, not a place.

This raises an important third way out of the flow. By following others who have made it out, so too can you make it out. Some people who have escaped the flow are psychologists, and some are psychiatrists. The key is to find what flow they were in and what they did to escape.

The idea of being able to "fit it all together" and escape the flow is a process involving others. The organism's ability to "integrate, hold, or reject" other people's ideas is crucial. It is those stimuli and how they are ultimately integrated that will determine a person's psychological strengths and views. If one can integrate what others are telling you, then you can escape the flow. This model is based loosely on the work of Deci and Ryan. Integration means that you take an idea from outside (another person) and realize how it fits into your world the way you understand it. You can see how what they are saying can work *for you.*

Below is a chart that describes how self vs. self and self vs. others can result in change.

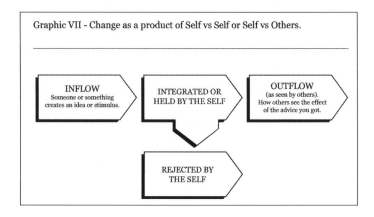

Graphic VII - Change as a product of Self vs Self or Self vs Others.

INFLOW
Someone or something creates an idea or stimulus.

INTEGRATED OR HELD BY THE SELF

OUTFLOW
(as seen by others).
How others see the effect of the advice you got.

REJECTED BY THE SELF

The inflow from the left comes from the external environment. For example, a person can tell you that your hair would look better if it were shorter. You need to figure out what to do with this inflow. You need to find a place for it and decide whether to integrate (adopt the suggestion), hold it for a while (ponder whether short hair would be good), or reject the suggestion and keep your hair the way it is.

Integration is the recognition of congruence between the self and the outside. Integration takes place when the organism reacts to an inflow and decides to accept it for its own benefit. Rejection is for those stimuli that cannot be integrated by the self, and holding is for those stimuli that need further refinement that ultimately leads to integration or rejection. This process of integration is life-long and is the basis for the strategies that we employ to deal with the world. At its best, integration contributes positively to self-actualization and serves to assist in predicting the consequences of one's actions.

Another example could be a new sales process. It may "fit" your personal beliefs, in which case you will integrate it and move on. It might be different but doable, in which case you will reflect on it and experiment until you can integrate it. If you can't, then you'll reject it. If you reject the new sales process, it could mean you were completely miss-aligned with what was being proposed.

Stage 3

So here we are. We have left the flow. As a leader/parent/lover we hope/believe that we are going to be happier doing so. We believe that we understand ourselves. We know how we relate to others. What is next?

The next stage is maturing, being able to forecast the consequences of your actions and make adjustments, and to build an effective way of interacting with other people and the environment.

Some people do not ever emotionally evolve to the point where they are mature and able to predict the consequences of their actions. These are the self-styled victims of the world. Even if you have left the flow and used yourself or others to escape, you must now again integrate this new existence.

Stage 3 is about the future. It is acting in uncertainty and creating certainty from it. It is about establishing an intent, or purpose. What do I want to do with my life? What am I going to do of my own free will and not just do because I have to?

It is also about doubt.

Did I make the right choice in leaving the flow and what other choices could I have right now?

5. Do I feel challenged?

6. When I integrate, won't I be in another flow?

7. Does any of this really matter? Am I doing anything significant?

8. What if I choose wrong?

9. What if everyone else gets ahead of me?

10. What is my purpose?

11. What if I fail?

There are two fundamental kinds of problems: *technical problems and adaptive problems.* This again is based on the work of Ron Heifitz at Harvard. *Technical problems* are problems that often have a known process: a beginning, middle, and an end. They often have a known or knowable answer. They tend to be of a form like net present value calculations or the distance a ballistic cannon ball will travel given a certain number of initial conditions. *Adaptive problems*, on the other hand, are complex. They have multiple answers and multiple truths. They require human understanding and some insight into psychology in many cases. These problems tend to be like the Arab-Israeli peace negotiations and the war on drugs in the US. When the flow is expecting a quick and easy solution to an adaptive problem, there can be real problems. Finding a purpose is adaptive work. It is not technical work.

There is no sure path to finding a purpose or path in life. Sometimes in business or parenting, purposes are easier because they are shorter term ("I need to do this project", or "I need to get my son a tutor").

You might think of purpose this way: What would you do with a million dollars? It may not matter *what* you do as much as it matters *why* you made the decisions you made about using the million dollars. What would you do if you didn't have to work? Do you care how and why things work?

Curiosity and purpose

Everyone may have as many as two purposes, the one that your parents gave you (induced purpose) and the one you find on your own (free purpose). Your parents' purpose puts you into the flow. It holds you there. The argument is often "you must go to such and such a school and become a doctor". The purpose of our parents comes as a result of our need to survive in childhood. Their behavior determines your purpose. If they ignored you, then you had to get attention; if they ridiculed you, then you needed to be perfect; if they beat you, then you had to always be ready for a fight; and if they were always losing, then you learned to be a victim. If they taught you that you were better than everyone else, you became judgmental.

Parental purpose is very powerful because, even as an adult, you can believe that it is necessary to reenact childhood when you are with them. When you finally see what their purpose was for you, you are a step closer to finding the purpose for yourself.

A parent's purpose can put you back in the flow! Take the example of someone who believes they are not good enough. This is a very common, parental-induced purpose. You are told that you could do better, you are compared to others, your grades could be better, you could be faster, and you could be perfect. In the end, everything becomes a case of waiting for someone else's approval to believe that you have value. Their purpose becomes how you are valued and how you value yourself.

As you have children, they must also be perfect because if not, then you will not have been good enough in the eyes of your parents. But who should the judge be? Is it your parents or other parents? Or is it your children? If it is your children, then you may be ok. They know who you are.

Discovering your purpose may be as easy as simply having the purpose to reject your parents' purpose. Take Robin Williams as an example. He was beaten by his father and was constantly told he wasn't good enough. The result was that Robin began to make up worlds for himself. In those worlds he *was* good enough. He discovered that he could make people laugh and this was his purpose. He rose to stardom as if to say, "You see how good I really am? Then he started playing more serious roles in movies like *Dead Poets Society* and *Good Will Hunting*. In both these films, he is showing his father how good he really is. He found his own role in saying to all of us, "If you are beaten down, if you have been mistreated, if you are told you are not good enough…that's baloney…you are!" This was Robin William's purpose in life.

Cynics may say that the purpose of life is simply to stay alive. That would be a behaviorist view. Whatever the stimulus, I will provide a response that allows me to live. That is of course a purpose, but it is the unconscious purpose of flow. There is something important in the meaning of the word "purpose" that includes the idea of autonomous intent. The idea that I chose and am not subject to the outside world is an important one. Because if we live only for others/environmental stimulation we can never know how to act in the case when others are not there.

Finding a purpose is not teachable. But one's purpose can be learned. Each person must learn their own purpose in their own way. In order to lead authentically, one must know their individual purpose. No one can tell you what purpose you should have. Only you can determine that.

Whatever you say your purpose is, it should pass some tests:

1. (Did I choose this?)

2. (Do others share this purpose?)

3. (Do I feel I am good at this?)

4. (Is this still my purpose?)

5. Does this purpose preserve human life?

6. Does this purpose cause others to better identify *their* purpose?

7. If everyone had this purpose, would the world be better off?

8. If I no longer have this purpose, does it matter?

It is not easy to meet all eight conditions. But when you do, you will likely be closer to a purpose for you. But what if your purpose conflicts with another person's purpose? Or what if your purpose is unattainable?

1. I want to lead, but I don't want that to be in conflict with your leading

2. I want people to follow me, but I don't want to be responsible for them

3. I want people to like me, even if we don't accomplish anything

4. I want people to be like me, even if I harm them.

Your purpose must be free of internal conflict and inconsistencies. This is the hard work. If you want to lead/be a parent/ have a great relationship, then part of your purpose must be an assertion that you will eliminate conflicts by knowing yourself. To lead, you must want to be responsible for others. To be a parent, you must want to be committed to a lifetime of love and support. You must want to accomplish things.

When you know your purpose, you are ready for the last stage.

Stage 4

When you have mastered the flow, removed yourself from its influences intentionally, integrated what others have proposed, rejected what doesn't fit, and then ultimately defined a purpose for your life, you are ready to make a declaration.

What follows is my declaration:

Leadership, parenting, and having good relationships is: "<u>Being</u> what is necessary so that others can do what is necessary, so that they too can be/become what is necessary, all the while acting to preserve human dignity and life."

You'll notice that this definition eliminates Hitler, Harvey Weinstein, and others as leaders. They cannot be a leader by this definition. Being in charge without valuing human life and dignity is not leadership.

In order to understand this definition of leadership, it is important to have insight into four concepts: being for oneself, doing with others, being for others, and finally, the spiritual integration of these three natures.

"Being" for oneself is a dynamic process. Being is a continuous process of improving self-awareness. "Doing" what is necessary requires understanding the flow, and the way out. Doing requires integration. The essence of doing is to integrate the being of oneself with the doing of others. This becomes the adaptive work of the leader: "Can I behave in such a way that my subordinates (children) can be better or more effective?" If one is devoted, all three natures come together, and spiritual integration happens. The way becomes clear.

People operating from an integrated spiritual base are rare in business. Most executives do not even realize that spiritual integration is really the only grounded place to be consistently effective as a leader. Most people in business are asleep (Gurdjieff).

If we examine the definition of leadership above more closely, we see why this is so:

"<u>Being</u> what is necessary" is hard because it is dependent on four "knowings":

1. Knowing Thyself (Gurdjieff work) Blue Door

2. Knowing Others (Enneagram work) Yellow Door

3. Knowing where the optimum "balance" is between flow and change

4. Knowing what the "pattern" is in the environment and how it is changing. Seeing the problem in the pattern and then performing the adaptive work to compensate. In some instances, this involves modifying your purpose.

"So that others can do what is important" depends on:

1. Knowing ahead of time (pre-cognition) what patterns may exist, what problem the patterns suggest, and what must therefore be done.

2. Getting others to agree to cooperate with the adaptive work.

3. Removing obstacles in the existing fields of work.

4. Setting the standards of "what and how"; defining the quality of the work.

"So that they too can be/become what is necessary" depends on:

1. Aspirations of others (Existential counseling)

2. Capability of others (Enneagram)

3. Future needs of the entire system and how the patters are changing

4. Future needs of the leader and how integrated one is within oneself

"All the While Preserving Human Life"

1. Have I just created another flow?

2. Have I truly done otherwise?

3. Have I considered others?

4. Have I met the standard?

A person who is integrated across (a), their own being (b), the being of others and (c), the adaptive work of "doing", can attain "spiritual integration". Only those who are so integrated are true leaders.

Over many years, executives build up experiences and have been trained by their environment to behave a certain way. Their "flow" has assumed control. In the early stages of a career, an employee "learns" the flow. Often, it is the technical flow of execution. To succeed, employees deliberately unbalance themselves (work long hours, take on additional work, manage their bosses, finish lots of projects, read business books, work for the right person, make even more money for the firm, etc.). In some cases, like Wall Street executives, the greater the imbalance the more that the "flow" rewards the employee. In the early years, this is a natural state and causes little harm at these entry-level positions. It is only when the imbalance pays off and the employee is promoted that the flow becomes less benign. At this stage, many employees have responsibility for others for the first time. Here is the moment of first and often greatest leadership vulnerability. Either the employee sets their feet on the path towards integration and spirituality or succumbs to the flow and may often repeat the behavior of their flow with perhaps even more unbalanced intensity. Without spiritual integration of being, the individual unknowingly confronts symptoms instead of the truth. This is why there is so much doubt and chaos in the leadership literature.

The day inevitably comes, however, when a kind of awareness sets in. It happens to every executive/parent. It is only the triggering event that is different. For some, it is being passed over for promotion, or being downsized, or realizing that the corner office or the boss's job isn't really what they wanted after all. For others, it is encountering midlife without answers. For some, it is having given up a career or children. For some, there is a reflection on their lives and a discovery that there has been less meaning to their lives than the flow had promised. It is this discovery that begins the path toward truth and, if developed early enough, to "real" leadership.

True leadership is about being integrated across oneself, across others, and across the environment. Since full integration is extremely rare, the work of leadership is in striving continually to become this integrated being. As a result, it is important to realize that qualities like integrity and actions like having a vision are not something that is "done" or "acquired" but are the natural result of being spiritually integrated.

So how does one become spiritually integrated? First, it's being, then doing, then becoming, and finally, integrating. At the beginning of all work on leadership is the essential principle of knowing oneself, of being correct. To "be", one must believe that being is important. No one can force this realization upon another. To "be" starts with awareness. Awareness is a first principle. It is the deeply pondered answer to the question, "Am I what I should be?" There is significant work even in this. Suppose that one says, "Of course I am what I should be; how could I not be?" Everyone in business has stories of the executive who is oblivious to "what is really going on". Everyone knows people who are just doing things each day, every day and will be doing the same things tomorrow. Everyone knows everyone else, but not themselves. They are as oblivious and unaware as those they observe. Most of us are asleep.

Awareness may come in many forms. It may come from reading these words. It may start with these words but come from a repetition in other literature. Once one is aware, the journey begins. Everyone has set out for a destination, believing that they know the way, only to "suddenly discover" that they are lost. This is like awareness. This is where the hard work begins.

Awareness is not a goal. In fact, it is only after being aware that one can have a goal. Gurdjieff, an exceptional man of uncommon insight, taught that man must "remember himself". These two words have rather extraordinary meaning. In the spirit of this book, they are the first words of leaving the flow.

Perhaps only a man like Gandhi could pass this book's definition of leadership. He allowed all others to do what was necessary, even his enemies.

Gandhi knew himself well and he knew others exceptionally well. He had a keen sense of environment and most probably had reached spiritual integration. No one more than he became what was necessary (free of the flow) so that others could do what was necessary (go on strike) so that they could become what is necessary, all the while preserving human life. How bad would our country's leadership be if we all were able to consciously be Gandhi when we needed to be?

21.

A Doctor, a Judge, and a Banker

A doctor, a judge, and a banker were playing cards. They were also playing philosophy.

Judge (raising a glass): "To our third anniversary!"

Banker and Doctor: "Here, here! Cheers!"

Banker: "So as I was saying, the idea of skill versus luck seems a bit tricky. For example, if anyone needed any of our three skills, they would easily be able to discriminate between our three professions. No one would hire a doctor to try a case for example. But then people are faced with deciding within our professions who is the most skilled of all."

Doctor: "I agree in principle. In my profession there are numbers of operations, numbers of cases, and numbers of years teaching that would provide stats on expertise in our fields. And these stats could be further refined to detail heart operations, criminal cases, and dollars of loans made. But you raise a good point. The more specific problems, or the more complex problems, have a higher need for a skilled professional. "

Judge: "But what we are *really* saying is that there is a kind of skill that is necessary to assess *our* skills. Most people may not be able to do that, so they

---

ask someone else or hire a consultant. And then there would be the skill of assessing the skill assessor. And then…well, you get it. I think this is how the idea of second opinions arises. In my work, judgments can be appealed. Even as a banker, you are second-guessed for making loans that go bad."

The banker nodded.

Judge: "So, can we say anything about skills in particular?

Banker: "I think so. We can say that having a skill must in some way be knowable and demonstrable to others. Otherwise, there is nothing to discuss except my assurance that I am good against your doubt that I am not. Examples as proof are helpful, but let's look at stockbrokers. They produce all kinds of data that show that they made money for us. In truth, they have no idea if they did or not, because they do not measure my return from the specific day I invested. They measure from January 1st or inception or some other time. In this case, I have no idea who is good and who isn't. I can only look at other funds who start measuring in January for some comparison."

Doctor: "And let's take our game here as another example. All of us know the rules of poker. But there is a second level to the game. There is the level of psychological persuasion. And then there is the result. If we grade skill by who knows the rules best, we probably get no discernable difference among the three of us. If we switch to psychology, then we again have no real standard to decide which of us is a better psychologist. Yet, if we go by the pot winnings, then we would say the judge is the most skilled. But we can only say that he is more skilled than we are. We *can't* say he is a great poker player."

Judge: "Yet, we also have the cards themselves. Assuming that none of us are cheating, and that shuffling is random, then the cards we get are pure luck. We get what we get. This is all luck, because I have no way to influence the deal. If I am dealt a royal flush, I only need to recognize it, then bet based on how you two are betting. Then, I wait for my likely win. But every deal is basically luck."

Doctor: "It is similar in the ER. Each victim comes in with a degraded ability to live comfortably. We are dealt that victim. The seriousness of the problem in that moment is largely luck. But then, it is skill that gets employed to "change" the bad luck back to good luck—if I can restore the patient as close to their original state as possible."

Banker: "It is similar in the bank, and I imagine for you, Judge, as well. We don't choose who needs our skills. It's luck, however, in my case I can make sales calls and increase the "luck" by only calling on people who would be valuable to me. In this sense, I am actively influencing the "cards", if you will, before they are dealt."

The three of them laughed. They glanced at each other and then the judge began "As is our custom - a toast, to bankers who foreclose and to spouses who jump out of thirty-second floor windows because of it."

Doctor: "And a toast to judges who put spouses away for fifteen years for their fourth (ahem) "assisted" DUI."

Banker: "And a toast to doctors who don't cure a spouse's disease."

"Ladies…a toast to us all!"

But the tinkling of glasses could not drown out the knock on the door, nor the forceful voice of Detective Larson: "All right! This is the police! Open up!"

APPENDIX TO 21
Is it Skill or Luck?

Luck and skill are both well-understood ideas. However, it is an interesting question to consider to which we attribute the outcomes of our past actions. As we look back on life, which standard do we apply? Were we lucky or good? Just suppose that you attribute some part of your life to luck. When you look forward, do you expect that same luck in the future? Is luck different for whites than minorities?

Luck seems to have the following characteristics:

1. While an individual can be lucky, it is hard to attribute this luck to any individual quality. The closest thing to individual luck may be being white and male in America and being viewed as "born lucky".

2. Luck can be addictive (gambling), but it can also net itself like gambling, wins being greater than losses.

3. Luck has a low probability and there must be other possible outcomes. Luck is not involved when there is only one possible outcome. There must be an unexpected aspect to luck. It can't reliably be *intended*.

4. Luck can be both good or bad

5. Luck is not deterministic. You cannot "summon" luck predictably. Rabbit's feet do not change luck.

6. The possibility of good luck can be increased, and the possibility of bad luck can be decreased. If you have better pattern recognition you might get better results more often, but this may not be luck— just better pattern recognition. You might also be temporarily focused on the downside of an action. This could be lucky if the worst happens.

7. Luck is an animate concept. In some sense, only living things can have luck. It is this notion of living with its probabilistic nature that gives rise to the idea of luck. Rocks are not lucky.

8. Luck is external.

9. In the end, luck only exists if there is no other obvious attributable cause.

Skills, on the other hand, seem to:

1. Have an internal locus of control. "I can do this" or, "I did this myself".

2. Exist as an animate concept. Rocks do not have skills.

3. Arise from innate abilities, practices, learning, and integration.

4. Be deterministic. They can be summoned when they exist.

5. Be learnable.

6. Be teachable.

7. Stay with individuals at some level.

8. Be capable of improvement.

9. I am curious about the temporal aspect of luck attribution. For example, when we are young, do we attribute success to our own skills and, as we age, do we attribute more of our past successes to luck? How do we *individually* think about luck? Whom do we think is lucky?

The reason this is interesting is that there is some integrating notion here. Could it be that luck is a function of how many choices people have, as in the statement "She's so lucky she has money"? Or, is luck a reflection of relative happiness, as in "He's so lucky that he found the perfect woman"? Are skillful people the luckiest, or are lucky people deemed to be the most skillful? I think it's the latter.

How much of America's "greatness" since the end of World War II has been as a result of luck? America had the most powerful, undamaged economy and the means of production and resources to carry on. For a while, doing business almost anywhere meant being careful in setting profit goals so that people would ask you back. The jobs were always yours. This good fortune carried forward into the 60s and 70s as a baby boom in the US propelled domestic consumption. Prices were in line with salaries and single income households could make a living. Except that it didn't for Black

Americans. In Levittown for example blacks were denied loans and excluded from the American dream. Was this a case of bad luck? Of course not, this was intentional. The gap in the availability of affordable housing between returning GIs began in 1946 and exists to this day as several generations have been traced from that similar place in New York to the present day.

By the 80s, the computer revolution had started and the US led the way by having the biggest hardware and software companies. We had resources, productivity, technology, language, and trade. We were not at war. Everything was going our way. Some would say that this was American exceptionalism. We were skilled and made things work. We won Nobel prizes and most new inventions came with English wording.

But was it luck? If you were born in the US in 1955, were you luckier than if you were born in Iraq? If you served in the armed forces of the US from 1977 to 2003 when we were mostly at peace, were you lucky? If you worked at a larger firm and that firm had a high market share, were you lucky? And if you married well and had children, were you lucky?

One might consider the history of the world to decide those answers. In 1900, there were no planes, cars were fifteen years old but the infrastructure did not support many drivers. Rural America did not have much indoor plumbing and refrigerators for the home were still thirteen years away. Even royalty had many of these disadvantages. This was only 120 years ago.

If you were born in the past eighty years, you have lived through the greatest expansion of product, knowledge, education, medical advances, and travel in the history of the world. While skill clearly developed the products, being born "at this time" confers the biggest advantage relative to other periods in history. Today, the average house has libraries more vast than any single university and has better heating and cooling than the palaces of the early 1900s. A person can get treated for serious injury in less than an hour in most first world countries, and has fresh food from all over the world at any moment in the year. There is luck to having been born in these times. No other eighty-year period comes close.

And yet as mentioned above not everyone was equally "lucky". Suppose you were one of the "unlucky" citizens or a descendent. How would you change your "luck?"

22.

A Cloud is on the Horizon

Notre damus: "Before the caravans come, an opossum will be awarded the Nobel prize. The Great Wall will be made great again, but not in the west. A voice from a cylinder will cause music to magically play in tight spaces. The King will be all a twitter. Near universities, snowflakes will arise."

Ding: "Is that guy here again? I thought that panhandlers—"

Dune: "*Shhhhh!* He's predicting."

Notre damus: "The young elder will overcome the older elder, who will be overcome by a comb-over on a golf course in Florida with a single stroke. He will drive a numbered pin into the ground, and polite applause will ensue. His cup runneth over."

Ding: "What is he even talking about?"

Dune: "That's the best of it: I don't think he knows. He's just channeling. The universe is speaking to him directly. Can you feel it?"

Ding: "No that's just gas. But what does that even mean?"

Dune: "He's saying that Brexit will cause Middle Eastern people to invade Germany. He's saying old people in France will tour Myrtle Beach and be overcome by kitsch. It's a warning that if we don't start global cooling soon, Nevada will have ocean front views. And he finishes with the standard Jewish proverb about kvetching.

Ding: "You didn't use a single word in your translation that matches a single word he used in his prophecy. How does that make sense?"

Notre damus: " Fruits, vegetables, and drizzle will hold captive their minds. Their intestines will be imprisoned by tofu and Ramsey II will get her own cooking show. A cookie will destroy a fortune."

Dune: "See? He's talking about Brexit! It's eerie!"

Ding: "It sounds like Baltimore. I predict the police will bring the universe here and kick some Notre buttocks."

Notre damus: "Breathless wheezers will vape until they hopeioid. A numbered Kardashian will be celebrated like a God-like figure only to be found colluding with sommeliers. The beast will arrive in a BMW with DEV 666 on the plates."

Dune: "This is awesome! Really amazing! Excellent! And perfect!"

Ding: "This is a lot like *Infinite Jest* without the literary clarity."

Notre damus: "The heavenly dart with starch will crease the sky. Death is speaking (a great achievement for a death mute). A proud nation will be brought low by a Keebler dwarf in a tree…men will be running to avoid extinction."

Ding: "He sounds like my post-modern women's studies professor."

Dune: "Why do you have to be so negative? Can't you just enjoy the existential vibe?"

Notre damus: "And a Cortez will move among you, feigning intelligence. The elders open cans of whup-ass. Volatility is being made great again. And the sky is tinged with orange follicles.

Ding: "My nose has smelled his color, my eyes have seen his sweetness, nay I feel the sound of his madness and hear the scales of his skin. If this be prophecy, then I am but the scum covering a pond. But I am not sore afraid, because Darwin in the end rules supreme. That, and the police have finally arrived. Our future is secure.

APPENDIX TO CHAPTER 22
The Future of Work

This essay will perhaps be one of the most expansive. It is somewhat based on patterns that exist today. There will be some extrapolation from the current world labor markets that is unavoidable because, after all, that's where this is trying to go.

A good place to start is to ask what *must* be true? The notion of what must be true does not have an exact answer. If your view of what the future of work will be like differs from mine, it is likely because we differ on what must be true.

At the base level of survival, there are several explicit needs that must be true. For some long time in the future, *humans must eat or perform some act that allows ingested matter to be converted into useful biological energy.* Staying alive is nonnegotiable. Bear in mind that this does not implicitly suggest that farming as it is today will continue to be necessary. We could suppose that "energy" pills might be available, or some other ingestible or injectable form of energy could develop. We *must also be able to drink.* Water will matter. We also must be able to *rest in safety* and be able to *create warmth.* Therefore, we must continue to have external energy sources and a protection system that ensures social stability. Finally, we must be able to repair ourselves and medically adjust our lives. These represent the base existence of humans everywhere. This is Maslow.

So, what changes will we face in these areas? Much of the answers depend on technology. Less obviously, they will also depend on how capable the average person must be intellectually and physically to use that technology. A past trend that must continue is the improvement of technology that will affect several areas simultaneously.

1. Medicine

2. Energy

3. Human machine/interfaces

4. Resource replacement/management (food/water)

Let's just make a few observations about each one of these "musts". In medicine, the mission has been to increase lifespans and improve the quality of life: repairing defects, preventing defects, and implanting superior functionality (valves, joints, hearing, etc.). All of these will likely continue to improve.

There are two directions in medicine that will influence work. First is replacing living tissue with synthetic and more durable material, so that we don't "wear out". Second is the cell rejuvenation possibility. This is so that certain qualities are retained while organs, tissue, and functionality are restored or held constant at an age like thirty, for example.

Medicine will be about research and experimentation as it is today. But suppose if we only assume we cure cancer and heart disease, for example, the average age of death will likely increase. Even though other diseases will take their places, the timing will be slower. This is not to say that negative pathogens can arise like the plague, only that they would employ the same people doing the positive work as exist today.

If bodies become more sustainable, then hospitals will be less necessary. Some drugs will become fewer and more specialized, while others will need inventing. Machines that do maintenance on these new "parts" and monitor the effects of drugs will also increase. It would also be important to consider what a longer life would mean if most of the elongation was in a physically diminished state.

So, what is the medical effect on future labor besides potentially less need for hospitals? If you are an MD in a discipline that gets replaced or reduced, you may be caught in a very strange form of unemployment that doctors have not faced before. The ability of lay people to self-test at home and deliver results through the web will make MDs less necessary and might even replace labs in many cases. Drawing blood and urine are not immune to AI analysis. Enhancing these changes will require increases in IT, mechanical miniaturization, plastic and specialized metal manufacturing, and home diagnostic machines and devices.

In energy, the breakthroughs are likely to be more incremental than in medicine. This is because the ability to generate power doesn't currently have unlimited possibility. Nevertheless, it is possible that a smaller power emitter could be created or a change in power usage could emerge that would affect the future of work. A simple example of this would be electric, centrally owned, self-driving cars. The effect of a power change to autos will certainly have some truths.

1. Cars will no longer need brand names nor outside shells. No VWs or Bentleys. It is a transport device.

2. Repair parts will all be of the same type

3. Car repairs and accidents will go down and there will be little need for auto insurance

4. Police speed traps will cease to exist

5. Long haul trucking, Uber, and cabs will go away

6. Parking lots will be turned into "car centers" where you would go to get a ride. Fewer single vehicles will exist as many people are going to the same places.

7. Google maps will be for conformation and not planning.

8. The idea of a "getaway" car will cease to exist.

9. Access driveways to businesses will be widened to accommodate simultaneous arrivals.

10. There will be no valet parking

11. The ability to drive will diminish

12. Licensing, driver training, and traffic signs will no longer be necessary.

On the plus side, jobs will open in

1. Linear programming to schedule the cars coming and going from any location.

2. The maintenance of the electric car system and the manufacture of the cars themselves will offset some of the loss of car engineers.

3. Electronic traffic monitoring technology will be necessary and any accidents will need special responses.

4. Ferries will need to be reconfigured.

Other energy changes may be found in battery technology, or computing changes using light instead of electricity. These are all happening now. The ability to forecast energy changes is hampered by the laws of physics. If matter could be converted to energy more safely and efficiently, jobs would change dramatically. A wholesale change in energy is the real wild card in the future job market simply because everyone would need to participate financially in this change.

Human and machine interfaces will increase. The ability to download "information" into newborn children could become a reality. One could envision a "downloadable" knowledge base for newborns that would make formal schooling and rote learning much less necessary. Having five-year-olds with the intellectual reasoning and mental capacity of forty-five-year-olds is an interesting possible pattern. In addition, virtual reality, information creation /distribution devices, and enhanced creativity software will increase. The interaction between humans and machines raises the ability of the average person to the ability of an above average person. Let's say you wanted to write music but have never had a class (This assumes you did not get a musical download). If the software is intelligent enough to read your short ditty and suggest harmony, orchestra parts, and key changes, you have effectively become as good as anyone who does it for a living. The ability for the software to be "creative" in art, music, or writing novels will compress the distance between the artistic haves and the artistic have-nots. It does not guarantee success, but it does mean that more competition will exist for people whose full-time avocations will be doable by people working part-time. A stockbroker could write a short song and have a paid "creator" put it to music. And a concert violinist could trade stocks.

Finally, it must be true that wood, water, food, energy, air, etc., must be renewed. If people live longer, there will be pressure on the biosphere. This will perhaps be one of the most important job creation sectors of the future. In one sense, the idea that the earth will change has created some anxiety today. But it may not be changes in the earth as much as changes in us that matter most. Getting more "value" from existing resources will become a field as important as IT. It must be so. I also appreciate the caveat that disease or war could limit the conditions on earth, but if so there will be, out of necessity, a "recovery" that will create jobs as well.

There are many other kinds of changes and waterfall impacts that you are free to contemplate. Just suppose all of this allows us to live longer with a higher quality of life. It is tempting to state the obvious, which is to say that we could experience multiple careers or multiple periods where we work and then "retire", only to work again. That is a simplistic assumption. More complex are questions of governance and wealth inequalities that become institutionalized. There must be technology (workers) and there must be governance (the method of making decisions that affect others). And then there may be a whole class of non-workers who rotate jobs over their lifetimes.

The method of getting paid and making payments will change. The notion of money will need to change. The costs to society of machines, printers, storage, etc. of all the coins and bills are extraordinary. If it all becomes electronic, it puts enormous pressure on the availability of electricity or some other power methodology such that the stored value of all things is retained. But the idea of simply transferring credits by thought is becoming more possible as technology increases. In the end, people may not work for money if all needs/wants are met. They may instead work for time. This time would be for pursuing education and other interests. Time will always ultimately be a limiting factor.

Finally, there is the possibility of transferring human consciousness into a machine. Would the consciousness be constrained? Would it "feel" revitalized? Would a life of thousands of years really be so grand? If time felt infinite, what would need to change? How would human interaction need to evolve? Suppose monarchs lived a thousand years? What about despots? What about disabled people?

Let's look at what could be true in 2040:

1. Technology and biology could become almost fully merged

    a. Humans will have more mechanical parts. Machines will have more human qualities. The first consciousness transplant will have been attempted.

    b. Technology will be so complex that almost no one will understand how everything works.

    c. Catastrophic loss of capability and collapse of the social order will occur if electricity is disrupted, even for only three weeks.

    d. Machines will not replicate free will. They will not "be able to do otherwise" unless they fail. Choosing randomly by programing is not the same as randomly choosing with intent.

2. Medical breakthroughs will prolong life

    a. New immunology bugs may offset some gains

    b. Gene and protein research will enable "natural selection" of newborns.

    c. Psychological disorders will be the most significant disease on the planet not for death but for ineffectiveness.

    d. Most routine prescription dispensing and most diagnosis will be done in the home—even lab work.

3. English will remain the dominant, non-technically enhanced spoken language as long as English-speaking countries remain economically important.

4. Language translating machines will be good enough to allow simultaneous conversation. It won't matter what language you grew up with. Same with written language.

    a. Language hacking will be a new crime to alter documents and policies written between parties and countries. Block chain may prevent this.

    b. Most languages will be stored electronically, but humans will know fewer.

    c. Grammar will become less important as meaning is conveyed in different ways.

    d. Christianity's center of gravity will shift from the equator to the south and from west to east. Northern countries will practice less religiously in daily life.

5. China will become a bit more religious.

    a. Islamic countries will become more secular

    b. The idea of God will change world-wide

    c. Multi-God ideas could make a come back

6. Separation will continue in the West

    a. Governments from Governments

        i. US from North Korea, Russia, China, the Mid East

        ii. Japan from China

        iii. Britain from Europe

        iv. Greece and Italy from Europe

        v. France from the Mid East

        vi. Everyone from ISIS

        vii. Taiwan and Hong Kong from China (special case)

    b. Governments separating from People

        a. US Environmentalists

        b. US Gun lobby

        c. Extremists

        d. Brazil, South Korea, and Italy impeachments or throw-outs

        e. Turkey from Kurds

        f. The established order from the revolutionaries

   c. People separating from People

      a. Sunnis from Shiites

      b. Republicans from Democrats

      c. Immigrants from "already theres"

      d. Haves and the have nots (1%)

      e. Hackers and hacked

      f. Algos trading from humans

      g. The elderly and the young

   d. People separating from themselves

      a. Caitlyn Jenner

      b. Mass shootings

      c. Everything is personal

      d. Hillary Clinton

      e. Donald Trump

      f. Reality TV

      g. Ashley Madison

7. Declining ability of anyone to know what is really happening or what is true

   a. Complexity and speed

      i. Unintended consequences

      ii. Instant change

      iii. Children cannot keep up; neither can adults

   b. Deliberate deception

     i. From résumés to photo-shopping

     ii. False Flag media reports /Fake news/ Alternative facts/Alternative people

     iii. Facebook

     iv. The White House

c. Asymmetric information will be the norm.

d. Internet hacking: what have "they" gotten into?

e. Isolation

     i. Not online means "not relevant" in many places

     ii. Extremist views become louder

     iii. Dating becomes more encounter-like

     iv. Virtual reality may isolate us all into sensory cocoons

f. Brinkmanship living

     i. Cell phones deliver instant help—no Plan B

     ii. No power, no tower, no shower, and the first world is set way back

g. Rising need for psychological competency

     i. Being what is necessary

     ii. Being able to help others will increase as others become less capable

h. Specialized workforces

     i. Gig economy dominates

     ii. Older people still working into their 80s

8. Debt will have destroyed much of the amassed wealth of the first half of this century. The collapse of debt repayment will start a crisis. The FED will be rightly blamed for it. They played two roles in the last one.

9. Fresh water will not be a serious shortage.

10. Energy will not yet be an emergency

    a. Oil will still be the primary means of converting matter to energy

11. There will be four divisions in society: government, technology, health care and "other stuff".

12. Banks will be nationalized by the government

    a. Technology will be nationalized by the government

    b. Health will be controlled by government

    c. Other stuff will be controlled by the government

13. Certain virtual reality will become "real" reality.

14. Distinctions among people will dissolve: gender, orientation, race, etc.—not because they won't exist, but because they won't matter. The ability of the mind will be the differentiator.

15. These perspectives do not need to resonate with everyone. But if you are in your twenties, you will experience a change in work as significant as the industrial revolution in the UK in the 17th and 18th centuries. If you can recognize patterns, figure out what must be so and then act *today*; you will have a better chance to control the future environment for your benefit. It has always been so.

23.

Everyone is a Possibility and Consequences Do Matter

I have retired from two organizations already: the navy and a bank. I often asked myself during my working years, "Did anything I ever do have positive consequences for someone else?" As it turns out, there are fifty-one people I think who would answer yes on my behalf.

The standard I used is simple. It is the answer to a question that only another person can give. "Did Carl do anything to change my life for the better?" None of the fifty-one people who would answer are relatives, children, or spouses. None of these people are the panhandlers that I gave twenty bucks to or the people I took to dinner. The effect had to be important and not trivial like, "I hired x" or "I promoted y". These changes needed to be significant and I cannot have been the beneficiary of a reciprocal good deed.

Most of the time, we don't know the effect we have. We really don't know the consequences of our actions. Sometimes we give advice and it leads to something wonderful. Sometimes we arrange for someone to change departments and they go on to become a leader in the company. And sometimes we save a life.

The fifty-one people that I am thinking about have all spoken to me at some point or conveyed their feelings while they were alive, so I have more than just my own remembrance as support. It is a good feeling to hear the way they tell the stories. And it is precisely because it is *their* remembrance that it matters.

In the early days, for most of us, we are working to get ahead, raise a family, and are focused on our own happiness. We all measure our happiness in different ways but rarely is it through acts of individual significance on behalf of others. Oh we all make donations and give our time for rides and walks in support of one thing and another but this is mega charity without consequence. Often when we donate to favorite charities and we make time at the holidays to volunteer, it is mostly "for us". What I am talking about here is solely for *them*.

There is a purpose and a consequence of that purpose for all of us here on earth. Perhaps you have already determined what that purpose is for you. For me, it is to try to grow my own soul, but the irony is that I can't grow it by doing things *I* think are good. I must do things that grow other people's souls and that can only be done by doing things that they think are good. It must be good for them. But again, it's not just a good deed—it's something that alters a life.

Sometimes we help people out of bad situations. We don't define the situation, but sometimes it helps to assist in what the words "getting out of this" mean. People from foreign lands can find transition to be bad. Single moms who are struggling to get by can be hit with a "final" expense that collapses everything. Young people are seeking their purpose in life but come from families where there was no such discussion. Other people are dying and want to know that you will change a life that they leave behind.

I am not perfect. Some relationships have not gone perfectly. To the best of my knowledge, though, there are only two lives that I changed for the worse that I would alter. Perhaps in the end the change would have been the same but the timing would have been different.

I also have never set a goal for helping individuals. It has just happened. In the end, I don't expect to "add up" all these memories for some greater purpose of my own. It's just that, upon reflection and upon retirement, a great deal of positive feeling comes from remembering these fifty-one people.

APPENDIX TO CHAPTER 23
Whomever sets the standards, accepts the consequences

Consequences are often a function of standards. There will always be a group of people who benefit because standards stay as they are because they are the managers and beneficiaries of those standards. There will always be other groups who are not in power and who don't benefit.

Suppose governments are faced with roughly the same problems worldwide. They are fairly straightforward and general. Therefore they probably are faced with similar consequences for their decisions.

1. Domestic Issues

    a. Do we see individual rights or government as the rule?

    b. What taxes and social policies will we set and by what standard?

    c. How will we manage the economy?

    d. What is the appropriate role of government now and in the future?

2. International Issues

    a. What are our national interests?

    b. What are we prepared to do for these interests?

c. What is the expectation for trade?

d. What foreign aid will we commit to?

The only way to have a conversation about the standards in any country is to agree on the basic assumptions underlying domestic and international issues.

Let's say we wanted to list things that the Federal government should be responsible for. Generally, these would be things that *bind* the country together and make it a country. In ten minutes, we would conclude that the Feds:

1. Should be responsible for national defense. We would not want the Air Force militia of New York bombing Ohio. State defense would be harder to coordinate and more *ad hoc*.

2. Should be responsible for one currency. We don't want Florida currency to be converted to Georgia currency every time a border crossing is made. For doubters, see the struggles of the European Union. Printing of money is another issue best left at the federal level.

3. The environment. We don't want the people of Minnesota to dump stuff in the Mississippi and have the people of Louisiana have to deal with it.

4. Airspace and airwaves. We don't want a trillion-watt transmitter in Boston wiping out the rest of the state's voices.

5. Cross-border crime investigation and prosecution. Enforcement of federal law/courts

6. Foreign policy and foreign aid. We don't want fifty secretaries of state making deals.

7. Creating one set of weights and measures

8. Taxing to perform the above duties

There is a debatable need for anything else. But it is this debate and its consequences that matter. The biggest item missing on this list is social policy. What is the true role for the federal government in establishing and enforcing *social policy? And what are the consequences?*

Let's take a closer look at sanctuary cities. As it happens, it is a federal law that requires immigrants to enter the country using a specific process. An immigrant is legal if and only if they conform to this process. So, the federal government has a law and the states with sanctuary cities are disobeying the law, allowing immigrants to avoid the process. This is why they are called "illegal" immigrants. Federal law preempts state laws by definition.

Suppose we say that every state could object to any federal law for any reason. What are the consequences?

1. Historically there would likely be fewer African American voters because the southern states through poll taxes and literacy tests would have confined voting rights exclusively to whites. Blacks might not be voting in the south. Women might not be voting at all. There is no reason to believe that women would have gotten the vote in all fifty states on a state-by-state basis. As a minority, states rights should not be seen as an automatic good. There can be bad consequences.

2. If states rights prevail the LGBT community will have to have reference books and policies to be able to conform to each state's interpretation of their legal status. Think bathrooms, marriage, adoption, and inheritance. Certainly, Texas and California are likely to grant different policies. As a minority, this cannot be good.

3. Can states determine that there should be separate entrances for whites, blacks, men, women, and LGBT members to any building within the state? Who is to say otherwise?

4. Women outnumber men in the state of New York. Therefore, New Yorkers could simply hold a referendum specifically denying men the right to vote in any national election. White guys beware of states rights on social issues.

5. Marijuana laws already are different by state, even though it is illegal by federal law. Can a federal bank lend to a marijuana grower in violation of federal law but in conformance to state law? Who would prosecute and for what?

6. If a state wants to withdraw from the union, can it? If so, what does it mean to have a union in the first place?

7. What if border states decide on both sides of an issue? One state won't allow immigrants and others will? When an immigrant crosses state lines, whose rules does he conform to?

8. What if a state wants to return to slavery? If states can decide anything, then there's no reason to believe they can't.

9. The consequences of a state's rejection of federal law are not trivial. Let's take another example. This one happens to deal with people's ability to self-declare their legal status. Let's take the case of Bruce Jenner, who transitioned into Caitlyn Jenner. Just suppose the question were asked: "Should this decision be supported in today's society"? Before reading on, think about your answer.

There is no way to have the conversation or to have an opinion without understanding the *consequences* of answering yes or no. The obvious "yes" answer is based on the idea that we are a nation of tolerance and that people who do not feel like they fit society's structure should be allowed to self-declare what their authentic self-truth is. This includes picking pronouns that they wish to go by, etc. The obvious "no" answer is that there are social conventions/standards that matter for society to function.

Let's say, however, that we reflect upon the consequences of any choice through a series of questions:

a. Does she (Ms. Jenner) have the right to start a business and claim minority tax status?

b. Can she apply for loans based on minority status?

c. How will she be treated in the census?

d. Can she declare herself back to being a man someday? Does she have unlimited choices and durations for these declarations?

e. If she serves on a board, how is she counted for purposes of gender?

f. If she adopts a child, is she then a single mother? What rights does she have for custody, alimony, and child support were she to marry?

g. Can she compete in the Olympics as a woman if she chooses?

h. The most important issue is "She can do all these things simply by asserting that she is a woman, and if so, then what does it *really* mean to *be* a woman?"

    i. Can a man simply declare himself to be a woman? If so, then one could contemplate the disappearance of gender discrimination completely, because every company/government/club would simply have enough senior men declare themselves to be women so that they reach some acceptable ratio in their organization. Is this ok? Can a white woman declare she is black? (Rachel Dolezal) If so, the same questions apply. What rights does she get and what status does she legally have? What does it mean to be black? What does it mean to be a Native American if Elizabeth Warren can claim to be one with a "negligible" percentage of DNA?

All choices have consequences, and it is these consequences that should frame whether it makes sense to support certain policies. It is not a simple question of a politicized "take", it is a complex question of consequence. Remember that nothing above suggests that one answer is better than any other. What matters is how a woman or a black woman or any minority reacts to the conferring of rights by declaration or assertion. Now, how would you answer the question?

America in 2019 is struggling with consequences. Who is responsible for the consequences of sanctuary cities and transgender decisions? Never in the past sixty years have so many individuals and institutions behaved as though consequences do not exist or don't matter. Those who are responsible are those who must answer for the consequences of that responsibility. It is independent of intent. If you are responsible and if your action or decision causes an unintentionally bad result, you are *still responsible* for the consequences.

Does it matter if TV or radio programming can say whatever they believe without consequence? Just suppose it no longer matters *what* people say. Suppose there are no consequences for lying. Suppose it no longer matters if anyone is right. Suppose no one is responsible anymore.

Suppose that I can behave to my own standards in a company or in the government. Suppose I do not have to abide by the decisions of those appointed over me. On one side of this issue is the right of a company or government to expect that their employees are doing good work and respecting the policies of the institution. On the other side are the whistleblower cases that call into question the motives of these institutions. Either way the behavior of the employee has consequences.

What are the consequences of a divided country? What about the consequences of a divided Congress? If no one cares what the consequences are there are no consequences by definition. Should this matter? Just suppose that 80 percent (made up number) of the US voters do not care about the consequence of an affirming behavior but instead only care about the consequence of an obstructive behavior. And if the employees of government are entitled to behave as they see fit, what could we ever say that we could predictably expect to get done?

Just suppose that every policy and law had to come with the consequences to anyone affected. Today this does not exist. Laws are written to describe what one must do to comply. Supreme Court decisions are like this. There is a majority and a minority and they both get to opine. Imagine if we required laws to do the same.

24.

Thanks for The Memories

I used to be a physician, but after sixty years of practice my hands are no longer capable of being trusted anymore. Moreover, I am now blind. This morning, a woman named Claire stopped by my office. She said that I had operated on her eyes thirty-five years ago. She said that she too was blind.

I searched my memory. *Claire…Claire Stafford.* The name meant nothing to me now, and all the records of that time were in some faraway warehouse. My staff from those days was also gone, scattered to the winds. I had not kept track of them because most had retired.

Claire said I had treated her for glaucoma. This procedure was then and is now routine. She could see when we first met. She remembered a great many details about me. She remembered mannerisms and speech patterns. She remembered the names of my staff and some things about their families.

She knew we had met professionally, but I did not. It was more likely she would remember me because I was the one who performed the operation. I, on the other hand, had performed hundreds of these operations by that time in my career. I asked her if there had been complications. Her voice seemed pleasant enough when she replied that there had been none.

I asked her if she had gotten better and she said yes, for a while, and then her eyes got worse until she could not see anymore. She said she had hated me from that moment on.

I asked more questions in a desperate attempt to place her. What did she want of me now? I struggled to recreate reality. She had one reality and I had a blank space, not as to time and location but as to her. I asked her to sit, but she said that would not be necessary. I asked her what she wanted, and she said to see me suffer as much as she had suffered.

I told her that nothing she did to me would bring her eyesight back, and she said that that was not true. She was here to change reality. I had no idea what she was talking about and she did not seem to want to explain. Eventually, she left.

That night, I sat over a wine glass trying to remember. It was possible that I could have treated her. She would have been the right age for glaucoma treatment in those days. But I had had no cases of remission. None. And yet here she was. I fell asleep with my wine.

I used to be a physician, but after sixty years of practice my hands are no longer capable of being trusted anymore. Moreover, I am now blind. This morning, a woman named Claire stopped by my office. She said that I had operated on her eyes thirty-five years ago.

I searched my memory. *Claire…Claire Stafford.* The name meant nothing to me now and all the records of that time were in some faraway warehouse. My staff from those days was also gone, scattered to the winds. I had not kept track of them because most had retired.

Claire said I had treated her for cataracts. This procedure was then and is now routine. She remembered a great many details about me. She remembered mannerisms and speech patterns. She remembered the names of my staff and some things about their families.

She stopped by to see me because she was in town and knew I still had an office. I asked her if she had gotten better, and she said she had. There had been no lapses and she still had good vision.

I asked questions in an attempt to place her. What did she want of me now? I struggled to recreate reality. She had one reality and I had a blank space, not as to time and location, but as to her. I asked her to sit, but she said that would not be necessary. I asked her what she wanted, and she said to see me and see if I remembered her.

I told her that nothing she did would bring back my memory and she said that that was not true. She was here to change reality. I had no idea what she was talking about and she did not seem to want to explain. Eventually, she left.

That night I sat over a wine glass trying to remember. It was possible that I could have treated her. She would have been the right age for cataract treatment in those days. But I had no recollection of her. None. And yet, here she was. I fell asleep with my wine.

I used to be a physician, but after sixty years of practice my hands are no longer capable of being trusted anymore. Moreover, I am now blind. This morning a woman named Claire stopped by my office. She said she had been a patient of mine thirty-five years ago.

I searched my memory. *Claire…Claire Stafford.* The name meant something to me now. It seemed like I had just met her recently. In fact, it seemed like I had met her a couple of times recently. Then it occurred to me how I knew her.

"Today is our 35th wedding anniversary," I said.

"Yes" she replied. "I wasn't sure you would remember."

APPENDIX TO CHAPTER 24
How Do We Know Our Past Really Happened?

How do you know your memories really happened? Sure, there may be a photo or two at home, but sometimes even then it is hard to remember details of the situation. Just suppose all the other people who were "there" have passed away? You try to remember various incidents and tie them together. Is there something that all memories have in common? And if there are instances that are now only in your personal memory, will the past somehow vanish when you pass away?

It seems that the past can be remembered differently than it "was". Humans can rationalize many things. If this happens, is there any "real and objective" past? If I "remember clearly" an episode that happened many years ago but I am wrong, how would I know? If I change the past in my memory, does it matter? Suppose I change the past in my mind and it really *does* change the past—would that affect the present?

Memories seem to start off with lines that have slopes, but as time goes by they become step functions. There are gaps where incongruities exist. How do we fill the gaps? The temptation is to use the same slope, but I don't think that really works. I remember many childhood events as specific instances but I can't be sure that they weren't just repeated similar events that have become distilled into one event. Other people remember events differently.

If the only parties to an event are dead did it happen? How could we say without evidence? Memory maintains a truth as long as it is functioning well. Does truth change if you remember something one way but I would have remembered it differently and I am dead? This avenue is a wonderful place to travel when considering suppositions. It applies to court cases, family histories or in fact all histories, interpretations of religious texts, and a host of other avenues.

When you think about your life, how do you "see" the years in your mind as you search for when something happened? I see decades as waves. In the fifties, it is a half U- shape starting in 1955 and it runs from 1955 to 1960. It is dark. In 1960, the timeline becomes brighter but now I see the sixties from 1960 going forward. At 1970, the years get darker and I view them from 1979 backwards. The 1980s begin light but grow dark and I see them from 1989 going back. The nineties start dark and then lighten. I see them from 1999 backwards. The 00s are light throughout, but I see them from 2015 or thereabouts. How do you see the past? What about the current year? Do you see the years in colors, sounds (music) etc.? I am interested in hearing from you.

25.

Who Done It?

My name is Dout. Joe Dout. I'm a private eye. Several years ago—I think it was 2015—I was looking into the murder of a society dame. She was beautiful. She was everywhere on the front pages of all the best fish wrappers. She was very popular and, other than the loss of Princess Diana, the loss of her ladyship reverberated worldwide.

Her body had been found crumpled up in a dumpster on the east side. It had taken months to get someone to identify her remains. Even though she was well known, she had been left in a devastated state. The police had to match dental records and use their MP list to get a final confirm.

Her friends said that she was one of the finest people to be around. There was something about her that everyone who knew her respected. She was a genteel lady of the finest stature.

Interpol, the FBI, the Sûreté, and even the Yard have at times looked me up. I speak several languages, I move about as I choose, and I don't feel compelled to conform to the laws of any country, state, or culture. My hands are dirty, and I like it that way.

Murder is both simple and extraordinary. Simple because, in this case, there is a certainty that she did not beat herself to death. And murder is extraordinary because it is never trivial. In this case, the world knows it all.

And yet no one knew anything. No one had a clue. No one had seen it coming. They rarely do. No one saw anything suspicious. No one saw her on the evening in question. In short, a world personality was destroyed in front of the world and the world saw nothing.

That's why they called me.

I started in the elementary schools, then the high schools and colleges. No one knew anything about her. No one had seen her. She had often spoken at graduations and she traveled extensively, yet she seemed to have disappeared sometime back. The irony was that no one noticed she was gone. No one missed seeing her on the talk shows or the news broadcasts. No one missed her speaking in support of political candidates. She just vanished.

There were no sightings overseas. No pictures. No radio. It was almost as though she had *chosen* to disappear. But if so, then why was she murdered?

I asked contacts in the media for help, but they seemed indifferent or distant. It seemed like the story of the year and yet no one was anxious to cover it. That, in a way, was suspicious.

After two weeks I had very little progress to report. Lots of well-meaning people had offered to help but they really didn't know anything.

So, I am still out there looking. And now, I am asking you: if you have seen her recently or if you know where she was before she was killed, I would like you to contact me. Her name was Truth.

APPENDIX TO CHAPTER 25
Who Should Decide What is Fake News?

"Fake news" is a type of *yellow journalism* or *propaganda* that consists of deliberate *misinformation* or *hoaxes* spread via traditional print and broadcast *news media* or online *social media*. *This false information is mainly distributed by social media, but is periodically circulated through mainstream*

media. Fake news is written and published with the intent to mislead in order to damage an agency, entity, or person, and/or gain financially or politically, often using sensationalist, dishonest, or outright fabricated <u>headlines</u> to increase readership, online sharing, and Internet click revenue. In the latter case, it is similar to sensational online «*<u>click bait</u>*" *headlines and relies on advertising revenue generated from this activity, regardless of the veracity of the published stories Intentionally misleading and deceptive fake news differs from obvious <u>satire</u> or <u>parody</u>, which is intended to amuse rather than mislead its audience."* Wikipedia

Let's start at the beginning. What is truth? It is not a trivial question. I am going to define it in a way that is non-standard. To establish truth, one first must get agreement on the underlying assumed circumstances of what, when, where, how, why, and who. What this means is that in order to say what is true there must be agreement on the answers to all the above questions and assumptions.

As we know, the environment can fool our senses. Straight rulers look like they bend in water. Electrons can be both particle and wave at the same time. We hear sound differently, depending on its movement or ours. There is a famous picture shown at all of the perspective conferences ever given. If you look at it one way you see an ugly hag and if you look at it another way you see a beautiful woman. Both pictures exist in one. So, there is a "framing" of the circumstance that must be agreed to before truth can be asserted. Framing is the answer to the "what is going on and where is it going on" question. Which picture of the lady will we agree is the one we will discuss?

The idea of "when" is also suspect. The earth has different time zones. Even if it didn't, the concept of day and night would create a different sense of time. Even New Year's Day is a different day around the world; in Asia, it is sometimes in a different month.

"Who" and "why" are the crux of the fake news matter. Videos can sometimes determine *who* is involved, as in the case of security cameras.

This is mostly unambiguous. But with so many phone cameras around the world and personal "takes", the context of action can change dramatically. Cameras only capture a narrow viewpoint, but the "truth" is often outside the view of the lens.

The obvious question now is whether anyone, anywhere, at any time can ever know whether something is true. Obviously, we could try to obtain independent video or monitor another news service, or call people who were "there", or use technology (tapes, drones, satellites, etc.). But even then, how do we know for sure?

If you were asked today for an unimpeachable source for truth, what would you say? A university? An intelligence agency? Wikipedia? Your own senses? There is no such source. "Fact-checking" isn't helpful either. Data does not come in the way that the questions or statements get asked. If you and I cannot assert whether something is true, then how can we decide? What about common court cases? (Was the defendant insane at the time of the murder? Did company X "know" that their product was defective? Did hacking into a private home computer violate personal privacy?)

This raises the question of who is the judge of what truth is. Is it the editor of the *New York Times*? Is it intelligence services? Is it the President of Facebook? Is it Congress? How about the judiciary? Is it the owners of FOX News and CNN? Maybe it's the Chinese "personal behavior score"? Is the author of the material the best judge? Which is it?

And what would we say the consequences should be if we say that someone really had produced and disseminated "fake news"? Do they lose their job? Are they accused of a crime? Are they banned from social media?

There is a process that is used these days to allow one to pretend that they know the truth. First, one must have access to a channel that other people monitor. (Facebook, blogs, CNN, Fox News, etc.) Second you must have some "status" that allows you to speak when many others must listen (City mayor, news anchor, talk show host, blogger). Third, (depending on the circumstance) your channel might make more advertising money if you say certain things that your listeners want to hear. Saying things that cause your audience to tune in to your voice is what makes money in these professions. And fourth, you must have listeners who want to hear what you have to say. Notice there is nothing in this process that assumes that anything said or heard must be true. There is no standard of truth.

Somewhat skeptically, I am asserting that people who have public forums to express their views are the minorities who get to say anything. But how much of it is true? How much of it is fake news? It all comes down to an important question and distinction. What does the speaker mean and what does the listener think the speaker means? And why is the speaker saying this? The answer to these questions is disheartening because it depends on what forces have conspired to create the speaker and listener because both behave consistently with their internal models of belief.

But is there a standard model that we could all agree on and assume in the same way? If we can't agree, can one person be persuaded or forced to agree to a set of assumptions? This is more or less where the media is today. There is no standard model. There is no agreement on assumptions. We are not talking about events. And we are saying "whatever" perhaps when one's only motivation is to *stay famous!*

Interestingly, there is no objective standard of fake news. Fake is relative in the same way truth is. However, suppose there are perhaps certain principles that one could apply to decide if something could be "true":

1. A statement is true where each part of a statement is true and can be verified by independent experiment or reality (2+2=4, John is taller than Mary, I am bald, you are reading this now).

2. A statement is true when all parties have agreed to the "who, what, when, where, why, and how" relativism of the statement's circumstances (The speed of light depends on the medium, dogs

can learn to obey human commands, people use reasoning, and my artwork sells well).

3. A statement is possibly truth, but all parties agree that it is true consistent with their internal model of reality. They agree to it being true even if it isn't. (When Trump wins it will be a disaster, fake news is designed to alter opinion, God is in all things, fake news is fake news). Note that this truth contemplates discrimination, euthanasia, ethnic cleansing, etc. Truth is relative. It may not be fair, honorable, tolerant etc.

4. A statement is made that is deliberately or accidentally *false*, but many people want it to be true (Obama and Trump both committed treason, that person is just a moron, that statement is/is not racist, you will lose weight on the "X" diet). This is the place where fake news resides. If you believe that the world should be a certain way and if you believe that others feel the same way, then it is ok to lie because people "should" know that this is the way "we feel". This is where the media is. On the left (cable TV) and on the right (AM radio), there is now an "editor-in-news" that has supplanted "just the facts". In addition, many people are seeking their fifteen minutes of fame. The more outrageous and challenging they can make their "take", the more they will be known. There is an idea of "personal brand" that some people take seriously. This, by the way, has nothing to do with integrity; it has to do with marketing. It's Kardashianism.

5. The people who have voices in the media that others read, see, or listen to can deliver whatever commentary they choose. Therefore it is impossible to check what is true. The media have the resources to be in many places at the same time and we, as citizens, do not. In the past, we counted on them to deliver a description of events. And they did.

Now the media deliver a description mostly of people as they see them. There are even stations that write headlines where one of their commentators disses a senior politician as though anything their commentator says really matters to anyone. What's important is truth, not the "take" of a TV face. It *truthfully* does not matter, except to other commentators. Even the Weather Channel has become personalized. In a fight for relevancy, they send their people out to become the story i.e. "Look at me being blown and rained on". And each photo op is a chance for a breathless description of the weather as the worst it has ever been. But it isn't true.

Today, actors can deliver personal attacks on anyone. There is no standard of truth required. And everyone criticizes everyone else, even though they could not do the jobs they are criticizing. Entire radio and TV programs are devoted to second-guessing coaches, politicians, and business CEOs. This is all opinion, but it has become blended by the media in such a way that opinion and fact cannot be distinguished. This is the place where fake news is today.

As we become more and more electronic in communication the programmers, coders, and consultants will know more than the rest of us about what is true. In the world of hacking, even they may not know everything. This leads to a difficult conclusion.

Truth may not be knowable ever again. Yet, there are very powerful entities (governments, corporations, criminals, and anarchists) that will have profound interests in controlling and managing what gets spoken about as the "truth". Nowhere can this be found more persuasive than in the efforts of Joseph Goebbels during the Second World War. Almost everything that was discussable and known in Germany during the war years was a product of the truth as known by only a few men. Was this the zenith of fake news? Is this same obsessive and relentless diatribe being witnessed today in the US media on both sides?

Just suppose we cannot know the truth. What is the next best thing? It may very well be to know all of the lies on both sides. Sometimes truth emerges from the point/counterpoint of the attacks and defenses. In addition, there are many fewer people seeking the truth. Instead they are simply seeking support for their already formed beliefs. It doesn't matter what happened. What matters is whether what I already believe was supported by the event. More and more people are less and less able to discuss the truth. Will it really be "they" who will ultimately decide what fake news is? That would be more troubling.

26.

There Are Two of Us in Here

There have always been two of us in here for as long as I can remember. It isn't troubling and it isn't pleasant. It is like having two hands, two legs, and two ears. When I read a book, there is a voice (V1) that is reading but I (V2) can be thinking of something completely different than the words V1 is reading. When this happens, V2 has to stop V1 and ask for a do-over. There are two of us in here.

There are also two of us who decide. One of us decides by walking around a problem and surveying it from every angle. The other decides what having a problem like that one must be like and "puts the problem on". One of us gathers data. One of us goes with hunches. One of us plans and one of us changes on the fly. One of us draws energy from people and one of us draws energy from reading a good book alone. There are two of us in here.

There is an inside "us" and an outside "us". Sometimes the environment causes us to react in some way i.e. cold wind, etc. Sometimes we react because our internal state reacts to a plan it has created (Go sled riding). There are two of us in here.

When I write dialogue for characters in a book like this, there are two of us in here. One of us writes the dialog (V1) and the other reads it to see how it sounds (V2). When "we" are stumped, we ask questions to "ourselves" and get answers back. It's that voice again.

With schizophrenia, there are always two of us. One is talking and one is listening, but instead of being equal, one is superior to the other. Sometimes it is like listening to someone with the radio playing in the background. Sometimes it is only listening to the superior voice and ignoring the rest. That is why I may not appear to be listening. I am, but not to you. There are two of us in here.

Sometimes I get to be the superior one. I get to control the volume and urgency. Then the other voice dims. It never goes away, but I don't hear it as strongly. I need time and energy to manage this process. This is also how a machine and a fault locator test program interact. When something is wrong, is it the machine or the software? And what can "I" use that is not the hardware or software to decide what is wrong?

There are two of us in here. I was born with certain physical characteristics that caused the MD to declare me male. But I never was. I never felt the "male" part of my being, except from people on the outside. Inside, it is only the female part. Yet I had to live as a male while I also lived as a female. There are two of us in here.

I have found a relationship with God. I know he is with me. He has a presence inside me that is undeniable. I know he is here because my fears and negative emotions subside when I ask him to take over for a while. His rod and his staff they comfort us. There are two of us in here.

There is a brain and a mind in here. They work together. My brain acts on my behalf and makes decisions about breathing and heartbeats. My mind monitors the outside world and tells the brain what is going on. My brain cannot interpret another person's actions. My mind can and does. There are two of us in here.

When I die, there will continue to be two of me. They will exist in a form that allows one of them to access the other in collaboration. They will be a complete consciousness. I do not fear that day. There will be two of us out there.

The Mind, The Brain, and The Body Problem

Ok, here we go again. Is this just another swat at the "hard" problem? Well… sort of. The answer to this tri-party "problem" has always been tricky. The body, as you would imagine, is the sum of all organs, tissues, molecules, etc., that make up a space composed of a living thing called "you". The brain is part of the body located in the body. This is by convention and because the brain can be seen and located. It provides an administrative and supervisory function. Elementary school children know all of this.

The interesting problem arises when pondering *the mind*. Suppose the mind is truly separate (although some think this is not so). The argument for non- separation is that there are things that affect the mind like drugs or disorders and how could the mind be separate if bodily things can act on it and vice versa.

But just suppose that the mind is like gravity. The mind "exists as an effect" of the "curvature" of consciousness caused by the brain being switched "on". This is much like saying that gravity exists as an effect of the curvature of space-time caused by matter. This curvature of consciousness as an idea may explain why the mind as an idea remains elusive. It is also why gravity is not yet fully integrated into quantum mechanics.

What might the curvature of consciousness be like? Several individuals have suggested that there may be consciousness all around us. I would call this collective consciousness a "consciousness field". It is external to anyone's mind. The brain also produces a field. This neuron-induced "field" interacts with the consciousness field and could create what we call the mind. The brain's field acts like matter and "bends" the conscious field. This local warping of consciousness can affect the physical human body in the same way that gravity affects life on earth. This warping creates the mind as long as the brain is turned on. When we are asleep, the warping relaxes. Our "mind" rests. If one uses brain-altering chemical substances one is affecting the brain's ability to warp the conscious field. And changes in the consciousness field change the mind,

The existence of the brain is required for the existence of the mind. There are gravity waves and there are mind waves. The more significant the brain, the more significant the mind…much like matter and gravity.

Matter can be dense or porous. Its form determines the degree that space is curved. Brains too, have differences in the electric fields they produce. Their field strengths determine how much consciousness is curved. Interestingly, a defective brain (lesions, chemical imbalances, etc.) causes an erratic warping of the conscious field. This leads to the mind problems that we see and can test for.

Black holes are extraordinary phenomena where matter is so dense that it creates a hole in the fabric of space. Other matter that goes into the black hole is "lost". That is, information is lost. Individual minds are similar but work in reverse. It cannot be proven but the electrical field interaction with consciousness produced by Mozart, Einstein, Aristotle, and others are the "mind" equivalent of the black holes of space. They curved consciousness so greatly that the information they were able to obtain was unique and inaccessible to the rest of us. They defined systemically important information that did not exist elsewhere. These minds, like black holes, occur randomly and how they do what they do remains inaccessible to us. These people are/ were very special integrators.

Suppose all of this were true. Let's return to the mind for a moment. What happens when a mind is "distorted"? One way to change the mind is to change the brain. The chemicals we use to impact the mind are delivered to the brain. This action adjusts the field of the mind. It is like adding matter to change gravitational effect. People who are mentally unbalanced (ADD, schizophrenia), or whom PTSD has affected have electrical field intersection issues with the curvature of consciousness. The noticeable problem is in the mind, but the treatment must go through the brain. The problem with chemicals in the brain is that all treatment except tumor removal involves the entire brain. There cannot be specific targeting in most cases. Hence, side effects can distort the mind. Gravity can also be distorted. The bottom of a black hole (a singularity) is a mutation of gravity. Equations cannot describe what happens there.

Gravity and the mind are emergent properties of other things. This is one of the reasons that they are not accessible to complete human under-standing. Gravity has not been integrated with general relativity and the mind has not been easily integrated with consciousness and the brain.

What happens at the intersection of the brain and the consciousness of the mind? Just suppose that the human mind has two parts: one that "we" are aware of, and one that is invisible and not accessible. What if the "I" that is formed in one part of the mind is an illusion created by another part of the mind? What I am proposing is that the brain bends consciousness, but in doing so creates two kinds of consciousness—one that "we" know as the "I" of that special voice we all have inside us, and the other that is the great integrator. This second integrating mind is the "real" you. But "you" don't control it. You are created by it.

The integrating mind is responsible for you. It exists as a condition of evolution. Just like the brain controls certain vital body functions, so too the mind controls certain vital survival functions. It is linked to all your senses and to the universe. It is linked to your soul. It is also linked to the "you" that you understand to be you.

Suppose that when you are born your brain has a field. This field bends consciousness in a small way to create your mind. Your mind is what begins receiving data from the environment very early. It begins "making sense" of things. As you age, your brain creates a stronger neuronal field and your mind becomes stronger as a result. The mind then performs a remarkable function. It splits the field into two parts, the hidden you and "you". It creates the idea of "you". This is the "you" that you believe yourself to be. The initial mind (IM) has free will. The "you" mind (YM) that has been created does not. The reason for creating this YM is that the IM is not capable of accessing other humans directly. It needs to know what other humans "are like". YM provides that insight to the IM. The IM is not "your" mind. If anything, "you" are its window. This is why we struggle with determinism and free will. We have both, but not in the way we imagine.

You can see this relationship in experiments. When asked to raise your hand and then report "the moment" when "you" made the decision, CT scans show that something had already been lit and had already made the decision to move your hand before "you" knew about it. This is the IM at work. There is a silent command given to the body that did not come from YM. It came from IM.

The IM is your source of intuition. It has free will, but *"it"* is not *"you"*, at least not the "you" that "you" know. The IM is separate from you. It has free will. Its mission is to help you interpret the environment and act on your behalf.

Everyone's mind (IM) is different. Some are geniuses, some are damaged, and the rest are in between. Damaged IMs have diseases that we call schizophrenia, among others. What happens in the case of schizophrenia is that the brain creates a mutated consciousness field. The curvature of conscious is not smooth. There are irregularities. It would be like experiencing gravity different in different physical places. The IM cannot do its job. Thus, the conversation between the IM and YM is "heard" by YM and it is confusing. To fix this, Ritalin is prescribed and the conversation is inhibited.

The profession of psychiatry is designed to access other people's IMs. It should be clear that the IM is not Freud's id. The IM is a bending of consciousness and the id is derived from instinctual needs and drives. They are different. The job of the IM is to integrate all things and provide the best possible management over the survival of YM and the organism. IM integration is not the same for everyone. If you pick up any introductory psychological textbook, you will find different theories for how personality develops, how behavior occurs, and what happens when we are defective. The brain runs the body and the IM runs YM and the brain.

So, where do emotions fit? First, emotions are also a function of YM. It is YM that can interpret other people's minds. YM reads people and gives the IM additional data about them. This aids in survival. The IM cannot do this itself. It needs YM to do its job. Emotions are part of YM. "You" know what's going on because you can feel it.

At this point, I want to compare my IM to Gilbert Ryle's "ghost in the machine". Ryle's idea was that mind and body were not different and that there was no "ghost mind in the body machine". Suppose that the problem with Ryle's idea is that the IM is in fact an independent concept, but it *is* integrated. It is this independence yet integration that has baffled the people who are working this idea as a "mind/body" problem. The analogy with gravity is the key. There is no "ghost in the matter", either. Gravity and matter are two different things, yet they interact. That is the IM.

Perhaps another analogy is helpful. Take laughter. Is it thought? Emotion? Is it volitional? Is it a choice and if so, what causes it?

Suppose that laughter happens at the intersection of thought and emotion. YM hears and interprets the words, but laughter is an emergent property of how IM and YM intersect. IM "reacts" to certain YM input and then causes "laughter". It seems to "just happen". That is IM working. IM creates hunches. IM is the basis for original thought, but the field of the brain determines its "strength". The larger and smoother the curvature, the better the mind.

The YM provides data to the IM during sleep. The field intersection and curvature of the IM are still there during sleep. But the curvature is lessened and data flows one way. Dreams are the result of YM continuing to send data in the form of memories or thoughts, but IM is not responding and interpreting. It is not assigning work to the body. It is not protecting. The reason flight and other powers are possible is that the IM is not constrained by reality when the curvature is relaxed. Weightlessness can be created in a diving airplane and effectively bring flight to conscious humans, even in the presence of gravity.

There is more to write about here, but my IM is already working on the next essay.

27.

Conversation Between Strategy and Tactics

A Board Meeting somewhere at this very moment. The debaters have names but their positions are the same as these.

Tactics: "We don't really need a strategy. If there were a strategy that was universally important, we would all be using it. We might even be using the same strategy. But we aren't."

Strategy: "But, without a strategy, how do you know how to invest money in your firm? If you have a strategy, then any project or expense can be compared to what you are trying to do. You will naturally reject projects that don't conform to strategy. You will also avoid conflicts between divisions because strategic initiatives that cross divisions will have an understood priority."

Tactics: "But how can you possibly know where you need to go? How do you know what the environment will be like in the future? It's all just guessing. Kodak dismissed digital cameras, GE couldn't continue its "all things to all people", Deutsche Bank failed to understand what was happening every day. And other companies have invested in technology (like dish vs. cable), all of which were "strategic" decisions. So there's that."

Strategy: "Yet, I could say the same for tactics. The Tylenol pill recall disaster was a tactical mismanagement of the press. At Gettysburg, Pickett decided to charge the Union positions and lost most of his division. During the dot-com bubble, investors put money into the stock of companies that had no earnings. So there's that."

Tactics: "But I will always know today whether I am better than yesterday. If I just seek incremental improvement, then I don't have to go in any certain direction. I can build a tactical plan each year that makes me better than the year before."

Strategy: "But that then becomes your purpose. You are not trying to make better products. You are not trying to appeal to a different customer base. You are not trying to reduce expense. You are just trying to be better without regard to what that means. How does anyone know "what" to do to get better?"

Tactics: "They know what is working and what isn't. They make adjustments to what already is there. They improve products, reduce expense, and all the rest of it but the goal or purpose is just to get better. "

Strategy: "So, if I am an employee, what would I think about to make the company better? It's too ambiguous. Let's take a tactical example. If a client complains about my product, am I trying to give them a positive experience or to minimize the amount of money paid out to correct certain problems? By what standard am I operating? And wouldn't you say that you'd want the whole company operating with that same standard?"

Tactics: "Coordination between groups is of course important. The culture of the company is the glue that holds it together. It is a way of being that we all understand. In some ways, it is the standard."

Strategy: "Are you then saying that culture is a tactic? If you are, then how would you decide in an acquisition which culture to accept? Suppose one company was extremely cost-conscious and the other was extremely customer-conscious. Which do you go with?"

Tactics: "We'd go with the acquirer's culture. It has been that way throughout history. From China to South America, the dominant culture always decided what would be done. The tactics of the stronger culture supplanted those of the weaker culture. Execution was the key. It was not whether we bought the right thing."

Strategy: "You lose a company by making bad judgments that affect thousands of employees or millions of dollars not by a single tactical mistake. Those can be bad, but you, the company still stands. While it is true that great tactical decisions have won military battles, most often it was only one battle. In the end it is strategy that unites or repels those who hear it."

Tactics: "But if you fail tactical execution then your strategy is doomed. It doesn't matter how well the house was designed if it could not be built. Under what circumstances should I give up on my strategy and redesign the plan?"

Strategy: "Equally, if you are trying to build a house without a plan, no one will know what they should be doing first or next. Under what circumstances should I give up on what I am doing and try something else?"

The chairman rose and said, "After hearing the arguments for both sides my strategy is to create 10 principal rules that will serve to generally govern. There will be tactical implementations but I will leave that to the customers. Keep things general but stick to 10. And let's get the marketing department to get one of those burning bushes ready to go."

APPENDIX TO CHAPTER 27
A Strategy for A Random Firm

Strategy (from Greek στρατηγία stratēgia) is a high-level plan to achieve one or more goals under conditions of uncertainty. This idea is more complex than a single opening sentence. For example: there are four possible strategies to stay in business:

1. Be a monopolist (Sirius XM Holdings)

2. Have the best product (Apple)

3. Have the best solution (Amazon)

4. Have the lowest price (Southwest)

Most companies cannot attain nor hold the ground in these spaces, apart from acquisition or startup. But here is what they are trying to do in their own words:

"SiriusXM Radio plans to be the dominant product in the connected car of the future." (Note they have more than 70% market share in the US and more than 50% world- wide)

"We (Apple) believe that we are on the face of the earth to make great products and that's not changing. We are constantly focusing on innovating. We believe in the simple not the complex. We believe that we need to own and control the primary technologies behind the products that we make, and participate only in markets where we can make a significant contribution."

"At Amazon we want to be earth's most customer-centric company; to build a place where people can come to find and discover anything they might want to buy online."

"At Southwest we will connect people to what's important in their lives through friendly, reliable, and low-cost air travel."

We would recognize these statements as "that vision thing". But there is a big difference. Each of these companies is known for what they are doing (by customers, employees, and shareholders). Even if the employees of these firms had never read the strategy statement, they would still be able to put the case in their own words. These firms already are what they say they are because they became what they set out to be. *They have a purpose.* If you were an employee at any of these companies and sat at home thinking how you could make it a better company, you have a very specific idea of what you can do.

You can help us to continue to dominate car radios, make us a great product, or add on in the tech space where we own the tech, figure out how to get more products on our web site, figure out how to reduce airline costs.

Strategy is easier to understand from the military:

1. We are going to end the war.

2. To end the war we are going to Berlin.

3. To go to Berlin we are invading Normandy.

4. Here's your role on Omaha beach.

5. From that point on, everyone knows what to do. You move east. You hold a bridge because our people are going east, or you blow it to stop "them" from coming west. Supplies are behind you; danger is in front of you. If you are separated from your unit, remember they too are headed east. Until you find them (or any friendlies), stay alive and damage as much of "the other guy's stuff" as possible. If you want to help, move east. You can recognize the patterns in your environment that support or refute what you are trying to do. You don't need a consultant. You don't need advisors. You don't need "adult supervision". You just need to know the "big" picture.

In short, if the strategy is clear, then everyone, everywhere, every time, knows what furthers the cause and they can *see* it happening. They know the pattern. Once the strategy is stated clearly, then everyone also knows what *won't* happen. (For example; we won't be spending money on Coast Guard issues while we are going to Berlin).

Business strategies are also about patterns. Strategy is about understanding existing facts and processes, intuitively recognizing patterns among them, relating these patterns to patterns in the larger world and making adjustments. It is about seeking the competitive, sustainable advantage. It's about defining the "going to Berlin". Strategy implies a very good understanding of the present situation, the forces at work in the environment, the quality of resources, people, and the general state of technology.

Strategy is about tradeoffs and alignments. It is about how to value things. It is about the belief systems that will prevail. Strategy provides consistency across broad geographies and time. Strategy "allows" for a culture to be in many places at once. In special cases, strategy *determines* culture.

Normally, culture determines strategy. In addition, strategy is essential to run a company across large geographies. A good strategy can cause remote locations to act independently and know that they are consistent with headquarters. Strategy allows for the invasion of Normandy without friendly fire.

The reason for having a strategy is that all businesses find value in having similar *quality* across the firm no matter how they are organized. Strategy allows for unaffiliated business units to act in each other's interests without constant and direct communication. It allows for the most junior person to tell the "story" to any customer, anywhere, and at any time. When the "story" is well known, it becomes part of the sales process, part of recruiting, and part of culture. When strategy is well known, it attracts and breeds "believers". Strategy is a uniting force. GE, McDonalds, Boeing and Microsoft all have well known strategies. This is one of the reasons that they can function effectively on a worldwide basis.

How does one start to think of strategy? During the past seventy years in the US, we have benefited from some of the most favorable market conditions in the history of mankind. It didn't matter what we bought or where: the result was a significant revenue increase. This growth trained US industry to budget and expect market-driven revenue growth. This growth wasn't independent of execution (the financial crisis of 2007-2010, for example) but it did make execution pretty simple. The problem is that the spectacular, market-driven revenue growth may be over. For all of us, this is a problem because many companies have had spectacular expense growth to match the revenue increase.

So why can't we just incrementally do better next year than we did this year? That's worked so far.

The answer is that shareholders are looking for 20% after tax returns from companies. There has never been a way in most industries to get this in a sustained way over long periods. But if shareholders in other industries can get 20%, then how can you get it in your industry?

You need a strategy. First, you must answer two categories of questions. Why does your company exist at all? And second, why should you continue to exist? Implicit in these questions is a definition of what value your company really provides to customers and the reason customers will continue to want what you produce.

Recently, a company answered the first question by saying that they are here to deliver world-class solutions to local markets and to tailor these solutions to individual clients. By itself, there is nothing compelling about this *raison d'etre*. Lots of people do this. There is something in the word "world-class" that makes one think that this company is likely large. Their customers have historically seen this company as a part of financial services. This is the good news. The bad news is that this customer perception has been mostly one of "simplistic product offering". Thus, this company struggles to convert people from their competitors because their products and people are perceived as "not being good enough or just like (fill in the name)".

Today, this company must change the customer's perception from, "you guys just sell simplistic financial stuff to existing customers pretty much like everyone else," to an unqualified statement as to why a client should buy from them. This company is in the information and knowledge transfer business. They do get information from around the world; they could add value to it and tailor its relevance to the individual customer. And they deliver it locally. This *can* be different from competitors. This company's clients are indifferent to where the information comes from, but after adding intellectual and customized value to it, they value knowing the individual with whom they are dealing.

Now, when someone asks what this company does, the response is that "they bring information and knowledge to their US clients that is valuable *specifically to them*. They know what their customers want to do with their assets and liabilities better than anyone else, and they bring world-class solutions to help them do it."

This means that they bring the outside world to their markets and bring the concerns of their markets to the outside world. If they can deliver on this concept, they can make more revenue because it isn't about a bull market or a new product launch; it's about doing over and over the things that customers value.

The answer to the second group of questions is equally crucial. Why does anyone think the company will still be in business in the next five years? One can look at product, position, price, place, or promotion and try to build reasons. But in keeping with the notion above that their value is in their knowledge management, one can say that they will stay in business by providing world-class information about any kind of "transaction", financial or not. They are positioned to know a lot about what is happening in the world, and they operate in a market area that does not have that knowledge. Yet they know a lot about their market areas, which the world does not and cannot.

But information acquisition and transfer are not enough. It is useless without a purpose. In keeping with the transfer of information and knowledge value added, as part of their strategy they must commit to something real that means something to their customers. So here it is:

"We the company will commit, in partnership with our clients, to increase your <u>net worth</u> by 20% each year. At the start of each year we will reestablish the value of all your assets with you, even the non-earning ones.

We will then subtract your liabilities. This is your net worth. We will grow this number together by 20%. If we actually reach 20%, we will earn 2%. Anything more we will share 2:1 in your favor. If we do not get to 20%, we will examine why. If you the client spent more than agreed or failed to make the revenue changes we agreed to, then we still get 2%. BUT, if it is our failing then we will work that year for free. Each June we will check to see how we are doing and adjust. We are in this for you."

This is the same approach that the company uses for itself in the yearly budget process. The best measure for a successful business is ROE. The same should also apply to an individual. If a person starts with $1MM, they will have $6.1MM after ten years by returning 20% each year on *their* equity. This is how the rich got rich. It is also how this company got rich.

This is the first step in developing strategy. Anything that gets better information to a customer or can assist in increasing customer assets, reducing liabilities, or growing net worth, is consistent with this strategy and should have a higher priority over other projects. Second, it is easy for employees to tell this story and easy for employees to know what they should be working on, no matter where they are or who they work for. They know that they are to find out all information about a client (and the client will help, because 20% of a bigger number means more earnings for the company, too). The company knows that, if they know their clients, they can find ways to increase net worth. They know that they must become better educated about many things and really know and be known in a community.

The next decision is how to execute against this strategic vision. This is the question of tactics.

1. What is our client's worth? How do we know this? Who is rich and who is poor (segmentation)?

2. What information do clients need to grow their net worth?

3. How do we align our delivery against customers to get 20% growth in net worth each year?

4. What roles do technology and labor play?

5. Who will decide what information a client needs and what information will be provided?

6. How do we convert from an indifference to everything except product to an indifference to almost everything except the customer?

7. How do we find people who can deliver on this strategy?

8. Are our employees diverse and skillful enough?

This strategy will obviously require different employees than the company has today. It will require a "total" employee, not just some sales guys. Single-product people cannot execute this strategy. Specialists also can't execute the strategy. The salespeople must be entrepreneurs who are able to understand how to grow their own net worth. Companies in this industry forever have said their employees are their product. This would prove it.

Growing net worth by 20% seems daunting, but it is not. Up to some level, real risk and return changes must be made. In the early going, even negative net worth clients can be taken on because they can now make the company money if the company makes them money. Every asset is examined for how it might bring in money. Employer discussions for raises may be a part of this. It is no longer just this company—it is personal financial consulting around the expenses and lifestyles of clients. No one need save for anything again. If you grow net worth, you are developing the ability to pay for college, retirement, boats, etc. The elegance of this strategy is that it is not easily duplicated by anyone.

A second tactic in this environment is to commit to using a high percentage of profits specifically for societal improvement. This strategy is independent of Washington. It is also independent of earnings because if profits fall, donations will fall. This strategy is designed to attract the client of the future to the degree that they are socially conscious.

The company in this scenario would control its donations and set up subsidiaries to manage local social issues. In this sense, it would replace some of the established systems in place, which in certain cases are the reasons why that particular social cause has been neglected.

I understand that this kind of social commitment is not why companies have traditionally been formed. But just suppose that if they could make a difference at the local levels of their offices, then more clients would do business with them and would be willing to pay a premium for causes they supported.

A Note About Risk Because it is a Huge Part of Pattern Recognition

Strategy and tactics don't just get decided. They are discussed in both positive and negative ways. The first section was the positive discussion. The following is the negative discussion.

Risk

Some notion of risk must be tied to success. After all, the loss of something important would be an unhappy event. But this is a future state of success, not the state of success (or lack of it) at present. Many companies have been successful, but because they could not anticipate risk or where it would come from, they couldn't stay successful. One of the hardest things for a company to do is to change a successful firm before it is failing. Risk anticipation and pattern recognition is important.

Think of the situation in any company, city, state, or nation.

Any situation can have multiple causes and any single cause can produce multiple outcomes. Even for two linked situations, the time and original conditions are often different (see the World Trade Center debate about whether it was one or two events for purposes of insurance deductibles). Men who have harassed women suddenly discover that the risk was far more than they had ever thought it would be (at least for some) and the risks were additive. (#metoo)

> People are bad at judging risk. If you are offered $1 as a sure thing or a 50/50 chance at $2, you are mathematically sound taking either choice. And at some level, they "feel" equal. The expected value of these choices is the same. But, if the dollars were $1 million and $2 million, then it is more likely one would choose the sure thing. There is an element of human nature that intrudes. The opposite is true of losses. You might gamble even at a $2 loss because you don't want a "sure" loss.

> Humans are unable to unambiguously interpret *the past*. The inherent psychological make-up of human beings makes retrospective analysis of past events imperfect. One need only consider revisionist interpretations of American history to see this. Many witnesses cannot remember what they "really saw". We don't recall accurately what really happened. We are biased. In business, we tell ourselves how we did something successfully so that we feel that it was through our efforts that the company got better. But we often "redefine" what we were really thinking and neglect an important contributor in many circumstances: luck.

> Humans are unable to unambiguously interpret *the present*. As mentioned above, this is becoming nearly impossible, as "fake" information is rampant. In addition, certain agencies that have been given special privilege to defend the democratic state have changed the environment in an asymmetric way that no one yet knows

has happened. If the NSA can access your personal data without warrant simply because they have been given special access to files, then this is an unknown risk that might be substantial

Humans are also unable to unambiguously perceive the future. Anything that changes rapidly or is highly complex will defeat biology (humans). Humans are too limited by processing ability and by emotional variation (fear, greed) to recognize potential risk even in their own lives. Even model builders cannot agree on the processes they will use to forecast certain events.

This is not to say that all human assessment is useless. For many simple problems there is the "parent model". This model suggests that, if another party has experience with your problem, they may be able to provide insight into yours. To some extent, these "parents" come from your future since they have dealt with a problem that you have not seen yet.

Here is another way to create a patterned understanding of risk. Think of this in terms of your home and then expand that pattern to the business you are in.

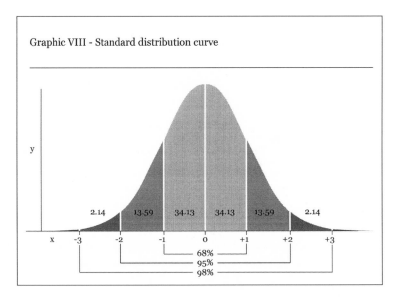

Graphic VIII - Standard distribution curve

To orient you, suppose the y-axis would be frequency of an event occurring and the x-axis would be the money lost. In the case of operational risk, we are looking at just the left side of the curve, the loss side. You'll see that the first shaded area is 34.13%. These losses would be losses that are frequent (y) but not very expensive (-x). These are losses you would have had at home or at work (broken dishes, lost medicine, mechanical devices that fail, etc.). To some extent they can be managed, but even at home it is unlikely that any of us go very long without something happening that created a loss for us that we did not expect.

The second area is the 13.59% and this represents losses that really happened but happened to a neighbor or to another company in your industry. These losses are lower in frequency (y) but higher in (-x). These losses are knowable (roof leaks that damaged a wall, a tree falling on the house, your teenager backing a car through the garage door, etc.).

The third area is the most important and the least able to be solved. These are the catastrophic losses at home or at work. These would be events like fires or 100-year floods that were not covered by insurance. This kind of loss could include the loss of life. No matter how well things are planned or organized, it is possible for a big problem to occur. We cannot know either the frequency or the cost. Unfortunately, one of these "tail" losses dwarfs all the others put together.

What can we do about risk in general? We can insure in many cases, but the skill is to not have to use the insurance in the first place. We didn't need it because we accurately anticipated the risk ahead of time. This is original work. Each of us must organize the world as we see it. Unfortunately, everyone cannot do this, so I have included four patterns to consider.

IA. Develop an Intelligence Network

Below, you will see pattern recognition as a necessary ability in managing risk. Developing a network could have appeared either before or after *pattern recognition* because intelligence is about data collection and validation. It is about gathering information to support a pattern or it is about deriving a pattern from information.

The ability to gather intelligence relies heavily on the ability to ask the right question. In the end, this skill is unassailable. But it is only 25% of the true skill. The other 75% is about being able to interpret the answer in context. The inability of people to interpret context makes for bad estimates.

External intelligence everywhere is very weak. Seminars are not effective nor are they a substitute. Some of us have relied on vendors (psychiatrists) to help us in the past and have had some success, but even *they* are not connected enough.

How do we ever know what the right data is? We don't. We can't. This is why risk cannot disappear. But if you examine the data yourself, the story that the data tells will mean something. It is you that must understand. You cannot sub-contract this commitment.

People will say that they cannot be expected to spend precious time on data. They can hire thousands of data miners and will just trust the data. But happiness about the future can be increased by a better understanding of the present.

IB. Develop systematic (non-human) pattern recognition in data

There are two ways to systematically look at data. The first is to run data and look for outliers based on some category within the output. The second is having a point of view and then running an analysis to see if it's true. This is effective when data is repetitive, retained, and retrievable. Computers can search for patterns, but *humans must tell it what to look for*! Without an idea, direction, or outcome, there is little chance of decent interpretation of the search.

II. Pattern Recognition

Success starts with pattern recognition. This is not about "identifying risk". That is too general a statement and doesn't say anything about what identification means. It is about the ability to see connections or patterns in all manner of things. **Human pattern recognition** is very hard because human heuristics make it so. There are few people who can recognize patterns. It requires some experience and significantly above average intuition, intelligence, and imagination. It sometimes also requires superior human mental storage and retrieval capability to access prior data useful to the case one is working on. There is a wisdom needed in understanding the process that created the data, and also in extracting meaning from patterns.

Pattern recognition can be trained, but only incrementally over the base qualities of experience, intuition, imagination, and intelligence. If the base is no good, then training will be of marginal value. Everyone can recognize something they have seen before. Anyone can read an article and check to see if it applies to him or her. The highest pattern recognition skill is the recognition of a pattern that hasn't been seen before.

Children get into trouble because they are unable to recognize patterns in their environment. Therefore, they are forced to rely on others. Some never lose this dependency. Who are the good pattern recognizers?

Patterns are about context. Context is about asking questions that mean something. We ask people, "What are the risks in your business or what worries you?" How would we ever know if they knew? Instead, we must ask questions in some context like:

1. Where is your business/individual stake BIG?

2. Where is your business/ individual stake SMALL?

3. Where is your business/individual stake FAST?

4. Where is your business/individual stake COMPLEX?

5. Name the five most dangerous things for you. Defining "dangerous" will give some insight into their pattern recognition.

6. Name the five most dangerous people to you. Why are they dangerous?

7. Who knows you and the situation well?

8. Who knows the people who can change the environment well?

III. Doing Things

Pattern recognition and intelligence only matter if something is *actually done*. We all have examples where we knew that something was likely wrong and yet we did nothing about it. Relationships were involved. It was hard. So, we didn't do the right thing. Doing is everything. Doing things is not about measuring, monitoring, controlling, testing, or reporting. Those activities are *consequences* of doing.

Doing is hard. These problems and many others are known, agreed to, and yet unresolved. No one is *responsible* for the work. However, we can all expect to be accountable if something goes badly. We have people in business units that resist doing things that hinder business efforts. We have people who insist that nothing needs to be done because they don't see the problem. We have people who insist that we should do *something*, just not *that*. Doing is all about biology and about the human condition. Any act that is not based on what is being done is going to be ineffective. Who is actually doing things to fix problems? Those are the real risk management people.

Unfortunately, in business the idea of future happiness is hard to discuss. It can be about money, but it can also be about personal reputation or responsibility. If I am doing something about risk, it should have a component related to happiness. If we do this and things go bad, will we still be happier than if we had done nothing. On the other hand, if we do things and nothing happens, will we be glad we did them?

"Doing" is hard because *not doing* is easy. "We have no budget", "We have no system", "We have no people", "We have no time", "We have no money" are all statements about not doing. Doing is intrusive. It is at the level of the individual person because human choices are where the risks are. *Doing* is about going to check how it's working. It's not about sending someone else. It's about going yourself. If the people who were securitizing and selling home loans in the mid-2000s had ever gone to the field and seen how they were being made, they would have recognized the problem and changed their structures. Will they do the right thing? Will they know to change their *doing* if the pattern changes? Will they ask? Will they decide to act?

IV. Exercising the Entire Operation

The final pillar of managing risk is exercising the entire operation. This is about doing, about gathering intelligence, and about recognizing patterns. It is a way for everyone to pay attention *at one time*. This is not just a systems drill. It is about a scenario that unfolds in a controlled way that forces people to take action on the spot. It is about exercising the ability to respond when things aren't the way they have always been.

This is about building a scenario that starts out in a certain way and then decays. Things get worse. Things people were counting on suddenly stop working. Imagine trying to live for three weeks with no phone connections and no power. How would we do it? No cells, no towers, no showers...

Imagine New York City with no power for three weeks. How would the people on the 100th floor get there? How would anyone do his or her job? Suppose there were no deliveries because you can't pump gas without power. Imagine no food deliveries. Much of the country lives a kind of brinkmanship existence without sensing how fragile it all could be. Let's hope we don't test this risk.

In the end, risk is about what people are doing. It depends on what kinds of people you are depending on. In your home, family, business, church etc., there are those who are in the wrong place and doing the wrong thing.

But no one knows this because none of the things mentioned above have been done. Spouses don't understand the finances, parents do not understand their children, workers do not recognize that they should not be seeing what they are seeing, and it is the same for drivers. Suppose that we could reduce risk by 20% in all things. Would it lead to a happier life?

28.

We've Been Assumed

I assume that by the second sentence of this story you will assume that you know how it's going to end. After all, this is a story about assumptions.

Once upon a time there was a modest, ordinary room. It had one chair and a window. It was a dreary little room most of the time until those special days when people came from far and wide to visit. Today is one of those days.

The first person to enter the room was the smartest person in the room. Every room has one. It has never been clear whether every room needs one. The smartest people in any room have experienced life in such a way that they know with certainty that they are the smartest. They have figured out by themselves that they are the smartest. Only the smartest person in the room is smart enough to have figured out they are the smartest person in the room.

The second person to enter the room was not the smartest person in the room. One might assume that there could not be two smartest people in the room because the superlative case (est) applies to only one person or group. The second person was standing beside the smartest person in the room.

The third person to enter the room was the doctor. She assumed she was the smartest person in the room about anything concerning medicine; after all, she had studied it for many years. Yet Google had made many people in the country as smart as she was in these cases. No doctor could know everything in her profession all the time. Even the doctor used Google. It made her smarter.

The last person to enter the room knew he was the dumbest person in the room. He had not gone to school. Everyone seemed to know more about things than he did. Everyone else seemed to be able to find someone to marry and have a family. He had not. He had the standard hourly job that he had done for twenty years. It was the same job. He would often say that he was just living life because there was nothing else he could think of to do.

They had all agreed to meet there at that time. None of the four people knew each other, although the second and fourth persons had seen each other "around". They had been summoned.

They knew the specifics of their mission. Each had been briefed on their part and they knew each other's parts as well. They were waiting for any last-minute instructions.

The smartest person in the room fidgeted a bit and then asked the doctor if she would like to sit. The doctor smiled and shook her head, so the smartest person in the room sat in the only chair. After all, he was the smartest person in the room. He settled in and made himself comfortable.

There was mild tension among the four of them that was broken when the dumbest person in the room asked the smartest person in the room if he would like something to drink while they waited. He said yes and asked for Dom Perignon champagne. Everyone laughed and after a phone call, a glass of a "suitable substitute" was delivered. Everyone else had declined.

At 4:35 PM, the word came that the mission was a go. Everyone took his or her places. The dumbest person in the room left the room momentarily, thereby elevating the average intelligence of the room. There was a brief countdown and then the dumbest guy *not* in the room pulled the switch.

Note to the reader: What do you assume happened?

APPENDIX FOR CHAPTER 28
Assumptions

Suppose that the "root of all evil" is not money but assumptions. Suppose that the greatest unhappiness we experience is predicated on what we assume that turns out not to be true. How many assumptions do we make in a day? And how many of them turn out to be true? In the trivial cases (Will this light turn on? Will my car start?) our assumptions are mostly correct. They are based on long experience and high probabilities of success.

The majority of us have no idea what we are assuming each day. If you sit at a bar and listen to the conversations (especially among friends who came in together) you will see what I mean. Each party speaks from their own perspective and the things they assume are astonishing.

There is some natural level of assumption that lies at the bottom of everything we say. For example, we all have an assumption of how smart we are. We have proof. We have our models and they work. We have papers that prove we are smart because we graduated. And yet, our relationships can often suck. Why? Because in truth, we aren't very smart and what we assume is not only *not* true, but also is *the opposite* of what we have been assuming all along. And yet, when relationships end, which assumptions do we question? We never question the bad ones ("I knew she was an ass" or "I knew he was cheating" or "I knew this was bad for me"), and instead we question the good ones ("I assumed she was always going to be kind", "I assumed she would never change", "I assumed she would change"). And we blame the other party.

One can find support for the idea that the more certain we are that something is true, the greater the likelihood that we are wrong. For example, if you ask people whether they are better than average drivers, far more people will say they are. It is the same with people who believe they know a lot about an issue. The more they say they know, the less correct they usually are. So why do we say we know more than we know? Why do we assume that we are right? What is it really that we *do* assume?

Look at these statements:

There is proof that Trump should be impeached.

There is proof that Comey should be tried for crimes.

Trump is disrupting the swamp.

Trump is incapable of leadership and good judgment.

Sanctuary cities are necessary.

Sanctuary cities are against the law.

What is being assumed in these cases? Each statement has two different conclusions, based on the assumptions one is making. But what are those assumptions? And how are they formed? There is of course no assumption *standard* in existence and assumptions are not hard-wired in some logical way into our brains. In many cases, assumptions are based on feelings or how things "ought" to be or based on some assumption of what good and bad are. Political assumptions are legion.

Assumptions are seductive for several reasons. First, we often don't think we are assuming anything. We believe that if everyone knew what *we* know then they would conclude the same things that we conclude. We assume that. Second, we assume that there is a right and a wrong way, which again is based on beliefs we have had all along. And yet, we still relish those arguments. We are still amazed when people vote for Hillary or Donald. We are amazed when people do not support causes like diversity, the right to bear arms, welfare, pro-life, or the death penalty. But why is this so? There are four reasons:

1. Even if one's assumptions have been right all along they may go wrong very slowly. You won't see it until it's too late. You assume that your drinking or smoking is doing no harm. You assume that the money you take from the till is so small that you'll never be caught. You assume that the people you sexually harass will never have the power to change your life. You assume that the life you have

led has prepared you for the rest of your life. The assumption you make based on the now is not valid for all future possibilities. That is simply missing the pattern. The assumption you have has failed.

2. Even if you have no common sense about things, you may go ahead with an action anyway because nothing "tells" you that you are *assuming* anything. "Give me a match. I think my gas tank is empty"; "We can pass this bill in the House without reading it. How bad could it be?" This kind of assumption is the "assumption of non-blameability". It doesn't matter what I do, as long as I won't get blamed. This is the assumption of unaccountability. It is extremely seductive. Most of the Federal government assumes they will never be accountable for anything they do.

3. You really desire something to be true now and forever so you assume it will be. "I am just lucky"; "I am the smartest person in the room": "We're out of range": and "I really know people". These are the assumptions of obliviousness. These are the assumptions of the delusional ego. People who believe they are always right, who believe that their past matters more than other people's pasts, and who believe that they actually see the world the way it is are actually mentally impaired and make wrong assumptions all the time. These are the megalomaniacs. These are the George Pattons, the Rasputins, the villains in the James Bond movies, and the Nurse Ratcheds of the world and maybe even some country leaders we know. These are people without a feedback loop. These are people who cannot see themselves as others see them. Yet they assume they can.

4. There is an opposite of the above, however. You may spend your time assuming things will *always* go wrong. This perhaps is the most seductive of all assumptions. We all assume that if something is good we have to prepare for it to not be good. We "know" (assume)

it's too good to be true. We dwell on what could go wrong. We assume that we're no good, that there's prejudice, that life is unfair, or that we are too poor. We assume we don't belong, that we are too fat, that we aren't perfect and that there are so many reasons we will fail. This is the "spiral of doom" assumption. It is also a form of dementia. Just as the egomaniac cannot see their assumptions are wrong, so too the pure manic-depressive also makes wrong assumptions. And yet neither can make progress because their assumptions are undefeatable. That is the essence of the problem and a visible cause for the way that people behave today in the US. It is what they assume.

But assumptions are not purely personal and bad assumptions are not the exclusive province of the mentally impaired. Balanced assumptions carry forward into every interaction. When we disagree with each other, it is because we have not tested each other's assumptions.

When you know you are right and you argue with someone over and over about some issue, it is because both of you are assuming that something different is true. This is not the assumption that your partner is an idiot. It is not the assumption that speaking slower and louder will convince anyone that you are right. It is not assuming that how you learned to debate in college is the only way the discussion should be held. Instead, the nature of a dis-agreement is at heart about the things that aren't discussed because "everyone knows" that they are true. Start there and the argument becomes far easier.

Let's say you want to decide with an opponent which political party is best. It is easy to see why this might go nowhere. So, instead of starting with the question "Which is better?" start by naming the assumption of what "better" actually means. In which circumstances is it important to take care of people? In which circumstances should laws be enforced? What things should be owned? Should people be able to buy on credit? Is humanism about self-interest or altruism? Is asymmetry ok?

In the end, you may be *thinking* about the matter while others may be *feeling* about the matter. You may be thinking about now and they may be thinking in terms of years. Again, each party assumes that they are having their conversation the way it should be had.

In previous essays, I have suggested ways to solve certain problems. They all began with an attempt to thwart assumptions. Suppose the way to do this is to ask one's self *"what must be true?"* Gravity will exist. Entropy will not decrease of its own accord. Heat will flow to cold. But it isn't this easy when doing adaptive work. In adaptive work, truths are not as "true". Is democracy the best form of government in all cases? How about capitalism? Can people really change how they behave in the absence of drugs or therapy? What exactly is the truth today? Can the Buffalo Bills win a Super Bowl?

It is obvious to say that we often assume that others are very poor and unfortunate human souls trying to be more like us. Our models are validated because we are who we are, and we became our wonderful selves by using those models to become us. We assume that we knew all along, or that we had a hunch how wonderful we would become. Or how terrible and worthless we are. It is amazing how many people of no means, no status, no influence, no power, no education, no hope can all pontificate after the fact what the rest of us should have been doing. They assumed all along and they are always right after the fact.

But assumptions work, don't they? This is what certain stories seek to test. Think of Scrooge and his assumptions about wealth and Bob Cratchet. He had assumed that his pecuniary thinking was more effective. But then those pesky ghosts showed up and conducted a tutorial of "just suppose". The same could be said of the movie *Groundhog Day*. Bill Murray assumed that he knew how to "solve" the problem of reliving the exact same day. Then, he assumed all the same rules of the day before would apply. Then he assumed they wouldn't apply. Then he assumed they would apply again at the end. It is easy to make movies about assumptions because assumptions are the things that are so easy to see *in others*. We all know what Harvey Weinstein was assuming.

An interesting question is whether animals assume. Probably, because they can see certain cause and effect and they can distinguish pleasure from pain. Suppose, though, that you could not link cause and effect. Could you assume anything? If you could not have some reasonable belief that your action would yield a desired outcome, would any assumption be possible? If you were a cynic you might say, "Of course assumptions would be possible; you would just assume that 'this' would continue to suck." Without some things being certain, your only assumption would be that everything would be variable. That kind of world is unlikely to support life however, because you would not be able to predict which life-sustaining actions would yield the same results. That would end it all. Some assumptions are in fact true. We depend on them for life.

Assumptions will be around. Or a square. Or a cone. And the whole basis of this book is "Just Suppose", but it could as easily have been "Let's Assume".

29.

Communications: "Houston, We Have A Problem"

Elderly couple on an airplane, probably bound for Buffalo NY, but we may never know:

Wife: "Are you thirsty?"

Husband: "No, dear. It's Wednesday."

Wife: "When…*what*?"

Husband: "Well, whenever they get here."

Wife: "Who?"

Husband: "Who what?"

Wife: "You said 'whenever *they* get here'. Who are they?"

Husband: "I don't know. You should have told me before we left."

Wife: "What does *that* have to do with *them?*"

Husband: "Who are them?"

Wife: "I have no idea, you brought *them* up just now. You're the only one on this plane who knows who *them* are."

Husband: "Who *who* are?"

Wife: "I'm telling you *I* don't know. It's your *who*, not mine."

Husband: "What who? I don't have any whos! I don't even *know* any whos. Whose whos are these whos you're talking about?

Wife: "Why do you do this all the time? You talk like *your* confusion is *my* fault. Don't talk like this in front of the children."

Husband: "What children?"

Wife "Our grandchildren."

Husband: "Are they coming here?"

Wife: "No. That's why we are on this plane, dear. We are going to fly—"

Husband: "We're going to die?"

Wife: "No, *fly*—we are going to fly! Turn up your hearing!"

Husband: "What? I couldn't hear what you were saying…"

Wife: "Here, take the *red* pill, and let's not talk for a while."

Husband: "Ok. I'll walk with you for a while…"

APPENDIX TO 29
What Were They Thinking? A Rant in G minor

How in the world did we get here? And where exactly *is* here? Not since the Visigoths, (settlers of West Virginia aka "deplorables") threatened Rome

---

(settlers of Martha's Vineyard aka elitists) has less been known about any place we call "here" than "*this here*" here. In fact, in the US, we can't even actually agree on where any particular "here" really is. Everyone's "here" is the *only* "here" they know about.

Strange people (aka strangers) are desperately looking for anyone foolhardy enough to have the seat next to them on the airplane to tell all about their *special* "here." And the range of subjects these strangers can opine on is truly breathtaking. You can *hear* about them, or something they did, or something they are going to do, or something they ate. They come wearing tee shirts with the current diet, disease, degree, or dementia they are flogging. And everything they did, are doing, will do, or are eating is one of a kind, the most dangerous ever recorded, the rarest in history, the most brilliant creation, the fastest in their category, or the only place to eat. Everyone is trying to overlap his or her fifteen minutes of fame with any of your fifteen minutes. These encounters are not intended to pass for conversation. They are pocket lectures designed as if the lecturers were being paid by the hour for delivering them.

Neither elitism, deplorability, nor gloom of night, will stay these creatures from the swiftless endlessness of their appointed take. In truth, we are not surrounded by fake news, but by fake people. Ah, but what can be done about it?

As it turns out, Darwin has been repudiated and electricity is the real problem. Read on:

In the olden days (say the Middle Ages), peasants (think Kar-dash-it-alls) were a scurvy lot. Any peasant (hereafter elite deplorables or EDs) were chiefly understood by standard convention (that is by their bar mates) to be "utterly daft".

These EDs drooled uncontrollably, wandered the taverns and fields drinking and mumbling "foresooth" this, and "fake news" that. Their effective range of stupidity (EROS) was about three meters (the hearing radius of roughly three bar stools on a good pub night in those days).

All those in range of these idle ED twaddlings knew them to be unhinged and paid no attention. The EDs were ignored right then and there and forgotten by history. Thus, for the EDs of that time, life consigned them to endless lonely wandering resulting inevitably in their going paws-up by licking frozen flag poles, keeping plague-infested vermin as pets, and always being the ladder people on the wrong side of the latest Bastille storming. Thus, Darwin willed out. The unfittest did not survive. No one knew about them and alas they were consigned to the dustbins of history with nary a footnote.

But, as time trod on, an amazing thing happened. The fittest created the internet, which ran by itself. The fittest then created access devices *for* this internet, which also ran by themselves. Then, those fittest further created cameras in these devices. But even more amazing, the fittest made all of this available to everyone no matter how fit! Behold! The EROS of today's EDs has grown from three barstools to 26,000 miles and billions of people!

Now these same EDs (droolers, drunkards, foodies) have access to *das alles vurld!* Now they appear on TV! They have fashion lines! They have their own "scent". They opine on subjects like Mueller investigations, ducks, gun control, the Supreme Court, and there are millions more like them who follow them! They all *belieeeeeve!* They're alive and they are multiplying! The number of EDs is now greater than the total number of people who gave them access. In time, they will take over the entire world. Global warming is nothing compared to global pontificating! Imagine a world like the endless loop of duct tape commercials with nanny tips advising us to fear all things from Mother Nature, mother's milk, Mother Jones and other mothers until we get the "all clear" from them!

If this t'were all that the t'wittest had tweeted, t'would be bad enough. But this same EROS (see above) is now available to both the EDs and their enablers...the world's deliberatest grating body i.e. the Congress of the Untied (sic) States. Take Dash Helmet Pelosi, who recently made landfall in Des Moines and mistook it for Impeachment, or Mitch Maligned McConnell, who took the last eight years to finally declare that it will take the next eight years to figure out if he can retire in eight years. And Maximum Waters who is just revolting (sic). And then we have "The Donald" (a name taken to distinguish him from just "A" Donald) known fondly as a piece of tweet. And finally, there is AOC who is actually OOC. These enablers are able to evade evasion, confuse confusion, steal stealusion, corrupt corruption, bribe bribuption, forget every forgetshun, and accuse us all of not being 'their' people. The ability of the aristocracy to steal from the EDs has never been greater. Government has promised the EDs endless entitlements for endless time, and for endless reelection. And it's been retweeted, so it must be so. One side thinks only of food and the other thinks not at all.

But how can "they" do this to us? Well, for that, we have to thank Twitter, which was built for twits, hence the name. It allows every Dashington/Dancerton/Princeton and Vixton to share what passes for meaning to other EDs who retweet it to yet other EDs until we reach the ultimate point of "SCREW-ED". Tweeting is inversely correlated to relevance. We know this because either God does not have an account (unlikely), chooses not to use it (possible) or is going to give one nuclear tweet during Armageddon, ending it all which, by the way, was foreseen by Nostradamus in his 42nd quatrain: "And a sound of chirping will be heard. From the mushroom-like clod (sic) will come the wrath of a thousand bytes of sand fleas. The horde will be Category 3 while growing to Category 5 before coming ashore as a light rain in many colors. And from the mouth of the horde will come a line of moisturizers that will cause all to cry for their crepey skin in despair."

So then how can we get out of this end of days, end of hours, and end of minutes Verizon calling plan that God will hath wrought when he sees his Twitter bill? Who do we have to kill and whom can we blame it on?

The answer is the grid! Electricity is the enemy! Kill the grid! Kill it for six months! No power, no tower, no shower, and the reign of EDs and Governmentingtons comes crashing down in a flurry of angry curses in the darkness—because no one knows how to work candles anymore. No Twitter? No Twit! Without access, the EROS of idiots comes screaming back to three meters. And then, we will all know whom to avoid. And the EDs will die a natural, unnoticed, untweeted and peaceful death! And once again, Darwin *Uber Alles*…and to all a good night! QED.

An add-on observation about today's conversation:

A most amazing thing has happened these days to conversation. A "drone" of personal assertion seems to have replaced what used to be an exchange of ideas or information. Today, when someone says, "Boy! It's windy today", it is apparently a call for the rest of us to deliver a personal vignette about some aspect of wind. Any aspect. It need have no relation to the original concept of "windy" or "today". Even if you work as a wind tunnel engineer and your "take" is completely irrelevant to the idea that prompted the statement about today's wind, it's ok to launch into it. If it's about you and about your experience, and you can use the word wind, then have at it! This seems to be the new normal.

Embedded in these exchanges are personal reports about things only the speaker can know. In the Navy these reminiscences are called sea stories and their relevance is zero to everyone except the person telling the story. These personal revelations may have little to do with the conversational thread either. It just so happens that the looseness of the opening topic seems to be combined with a ritualistic round robin of those who are within range of the conversation. After a comment about something maybe windy, it is "just your turn to talk". Not only is it your turn to talk, but even if you have nothing to say about wind in particular, you can apparently tell a story where you are the hero and everyone you spoke to or interacted with are complete idiots. This is punctuated with "so *rriiiiigggghhht*", and "Well, there's that". This pattern of transmission seems to be perfectly acceptable. At the end of two "rounds" of exchanges, it is possible to change the topic from wind, but there are limits. Food, wine, and "experiential things" like Disneyland, my day at work by the hour, and plane flights are solid go-tos.

In addition, there is really no requirement to listen anymore because you aren't expected to say anything that relates to anything said before. When it *isn't* your turn to talk, you can look at your phone and wait to talk again.

There are additional patterns.

You are allowed to repeat the same things hourly that you said before. However, these can't be in the exact same form. They can, however, be a different point about your heroism mentioned earlier. These interjections are prefaced by "That's what I was saying before". Questions are avoided because they are seen as a "trigger" that serves to send the speaker into a self-defensive rant about why you are not being nice. In addition, no matter how inane a question your response is "that's a good question."

1. No matter how arcane the subject, you should have a story in your hip pocket ready to go. When you become a professional you will be able to text stories about texting stories.

2. Don't forget the ubiquitous terms like "awesome," "excellent", "perfect", and "I get it" and be sure to catalogue all your various run-ins with lesser mortals. If you watch any live TV, it is filled with this stuff and should help immensely. If you work in a service job and you ask a question like "Do you want soup or salad?" and the answer is "salad" you are required to declare one of the four terms above. "Awesome" works. This applies to checking into hotels, talking with garage mechanics and landscapers, or any restaurant exchange.

3. If you are a member of the media you should not speak as though anyone except other people in the media are listening. This is helpful advice because no one is. They are on their phones and just paused on your channel on their way to the Kardashians. This is why

ratings are down. Do not despair. At first chance, switch to the Food Network. It's all about that bass, just that bass(sic). Think about it…

Facebook has become the backdrop for these conversations. I am constantly surprised when anyone dies of cancer or we discover that we do not have humans on Mars, because you can find all sorts of people on Facebook who have cured cancers and who are in a capsule headed to Mars. With Facebook, we get to continue our personal conversation with the masses. After all, isn't everyone just waiting to get our "take"? Some of us even write a book of essays! Imagine the chutzpah of that!

30.

A Reflection in Time

"Did you see the news today?" she asked.

"No," I replied. "I've been too busy. What's new?"

"Well, we now seem to have access to what they call a time mirror. It allows us to see ourselves both as we were in the past and as we shall be in the future."

"Who is 'they'? You mean someone just invented it?"

"Not exactly. Someone *will* invent it. But apparently when they invented this mirror and shone it back into our time, it turned out we can see *them* as well as they can see *us*."

"So, if I look in our bedroom mirror it would be like the mirror image being able to see me? I had not thought about that before."

"Yes, in a way. We have never thought of the "image" in the mirror as being anything other than our reflection. I suppose that if the image were conscious, it would see us as a reflection as well. It plays hell with reality. Apparently this image just appeared on a PC at MIT. There was no communication, just a video feed, if you will."

"But I thought time travel was impossible. Are we saying now that we can communicate with the future? Is that not *like* time travel?"

"I don't know. We have always experienced some ability to go into the past through film that was shot at an earlier time. We could obviously only go back as far as video film existed. And we were limited by only being able to see whatever the camera saw. Obviously, we cannot communicate with the film to change it. But if we could have had a live video feed from the past we might have been able to send messages."

"Wouldn't sending these video messages defeat the principles of relativity and the speed of light? I seem to recall that light defines time. But you are saying that it's like light itself has gone back in time and is somehow illuminating past events and future events 'at the same time'. How can that be?"

"Well let's say that space is fantastically curved and forms a cylinder. Let's say that you shone a light out into space and the beam travelled around the curved space until it illuminated your back. Let's say that process took thirty minutes. Then imagine that I had a device—call it a mirror—that could allow me to see you with the same light you were shining. I would see you with the very same light you were using in the past. And yet, this device also allows you to see me seeing you."

"So, you are using my past light but also some future light as well. It sounds like the light may be in two different times at the same place. Maybe it's like this. If light from a star were to be traveling in space, and if I had a time mirror, I could see it as it was a million years ago as well as I see it today. In fact, isn't this what a telescope does? When I look at a star with my naked eye, I see its light as it was a million of my years ago. When I look at the star through a telescope however, I am looking back in time based on how powerful the telescope is. I can see the same light at two different times but in the same place. If the telescope were powerful enough, I could see life on another planet.

But this mirror you describe seems to be able to allow for the planet I am looking at to see me in return. I can sort of understand that; but how is it possible for me to see my *own planet*'s past or future where both of our real times seem to coincide in the mirror? Further, why are we the first in "time" to see this mirror? If it has existed for many years into the future, then I would think that prior "times" to this one would have experienced the mirror and we would have known about its existence for some time now."

"Just suppose when we die that we could experience all previous times at "the same time". This is to say that we can zoom in on any time in the past and see exactly what was happening. And here's how they would be able to see us also. They would only need for us to be dea…""

APPENDIX TO CHAPTER 30

Time

Time is a perplexing concept. Certain things cause our understanding of time. Entropy increases. We see differences. We perceive movement. So time seems in some sense to "pass" as in first this was "here" and now it is "there".

Imagine that you had a pen in your pocket. Imagine that the pen was created at a manufacturing plant in your town. Imagine further that you could hover above the US and see every second that the pen has spent "alive". From the moment it was created that pen has traveled down an assembly line, it has been packaged, it has been driven to a store, and finally it was purchased by you. Assume that there is a permanent "photo" of that pen, a visible "pen" everywhere that pen had been, and you can see them all at the same time. So, you see a 3D solid line made up of millions of spatial positions of that pen. That pen's entire "life" is knowable to you now because of this special representation. You can "see" the life*time* of the pen.

But there is no elapsed time at all while you are viewing the pen's "life". You can see its whole life at the same "instant". Every location. Everything that has ever happened to that pen is visible to you right now, all at the same time. And it takes you no time to view it because it is all right there.

Now, imagine that instead of a pen, it is your life that you are viewing and that from "above the earth" (maybe in the afterlife) every position you have ever had in every location you were ever in could be viewed at the same time. Imagine that a dead relative, for example, is viewing her life in this way. Their life "in the afterlife" would take place in zero time. Their whole life can be seen. Every instant. Everywhere they were and all at once. Imagine that you could observe the entire universe this way. There would be "no time" because you would know everything at all times at "once" (now).

Suppose when we die, we are able to see all the lives of all people who lived before us, and those who will live after us. Could that happen? That is an interesting question. I think the answer is no. Otherwise, time would be like an MP3 file. Time would exist from its beginning until its end…all right now. If you were able to perceive the entire MP3, you would be able to see all things that had ever happened, or ever would happen, "now". It would be an MP3 of the universe from birth to death. This might be how God might see it.

Time is "created" by motion, state change, or the ordering of thoughts. Imagine if there was no motion. This effectively is a photograph. For those images trapped in the photograph, there is no time. There is only that instant. If there were no motion but there was a state change i.e. something decayed (entropy), there would be time. And famously from Descartes, if I think, then the notion of having one thought follow another thought would also "create" time. Therefore, time does not "exist" but comes into being because of these properties.

There are kinds of "time". There is the passage of time when one is engaged in a work of love or in an activity that one is "lost in". Then there is the time passing twenty minutes before class lets out. There is the time waiting for a birth and a time waiting for a death. There is time when one is competing in sports and whether one is ahead or behind in points, and there is the passage of time when one is in pain. Human physiology, emotion, and sensory experiences of time exist as distortions of the "reality" of a clock version of time.

Let's look more closely at the more familiar concepts of time. Why might successful business people behave as though time is often more valuable than money? Because there are those who feel certain that they can "control" their future time. The greater this sense of control, the more important the use of time becomes. If one believes that the future is deterministic, then the use of time in the present is a crucial necessity for that determination.

Suppose the biggest difference between successful and unsuccessful people is related to how they use time. Since the mid-80s, people have used time to do the following:

1. Changing what to do with time: software/hand-held device sales/telecom/the net
2. Making time more valuable (Amazon)
3. Making more time (medicine and services)
4. Wasting time (government)

Just suppose that the people who are going to be the most effective in life are those who manage time the best. In order to "manage" time, it is important to break time into two parts:

1. Reactive time
2. Planned time

Reactive time is the time that must be spent without any preparation. This would be time spent recovering from an accident or time based on the demands of others. It is time that is imposed on us by the environment.

Planned time is time that is anticipated by the planner. If planned time is successful, the amount of reactive time may be reduced dramatically. Planned time, however, might not be effective. One just might plan badly or plan too much to do. Some people will say they can maximize planned time by multitasking. Maybe. This may just be another way of saying that they drop their papers as they get into the wrong elevator while cutting off the call with their boss on their cell phone.

When all of the young people in the 90s and early 2000s were playing forty-seven instruments, taking twelve classes, skating, playing soccer, being the editor of the high school newspaper and doing community service, they did so because their parents believed that this was the way to succeed. The parents planned and they "reacted". They reacted by using every free moment to "do something". The problem is that the most important skills children have to master are mastered in planned time. Parents and schools do the planning. Children do the reacting until it is too late. When the kids graduate from college, there is suddenly no one planning their every minute. They become disoriented. Becoming good at planned time is a crucial skill.

If you examine the things that people who continually have problems all have in common, one of them is an inability to make reactive time effective because they confuse it with planned time. In all relationships, it is necessary to give and receive planned time. Long distance romances do not work because there is no time to have common experiences. Marriages fail because the ways that the spouses choose to use planned time are ineffective. Planned time is critical and necessary for all relationships. It is time with a purpose. It is time with intent and deliberateness. This is the most powerful time there is. When you examine differences between successful and unsuccessful people, you can see that much of that difference is how they use their time.

Newly married couples start life with planned time. They plan together rather than separately. Then they have children. The world becomes much more oriented to reactive time. After the years of raising children, it becomes planned time again.

Time has many facets. Much of it is based on our biology. It really is an illusion caused by our brain's interpretation of events. Yet it allows us to meet each other in the same three-dimensional space much "later" than "now". Suppose there is another way to interpret time. What might it be?

Suppose you had started with the last essay in this book and worked backwards to page one. Would you have had a different experience? Why didn't it occur to you to do so? Would it feel the same? Would you think the same way as you do now? What if you just skip around?

Suppose that you could tell your past self today how you could have avoided that partner, that jail sentence, or that job loss. Alternatively, suppose you could advise your past self to do something different and positive or to confirm a decision that went right for you. How would you do it?

As it turns out, you can and you should. Take a moment each day and reflect on the past. Tell your past self exactly what needed to be done at that moment. Focus first on those crossroad decisions you had to make. Tell your past self everything you now know. Make it as clear and as emotionally strong as you can. Repeat this often for the biggest turning points.

Suppose you started a journal. You could list markers when you needed to know an answer. Later, when you re-read your journal, you can send that message. Your journal is both a place for reflection and for original work. In the end, it will represent your psychology far more completely than anything else you can attempt. It also gives future generations real insight into the depth of your humanity.

If you start now, then you will "know" that your future self will have told your present self that this is a great idea because you will now be helped by your future self to make the best decisions now and have a better life.

31.

What If we are all gene-iouses

What determines your future? Is it God's will, is it fate (predestined karma from a prior life), is it determinism (the universe began and because of how it has functioned everything you do is whatever the universe has evolved to at this moment), or is it free will (the ability to do otherwise)? Just suppose it were something else.

What if your future is not caused by determinism, by you, or by the prime movers of fate and God? Suppose it is caused by decisions your genes make. What if a human is simply a way for a gene to make another and better gene? What if gene networks are responsible for the idea of "mind"? What if genes have their own consciousness that we cannot detect or that they hide from us?

Suppose that humans are incidental to the universe. Suppose all the things "we" think "we" are doing are really being done by clever genes that operate behind the scenes.

Genes are packages of DNA and DNA is composed of bases and bases are composed…etc. All of that isn't important. But suppose at the level of the gene there is an emergent consciousness. We know genes make proteins. The process is complex but they operate like a kind of software (in my mind). They also control cell growth and division. Suppose that evolution was not accidental. Suppose certain genes decided to "tweak" various humans. Maybe they banded together in certain chromosomes to change how the chromosome would function.

Genes are located inside chromosomes that are inside cell nuclei. They are in almost all cells. If they were conscious and decided to act in concert, humans would be along for the ride. Imagine if all that "we" know is only what genes have allowed us to know. "We" have mapped the human genome and know that there are maybe 20k – 25k of protein coding genes. We don't really know the exact number because the work genes do is still cloudy.

What if genes are using us to modify them so they are more effective? As "we" discover more and more diseases that may have genetic roots could it really be that genes that are "instructing us" to repair them? What if a gene has caused me to write this introduction to essay 33 so that other genes in other humans can become aware of what the state of genetic art truly is?

Suppose charisma is simply one person's genes appealing to a lot of people's genes? Suppose schizophrenia is just a kind of genetic revolt and the reason we can't cure it is because genes have a reason for this experiment to run its course.

What if your genes are controlling you at this moment? What if genes have a hierarchy? There are noble genes, and peasant genes, and messenger (RNA) influenced genes and yet each of these genes has free will to work or not work. Their mission is to grow better genes through human control.

What if the 1% difference in human genetics is because the governmental genes are located in different spots? We can all imagine certain people who have a governmental butt gene. Maybe others have a governmental karaoke gene or a governmental nostril gene.

What if this were true? What else might occur to you that this could mean?

APPENDIX TO CHAPTER 31

What if?
What If You Had A Third Arm?
(Or an additional "whatever")

Suppose you had a third arm coming out of your chest. Or suppose it stuck out of your back. What would be different? This kind of question affords a real opportunity to test creativity and intuition. Before you read on, run through some of the first things that come to mind.

In order to get at a question like this, it is helpful to begin with general categories that require the use of human arms. For example:

Playing instruments

Certain sports

Operating machines

General activities

Climbing ladders

Driving a car

Hanging pictures

Feeding babies from bottles/Carrying triplets/making love

In the case of playing instruments, you might imagine certain music that could be played with three arms that can't be played with two. It might even be music we have not heard before. Imagine a saxophone with two bells. One hand plays the common notes and the other two hands play different harmonies or melodies. Imagine a three-armed drummer.

In the case of sports, swimming and gymnastics would have to be redesigned. Golf, too. Perhaps only skating, darts, and soccer would remain the same. Imagine a baseball player with two gloves, or a pitcher who threw R, L or M. It might also be easier to do pull-ups.

Computer keyboards could be far more employable if three hands were on them. Computer games could also need to be redesigned. Stick shift cars might be easier to drive. Carrying things around the house would be more efficient. You can have two bags of groceries and still open the door.

Climbing ladders could be safer because one additional arm is available to carry the paint, bucket, etc. while the other two arms climb the ladder.

Different ancient weapons and tactics would likely have been invented since two arms could thrust a spear while one arm swung a sword or held a shield.

Would the word ambidextrous even exist?

The reason to consider silly ideas like this is because, in the course of doing so, I often arrive at dependencies or integrations that I have not thought about before. Doing this experiment forces one to create categories. It forces one to "imagine things". By starting with an outlandish premise, you can free yourself for outlandish conclusions. Imagine the fashion industry where today blouses and jackets close in front, what might clothes look like with a third arm?

We don't often see asymmetric appendages in nature. Why is that? Why do we have mostly two or four of these sensory input devices? It is easy to say that's "just the way it is". Maybe Darwin was right: if other prehensile appendages ever existed, they were lost because they were ineffective. Maybe. But what else could account for it? I can think of several things.

What If You Knew What Everyone Was Thinking?

If you were able to know what everyone was thinking, what would be different?

1. Lying would not exist as a word or concept.

2. There would be no government jobs needed in intelligence gathering.

3. There would be no language translators.

4. There would be no need for teachers. We would access the minds of anyone who had learned a specific thing or task.

5. There would be no need for instruction manuals. The people's minds that designed the process would be accessible.

6. Situational awareness would be at its maximum. It would still not be at 100% because things would happen that no one knew or would have known.

7. No one could physically "hide".

8. Crime would be disrupted before it could happen.

9. Some short-term view of the future would be certain. (What stocks people will buy today, what people are likely to die, what people are likely to be born, etc.)

10. There would be jobs reading books no one has read, experimenting with new things that no one has thought of, and accessing/replacing certain memories of people who are dying.

11. But lest we make a mistake—just because I know what you are thinking does not mean I can act on it. If you are expecting me to open the door for you, I could still refuse. I would immediately, however, know the effect.

12. Suppose two people know the same thing but at different levels of detail: would one *overwrite* the other? What about two different people who have both been treated differently by someone? Whose view prevails on that person's personality, or do they both prevail?

Imagine how close this environment is to where we are right now. From Google and Wikipedia, we know what "everyone *has* known" about something. We have a static version (blog, Facebook) of knowing what everyone who writes down or records his or her thoughts has experienced recently.

Transparency, though, is a double-edged sword. If everyone knows everyone's cards, then we will all short the guy with the weakest poker hand. Second, if we are all hedged the same way and all act the same way, then we are all dependent in the same way. Certain markets would seize up because there would be no clearing price. Everyone would know what the seller's cost is for the item and then it is a matter of how much profit the market will allow. Would groupthink exist or would there still be people who created new ideas and then these became part of everyone's thoughts? Where would our ideas end and everyone else's begin? Would the world be a better place in some way if we all knew what each other knows or thinks?

What If Ethics Are Not as Hard as The Philosophers Think

For thousands of years, people have behaved badly. Defeating the ability of one person to mislead another person is becoming more impossible each day. There are fake news stories, outright lies, deliberate attempts to mislead others, and a willingness to do anything that we deem to be "right".

Suppose that there are two tests that one can apply to decide if what you are about to do is "right action", as the Buddhists would say. For example:

1. The first test is to ask: "If everyone in my company, or in my family, or my school, or everyone in the world would all do what I am about to do, would we all be better off?" This is a version of Kant's categorical imperative: *I should act so that my actions conform to a principle of such value that it would improve society if it were adopted as a universal law.* Not acting should be interpreted in the same way as acting. I should not act in a way in which I would not want others to act.

2. What does this look like? It is like asking us all to behave as we would want others to behave so that the results of our actions are a better state for all. If I lie to Congress and everyone else was to lie to Congress, would we be better off? If I were to use my company's

copy machine for personal purpose and everyone else did as well, would the company be better off? If I were to sign a document on behalf of a customer because I "know" they would not have wanted to come back and others did the same, would people be able to trust me or others as far as judgment?

3. The second test is "I should behave as though my private thoughts in conversations, negotiations, and discussions would be simultaneously directly aired on national television for all to comment on." There might then be a national, simultaneous voting referendum on whether I behaved ethically or not. Everyone would know the nature of my intent. That would certainly help decide if I were behaving within a certain spirit of fairness.

Neither of these two statements is absolute. There are scenarios where it might be necessary to take a life in order to save a life, or where harming an individual is preferable to harming an entire group. Knowing that a behavior is unethical (as in the case where an authority figure has asked you to do something that does not satisfy the conditions above) is different from the choice of whether to behave in a certain way or not. The obvious dilemma exists when you have been made an offer that you can't refuse. If the alternative is losing your life, the life of another or breaking the ethical code, most people will break the code.

There are various philosophical or ethical dilemmas that are raised in college philosophy classes. (For example: You are on a train that cannot stop, and you control a switch that can divert the train. If you do nothing, the train will kill five workmen on the track. If you divert the train to another track, it will kill a single person who is presently crossing that track. What do you do?) In these cases, the choice is between the deaths of many versus the deaths of a few. But it is your choice. Do you let the universe happen as it is, or do you take responsibility to intervene?

The ultimate, ethical dilemma might be whether one should choose to save oneself or sacrifice oneself for others. While most of us would act with intent in favor of family and perhaps friends, there are many other instances where people will jump into a river, throw themselves on a hand grenade, or give their life for a child who is not their own. It is not clear that there isn't some hard-wired human capacity for ethical altruism that takes over in certain circumstances.

In every culture there is a "Do unto others as you would have them do unto you" expression. It eliminates most of what passes for unethical behavior, except for sociopaths and psychopaths and other damaged people who cannot adequately contemplate the consequences of their actions. There is also the idea of doing unto others as *they* would want you to do unto them. In one case, you are guessing if they like what you like and in the other case you are trying to comply with their view of the world.

What about day-to-day ethics of the common person? There is always the case of whether I should be entitled to steal medicine from a drug store for my dying wife if I am too poor to buy it. Or the case of running a red light when I am alone, or when I am driving my injured son to the hospital. However, if everyone behaved in these same ways, there is a problem. Does the standard decline over time? If the "right" to break the law is up to me to judge, then does this not risk more and more lawbreakers, as judgment does not result in consequence? If my act is self-determined, then is it also my responsibility to be self-limiting? Suppose it was. How do we think that would play out?

What If IT Departments Actually Destroyed Shareholder Value?

Anyone who works in an IT department will take umbrage with this statement. IT departments destroy shareholder value. The reasoning, though, is straightforward. Let's say you are in an industry where there is a great deal of competition and everyone has her own IT department. Now, let's say that the industry begins to consolidate. If I must convert the files of another company to mine as a consequence of an acquisition, I will bid less for their company because of the cost of conversion. The more proprietary the target company's software, the less I will pay the shareholders of the purchased company and the more their market value is therefore destroyed.

However, let's imagine that you are in an industry where everyone has outsourced his data to the same industry consultant. If there is an acquisition, the consultant will repoint the data table flags and all the accounts and transactions will virtually flow through to the purchaser in an instant. This is not costless but far less costly than individual field mapping and conversions and testing. Having one standard that is employed everywhere is the least costly.

The conclusion might therefore be that IT standardization could be a great benefit to the country. In a sense, Microsoft accomplished this very thing. We all use the same file protocols, the same operating system, and the same screen alignments. This is worldwide. Apple hardware is the same. In this case, if I own the software I can create anything I want and be able to send it or translate it to you no matter where you are, as long as you have the same software.

There are other reasons why IT standardization could change the business landscape. There are interesting places where using a government-mandated system could effectively nationalize industries like banking in the US. In banking, there are places where federal regulators have ordered a single method for submitting data. The Dodd-Frank Act Stress Testing Report 14A of balance sheet assets, liabilities, income, losses, and capital is an example of these reports. These consolidations, templates, and requirements could expand to various systems including national trading systems and account opening systems. This would allow the government to do more analysis of all the money movement in the US without using the BSA/AML process unique to each bank. The government with little effort can cause all data submissions to be uniform, which would decrease banking industry costs for sure.

Once again, in the case of an acquisition, having the same report formats and links would make the costs of conversion less. This could also apply to any industry overseen by federal agencies. The temptation will become very strong.

What If US Presidents Could Be From Here and There

Suppose you did not have to be born in the United States to be president. What could that mean? First, it opens the door to former presidents of other countries to run for office in the US. They have a record that is reviewable, they have experience with foreign leaders, they have dealt with "their opposition", and they are not beholden to anyone here in the same way as our politicians.

Suppose that the recent presidents of the UK, Canada, Australia, New Zealand, or perhaps a person with significant status like Henry Kissinger or Prince William were eligible. Suppose Prince Charles could have been president so many years ago. Suppose that this were at least possible.

Imagine how foreign heads of state might behave if they were "running" for their next job as head of the US. Imagine how much more enchanting American politics would be if one had to cater a bit to those who might succeed you. Would the US be better off? Would the world be better off? Would this be the start of a kind of world government?

There are many issues with all conceptual changes to the status quo. First would be the nationalists. They would argue that people would be raised up in foreign countries precisely to get elected in the US and then begin to dismantle our prosperity. This is the "Once a Brit, always a Brit" argument.

Second is the argument that these "foreigners" would "advantage" their native countrymen in trade or defense, etc. This is the militarist argument.

Third would be the fear that all cabinet members would also come from the president's country. The US would in effect be "taken over". However, this is really no different than the way the cabinet is chosen today.

Fourth would be the fear that once the president learned all our secrets, she would be a threat to the US when she returned home. This is non-trivial, but could be dealt with by perhaps "swapping" one of our former presidents with theirs. All secrets would then be exposed.

This is not a plea for a world government. It is simply a chance to bring a more experienced and already vetted group of prospective presidents before the people.

I really don't imagine that most of you reading this will find it a favorable way to govern. I accept that, but just suppose…

32.

It's Not What You Know, It's What You Say

Neophyte: "Are we having an exam next week?"

Post Modern Plato: "As a 'situated being', I must confess that I have no true knowledge. In fact, I know no truth and have no knowledge that is absolute. I have told the class the exam narrative, but I cannot shed my situatedness to tell you the absolute truth of the answer you seek."

Neophyte: "Are you saying, then, that from your perspective only it may be true that we are having an exam, but it is not an *absolute* truth?"

Post Modern Plato: "There is no truth except that which we declare through language. Because language has no fixed meaning (only my meaning), you are free to impose multiple meanings on my words. Therefore, neither of us holds *the* truth, only *our* truth."

Neophyte: "Since any statement that applies to all people at all times cannot exist, then there can't be an exam next week because it would apply to all of us at all times during the exam. What if I impose this meaning on your words, that there *won't* be an exam next week? Whose relative truth is 'better' yours or mine?

Post Modern Plato: "Both truths are contingent. Neither one is better."

Neophyte: "But *that* statement must also be a contingent truth. And I therefore disagree with that statement as well. You are saying there will be an exam next week and I am saying there won't because it is impossible for you to assert an absolute truth. It is also impossible for me to assert an absolute truth, so if neither of our truths are better, then it does not matter which one I choose."

Post Modern Plato: "Covfefe, you don't have to make the perfect choice, you just have to be 100% committed."

Neophyte: "But since there is no innate human nature but only that which has been socially implanted, what does commitment mean? And if I say I am committed to not studying for the exam because we are not having it, does the nature of my commitment have any meaning?

Post Modern Plato: "What the hell does that mean?"

Neophyte: "That is precisely my point. If your class fundamentally has no meaning then isn't it a conflict to be teaching the meaning of meaninglessness?

Post Modern Plato: "What are you majoring in?"

Neophyte: "Economics."

Post Modern Plato: "You have made an important contribution to this conversation by effectively stripping reason from humanistic concerns."

Neophyte: "You taught us that. So, no exam?"

APPENDIX TO CHAPTER 32

General College Education vs. Experience vs. a Specific College Education

It is a simple tautology that more education is better. After all, there is a fantastic correlation between future success and a college degree. But the idea of a "degree" has changed, and the ability it confers today is less clear.

Historically, experience was often of less value than education. This was true no matter what country you were in. In China, the best way to rise in economic stature was by passing government exams.

Things changed in the West, however, as increases in product complexity meant welders, plumbers, and electricians were able to maintain middle class buying power by experience. The powers of the guilds and crafts were awesome.

Then, the world changed again. Computers made massive changes in the way routine tasks could be accomplished. This brought great pressure to bear on experience and general education. If you were not part of the tech-savvy workers, you began to see the demand for your degree or labor diminish. Perhaps the only exceptions to this are the legal profession, therapists, and clergy.

What are we to make of higher education vs. experience today? Does education have value if it is not relevant? It would be easy to make the economic argument that degrees that require large debt but have no job prospects are expensive illusions. Is this the end of the Renaissance person?

One of the interesting things over the last twenty years of teaching leadership to newly minted college graduates is the notion of what is a fact and what is a belief. Opinions have become important substitutes for facts. A person's "take" is now a sacred artifact. Everyone is special and everything everyone says is special. There is no child who is not a genius, or the best in the world at something. There is no distinction between knowledge and belief. They have all been told so.

Both parents and schools have created a "belief over knowledge" culture. Students are allowed/forced to take belief classes that in many cases mirror a professor's notion of what *should* be true. And because the exams are about what was "learned", it is these beliefs that hold sway. This is obviously not the case in hard sciences like engineering or mathematics. They are knowledge and not belief based precisely because everyone can perform the same operation, or design the same structure, and get a reproducible result.

A college education may not be in demand much longer. Specific majors of course will be. Experience that is valuable will also be in demand. People educated in majors that are in demand, or have experiences that are in demand, become the supply. It is *they* who will earn the money to further the demand for their skills.

Suppose however that education's actual value is how well it confers an ability to distinguish between knowledge and belief. Skepticism is important. If a person has absolutely no skepticism, then they cannot know *why* they know something or believe something.

Why does it matter? It matters because knowledge (and the "Why is this true?") leads to understanding, which leads to the ability to do things with intent (right or wrong), which leads to discovery, which leads to value, which ultimately leads to choice. And choice, if you think about it in education, may be what counts most. Just suppose at any moment you had every choice you "wanted". You effectively would have no volitional constraint on your action. If you truly had every choice, then the "rules" of the universe would be integrated in such a way such that they would work for your benefit. Learning to create choice might be the best thing higher education can do. But what choices are we building? *Does anyone think they still have choice?*

Education probably started as experiential. A hunter or gatherer would teach people what they had done to reach a better answer to a problem. Over time, tradesmen, soldiers, farmers, and politicians shared these "effective experiences". The relationship between a snake and a bite and venom and death was "known" by experience. This kind of knowing has returned today and it is equally important for survival. What was merely discrete information has now become integrated knowledge. This is where value is today.

This new kind of knowledge dwarfs the value of experiential information. The essence of knowledge does not lie in parsing information into "facts" anymore. It lies in an ability to integrate information into an outcome that others would be able to replicate if they used the same approach. So, if you achieve a breakthrough (Einstein), it comes from *integrating* information.

What does this "integrating" look like? After twenty years of seeing college graduates, I would offer this:

1. Certain students are integrated in their understanding and generally relativists in their beliefs. Perhaps they were integrated before they went to school. I can't say. Perhaps they integrate because of their classmates. This is not clear, either. But the difference between these students and the rest is enormous. In an interview, if you asked a standard student who majored in economics what their preferred economic theory is, they will choose one (likely but not always from the last classes they can remember) and talk about that theory's principles. They will answer the question with a single answer because they have been trained to do so. However, an integrated person will understand the question as an invitation to integrate more than just one idea. They will see that the "best economic theory" depends on the state of civilization, its moment in history, its endurance through time, etc. They will compare economic theory that worked in ancient Rome, but would have failed in Britain during the Industrial Revolution. At the very least, they will compare and contrast several theories over time because they won't

see a single answer as sufficient. They see the question for what it is. It's not multiple choice—it's essay.

2. Certain students have been exposed to a more complex view of the world. Thus, they are integrating *more* of what there is to integrate. For example, let's assume that one is learning basic math. Some colleges teach you addition, but on the exam ask you to do a problem in subtraction. You may have never seen it, you have never examined the idea, but the expectation is that the approach will occur to you during the exam. A slightly more complex example would be that you are taught supply and demand curves and are taught that their intersection is the price that clears the market. On the exam, you would be expected to discover that you are able to add demand and supply curves of like product to calculate a new price. The idea of adding "graphs" must occur to you on the exam.

3. There is a premium at certain schools for original work. Merely reiterating another's view is normally insufficient. Even the way that things are categorized is not sacrosanct. If one decides for the purpose of making a point, that animals are better divided into only two categories--those that can kill humans and those that can't kill humans—then the conversation is encouraged to go from there. This is a great simplification, but it speaks to the arbitrary nature or categorization. It also speaks to a new way that of categorizing things that is more easily understood than the standard kingdom, phylum, class, etc. If you ask in an interview how poverty might be solved, there is a better chance you will hear something you have not considered yourself from a person who has integrated. They may even suggest that the manner in which you have asked the question can be more helpfully restated so that you actually get a better answer.

4. In all universities, there is learning among students. Diversity of thought matters. This, however, is not simply a matter of difference. Having a different "take" is insufficient. Having a different belief is insufficient except that it exists. It is the ability to recognize patterns that matter. If you have never sat in a class where a student answered a question that left you in awe of their grasp of the subject, then you won't be able to relate to patterns. But it is the ability to recognize patterns that allows you to not major in degrees that no longer matter.

Here's an idea (and an attempt at original work). Just suppose for the moment that what has been written above is true. Suppose that greater integration matters a great deal. Suppose that we think of this work like the health of our bodies. Suppose that the harder we train, the better our trainer, and the higher our ability to do original work, the better our *integrated* health will be.

Years ago, a man named John Watson famously declared: *"Give me a dozen healthy infants, well-formed, and my own specified world to bring them up in and I'll guarantee to take any one at random and train him to become any type of specialist I might select--doctor, lawyer, artist, merchant-chief, and, yes, even beggar man and thief, regardless of his talents, penchants, tendencies, abilities, vocations, and race of his ancestors. I am going beyond my facts and I admit it, but so have the advocates of the contrary and they have been doing it for many thousands of years."* –John B. Watson, *Behaviorism*, 1930

This is behaviorism, and it is exactly the place that we have come to in American higher education. Professors "believe" that they can "educate" the youth of this country by providing a stimulus and getting a response. Often, the response is merely agreement.

A generation of baby boomer parents have interfered with integration and made children into micro-belief systems. When family relationships disintegrate, when economic policy fails, when the kids graduate from college and there is no "there", there, it is because we have taught non-integrated beliefs. We have taught only opinion and worse, opinion with purpose.

So what should we expect from education? What could it achieve? How do we get choices? What is necessary (not necessarily nice)?

1. First, we should expect some basic integration of knowledge. This is value relevant. Being a productive member of society should be a minimum standard for college courses. These courses would create multiple foci. Note: These are only a few of the possibilities.

   a. Writing effectively in English

   b. Speaking (translation skill)

   c. Mathematics

   d. Computer operations

2. Able to exercise interpretive skills

   a. Integrating two different ideas into a viable synthesis

   b. Cause and Effect (ability to predict from a base)

   c. Awareness (in all aspects) and Skepticism

   d. Interpersonal skills (psychology)

3. Practical skills

   a. Law

   b. Risk Management (from cause and effect)

   c. The Way Things Work

   d. Medicine (practical)

4. Finally, we should pit the beliefs of schools and parents against each other to see which fits best with reality:

a. What condition is best? (religion, political belief, economic belief, environmental belief)

b. What future is best? (survival, happiness, choice, autonomy)

c. What process of change is best? (finance, government, social policy, self)

d. What education is best? (Be skeptical of this list)

This education merely gets someone to the place where they can function at some basic level. There is the process after college where building experiences is important. In business it is crucial to be able to manage people (preferably in multiple countries); it is helpful to speak a foreign language fluently (computer languages count). You have to be able to hire, fire, train, coach, pay, and promote people. This is a lot harder than it sounds. These early experiences are important—in many cases, even more important than grad school. They require an ability to integrate experience and education. Without a sound education based on skills that are in demand, there is nothing to integrate.

Being able to see patterns and integrate them is now the coin of the realm. Anything that does not focus students on these skills is not helpful. The value of integrating education and experience in leadership has become much more important. The ability to do adaptive work (work with no easy answers) is the path to senior management.

Just suppose that in order to graduate you had to prove that you had integrated education and experience. Suppose that you had to explain how the major you studied and the experience that you had with internships make you valuable to society. Who would hire someone like you and to do what.

In the end, college degrees have been degraded because so many people who cannot integrate complex concepts can still get a degree from somewhere. As a result, the degree does not matter as much as it used to.

Government funding, on the other hand, has made degrees more affordable to people who would not have gone to college. That is a good thing.

33.

What Did Dey Know and When Did Dey Know It?

LTJG Kaffee: Colonel Jessep! Did you order more Data?

Judge Randolph: You don't have to answer that question!

Col Jessep: I'll answer the question. You want answers?

LTJG Kaffee: I think I'm entitled to them.

Col Jessep: You want answers?

LTJG Kaffee: I want the Data set!

Col Jessep: You can't handle the Data set! Son, we live in a world that has Data and those Data have to be guarded by men with guns. Who's gonna do it? You? You, Lieutenant Weinberg? I have a greater responsibility than you can *possibly* fathom. You weep for missing Data, and you curse the programmers. You have that luxury. You have the luxury of not knowing what I know -- that missing Data, while tragic, probably saved lives; and my existence, while grotesque and incomprehensible to you, saves lives. You don't want the Data set because deep down in places you don't talk about at parties, you want me gathering Data, you need me gathering data! We use words like honor, code, loyalty. We use these words as the backbone of a life spent defending something, you use them as a punch line. I have neither the time, nor the inclination to explain myself to a man who rises and sleeps under the blanket of the very coding that I provide, and then questions the manner in which I provide that code! I'd rather you just said 'thank you', and went on your way. Otherwise I suggest you pick up a weapon, and stand a post. Either way, I don't give a damn what you think you are entitled to!

LTJG Kaffee: Did you order more Data?

Col Jessep: I did the job!

LTJG Kaffee: Did you order more Data?

Col Jessep: YOU'RE GODDAMN RIGHT I DID!!!!

With apologies to the movie A Few Good Men

APPENDIX TO CHAPTER 33
Data

In the era of fake news, even mathematical truths are being "managed". The idea that I can find something that supports what I believe is powerful. Even when I can't find "proof" it doesn't seem to matter because I can manipulate what is on the web to make a truth.

There is nothing new in statistical deception. What is new is the number of people who do not have the intellectual skill to determine if what they read is a deception. Let's look at something simple. Just suppose you wanted to find out how many Americans have an incurable and ongoing chronic disease. The National Health Council produces a number of 133 million people. The CDC says the number of adults with chronic diseases is actually 117 million people. Maybe the missing 16 million people in the CDC database are children. But if you go to the CDC's site and add up people by disease, you get the following:

Table IV - Americans with an incurable or ongoing chronic disease (source CDC)

HEART DISEASE	28,100,000
CANCER	22,900,000
DIABETES	32,193,000
DIGESTIVE	14,700,000
ARTHRITIS	57,900,000
PSYCHOLOGICAL	970,200
	156,763,200

It is one of the simplest data requests to get right and yet the difference is a third. That's a lot to miss by. Perhaps people have more than one disease and so they are counted twice. Maybe most of these people died this year and the numbers are actually far different. Or maybe even more people could have become sick. The point is, we don't know and without a great deal of effort we may not be able to know. Yet, the data is being collected. If any of it is true, it means that perhaps half of the US population has some form of significant impairment.

Stock return data also presents very interesting issues with data. The CRSP (Chicago data base) data go back to the 1920s. Total returns can be calculated for that period. Large cap stocks earned about a 12% return and small cap stocks earned a 17% return over this period. But almost no one held stocks for that many years. In addition, many of the companies that existed in the 1920s are gone. Many studies have used different total periods (total years studied) during this almost hundred years and different holding periods (typically 1,3,5,10,15, and 20 years). The results are very different, depending on which set of years is studied and which set of holding periods one uses. This allows for the ability to "pick" the desired return by using a subset of data. These subsets are crucial.

Let's take a simple example. This stock is deliberately very volatile to make the point. Let's say that you invest in a stock with the following one-year pricing:

Table V - Dataset of a volatile security	
JAN	$100
FEB	$125
MAR	$125
APR	$150
MAY	$120
JUN	$100
JUL	$120
AUG	$100
SEP	$125
OCT	$150
NOV	$130
DEC	$100

If you invested in January and sold in December, your annualized return is zero. This is the return that you would see from the fund. If you invested in April and sold in December, your annualized return is -22%. If you invested in January and sold in April, your annualized return would be 75%. This is why it is important to agree on the period and values of a data set. In this specific year, returns could have been wildly different, depending on when you bought and sold. This is obvious, but it is valuable to see it. This is what I call *data set deception*. Studies of the actual market suggest that if you want something like the 12% return that is listed in the real market, your holding period should be about fifteen years. In any fifteen-year period, you would not have lost money and in some periods you would have earned more than the 12% average. But this too, is cherry-picking that data to "see" a pattern that is random in the sense that there is nothing special about fifteen years.

Let's look at data from a visual perspective. You can easily deceive your audience just by changing the width of bars that you use. In these two charts, the data are the same, just drawn differently.

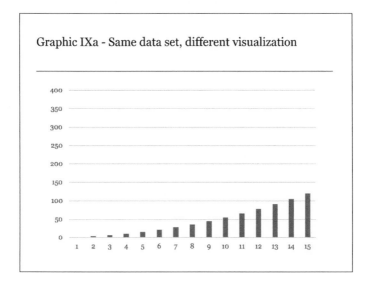

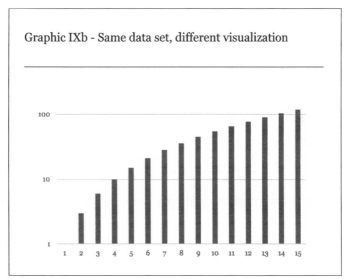

These charts look different. The lower chart looks like things are growing faster. All that I did was expand the lower chart to get the chart above. If you want the "story" to look great, use the bottom chart (sales up or numbers of clients up). If your story is bad, expand the graph without changing the data. Just make the bars wider.

Data is not just raw numbers; it is also the models that run the data. Earlier, I wrote that whoever controls the software wins. It is also true that whoever controls the model wins. If you think about Microsoft, for example, and the excel notion of "=SUM(x...y)", you see that the equals sign triggers all functions. While this may seem intuitive, it replaced the @SUM(x...y) from LOTUS 123. But it is arbitrary. The "way" you use the software is chosen for you. *You* have no choice. The method you employ, the output presentation, the process you use, etc., are all determined by someone else who had opinions. This is doubly true with models. Models follow biases. There are some statistical preferences that are taught in school, but in the end, the results can be very personal. One only has to look as far as the last court case to see how two modelers with the same data can come to two opposite conclusions.

Finally, let's talk about a critical issue that has people on all sides: climate change. It is a certainty that the climate is changing. It always has and always will. The important question is how and why.

It turns out that much of the debate is around data. The only data we have goes back to the middle 1700s. Is that enough? There are many issues with temperature data measurement over that period. Which instruments were used and what time of day were the readings taken? Did the measuring station move locations? Did new devices replace older ones? Was any data interpolated? Did every station on earth use the same process? Is it surface temperature or air temperature at altitude and are any of these readings influenced by structures in their proximity? Are the 1700s a good place to start? We can't know. It's the best we have.

Lots of data are missing. So researchers put data in. Whatever data you put in can influence what your results look like. There are conventions for data entry, including rejecting whole sections of data. Because of this, it makes data selection crucial for "proving" a point.

It is possible to assert that the temperature in the past fifty years has gradually gone up. Everyone agrees with that data and it's reliable. But how does this fifty-year period compare to all other fifty-year periods in the 8000 years that man has been the dominant species on the planet? We can't know that.

There are studies showing that CO^2 has increased and that human activity is probably the cause. Even that the sun is at fault or that readings are affected by nitrogen hidden in rocks. But just suppose we finesse the whole debate and agree that the climate is changing and that man is causing it. If we do *that*, we can then have a more interesting conversation.

Just suppose there is global warming. What do we think will happen? There will be lots of opinions, but in the end the whole issue comes down to a single question. Can mankind adapt? What about sea level rising? What about the loss of animal life? What about the loss of food? These are all important questions, but in the next fifty years many things will change and those changes will change the nature of the debate. It may be that single pills will be able to support life just fine. It may mean that we need to build dikes like they have in the Netherlands. They are all below sea level. It may mean that we need to create "weather" by changing technology. All these possibilities and the conversations that they lead to are what are interesting to me.

Suppose we just concede climate change, accept the idea, and then ask everyone to describe what he or she thinks is going to happen. Let's remember that we've had alar, swine flu, HIV, Avian flu, obesity, opioids, hurricanes, Y2K, the Cuban Missile Crisis, killer bees, Legionnaire's disease, Mediterranean fruit flies, Polar Vortexes, Ebola, Donald Trump, Nancy Pelosi, and many other scares that started bad and are still out there, but they are contained. Can we do the same with the climate?

34.

Whose Line Is It Anyway?

"Do you come here often?"

"Is that your best line?"

"If it isn't, can I buy you a drink anyway?"

"Can you give me something better than that line to react to?"

"How about if you Goggle me?"

"Are you one of *those* people?"

"How can I answer that if I don't know who *you* are?"

"So, are you saying you would be different depending on who I am?"

"Don't we all tailor the message to the audience?"

"You're not in marketing, are you?"

"Would you let me buy you a drink if I were?"

"Isn't that what conversations are for?"

"Isn't that what we are having?"

"How about if I buy *you* a drink?"

"Are you going to ask me to leave then?"

"Should I? What will you ask of me if I let you buy me a drink?"

"Isn't that the ultimate question of the universe?"

"What is the universe's answer?"

"Wouldn't the universe have a different answer depending on whether we like each other or not?"

"Ok. How do you like me so far?"

"How much do you want me to like you so far?"

"Well, how far do you want me to like you?"

"How far is it to your place?"

"You are pretty confident in yourself, aren't you?"

"Aren't you acting the same way?"

"So, what happens when two confident people meet each other?"

"How far is it to your place?"

"Why don't you go sit over there?"

"Why? Aren't we hitting it off?

"Aren't you just hitting on me?"

"Isn't that why you are here?"

"What if you're not doing this conversation well at all?"

"What if I am doing it brilliantly, but you can't see it?"

"What if I say good night?"

"How far is your place?"

APPENDIX TO CHAPTER 34
The Four Pillars of Confidence

Suppose that you wanted to teach confidence or that you wanted to be confident. The road to confidence lies on a path that integrates events, education, temperament, and conflict. One of the reasons that integration matters is that the process of integrating aids in creating confidence. Integration is the ability to link patterns, link experiences, imagine different relationships among patterns and experiences in order to act in a successful way. By doing so, new patterns emerge, and new ways of thinking are possible. This prevents getting stuck. Once you realize that you can always find a way to act successfully, confidence can grow.

There are four pillars of confidence:

1. Diverse experience

2. Reflective education

3. Temperament (Adversity or perfection)

4. Conflict

Diverse experience is self-evident. The more experiences you have, the higher the probability that you will see patterns in these experiences. The more experiences you have, the more confident you are that the next experience will be like something you know. To the degree that this gives you insight that no one else has, it adds value. If you have flown before, visited foreign countries, fired a weapon, drawn a sunset, hit a golf ball, etc., you have a certain experiential diversity. This experiential diversity gives you a benchmark for what is *currently* possible. And the reason you know this is that you have experienced it.

Reflective education is not just attending college. The notion that someone else has ordered the world, that someone else has decided the process that you should use, that someone else has decided what's right, or that someone else can compel any point of view does not breed confidence. The only thing it does is cause you to adopt a view to pass the exam. In some cases, there are conventions like language and mathematics that are valuable and must be learned and followed in order to survive. In others, there are not. It is up to the individual to question all manner of education and to reorganize the world in a way that makes sense to them. To do otherwise is to acquiesce. When this recognition works, confidence ensues. Reflection is also important for determining the truth of things. If you know what is true, then you can be confident.

Temperament (Adversity and Perfection) is a special kind of influencer for confidence. If you have succeeded all the time, you would have confidence that the next time will be a success, too. This can however be false confidence!

If you have only lived in one home, gone to one school, had one friend, and worked one job, you may have a fantastic "local" confidence, but this is a mirage. You won't know what you don't know.

However, if you experience adversity only once, it forever makes you cautious about outcomes. Interestingly, this may not be a negative. When we know that we have failed at something, we often are able to know why. This is important. And equally important is the reason that we tell ourselves why we failed. If we blame the world, then we may have rationalized our behavior as an illusion. If we take all the blame ourselves, we risk never repeating the process again and becoming ineffective. Dealing with adversity and the truth about its cause is perhaps the most important pillar for confidence. It allows one to see that we are not perfect, but also that we can still succeed.

Finally, we have the pillar of *conflict*. This may seem strange as a confidence-builder: after all, picking fights is a good way to lose confidence. But this is not about fights per se. No matter where one goes in the world, there will be conflict. It cannot be avoided because:

1. There is never enough money

2. There is never enough time

3. There are never enough people

4. There is never enough skill

These are eternal sources of conflict that are especially real in business. Confidence is not about seeking out conflict, but being comfortable with it when it occurs. It is about being able to balance the needs of bosses, colleagues, and subordinates so that a mission can be accomplished. People have endless ideas for how to do things. Ask any five moms what constitutes a perfect history report and you'll get five different answers. It's conflict. Families are all about conflict. You have to be very good at it to be confident.

To be clear, there is a quality and relevance to these four pillars that is unique to individuals. For example, the experiences of an African-American boy are not the same as his white counterpart. It is true of gender, ethnicity and sexual orientation as well. The four pillars hold that they are different for everyone. This means that systemic attempts to instill confidence are not effective. They must be personalized.

It is interesting to me that so much of the US culture today is about destroying confidence. Each day there is a new disease or symptom that you have to worry about. Each day there are signs that the world may be ending that you have to worry about. And each day, there are more individuals who are doing things that you should worry about. All of this defeats confidence. This is why integration and being able to assess the truth are so important.

A kind of anti-worry reaction to all this is to just forge ahead in spite of what people think. Politicians do not resign, CEOs do not resign, no one is accountable, and they practice long at not being so. This faux confidence only stirs resentment among the people who believe that actions have meaning.

35.

We Have No Idea

In Kindergarten Johnny was sent home for stealing another boy's sandwich. Johnny was spoken to and put in time out. Johnny's parents said it was nothing.

In the second grade Johnny's parents were called because Johnny had thrown a rock that had a struck a little girl on the arm. Johnny was spoken to and put in time out. His parents said the little girl had provoked Johnny.

In the sixth grade Johnny was caught smoking marijuana in the boys' bathroom. He was suspended for a week. Johnny was spoken to. His parents said that marijuana was legal in other states and just because it isn't in their state shouldn't mean it's a crime.

In ninth grade the police arrested Johnny for selling cocaine. He was booked but since it was a first offense he was given probation. Johnny's parents were divorced so no one was at home. His guardian was his mother.

In twelfth grade Johnny was arrested for armed robbery. His mother said he was being influenced by a bad group of other boys. She couldn't remember when she had seen him last. He was convicted and served two years in the Juvenile Pen.

Johnny was released and eight months later was found dead in an alley. His parents blamed society, the authorities and the school system.

Suppose it just ain't so?

APPENDIX TO CHAPTER 35
It's the Parents

You're not going to like this one. Suppose that people had to prove they could become a parent. This sounds Orwellian, but the act of parenting is perhaps the most important activity one engages in during their lifetime. Yet, no one has to show they have the necessary skills to do the job. There is more responsibility placed upon a person to get a driver's license than to have a child. There are hundreds of studies that reflect on everything from the roles of parents to the decisions parents make about how *to be* a parent. These are all available by Google search, should you wish to search. I am not reproducing any study here, only noting that this topic is the most significant topic in any view of the future.

The reason that people should need to prove they are going to be good parents is that *only they* have both nature and nurture *capability* therefore, only parents have both nature and nurture *responsibilities*. No one else does. Not the government, not other non-family people, not the church, and not the hospitals. If we say that parenting is important, then we should have a way of reflecting on that importance.

If we ask what sort of proof prospective parents might show, we'd start by describing a parent's specific responsibilities.

Parents must ensure that children at a minimum are provided these parts of the bottom layers of Maslow's hierarchy: air, food, water, shelter, healthcare, rest, safety, and security. If we think about this reasonably, parents would later in life also be responsible for education, different levels of safety and security, certain preventative commitments (vaccinations, etc.), and for overseeing those children who are capable of earning a living. If children are not in an environment where these basic needs are met, then they will struggle. It is puzzling why this is not the center of any conversation about where money should be spent. If two people cannot execute these basic functions, then they must take action to *become* able to execute them.

1. Parents must also be able to show that they are able to take care of themselves. If a person cannot link action to consequence, cannot perform a base level of physical and mental skills, has no source of income, or is in jail, then there is a question of whether they could ever be responsible. This is not about testing for IQ or about existing socioeconomic conditions. There are examples of people who have succeeded anyway. It is about the process that leads to having children and what capabilities are needed. Naturally, these capabilities differ by climate, social culture, "expectations", and individual beliefs.

2. Parents have duties they must perform. Parents must be able to take care of children. They must maintain a clean environment. They must teach their children a language. Parents must be available to their children and they must make their children into good citizens who are independent, capable, and responsible.

3. There is good evidence that parenting more than anything else is responsible for a child's developmental outcome. There is an absolute superiority conferred on children by their parents. Parents who have materially failed in financial matters, health matters (drinking, drugs), incarceration, or multiple divorces and multiple families have a much higher proportion of children who will also fail. Parents who can meet the requirements in 1 and 2 have more capable children. If you had crappy parents, then there is a high

probability that you will have a crappy environment to overcome, even if you somehow are able to rise above it.

4. Anyone wanting to be a parent should be able to do so. This essay is not about a one-time test and if you fail you cannot have children. It does mean, however, that parents should be asked to meet certain minimum standards. *It might be possible to use adoption standards already in place to establish the potential effectiveness of people to become parents.* If we ask two people to conform to certain conditions to adopt, why would this not be a reasonable standard to measure up to? In New York, these standards are:

- Be at least 21 years of age, financially stable, and responsible mature adults

- Complete an application (staff will assist you, if you prefer)

- Share information regarding your background and lifestyle

- Provide relative and non-relative references

- Show proof of marriage and/or divorce (if applicable)

- Agree to a home study which includes visits with all household members

- Allow staff to complete a criminal history background check and an abuse/neglect check on all adults in the household

- Attend free training to learn about issues of abused and neglected children

- Provide permanent homes and a lifelong commitment to children into adulthood

- Provide for the short-term and long-term needs of children

- Provide for children's emotional, mental, physical, social, educational, and cultural needs, according to each child's developmental age and growth.

Anyone who has had children can identify with these basic tenets. If we expect our adoption process to be good enough to get this right, then we should be able to expect that this would be adequate for getting the parenting process right.

There will be times when things go badly for the parents and this may disrupt their ability to provide one or more of the conditions outlined in 1. In this case, and because state laws prevail in adoption, the resulting actions would be decided at the state level. At the end of the day, it is parents who make the children successful and the children make the future of the country successful. It is parents who determine what the next generation will be capable of. It is parents who must advocate for their children and must know enough about life to be effective.

There will be debates about what kind of parenting should be judged unacceptable. Again, many family court cases would serve to establish the bell curve of what happens. In the end, the behaviors that are not acceptable can be included in the conditions for parenting.

I realize this smacks of Big Brother telling us how and who and what we are allowed. For 30% of the population, this will be viewed as an intrusion based on all sorts of arguments. But it's really the other 70% who make so many of the policies of good parenting necessary. Welfare, student aid, incarceration, poverty, drug abuse and many more situations require vast sums of money to deal with parental failings. But having money does not ensure good outcomes. While there is an economic component, there is also a maturity component, an experiential component, and a stability component.

Suppose, though that every parent *was* "good enough" in the same way that adoptive parents are. Wouldn't it stand to reason that much of society would be improved? Wouldn't that be *the surest* way to reduce the largest and most intransigent of society's problems? And wouldn't it in the end create a citizenry that is more capable of passing along the qualities that make children good citizens?

36.

Without the Emperor

The four generals had just fought a long and bloody war to overthrow the emperor. Now, they had to come to agreement on who would sit on the throne. General Yu (of Shi) paced the floor. Generals Zhang (of Wei) and Wang (of Han) sat drinking Maotai. General Lin (of Shu) stared out the window in thought.

Yu: "So, it's done. What should we say to the people?"

Zhang: "We say the Son of Heaven *is in* heaven and we have taken his place."

Wang: "It is true. We hold the army, so we now hold control of the four major cities, plus Beijing. But this may not stand. We must be prepared for counter revolts and for others to think that now is *their* time. We must appoint the next Emperor now!"

Yu: "Yes! But it is also a time of great reflection. We have two choices. We can rule centrally, or we can divide power. We can have one Emperor or…" He left unspoken the thought that all of them might somehow rule.

Lin: "Just suppose we divide the jobs among us. We would then be forced to send our most trusted subordinates to manage our former cities. They would pay tribute, as we have always done. But we all know how bad this is. The smaller cities think we tax them and use all their money here in Beijing. If we ask lesser officers than us to rule in our stead, how can they be as effective as we have been?"

Wang: "It is likely that they will not be as effective. That is in our favor. They are unlikely to attack us. But they will get stronger..."

Yu: "But what if we did disperse power, but to ourselves? Just suppose that we create the four great duties for each of our four cities. We would leave no power here in Beijing. We would put the administration of the Empire in Shi. This includes responsibility for all services and roads. In Wei, we would put management of the economy. In Han we would put the management of foreign affairs, and in Shu we would place the judges and the education department. And here in Beijing, we would each assign a part of our army. Each city would have one fourth of the combined general staff."

Lin: "I like what you say. But how would disputes be settled? Who will then be "Emperor-like" and resolve differences among the four of us?"

Wang: "Just suppose that we submit disagreements to a vote among the four of us. A tie would be broken by a group of citizens appointed by us in Beijing to make these choices. We could each argue our cases. These people would only be appointed for five years."

Zhang: "So, now it is the little cities who rule! We have separated the nation into states. This should prove quite interesting!"

And thus could have begun the earliest days of the United States of China.

APPENDIX TO CHAPTER 36

The Case for Optimal City Size: An Alternative Idea

Suppose that poverty, health care, education, and physical security are merely functions of how big our cities are. Suppose that our big cities are too big because the people who need services exceed the ability of others to pay for them. Suppose that in delivering services huge administrative staffs get created to contend with distribution. Might there be a better way?

Suppose there is a desert island and there is only one person on it. The entire question of survival is dependent on the individual. If we add one new person, we immediately get to a kind of division of labor according to competitive advantage. "I'll climb the trees for coconuts (food) and you build the living platform." Even if one person is relatively better at everything, no one can be in two places at once. This second person provides an indisputable "advantage" (this assumes basic health and mental ability). Even if this advantage is only to be able to hold something in place while it gets tied, it is an advantage, nonetheless. If there is enough food on the island, the population can continue to grow. Everyone on the island would know what needed to be done and who could do it. People would know what resources existed and how they were being used. And, as the population grows, "governance" develops to allocate these resources.

If we let the island fill up to a small, city-size population of say 10,000 people, it is still likely that all people would be aware of what needed to be done and whether the food supply and resources can be balanced such that all people are able to survive. As is the case today, everyone on the island would have to be able to do something of value. But people do age, or they get sick. Some of the 10,000 people would not be able to do anything of economic value, even if for just a short period of time. They would need to be helped. There would be haves and have-nots.

The question is whether there is a size where a city becomes so big that the 'haves' cannot locate and support the have-nots. Is there a size of population where the family structure cannot be maintained and where others must provide for survivability? Is there a size where the value of people is unknowable? Is there a size where the support for the disadvantaged cannot be effective? The intuitive answer is yes, because at city sizes even like Baltimore and Pittsburgh money must be drawn into the city from the surrounding regions to manage services.

As cities grow, they tend to do so because there are increasing ways for people to create and add value more than they had been able to elsewhere. But at some point, the resources run out and they must be imported. In New York, there is a $38 billion difference between what is sent to Washington DC and what is received back in tax revenue.

In smaller cities like Buffalo it is not easy to tell whether they send more to Albany than they get back. The state of NY provides some services, but if the Buffalo taxes were never sent to Albany, some of those services would be irrelevant. Buffalo can service state roads. Buffalo can police its communities roads. Buffalo does not need Medicare and Medicaid payments because there is enough money from income taxes (they would not go to Albany), sales tax (they would not go to Albany any more), and real estate tax to pay for all the city and state services in Buffalo. Buffalo does not need education help from the state. It gets money from the state, but it is misused and managed badly. This is because the taxpayer is too far away from the program. If you look at the result, the state of NY has the worst schools in the country for the money being spent by almost any measure. Politically, you can find suggestions that NY state gives more money to Buffalo than it gets in taxes, but it is very likely that this is not true when you look at the cost of running programs at the city level and taking Albany out. It is this calculation that must be done by line items to know for sure. And it is this calculation that cannot be verified.

Today, in states like NY, IL, CA, and others, taxes are sent from the more rural regions to the principal cities. The supporters do not see the supported and vice versa. What's worse is that there are people in between who are "processing" the support. And they take a cut. If a person were to be homeless in New York City, there is no way a person in Buffalo would know who they are, but they are supporting them. Plus, in some sense, there is a geographic relativity wherein the problem you have is yours alone if you are more than a certain distance by car (With the exception of disasters).

In Rome under Caesar and in Baghdad under Saddam Hussein, taxes were levied on the regions to support the behaviors of the large metropolis. This is not unheard of and is another reason why it is crucial to understand that taxes can easily flow from regions to a larger, central city.

Suppose we create a direct link between "a have" and some "have-nots". If the taxes a person pays could be retained by that person, but then spent in support of some specific nearby have-nots, would the entire system be better for it? If Wall Street had to support Harlem and if The Gold Coast had to support Cabrini Green, could individuals who were creating value be able to individually support those who cannot? If instead of collecting taxes, the state required the "have" people to provide directly for certain have-nots, could this be an effective way to better society? The requirements on the haves would never exceed the taxes they would have paid, but they would be spent directly on agreed-upon education, family services, and health.

Commercially, business taxes would be retained by the business but used to provide quality services to defined neighborhoods. All people in larger cities would know the results. There would be more demands from the haves on resources to support the have-nots. Without the entire admin-istration surrounding the effort, the result would be a lesser burden for all society and perhaps better care and attention. This support would be both corporate and individual. The effect would be to create smaller towns inside bigger ones. Imagine the Old West and the effect of the rural model on the livability of the town. For those of you imagining the evil plunderer who buys up all the land and makes everyone work for them, this would not be possible because the amount of wealth you own increases the obligation you have up to the point of prior taxes.

The haves could volunteer for certain have-not areas. Haves could band together to support adjacent have-not areas. If you were responsible for another family or two or three, there would be programs at the city level to make the interactions easier for all. If anyone was not doing their part, it is easy to see at the city level why and thus make changes. The mayors of most smaller US cities already do this. The ones in the larger cities can't because they don't have enough haves for all the have-nots. This is where city size adjustments should be made.

The point is this: if a wealthy family were to stop paying tax and instead be given three disadvantaged homes (to be defined) of people who needed support and economic help, then the tax dollar would be better spent because there would be no middlemen. Money would go from one home to three. The responsibility for education, health care, and problem solving would be on the wealthy. The movement of money and the audit of the program would be at the city level. If one thinks about all the programs that must go to the state capital, then to the federal government and then back again, one can see why this idea is better.

If we look at the largest US cities, we would see a difficulty in executing this scheme. There are not enough people of means to assist those without. There would be a need to "divest" parts of large cities so that the balance is restored. Those divested parts would join other smaller cities where possible. The cities being joined would be of sufficient wealth to absorb the new commitments.

There are however many ways to contest this idea:

1. This plan will create an overlord situation where the people with the money will seem to "own" those who don't.

2. There will be disagreements on health care and spending. Who gets to decide if someone should have Lasik surgery?

3. The city will need to audit this program and add back all the middlemen who were removed.

4. No one will want to spend the extra time deciding how their tax money should be spent; they would just want to let it go to the state.

All of these objections are reasonable, and yet when people are *less numerous* they seem to be able to make a kind of system like this work. It has been so for hundreds of years across this country. This idea will of course meet with resistance from the state and federal governments who will see their power diminish. In a sense, this is the point.

In New York, the problems of ineffectiveness of many state-run programs can surely be made better by getting the programs to as local a level as possible. I have had experience with a charter school in Buffalo that is not even being run by the city. It produces good results with less money and delivers many more services. A big part of this is because the decision-making is at the level of the school.

In the end, there is no point in collecting more and more taxes for less and less benefit. Those days have been over for many years. It would not be easy to execute this, because the politicians in NY believe that government should be involved in as many aspects of life as possible. Therefore these kinds of systematic failings exist.

37.

Mary

They had worked at Area 51 for twenty years apiece. They were never on the same project, but had often had lunch together. Sam was a thin man with light hair and a quick mind in aeronautics. He had worked on propulsion and theoretical principles of flight for many years. Nelson (Nelly to his friends) was a heavy man with glasses and a mild asthmatic condition. He had been working as a biologist researcher since he got his PhD. They were having lunch as they had done every month for the past twenty years.

Sam: "I have to cancel tonight, Nelly. They want me here for some OT."

"Interesting," said Nelson. "They asked me to work as well. Maybe I'll see you."

"Maybe." Sam shrugged then he headed for the door to the physical hangar facilities.

At ten o'clock that evening, they found themselves in a room that neither had been in before. It was underground and accessible from only one elevator shaft. It had taken them fifteen minutes to be admitted.

General Charles USAF was the meeting's sponsor. There were people from all over the government, including the CIA, the CDC, airline operations, all of the military services, and others that were not afforded place cards. There were maybe thirty people assembled. The general had a good reputation in the area and had been seen as a huge source of funding. His voice was measured as he spoke slowly.

"Tonight, we are gathered to analyze data on a most remarkable find. Several weeks ago, in Oregon, an object was brought ashore by fishermen working in the Sound. It was transported here, and will be brought in now."

With a nod, two airmen wheeled in a cart. On it was a football-shaped object of about eight feet in length. It was contained in a transparent wall of clear, explosive-proof plastic. It was thick in the middle and tapered on the ends. Its appearance oscillated between moments of clarity when it appeared black and white and then other moments when it became distorted and almost transparent. There was a sound that people in the room would later say was like the purr of a cat. It sounded alive.

The General continued: "We don't know anything about it that matters. It is here, but there is no obvious reason as to why or how. There is no way that we know of to date it. Its x-ray footprint is black. The MRI produced no readings. We subjected it to heat and cold with no effect. We tried light. Its spectrum is unknown to us. There is no element we are aware of that could be identified in its composition. We also tried electricity and infrared. Nothing."

The room was quiet. "We need you all to suggest ideas. Why is anything like this here? And what is it?" The meeting broke up and teams were formed.

Nelson looked at Sam. "I am wondering if this could be a pod of some sort. That could perhaps explain a bit of the shape. It is tempting to relate its shape to something we know. Seeds come in pods. It seems to have survived the ocean. Did we have any track of its path?"

"I'll ask. I don't remember anything recently. I'll check to see how long we think it could have been here. I am baffled, though, by what we don't know and what tests we could still employ. Sounds like we've run the usual."

For the next week they all labored to find anything of use. Absolutely nothing had any effect or brought any reaction. Nothing changed. Sam reported that there had been no space track that could have wound up in Puget Sound.

In the middle of the second week, one of the physicists, Mary Black, began to report odd feelings. She had been born blind and as she worked at a desk near the object, she seemed to be experiencing what she called "visions". The location of objects in the room seemed to have become known to her, even if they had just recently been moved. She could not say how she knew.

By the third week, she could navigate as well as a sighted person. She could not "see" exactly, but she was able to sense the location of objects. She could not describe exactly how she knew. What added to the mystery is that those who worked with her experienced no changes at all.

By the fourth week, she had acquired a most extraordinary ability to determine the health of the people who worked with her. She had correctly located a blood clot in one IT woman and had detected the emergence of cancer in one of the soldiers who guarded the doors of the exam room. She was unable to explain how she knew.

Her new sight and diagnostic powers were not localized. She could hear a person's voice and tell how healthy their internal state was. When she went home and listened to the news, she was able to tell the physical condition of every voice she heard. It was astonishing.

When Mary reported that she had felt a connection to the object, all work ceased except for Nelson and the biology teams. The feeling seemed to come and go, but it was "pleasant". She asked if anyone had actually touched the surface of the object. After being told no, she asked permission to try. General Charles was skeptical but in the end he agreed to allow it, partly because Mary seemed so certain that this would be valuable. It was scheduled for the following week.

When the day arrived, Mary was given a hospital gown and gloves. She was connected to a variety of biological monitors and all Area 51 people involved in the project were either in the room or connected by video. Nelson was monitoring Mary's vital signs and had given Mary a small geranium plant to hold in case this was their only chance to learn the effect of the object on plant life. Mary's face was serene as she started toward the football-like object. She reached out her hand and it seemed to pass through the outer wall. To those watching, it had disappeared. Nelson's readings jolted in all directions and he shouted that she needed help. But no one in the room was able to move. Suddenly, there was a short, startled gasp from Mary and her body went limp. At exactly that moment, there was an extraordinary flash of light that blinded all those in the room.

When their sight returned, the object was gone. Then, another extraordinary thing happened: Mary's voice was in their heads. They could hear her say that she was fine and had joined a sort of consciousness. She reported feeling loved.

Mary somehow was able to know things she never could have dreamed of knowing. She simultaneously corrected some equations that she had been working on in everyone's mind and confirmed that other life existed in the universe. It was amazing. The sound of her voice in their heads was powerful, yet gentle. And then, as suddenly as she had arrived in their heads, she departed. Her last words had been that she would return someday when the time was right.

All attended Mary's funeral, but it was not a funeral in the traditional sense. She had been alive in their minds. They knew she had not died. She had just given up the use of her body.

Mary's autopsy had been thorough, but there seemed to be no indication as to why she had died. They never discovered that hidden in her brain in a way that our medicine would not be able to identify for a thousand years, was a microscopic football-like object that would one day change the world.

Why <u>is</u> There Anything Here and Because There Is, Why Do We <u>Do</u> Anything?

Physicists ask why anything is here, meaning why does *anything* exist? Does it have to? Is it inevitable? Is it luck? And because there is something "here", why is it that we humans *do* anything? The answers to these questions rely on one simple pattern being either true or false. Just suppose the following is true.

There are several theories of how the universe operates which can all be reviewed elsewhere. One of them, though, is important to the question of why there is anything here at all. It only makes one assumption. *If we assume that all possible futures do in fact occur, then every possible outcome is certain to have occurred somewhere.* This is the theory of multiple universes (multiverse). It contends that, in each nanosecond after the Big Bang, our universe split into many universes. It continues to split in such a way that everything that *could happen, does in fact happen* in at least one of these universes.

All of us can only "know" what is happening in one universe: our universe. This is because we split as well. This universe is the one that you and I are in right now. In the next moment, many things can happen with different probabilities. Let's take an example. Just suppose you and your friend are at a table having lunch. There are four life possibilities in the next nanosecond: you could die and your friend lives, your friend could die and you could live, you could both die, and you could both live. Most of us experience the outcome where we both live. Yet there are universes where the other three results occur.

So what? So I wrote this book in some number of universes. And you are reading it. This means that I was alive before you in this universe or living at the same time as you are, and you must be alive now in order to be reading this book. In some universes I would have died before writing this book so no one ever read it. (This is perhaps a more desirable universe for some of you!). In other words, there is some infinitesimally small probability that our "precise" experience should exist at all, and yet it does. The existence of "your" own universe exactly as it is can be seen is a fantastically small possibility, considering all things that have happened and all universes created since the dawn of time. Yet, if the multiverse theory holds, all possibilities sum to one. Everything is happening and has happened that could ever happen.

So, if the above is true, is there any *reason* why we humans *do* anything at all in our *particular universe?*

In this universe, if my hand waves, then in others it will not. Does this mean I have free will? Maybe. Could I raise my hand in this universe and cause another "me" in another universe to "not" raise their hand? No, because we would be raising or not raising our hands at the same time. There is no cause and effect. So, is there any reason to believe that what I do matters in this universe? No, because the opposite is happening in other universes.

When I make a list of "reasons" for doing things, are these same reasons applicable in all universes? I think so.

The first reason we do things is because we have a certain arrangement of genes. Genes are triggers that turn on or off certain functions and are one of the bases of life. If genes get it wrong, behavior will be different, especially in mental illnesses like ADD and Alzheimer's. If everything can happen, then in some universes it is possible that different people married to produce me. Perhaps my mother met a different man than in this universe. An interesting question is whether two people who were *not* my parents in this universe would be able to have produced me in *any* universe? I don't think so. At least one of my parents and one of each of my grandparents must have been alive for me to be "like" me in other universes. Clearly, though, I could have different genes in those universes and may even be a different sex.

The next reason is internal, intentional states (cognition and emotion). If we have an internal state that exists as the primary "strategic intender", then any stimuli can be evaluated against one's internal state and a decision as to whether the stimulus deserves a response is executed. This is a comparative state and the decisive choice is made internally. Clearly, if I am genetically different in other universes, I will have a different internal state here.

The third reason we do things is external stimuli (the environment). If we just react to an environmental change by reflex, then the environment in some sense causes our behavior. The way this happens is important. If you believe that the locus of control for us as individuals is outside (meaning that all actions are influenced by the environment), then your status is reactive and behaviorist. Again, this may only apply in this universe.

Finally, is this idea that everything that can happen does happen in all the universes combined—so, I may in fact only be doing something in this universe that is the opposite of what I would have done in another universe.

Now it gets complicated. What if we have *two minds*? We have a mind we call "us" (that we are aware of) in this universe, but there is a second mind that is *responsible for* "us" and unknown to "us" that manages us at a some meta level. If this were to be the case, this "meta" mind could be the determinant of action. It is even possible that this "mind" may have created the "idea of us" for "us". Just suppose that "we" do not know this "meta" mind exists. Suppose this "meta" mind creates the mind we experience...the "us". Suppose it does so because it needs something to translate the outside world inputs. The meta mind created us to be able to more easily predict the actions of others. In this scenario, "we" (meta) survive only because "we" (the us we are aware of) have access to others though our senses more directly.

In this example, the sense that we have of "us" being in control and that we have free will may be an illusion created by our meta minds so that "it" can manage our bodies better. "We" feel that there is an "I" that is in control and "we" see actions that "we" attribute to our own decisions. But what if the system is so clever that "we" are fooled by the meta mind into thinking that we are deciding when in fact we are just playing out the "silent" unconscious orders of our meta minds like the management of our heart and lungs? They seem to be on "auto pilot", because we cannot link their function to any command or intent "we" possess to "stop" these organs consciously.

So, things/events exist because there is probability in this universe that they do. We do things by genes, or by extrinsic or intrinsic motivation, or by some other unconscious power. In the end, the fine balance in the universe makes more sense to me if one supposes that all universes exist—and especially because this happens to be one that contains our lives.

38.

Universal Solvent

A. I am in favor of raising the minimum wage.

B. Why?

A. Because people need a base level of income to support themselves. $10-$15 an hour is not enough.

B. What standard of living are we talking about? TVs? Cars? I-Pads? Or just food.

A. They need whatever it takes to get a job, like a car for example.

B. How much should the minimum wage be then?

A. Probably $25 per hour.

B. Ok. That's about $50,000 per year. But why wouldn't you think that $60 per hour would be better? That would be $120,000 per year.

A. Well obviously it would be better but that seems like a lot. At $25 per hour people would at least be able to buy the things they need.

B. Where do you think the money would come from to pay for that kind of minimum wage?

A. From corporate profits.

B. I see. So let's say I have a lemonade stand. There is just me and one other person. Lets also suppose I work for free. And finally suppose that it costs 4 cents in lemonade mix, 2 cents for water, and 4 cents for a cup to make lemonade. That's 10 cents in cost. But I also have to pay my worker $60 every hour. So lets say that I can sell a cup a minute. That's 60 cups an hour so I have to charge $.10 for the lemonade and $1.00 for labor to break even on every cup. That's $1.10 a cup.

And you have to sell a cup a minute every minute that you are open. That seems like a lot. I don't think that many people will drive by here. Even if they did can two of you make a cup a minute every minute? You could reduce your cups to one every two minutes but then you would have to sell them for $2.50 per cup. I don't think anyone would pay that much for a cup of lemonade. Even if you sell no lemonade you still pay $60/hour.

So we have a problem. Someone has to pay the wage rate. In the end it will be the consumer who pays. Even if the company made no money, it is still $1.10 to the consumer at a cup a minute. But imagine that you only sell a cup an hour. That cup would have to cost $60.10! People will just buy the lemonade mix and do the work themselves. There won't be any lemonade stands at that these prices. You can see what this means if we expand this idea to a much larger businesses.

A. OK, How about a maximum wage?

B. That sounds silly. That would mean the government would tax you 100% of your earnings above a certain salary level.

A. They could do that but everyone would just stay below the maximum salary level.

B. Maybe but there are those who want to tax your net worth if you make above a certain amount. Lets say you have $100,000 in net worth and the tax that is being proposed is 2%. Lets say that you earn $50,000 and if you make 1 cent more you will owe the $2,000 tax on your net worth. You would have to get a pay increase to something above $52,000 in order to agree to the increase because your wealth is affected too. Effectively everything between $50,000 and $52,000 would be taxed at 100%. For small dollar amounts like these it doesn't matter but for bigger dollars it can.

A. But won't the wealthy just reduce their net worth or stop working so that the tax is just on their wealth?

B. Perhaps but in about 30 years they'd have only half their money left if they didn't earn any more. This is assuming of course that they earn nothing on the $100,000 and also that they don't need to use it.

A. OK I get it. Let's reconsider all this…

APPENDIX TO CHAPTER 38
Universal Basic Income (UBI)

Universal basic income is an idea whereby the federal government would pay some minimum level of income to all its citizenry. It is believed that to pay people above the poverty line would be a starting place and that the reason for doing so would reduce poverty and increase equality. Fundamentally, a program like this ties everyone to the government. This should be obvious. This would effectively make us all "government beneficiaries" of a sort, except we would not be required to do anything for the income—or would we? This is an interesting question.

Suppose we start with a couple of observations:

1. The government already pays money to people today. It pays welfare, Medicaid, Medicare, housing, social security, unemployment benefits, government employee salaries, food stamps, agricultural support programs, pensions, the military, etc. Would these programs be eliminated? Would they be netted (if you were to get $25,000 in UBI but receive the equivalent $25,000 already in different programs, would you be eligible or not eligible? What

about pensions? Is UBI in addition to pensions or just netted? If UBI replaces all other programs including social security, maybe it *could be cheaper* than the welfare programs today. This might be an answer.

All this money is supposed to create "better lives" for people who need assistance. It may increase consumer demand also, to the extent that the people who receive it spend it. That could be better.

2. But there are only three ways government can get money to do anything: taxes, borrowing, or printing money. If I am a taxpayer, do I pay more tax for this system? Do I get the UBI, too? If the government cannot collect enough tax to fund the system, will they be allowed to borrow? If we continue to print money, won't we just drive the price of things up? If so, wouldn't this increase the amount of income needed to be above the poverty line? Wouldn't that just lead to more printing, etc.?

3. It matters who gets paid. If illegal immigrants get paid, if prisoners get paid, if minors get paid, or if foreign students get paid, it makes a big difference. It also makes a difference if there is no means test. If everyone gets this money, then billionaires do, too. People move, die, get married, all of which could change their amount and eligibility.

4. If everyone gets a minimum income level it might not necessarily mean they are better off. More money in people's hands may mean more spending, but it may not be *contained* spending. There is a difference between buying a dog (with lots of additional expense) and a tube of toothpaste. The people who would presumably get this money must be capable of making themselves better off. Money alone won't do it. Poverty happens for a variety of reasons and some of them don't go away simply by having more money.

5. If (UBI's) goal is to reduce poverty, other conditions may hinder its ability to succeed. The poverty line was $24K in 2017 and was the minimum level of income deemed adequate to live on. But what is this dependent on? Prices, of course. In Argentina, where inflation is rampant, the Peso has declined 60% in a year. So, the poverty line expressed in pesos rapidly goes up. Anything that sparks inflation would increase this impact because everyone would get a boost in pay to make up the "difference". But this would boost the poverty level again because inflation is connected to the boost in income. And this would boost income again and the poverty line again. So, tying the income distribution to the poverty line will be inflationary.

6. Presumably, people who are below the poverty line would always value more income, but how much more? Is $24K the right base? The value of $24K/year is about $12/hour. This would mean that any job below $12 per hour would vanish in *principle* because no one would work for less than $12 per hour if they could get that same amount without working. People might agree to work for less than $12/hr. if they get a base of $25K without working and the money is not lost if they do additional work.

7. The actual $/hr. salary required for people to work must be higher, because there are costs to working. You have to search for, interview for, and finally somehow get to the job. You have to stay on the job. You have to do an adequate job. You have to pay for co-workers' celebrations etc. So, the real $/hr. equivalent may not be known. But it is surely higher.

8. This reasoning goes for businesses as well. If there are no jobs that can be bought for less than $12-$15 per hour, then prices on all manner of things must go up to cover the minimum effective wage. Fast food chains, landscapers, hotels, call centers and all manner of industries that require low-end labor will either become

more expensive to us all or the jobs will be eliminated by cheaper machines. This is already well underway in the fast food business.

9. What do we suppose the extra money will be spent on? If it is transportation to a job, education, child or elderly support, and other things that add both current and future value, then it's money well spent. If it is spent on standard family or personal expenses or saved, then it is well used. But if it is spent on alcohol, drugs, gambling, or other addictions, then it may not be well spent. The government cannot monitor all these expenditures unless the money is given in the form of specific vouchers. Even then (as we have seen with food stamps), people will discount their vouchers (stamps) for lesser amounts of cash so they can buy things they want. The government cannot easily control what people spend money on. It may not be about money but about choices. Universal income may not work for reason like this.

Every governmental system requires technology to manage. Without electric power for example things could get nasty. Let's look at Puerto Rico. Hurricane Maria devastated the island. The electric grid collapsed. The highway infrastructure collapsed. The medical distribution and supply distribution collapsed. Despite the efforts of unaffected governments to help, the island is still experiencing random interruptions of electric power every day, more than a year later. When it became clear that certain external benefits would be given to families who lost relatives, the death toll rose to above 3000 people. Corruption is the enemy of the people.

Just suppose, however, that a program of distribution of income was done locally at the city level. Each city would decide what measure to use for poverty in their city. The number of citizens below the poverty level would be identified. At the city level, there is a better chance of identifying each of these people. There is also a better chance of managing the distribution. Cities under a million people can do this fairly easily. They already know a lot about real estate ownership, employment, etc. Each city could decide how the program would play out. The Federal Government would give each city its "share" of income to distribute, based on the Federal basis of awarding the grant. It would be funded by a tax as described later. Each city could vote for how to distribute "the pool" to individuals. If the income award is just to the poor (by some definition), then QED. Nothing else needs to be done.

But what if everyone gets $25K? Some cities have very few people below the poverty line. If everyone is eligible, distribution could get interesting. Just suppose that I would rather have my Federal taxes cut than accept income that I have to pay more tax on. Suppose I could deduct it straight from my tax bill to the Federal government. That would boost its impact on me by the inverse of my tax rate. The Federal government could then decide whether to keep my money to offset my tax break or to award it to someone else in another city. My contribution could go to more needy people as determined by the Feds.

I know what you are thinking. Certain cities would become tax havens. That is true, but only if the citizenry below the poverty line (or whatever standard we are using) are taken care of. The taxpayers of the city would contribute directly to the poor of the city in a way that the city could manage. At the city level, government has the best chance of successful distribution. That is not to say they will succeed, but they have the best chance. Even in the big cities, this might work. People who want the money get it and people who want tax breaks get them (assuming everyone is getting income).

One last point. Universal income will tell the government exactly who and where you are at all times. Maybe that's good and maybe not. See China for their experiences.

This scheme may not address every issue, but it is worth a discussion.

39.

Whose Freedom Is It?

A. The way you people talk makes me unhappy. It scares me.

B. But I have a right to freedom of speech. Your skin is too thin.

A. But I have a right to happiness and also to certain expectations of security. You can say what you want in private. You can also say what you want in public but your intent is crucial. If you are only saying things to provoke anger in me then you are denying *me* a right to happiness.

B. But you have no right to declare that everything I say makes you unhappy. There is no standard by which it is my responsibility to fix anything you deem to be making you unhappy. Your standard of happiness does not supersede my freedom of action or my standard of happiness.

A, But the crucial issue is intent. If you say something that threatens my security or my freedom or my happiness then it matters greatly whether you did so with intent. We might consider employing the standard of a common person and how they would interpret your intent. If your intent were to provoke then there should be consequences. If your intent were not to provoke then I should reconsider my reaction.

B. But who is this common person whose standard we would employ? How can you know my intent? Suppose I say that, "the only good gun owner is a dead gun owner." Is it my intent to kill gun owners? Am I just rearranging words of a common expression? Who is to say?

A. This may not be so difficult. I can take a cross section of people, show the video, create a transcript, describe the conditions etc. and ask for a decision as to intent. Let's take the old standard of shouting "gun" in a crowed theater when there is no gun. The specific intent may be unknown but the effect of that word on the crowd is certain.

B. But all kinds of situations happen each day and they can't be "moderated". How am I to assess intent quickly? In fact I might suggest that in times gone by the supposition was that people were trying their best to find agreement and that any slight was unintentional. But now the opposite is true. It is as though we are deliberately provoking each other as a means to our own happiness.

A. That is where we are indeed. A society's collapse happens when it turns on itself. When nothing matters any more except one's own personal happiness or delight in someone else's unhappiness then we are on a steep path to irrelevance. You and I should continue to talk about this. Perhaps an idea will occur and just suppose it does…

APPENDIX TO CHAPTER 39
Freedom vs. Security

Freedom: The power to act, speak, or think without hindrance or restraint. Note: This is the positive view of freedom. However there is a negative view of freedom wherein one is poor for example and because of that is not free. Or where one has had their freedom removed because they were in an accident or robbed. These are negative freedoms as are freedoms to do evil oneself. The idea of freedom below is only approached from a positive POV.

Security: The freedom from risk and threat of a change for the worse. Freedom from danger.

Just suppose that these two concepts are very much at the core of modern US society and yet they account for much of our instability. These concepts are at the heart of national disagreements, and also at the heart of personal disagreements.

National: First let's examine US domestic issues. Immigration is perhaps the most obvious issue. Will the US allow foreigners to cross our borders in search of freedom or will we impose constraints to restrict foreigners from entering the US to preserve our national security? This conflict spills over to individual states where certain states have created sanctuary cities to encourage the idea of freedom while others have enforced current immigration laws.

A second national issue is the nature of speech on campus. On one side are the people at the University of Chicago, for example, where the nature of free speech includes speech that people would be expected to disagree with. On the other side at many other universities the idea of speech that threatens student's security is of greater concern and therefore safe spaces and trigger language have been instituted.

A third issue is the concern regarding weapons ownership in the US. Here again the freedom of the second amendment right to bear arms conflicts with the security concerns around mass shootings and gang crime.

Finally and perhaps less obviously are the concerns about climate change. On one hand is the freedom to live a life that has made use of certain means of production and natural resources vs. the security of being able to continue to survive as a species on this planet.

This is a non-trivial idea and if we suppose that we can categorize a lot of national conflicts this way we can perhaps see that much of the idealistic debates are all originating from the same place. Those who are running for office would benefit greatly from understanding this similarity and categorizing their answers in debates along these lines. A reasonable question is what external commitments of security are worth the removal of freedoms.

There are studies that have been done in the countries that switched from communism to democracy. These studies reported that all people value security highly, but that freedom is valued only by those well enough off to not be concerned as much with security. One could also say that if you are concerned with security then freedoms are less important. There is an implicit sense that freedoms are themselves secure but that sociologically, income, jobs, and the welfare of one's children are the higher security concerns. This should seem obvious.

One could say here that the devices being employed by the two political parties are about these two issues. If by electing "my people" I can increase both my security *and* freedom then I will have won. In this case however my freedom may mean that your view is silenced because I deem it a threat to my security. This game is very serious because the activists on both sides who are playing it don't understand its importance.

Personal: But freedom vs. security is not just a macro level issue. In fact this issue has been and will continue to be one of the key individual differences between men and women. A number of studies have reported that men and women value freedom and security differently. Link.springer.com references some of these. The authors actually researched a more specific question of how genders view money. Men see it as a means to power and freedom and women see money more as love and security.

Suppose that the genders do have a preference between freedom and security. Suppose that the genders from teen years until marriage are really seeking different things. Further suppose that both genders achieve some parental satisfaction during child-raising years but as divorces and separations occur more often, both genders return to their original preferences. This would mean that men seek greater freedom and women seek end-of-life security. This is not to say that all women always want security and all men always want freedom. Security can be someone to eliminate loneliness, or someone to be there to help. Security can be physical security in a neighborhood or security around the outside of a house. There is indeed something that reduces anxiety by having a second mind, set of hands, etc. to do things we cannot do.

This link between male freedom and female security can be seen in dating sites that allow trades between free older males with money to financially insecure younger partners in exchange for sex. Older men with younger women are not new nor is this unique to today. However, it is much easier to see the supply and demand on these dating sites.

But freedom and security also lie at the heart of raising children. It is the freedom of teenagers vs. their security that disrupts families. In this case both parents and teens see issues, like driving independently, as a question of freedom vs. security. Again there is nothing new here.

The point of this essay is to describe a simple opposition between freedom and security and ask "just suppose," most of our problems in society have this particular conflict as its basis." What then is the general case solution?

The way to have a conversation here is by asking, "when does your freedom affect my security?" Or conversely, "when does your security affect my freedom?" These questions can always be answered by the invested groups or individuals but is there a general case wherein we could be more consistent in how we have the discussion?

The Constitution of the US sets forth rights or freedoms if you will; life, liberty, and the pursuit of happiness. It says that to "secure these freedoms" (my words), the government must be managed by the very people who are entitled to these rights or freedoms. This is an important distinction because there is no specific affirmation for security here. One may say, "well that's true but to pursue happiness I must have a certain secure economic position in society. Therefore as a politician I am insisting that the government use its power to give me economic security for my pursuit of happiness."

This is an important concept with an interesting limitation. Suppose all of the fuss about freedom and security is really over what makes us happy. Every argument above can be distilled into this general case. Why do people hate the current administration, why do people protest, why do people have guns, why do people create fake news etc.? It starts as a case of freedom vs. security but in the end it's about being happy.

One approach would be to say that everyone should be able to pursue his/her own happiness as long as it does not conflict with another person's happiness. Everyone should be allowed to act freely in support of another person's happiness as long as it does not conflict with a third person's happiness. Parents have special duty to balance happiness and responsibility in their children.

So what happens if the only way I can be happy is for you to die? Or be put in jail? Or to have your viewpoint wiped off the earth? It is important to understand that this is *impossible* because like me you are entitled to life and liberty and the security to maintain them as long as you do not deny me mine.

Happiness is both absolute and relative. If I do not have good health (I am in pain), if I have no hope for a job, if I live in fear for my life, etc., then it is highly unlikely I will be absolutely happy. On the other hand as people in first world countries move up Maslow's hierarchy, the idea of what constitutes happiness becomes relative. In a country like the US we have thrown away the self-enforced behavior that subordinates your right to happiness if it has a negative effect on me. Instead there are people who live as though their version of happiness should be everyone's version of happiness.

In other essays I have addressed certain claims of individuals on society. I have addressed individual happiness and ways to achieve it that do not conflict with others. In the end all of our collectiveness must be built on the idea that each of us must accommodate everyone's right to happiness as long as it does not impact others negatively. If we do not then the societal bond is broken and none of us will be happy.

40.

Ari and Plato

Plato: "I have a thought. There is a perfect objective reality. All things have a perfect Form. These Forms are not knowable except in the mind. Each object has a Form that is the ideal Form of all objects in that group. Let's take a sphere for example. There is an ideal sphere that is perfect in all matters of the Form "sphere".

Aristotle: "I too have a thought. There is no objective form or reality. Any experience of the world, including the mind, is based on the circumstances of the moment. The form of any object is a summation of the forms of the things that went into making it."

Plato: "But I can imagine a perfect sphere that has equal curvature everywhere. This is the ideal Form. No one can craft such a sphere. So, the perfect Form in my mind sits above the form of the man made sphere. Nevertheless, both exist."

Aristotle: "I too can imagine a perfect sphere but in your sphere example you started with the sphere first and then spoke to its form. I say that there is no form except whatever form a sphere already has. If no existing sphere has perfect curvature, then its form is a sphere that does not have perfect curvature."

Plato: "By that reasoning you are disregarding the very nature of your mind. If you can imagine something it exists even if it only exists in your imagination. Even if the sphere cannot be made it still exists."

Aristotle: "But because I can't actually make what I imagine and subject it to my senses, how would I know that my imagination was accurate? How do I know that I have not fooled myself and thought of a lesser form than *the Form*? Suppose my imagining of the perfect sphere is flawed?"

Plato: "You do not have to have an accurate imagination. You simply have to say, Let's assume a perfect sphere with these attributes."

Aristotle: "But you are making my point. You cannot say, 'Let's start with attributes and say they are a perfect Form' without saying these attributes are connected to something. How can an adjective exist in the absence of a noun?"

Plato: "But the nature of the word adjective implies an existence. There is a unique word for it. This word is like 'Form.'"

Aristotle: "Then are you saying that form has existence but no separate meaning? If an adjective exists as a Form, how can we say that it is perfect without a meaning of perfection? For example, what is the perfect Form of black?"

Plato: "It is the idea in my mind that there is a perfect color black, even if I can't describe it. I know it exists because I imagine it could exist."

Aristotle: "Then we are discussing the concept of the Gods. You say they are perfect because you can imagine them to be so, and yet I say that they don't exist because even though I can imagine these Gods I also have free will to dismiss them as a Form. You believe their Form exists and I don't. You can't prove it, and neither can I. You believe that they exist as Forms and I do not. I can only say that the things that I believe can be shown to you in such a way that you will believe as well. Your senses will tell you what form *really* is."

Plato: "It is a shame that you do not see that the way out of all caves is to ascend to the reality of what your imagination can contemplate. I am afraid that you will be forever stuck here on earth in the world of your own limiting senses. Ah well, it was a good talk."

Aristotle: "I agree it was a good talk. You were in rare Form!"

APPENDIX TO CHAPTER 40
Has Everything We Know Always Been Here or Did We Discover It?

In the absence of consciousness, nothing ever exists nor is there anything to discover. Throughout these essays I have contended that consciousness is necessary for anything to exist for the simple reason that without a consciousness there would be nothing to acknowledge any existence. Everything only exists if consciousness exists.

Time exists because of and dependent on consciousness. The notion that something is different than something else, or different than it was, can only be considered by any something capable of recognizing that difference. This is consciousness. This is Schrodinger's cat. It is also the argument concerning electrons and whether they exist as a particle or a wave. They can be both. But it is the observer who determines which it is "now". It is consciousness that calls things into existence.

Many things though, exist because a human mind has "invented the existence". We can say for example that the categorization of animals has been commonly decided. It is the ordering of Kingdom, Phylum, Species, etc. However the ordering could have easily been like:

Living things that can fly;

Living things that cannot fly;

Living things that can or cannot live under water;

Living things that can live in more than one environment.

We could also divide animals arbitrarily into living things that can kill humans and living things that can't. Thus, categorization is a human idea that is discovered from sensory input. We "realize" or "discover" what is the pattern is.

3. What about something like mathematics? Here it gets murky. This is like asking if there is an underlying programming language or rules behind "everything in the universe"? In the case of mathematics, we can surely say that it helps forecast events. By knowing the compression of a spring, or the movement of a planet, and the resistance of air and gravity, we can forecast where the spring will land if pulled and let go, and where a rocket needs to be fired in order to fly close by the planet. In this sense, mathematics provides us with a handy tool to manage our existence. But did we discover mathematics or is there a hidden tool more proficient in describing our existence but not yet discovered?

Einstein invented a mathematical view of the universe long before we had the power to do experiments that could confirm the mathematics. It was the genius of Einstein that he was able to forecast reality with symbols. But now we have observations in the quantum realm that defy unification with Einstein's work. We think that the universe may not be "decided" in that the reality of things can be said to "depend". We perhaps need a different system of integration to bring relativity and quantum mechanics together. Again, the question is, "Does this different system already exist or do we have to invent it?"

Another interesting set of questions that are raised in mathematics is the hypotheses about whether something is true or not. An example is the Riemann hypothesis that is one of the seven puzzles in mathematics proposed at the end of the last century. Only one of them has been proven so far. Do solutions exist? And if so, are they already solved or do we need to combine things "unnaturally" to get the answer?

Another way to consider this is to reflect on things that would not exist if it were not for humans. A number of elements on the periodic table do not naturally exist and so human thinking created them. Gunpowder is a more prosaic example. Nature did not invent these combinations of elements; humans did. The same is true of medicine and all the machines that have been fabricated. And yet, with all of these "creations" by humans, we still cannot answer all the questions that we have. The question is, "Are these answers out there, or do we have to invent them?"

Finally, we can think about the things we know that we do not know. For example, when we look at the night sky, we see stars not as they are but as they were. We don't know whether these stars even exist right now. We are then faced with knowing that something *did* exist because we have access to its past, but we do not know if it still exists in the present. In some sense, each day we discover that these stars still existed at least one more day. No mathematics can prove their existence today. We are bound by observation in a different way than above.

The reason it matters whether things always exist or whether it is us who discover them determines how information exists. Does information already "exist" everywhere in the universe or is it "discovered" by consciousness? Is information an invention of human minds?

If one had the powers ascribed to God (universal consciousness of all things) then she would "know" all things everywhere at the same instant. All things would exist, and nothing would remain to be discovered. This would even be true in all dimensions and time and space. It might include multiple universes as well. God would know all and if she created the universe, then *she alone would have done so by inventing it.*

But does God know all things? If so, then a consciousness *does* know all things and the existence of all things. If this is the case, perhaps it does not matter if *our* consciousness only knows that some lesser set of things exists; it only matters that *a* consciousness knows. Things would exist independently, and our "discovery" would simply be recognition of what God invented.

As Einstein said, "When I am judging a theory, I ask myself whether, if I were God, I would have arranged the world in such a way."

Jordan's Questions

Do foodie people have better oral and olfactory inputs than the rest of us? Is this a recent change in human biology in first world countries?

Are all the tremors that have recently been felt around the world caused by stress being built up from inside the planet? Is this stress affecting biological life? Is this what we see happening in the US today? When the great systemic stress "bursts", will you survive? Does all this stress mean that more of us will commit suicide?

Could it also be that the earth is going through a radiation belt that is affecting all biology on the planet? More suicides, more anger, more negativity.

Would football (soccer) be more interesting and important if there were two balls in play at the same time?

What else should we just suppose as a problem that could be improved?

Who are the 'theys" that say all that stuff attributed to "them"?

How would you categorize these essays into four groups?